Stan
a Hammock

Standing in a Hammock

PAULA CLAMP

POOLBEG

Published 2002
by Poolbeg Press Ltd.
123 Grange Hill, Baldoyle,
Dublin 13, Ireland
Email: poolbeg@poolbeg.com
www.poolbeg.com

13 5 7 9 10 8 6 4 2

A catalogue record for this book is available from the British Library.

ISBN 1-84223-096-4

Cover Designed by Vivid
Typeset by Patricia Hope in Goudy 11/14.5
Printed By
Cox & Wyman Ltd, Reading, Berks

About the Author

Born in Nottinghamshire, England, Paula Clamp has lived in Northern Ireland since 1986. She is married with three young children. A theatre studies graduate from the University of Ulster, her plays have been performed in Belfast and Dublin. She has Masters degrees in Cultural Management and Anglo-Irish literature. She is a keen volleyball player and has played for Northern Ireland. *Standing in a Hammock* is her first novel.

Acknowledgements

Thanks to Jordan and Yana for going to bed on time and Jay for giving me the craving to eat cream-cakes as I typed. Hence the 11lb 11oz bruiser who popped out two days after I finished the book. To Kieran, Gaye and Paula at Poolbeg for that first meeting that set the ball rolling. To the Arts Council of Northern Ireland for buying me time. To my editors Gerry – and Gaye – for their encouragement and annoying habit of correcting me. To all the team at Poolbeg.

Thanks to my husband Gerry for everything.

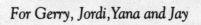

For Gerry, Jordi, Yana and Jay

Chapter 1

"Anything else?"

"Aye, Frances, something nice for a cup of tea."

"Aye, Fergal, but anything in particular?"

"No."

"Just anything?"

"Aye, you know, something nice."

"Like what?"

"Anything."

"Give me an idea."

"You choose. Something nice."

"Something like biscuits?"

"Something a bit more exciting."

"Buns then?"

"Nothing sticky."

"A pastry?"

"Not really."

"Cake?"

"Too sweet."

"What then?"

"You know, get something nice for a cup of tea."

Frances Coyle grabbed at her purse and rushed out of the house. Slamming the door of her husband Fergal's Vauxhall Vectra, she hurried out of the estate and onto the main road. She quickly made a mental correction: 'development'. They lived in a development and not an estate. Ashbury Development consisted of twelve redbrick detached residences with white arched windows and mahogany doors. Friday night and house numbers 8, 6 and 4 were mowing their lawns. Number 5 across the road had one white and one pink balloon pinned against their garage – the universal signal for 'children's birthday party within'. The black windows of recently divorced Number 7 denoted another evening out. The third this week. A quick left off the main road and Frances came to an abrupt stop outside the local Spar. As she pulled the shop's clearly marked 'push' door, Number 7 was trying to pull the door open from the other side. Immediately Frances regretted throwing on her grey tracksuit bottoms and Minnie Mouse T-shirt when she arrived back from work. There was a standstill for what seemed like an hour, but in real time a matter of seconds. It was long enough for Frances to study Number 7 in detail. She looked stunning. Blonde curls framed grey eyes and honey-toned skin. Slim hips and obscenely elevated boobs were wrapped in a delicately cut pale-blue shift dress. Frances cheered herself for a moment with the phrase 'high maintenance', but this dissolved as she caught a glimpse of her own reflection in the door. The distorted glass made her head look enormous, and squeezed in the middle were tiny eyes, nose and mouth. Her chocolate-brown eyes looked like tadpoles and her fair hair was transformed from its usual bob style to a frizzy blur.

The door finally gave in to the stronger of the two women.

"Sorry, Frances, did I hurt you?"

Bitch. She's nice as well as gorgeous, thought Frances.

"I'm fine. Off somewhere nice?"

"One of those parties where the married men are frightened to come near me and the single ones are scared of becoming biological-clock victims."

Frances and Number 7 were the only ones in the cul-de-sac to be childless, or 'childfree' as Number 7 preferred. That and being 34 years old was where the similarities ended.

"Still, a party's a party," said Frances.

She wondered whether to add that she was off to the gym, hence the slightly grubby-looking sportswear. She liked to view her image as the athletic type. This was her rose-tinted view of herself – usually after two glasses of wine or a jolt of high-caffeine cola. Right now, however, was not one of those rare moments. How was she going to explain this one? She thought for a moment.

"Frances, you make me so envious. I'll be stuck between the accountant and the mobile-phone consultant, when I should be off to the gym with you. You're so disciplined to go exercising on a Friday night."

Bitch. She really is nice, fumed Frances.

"If you bring me back a doggy bag, I'll show you how disciplined I am."

"I'm sure with all your basketball training you can eat whatever you like."

"Volleyball."

"Oh yes, volleyball. That's where you do this, isn't it?"

3

Number 7 pushed two clenched fists up into the air. At that moment a white van overflowing with floury-looking labourers hurtled past. They whistled and cheered as her raised arms gently tugged her dress over brown slender knees.

"The action's a bit more like this."

Boosted by the gentle confidence Number 7's kind remarks had given her, Frances motioned the correct action, precisely drawing her open palms from her forehead straight up in the air.

"Hey, missus, you're a bit old for raving!"

The shop door had once again flung open and two spotty youths chomping on crisps caught sight of Frances in mid-flow.

Driving home with her grocery bag on the seat beside her, the heat from Frances's face slowly subsided. She had been masquerading as a social, sporty volleyball player for the three months she and Fergal had been living in Bangor. The reality was she had lost contact with her old team over six months ago. At first her reply to concern about poor attendance at training had been the hassle of heading into Belfast twice a week. When her team-mates were ringing at least three times a week, her excuse had become a recent promotion to committee clerk for Belfast City Council. When the calls got down to once a week, her ankle was playing up, and now on the once-in-a-blue-moon call, she said she had got out of the way of it. But when it came to new-neighbour introductions, volleyball as a subject had given her something to hang her conversation on. However, it was starting to become a burden rather than a conversational opportunity; she was starting to feel the pressure when faced with questions like 'Any matches lately?', or 'Out with the team last night?'.

As the Vectra made the sharp turn back into the

development, Frances hatched a plan to announce that her doctor had said that one more volleyball match could leave her crippled and wheelchair-bound. She had the image of the boxing contender who, faced with a diagnosis of a brain injury, decides whether or not to challenge for the championship. She took this image further and pictured herself as special guest at neighbourhood parties, receiving heaps of sympathy and concern.

With this vision blurring in and out of focus, she slowly pulled into the cul-de-sac. Three cars were parked outside Number 5, as parents picked up their chocolate-clad youngsters from the children's party. They poured out of the front door, carrying party bags and small silver parcels of birthday cake. Dressed in midriff tops, long pencil skirts and silver platform shoes, the girls looked six going-on sixteen. The boys reluctantly gave parting kisses to the birthday girl and quickly erased the moist impression left on their lips with a sharp rub. Number 8's lawn was looking pristine as usual, as he perched himself on his front step and meticulously cleaned the mower blades with a toothbrush and sponge.

Frances pulled into her drive and sat in the car for a moment, gently soothed by the purr of the engine. An old collie dog waddled towards her and wagged its grey tail as it saw her beaming smile. Fergal and herself had moved into Ashbury only three months before and theirs was the last house to be completed. She thought back to the first week in their new home. Half of the upstairs had still to be plastered, the front door leaked and there was a nasty smell coming from the attic. When she had come home from work one day on the last week of their move, she discovered the workmen had let her Labrador Murphy out by mistake. As Frances had searched through the house, she came upon this Labrador sitting at the top of the stairs. But it wasn't Murphy. The workmen had gone out and got any old Labrador and assumed that Frances and Fergal would be none the wiser. The dog just sat there on the stairs as if to say, 'Who the hell are you?' After placing a number of notices in the local shops, the poor dog's owners were eventually found, but Murphy was still missing.

The old collie dog turned to continue its purposeful journey, but not before lifting its leg and urinating against the wheel of Frances's car.

Throwing her grocery bags onto the kitchen counter, Frances hunted out two toffee-flavoured pancakes and two tubs of vanilla ice cream. She plonked her feast on the living-room coffee table and pulled up the brown leather armchair. The heat of the evening had made her soft, fair hair glue in spikes to her forehead, and her mouth felt dry. Fergal was laid out on the sofa, his feet perched on the big fluffy hippopotamus that he'd bought Frances their first Valentine's together almost ten years before. She plunged her spoon into the core of the ice cream and pulled out a dripping icy lump. Frances momentarily thought back to her Hall of Residence room with herself, Fergal and the hippo squeezed into a bed not much wider than three foot.

"Fergal, move over. Get off, you dirty wee shite!"

The hippo had taken up the lion's share of the bed. Frances' lover had reached over past the cuddly toy and was now cupping her breasts in each hand. Frances didn't resist.

"Go on then, Fergal. What are you going to do with them?"

"Well, I can squeeze them, I can fondle them, I can hug them, I can . . ."

"You can lift them."

"I can press them."

6

"You can weigh them."

"Oh Frances, I can certainly stand back and admire them."

"You can count them."

"Canoodle them."

"Juggle them."

"Milk them."

"Push them."

"Pick."

"Point."

"Press."

"Ah, ah Frances . . . I've already said that."

They had made love all night and the hippo had looked on approvingly.

Frances carefully peeled back the lid on the second ice-cream carton. Fergal's eyes were glued to a 'get someone else to do-it-yourself' television programme.

"Met Number 7 in the shop. Ursula, is it? Off gallivanting to some party or other."

"Nice."

"Lawnmower Man at Number 8's even managed lines like a cricket pitch in it this time. He mows that lawn like he's on autopilot. I wonder if we pulled down our fence, would he just keep going and mow ours as well?"

"That's nice."

"You're not listening, are you? I'm going to ask Number 8 to mow ours as well. Do you think he'll do it if I give him a blowjob?"

"Good."

"We might get our borders planted if you give him a blowjob too."

"That's nice. Get anything for a cup of tea?"

7

Chapter 2

"You know, get something nice for a cup of tea."

Frances had slammed the door on her way to the shop and Fergal felt the tremor across the wooden laminate living-room floor. Yet again his wife had made a big deal out of nothing, he thought. He took the opportunity to change out of his work suit and pull on a pair of moleskin jeans and a grey polo shirt. He squeezed a blob of hair-wax into his hand and gently warmed it before applying it to a few stray tufts of hair. At 35 years of age, he had a warm open face, pale grey eyes and strong shoulders. As he looked in the bathroom mirror he saw something else. All was grey. Dull grey hair faded to a dull grey face down to his grey clothes. He quickly pulled off his polo shirt and dressed in a bright orange casual shirt. Fergal pinched his cheeks, a beauty tip often recommended in Frances's women's magazines which were an interesting toilet read. Unfortunately, he broke the skin and spent five minutes mopping up specks of blood with toilet paper.

How did I get to be like this? He pondered the question as he sauntered into the study to dig out some work reports. As new accounts executive for a city-centre building society, he had a presentation to make at 8.30 on the Monday morning to a group of businessmen in the Europa Hotel. He hadn't got home this Friday evening until way after seven and Monday looked like it was going to be a long day as well. Fergal kept his study scrupulously tidy. All files were catalogued and systematically ordered along five maple shelves. A black leather chair completed the work area, set against a desk made from a curve of similar maple. The desk was placed against a large window devoid of any clutter, other than a plainly framed photograph. Fergal picked up the photograph and sat in the office chair. With small side steps, he began to rotate the seat. Staring out of the photograph were two young men. He gazed at the taller of the two, whose hair was slightly greasy and lay in waves on his shoulders. His coat was shabby, decorated with tassels and buttons the size of old pennies. Flared jeans, muddy at the hem, betrayed the era the picture was taken. Aloft he held a dead salmon. Fergal flicked off a speck of dust from the edge of the picture frame and replaced it on the windowsill. He gently re-positioned the frame until it was exactly where it had been before.

Frances's 'stuff', as Fergal called it, took up the bottom drawer of a silver filing cabinet. She had left the drawer slightly ajar and various pieces of white paper, old trophies and bits of cardboard were sitting out. As he opened the drawer, a porcelain doll's head rolled out onto the seagrass floor. Smiling, he rolled the small face, with faded pink cheeks, between his thumb and forefinger. The moment passed and he quickly stuffed it back in its home and shoved the drawer closed with his foot. The report he was looking for was balanced against a pile of motor journals and Fergal folded it in three and buried it in his top pocket.

From the upstairs window of the study, Fergal could see his neighbours below. He was disconcerted to see three of them cutting their grass. His hadn't looked too bad until now, but his initial thoughts of Saturday morning golf were beginning to fade. Alex, at Number 5, had asked Fergal several times to make up a golf foursome. Frances was constantly 'at' him to go along and 'get to know the neighbours'. He wasn't so keen. Once the chat about the best feed and weed formulas and problems with cracked plastering had dried up, Fergal was lost. The sexual innuendo about each other's wives then usually followed. At this stage, Fergal usually asked about his neighbours' children, which quickly ended all conversation. He could see Ursula at Number 7 was out again. Bugger, he'd missed her leaving. He could talk to that one all day.

Back downstairs, Fergal lunged onto the sofa and proceeded to methodically flick through the television channels. He was shattered. As a young man growing up in the ghettos of Derry's housing estates he had had boundless energy. That young man bore no resemblance to what he had become as he approached his unwelcome forties. He stopped briefly to notice how his stomach rose when he inhaled, but didn't go back down that far again when he exhaled. This meditation lasted only a moment before he returned to his task of channel-hopping. The sun's reflection on the television screen created a blur of dull shadows, blanketed in tiny specks of dust. Fergal reluctantly got up again and closed the curtains. Seconds later he was back on the sofa and within a few minutes he had fallen into a light sleep.

Fergal woke to find a small pool of saliva on the cushion and his left arm completely numb. As he lifted his head to wipe his cheek with the arm with any feeling left, he saw Frances looking down at him. Her cheeks were slightly flushed and translucent. She looked beautiful for that moment. As he smiled she furrowed her brow and the translucency turned to pale white with bluish tones. She bit into a pancake and started chewing rapidly. Only a spearmint-gum-munching football manager could match her chewing speed and vigour at times like this.

"That's nice. Get anything for a cup of tea?"

Chapter 3

With only the twins left to be collected from down the street, Christine Watson from Number 5 breathed a slow, long sigh. Molly, her daughter and birthday-girl, came rushing through the hall with a bright smile.

"Mummy, I'm having another baby."

"Who's the father this time?"

"Ricky Martin."

Molly was an eight-year-old mother of two already. The other two fathers were of course Leonardo de Caprio and some boy-band member who Christine didn't know. Christine and her husband Alex had a family of three girls. The eldest, Ruth, was twelve, then there was Molly in the middle and then The Baby. The Baby's name was Helen, who at two years old was perhaps no longer a baby, but she was still the Watson's baby, or rather Christine's baby. The name on her birth certificate had long since been forgotten. Molly's birthday present from her parents today had been a miniature Silver Cross pram. Molly was sitting on the porch admiring the black veneer of the pram, the speckling of delicate roses on the hood and inside the kitten-soft pale-pink blanket, which her mother had knitted. The purchase of the pram had caused severe ructions in the Watson household over the past few days. Toys 'R' Us had witnessed quite a to-do the day the pram was collected.

"The price of that bloody pram, we could have got a real one."

"But, Alex, she's saved up nearly half the money herself!"

"It's not right the way she mothers them damn dolls. It's not healthy."

At this point, they both spotted Molly squatting in the cuddly-toy aisle with her jumper pulled up over her stomach, attempting to suckle a very contented baby sister.

Christine was herself concerned. But she wasn't going to share this with Alex. His way of dealing with the problem was to force Molly to take an Action Man to bed with her. But the girl really wasn't interested. Ruth, their eldest daughter, was also presenting her own set of problems. Only that morning she had jumped into the bath beside Christine and announced she wanted to be a lesbian.

"Ruth, if that's what you want, dear, that's fine. But where has this come from all of a sudden?"

"At school we're doing about how babies are born. There's no way I could go through all that."

"But, love, you don't have to be a lesbian not to have babies."

Christine hadn't shared this conversation with Alex – she had been too busy getting Molly's party together. After her bath, Christine had plonked The Baby in front of a Disney video, packed Ruth's overnight bag (she was staying with friends for the night) and simultaneously curled Molly's hair around old-fashioned plastic rollers. Molly had protested vigorously at her shoulder-length auburn locks being pulled and positioned. She also managed to throw up. Extreme, but effective. Alex had arrived back from the supermarket, just in time, with four bags of party nibbles, fizzy drinks and ice cream. Alex loved to clean. Christine was the envy of all her friends and neighbours. A man who loved to clean, and who was good at it into the bargain, was not only a novelty, but a prize possession.

"Alex, not her face!"

He had forgotten it was a scourer he was using, and not a sponge, and in the process of cleaning up the vomit, had taken the top layer of skin off Molly's very red and now blotchy face. He consoled a wretched birthday-girl with a barrage of kisses and the two of them continued the cleaning together. Returning from leaving Ruth off at her friends, Christine began preparing an assortment of tray bakes. While they were in the oven, she popped in another video for The Baby and began making sandwiches and sausage rolls. Alex and Molly had turned the job of laying the table into a game of commando.

"Cover me, Molly. I'm going in."

As Molly patrolled the living-room, her father slid onto his belly and squeezed under the dining table. Alex, a general practitioner, always had his medical bag at the ready and Molly had imaginatively transformed a medical syringe into a Kalashnikov rifle.

"Daddy, I've covered all the exits. Watch your back."

"Hold your fire. I'm going to try and grab the hostage."

"Kick ass, Daddy!"

14

Alex dived behind the back of the sofa and pulled out Suki, Molly's favourite dolly. Suki was a slightly balding blonde and, with one glass eye permanently stuck, had an unnerving sardonic expression. He held Suki aloft by her podgy plastic ankle. A tiny tear film covered Molly's oval brown eyes and her bottom lip slowly pulsated. A mighty roar swiftly followed as she fell to the floor in floods of tears.

"It's OK, Suki, my love. Mummy will make it all better."

Alex looked over at Christine, but there was no conversation. There was no need. Christine could read a million words into his one expression.

Christine was pleased that the party had gone well. Molly's friend Patrick, the only Catholic in her school, had cornered Christine within minutes of arriving.

"Missus, what's Holy Communion?"

"I guess it's when you are given a small piece of bread as a symbol of God."

"Is God made of bread then?"

"Not really. But God is everywhere. He's in the stars, in the trees, in the moon."

"Is he in my egg and onion sandwich?"

Three hours later, with the birthday party eventually over and the guests finally away, Christine went outside and took down the balloons hanging from the garage door. She used an upturned bucket to reach up and yank them from their hook. The pink balloon burst. The popping sound momentarily took her back to her own eighth birthday party thirty-one years ago. She had been a gawky youngster, all arms and legs and a shock of reddish brown curls. Her mother had been working in the office at the shipyard all day and had cobbled a few egg and onion sandwiches together. The home-made birthday cake had been assembled the night before and unfortunately had sunken in the middle. Her mother had cut out the centre and replaced it with a Granny Smith studded with birthday candles. She had been too busy to organise any party games, but Christine and her three young cousins had improvised with some old newspapers and a few sweets from their lucky bags. Her mother had looked tired, but smiled and laughed and chased after them with the hosepipe. Bang, the second of the balloons had popped; Christine was back to the present. Her long lanky legs, dressed in smart linen slacks, stepped off from the bucket and a lock of red-brown hair escaped from her neatly coiled French plait. Quickly she scooped up the wayward curls and re-pinned them tightly.

"Lovely evening, Mr McAllen," she shouted across the street and Mr McAllen at number 8 gave her a brief military wave before wheeling his sparkling lawnmower into the garage. He tentatively walked along the stone border dividing up his newly mowed lawn and his recently laid red-brick drive. She noted his excellent balance as he avoided stepping on either side. Frances and Fergal, the new couple across the road, had drawn their curtains. Having a bit of hanky panky, she thought to herself. As she walked back to the front door, she glanced through the front window. Alex had changed into a pair of old workman's overalls and was conscientiously on his hands and knees removing crusted bits of marshmallow and toffee sauce from the kitchen floor.

Alex hadn't seen his wife and had obliviously fallen into a cleaning trance. His sleeves were rolled up and sinewy arms flexed and relaxed as his sponge danced along the floor. When they had first met at the Young Farmers' twenty

16

years previously, he was twice the size he was now. Christine had admired him from afar, but he was very shy and would tremble if she came within four feet of him. He wasn't that great at conversation either and was embarrassed by silences. He filled them by whistling. Needless to say, the start of their romance wasn't exactly the fourth of July. It wasn't until three years later that they met again through their church. Alex was about two stone lighter and a medical student at Queen's. He had offered to take Christine's pulse at a car-boot sale in the church forecourt and three months later they were married.

Alex stopped scrubbing and looked around him. Christine reached up on her tiptoes and waved, but her husband didn't see her. The Baby was watching her fifth video and the tired-out birthday girl had fallen asleep on the lime-green chenille sofa. The carefully manicured ringlets had rebelliously fallen out and her natural frizz of auburn hair cushioned her sleeping head. Molly's three sleeping babies were laid in her arms. Alex stood up and walked carefully over to Molly. She continued to sleep. He then lifted down his medical bag, which had been stacked on the top of the bookshelf out of harm's way. He reached inside and fumbled for a few moments. Christine waved again, but with his shoulder slightly turned against the window, she couldn't attract his attention.

Looking around him again, Alex pulled out a syringe and an elastic strap. He quickly yanked up his left sleeve, pulled the strap tightly around his upper arm and injected the needle.

Chapter 4

Maurice McAllen kept himself to himself. That was the way he liked it. Out in the garden it was sometimes difficult to do that without coming across as downright rude. The satisfaction he got out of tending a few borders dotted with chrysanthemums and fuchsias was worth the daily battle of diverting stares and mumbling a few hellos. His lawn was his pride and joy. When he'd first moved into Number 8 during the previous summer he'd won a tough battle against weeds and thistles. The soil was also waterlogged in the corners and patchy at the front. Maurice had erected an eight-foot wooden fence all around the back of his garden within weeks of moving in. Now, a year later, the result was a lush secret world, with shafts of emerald grass bordered by plump scarlet and purple flowers.

Tonight was one of those rare balmy evenings, perfect for grass-cutting. The lawn appeared to slowly release the heat it had endured during the day. Maurice decided to take his shoes off and continue his gardening barefoot. He felt the warmth of the grass between his toes and the soft evening dew darkened the edges of his blue corduroys. As he crouched over the lawnmower, removing cuttings and loose debris with rounded shoulders and his chin hanging heavy towards his chest, from a distance you'd guess he was in his late fifties. His wide-brimmed cricket hat would also suggest the fashion of an older man. A bee buzzed past his ear on its last trip home for the evening and Maurice abruptly stood up and removed his cap in order to flap away the unwelcome intruder. Up close, his image was starkly different. At six foot three, he cast a vast shadow across the lawn. Maurice's eyes were cobalt blue and were squeezed into a slight squint. Threads of grey in his dark-blond close-cropped hair betrayed his real age of early forties. He ran his long fingers through his hair leaving behind soft slivers of damp grass. His green cotton shirtsleeves were rolled up to reveal strong forearms, dappled with the same dark-blond hairs. He wore no jewelry, only a plain-faced watch. The bee knew he had met his match and made a sharp detour through Maurice's legs and over the fence. Hat on again, Maurice crouched back down on his haunches, and his animated moment dissolved.

"Lovely evening, Mr McAllen."

Maurice looked up momentarily, and briskly returned a wave to a cheerful Christine Watson. Most of his neighbours seemed happy to leave him alone and get on with their own business, but this one refused to let his coolness deter her. She was always the first to pass commentaries and compliment him on his garden. Last Christmas she'd sent the little one round with a home-made Christmas cake for him. He'd started to think that maybe he had become her pet project. He imagined her sitting with her many friends discussing how she was going to get that 'strange man on his own at Number 8' to come out of his shell. Ignoring her for the first few months didn't work, so now he thought a few pleasantries or brief gestures would pacify her thirst for sociability. It appeared to be working. Christine had now turned her back on him and was standing peering in through her front window. Obviously admiring her crop of wee daughters, he assumed. Maurice slightly tilted his cap, enough for him to look at her without letting down his guard. He had thought she was terribly old-fashioned and sure to be a leading light in the local Presbyterian Women's Association. He found it hard to guess her age, but reckoned she must be older than him. Mrs Watson reminded him of his old schoolmistress. Since moving into the Ashbury development he had looked at her with primary-schoolboy eyes. As she now poked her nose against the window glass in order to get a better look, he could see in detail the outline of her figure. For the first time he could see the faint outline of the woman rather than the mother. Her linen trousers clung to a very slim waist and fell in soft folds down to a rounded behind. Mrs Watson's legs were long and slender and the trouser fabric clung to her thighs and her calves. She slowly eased up onto her tiptoes and the muscles in her legs flexed and tightened against the linen. Feeling uncomfortable at this secret intimacy, he pulled his cap back down to its previous position and re-focused his thoughts. He removed the last stubborn piece of grass jammed in the mower blades and, pleased with the result, replaced all his gardening tools in the garage.

Maurice's labour had given him a thirst and after

banishing the outside world by turning the lock in the garage door, he made his way towards the kitchen. Looking through the garages of his neighbours' houses he had studied the inner doors, which all opened directly onto the instant warmth of yellow and amber tones of the busy kitchen within. The mood within Maurice's house, however, very much echoed the cold empty atmosphere of his garage. He had the necessary kitchen equipment, the cupboards and even a few decorative items such as an assortment of vintage kitchen utensils but there was no warmth. There was no life. He grabbed a bottle of concentrated orange juice from the top of the fridge. He ran the base of the bottle across his hot brow and along the back of his tanned neck. After opening it, he drank its contents swiftly in one gulp and wiped the orange residue pith from around his mouth on his bare forearm.

Maurice threw the now empty bottle into the sink and picked up a bunch of car keys. Leaving the house, he methodically ensured that the three locks on his front door were properly secured. He then hopped onto the granite border which separated the lawn from his newly bricked drive. Maurice caught sight of the new couple across the road at Number 2 who were opening their curtains. He imagined what a rare duck he must seem to them all and the discussions they must have about him: 'he doesn't seem to work', 'but where does he go to in the evenings?', 'strange man living all alone', 'how come nobody ever visits him?'. Almost losing his balance, he re-focussed and walked the self-imagined tightrope to his red Golf GTI parked on the road. Maurice looked down at his watch, which read nine-thirty, and looked along the road in the direction of

Number 7, Ursula Richards' house. All was dark. He closed his eyes for a moment and then quickly regained composure and opened the car door. Seated inside, he started the engine and reached over to the glove compartment. He unlocked it and lifted out a cloth, which he used to wipe away the moisture from the inside front window. He felt warm and sticky and small beads of sweat had formed across the bridge of his nose and along his jaw. He wiped them away and then wiped his bronzed strong hand across his trouser thigh. He reached back over to the glove compartment, to return the cloth. As he did so, something fell out and made a thud on the carpeted car floor. He slowly started the car moving and turned in the direction of the main road. As he indicated left into the Old Belfast Road he reached down to the floor and lifted the fallen object. He replaced the handgun and re-locked the glove compartment.

Chapter 5

Ursula couldn't get the shop door open. The new woman from Number 2 was having difficulties at the other side. Ursula stuffed the recently bought copy of the *Bangor Times* under her arm and gave a swift pull. She was going to be late again, with the party starting with aperitifs at 8pm sharp. Ursula's best friend Carla had badgered her to come along to her Russian theme-night. There was always a theme and Ursula was starting to tire of them, but a night in Carla's company was always worth it. Carla had hatched the plot over coffee in the canteen of the BBC where they both worked. Ursula worked as a fashion researcher and Carla, her Spanish friend, worked in travel.

"My darling, we must have another party for you."

"Give us a break, Carla!"

"Really we must. I've met a couple of super new guys from Portaferry in my flamenco class. They're both very single. They'll just love you."

Carla taught flamenco dancing classes every Thursday

night in the local sports centre. Ursula had attended the first few, but she hadn't found the squash court, where the lessons took place, all that conducive.

"Look, Ursula, I have some absolutely tremendous recipes from my last trip to Minsk."

"I suppose you'll want us all to dress up again. What will it be, furs?"

"Yes, fur coats and no knickers, perfect."

Carla was Latin-blooded in every sense of the word. No one would describe her as beautiful, unlike her classically sculptured friend, but she was sexy as hell. A few years older than Ursula, her long jet-black hair betrayed a few wisps of grey. She was slightly overweight and this was concentrated on the bottom half of her body. If you dissected her features, there was nothing remarkable about Carla – in fact with her over-sized hips, slightly snub nose and a chest the size of a pre-pubescent boy's, you would think she had very little going for her at all. But, she oozed sexuality and when she danced . . . she was sex personified. And she knew it.

After exchanging a few pleasantries outside the shop with her new neighbour Frances, Ursula got back into her car and sped in the direction of the marina. Precariously balanced on the back seat was a giant silver pot, brimming with beetroot soup. The borscht had taken nearly seven hours to prepare; an hour to peel what felt like ten stone of beetroot and nearly six hours to simmer. She'd popped into the shop on the way to the party to pick up a tub of sour cream, to finish the soup off when she got to the party. She had reluctantly been carried along with the dinner-party plan. They had spent every lunch hour of the previous week discussing menus and table decorations. Ursula had to

24

admit to herself now that she was quietly looking forward to the evening.

Within a few minutes she pulled up outside Carla's house. The Georgian terrace facing onto the marina and out onto the sea was the only one in a block of seven that was not a bed and breakfast. The other six were painted in pastel blues and yellows. Carla's was turquoise with a ruby-red door. Ursula began to carefully carry the giant pot of soup up the steep steps to the front door. She was struggling. The lace on her hem had accidentally got caught between her hand and the pot handles. As she tried to release it, her little finger jammed in the lid.

"Need any help?"

Shouting to her from across the road was 'Walk the Bike'. He was Ursula's window cleaner, and christened 'Walk the Bike' by Carla, as a result of him never being seen actually riding his bicycle.

"That would be great, thanks. You really have become my knight in shining armour."

Ursula's move into the development several months earlier had not gone without a hitch. The deliverymen, refusing to move furniture after 5pm, had left Ursula stranded with five crates of clothes and knick-knacks on her front step. 'Walk the Bike' had been passing and within minutes had all the boxes safe and secure in her front room. From that moment on, he was taken on as Ursula's window cleaner and in the months since, he had helped her out countless times. Ursula guessed he was about ten years her junior at around 24. His outdoor work had given him a tan the colour of treacle, plus the build of a rugby player. This evening he was dressed in his usual plain white T-shirt and faded blue jeans. Ursula had never really got a good look at his face, as it was always hidden by straggles of chestnut-brown curly hair. He was quiet and shy and, unfortunately, occasional victim to Carla's sexual innuendoes. He awkwardly bounced across the road and took hold of the pot of soup.

Ursula and 'Walk the Bike' carefully manoeuvered up the half-a-dozen steps to Carla's front door, in silence. Side by side, they stepped crab-like. As Ursula rang the doorbell, 'Walk the Bike' turned to go. Wanting to thank him, she quickly grabbed hold of his arm. The firm warmth of his skin surprised her as she was expecting a soft cool feeling. Her ex-husband had felt soft and cool at all times and this was the first time she had felt a man's skin for some time. 'Walk the Bike' was now standing three steps below her. He stopped and turned his head upwards. His curls hid most of his face except for a slowly widening smile and his slightly parted lips revealed the pure white enamel of his teeth. Ursula maintained her hold. The door opened.

"What are you two up to?"

Carla was dressed in a crushed velvet purple mini-coatdress. She had knee length patent black boots, which she had edged herself in brown fake fur. She had also created a hat out of the same fabric. 'Walk the Bike', pulling his arm away abruptly, raced down the steps, jumped on his bicycle, and disappeared around the corner.

"Ursula, darling, we're going to have to change his name to 'Ride the Bike'."

Both women laughed and Carla greeted her friend with kisses on both cheeks. Ursula usually got this wrong and never could quite work out when one cheek was preferred to two. She was frequently teased by Carla, who said that hugging her was like squeezing a cardboard box. As Carla helped with the soup, a couple in their early thirties arrived at the door carrying two large Tupperware containers.

"Carla, you look scrummy. We've bought some borscht for the party, hope there's enough."

Once inside the house, Carla continued with the meal preparations in the kitchen and Ursula made her way into the front room. With its enormous bay window facing onto the marina, this was the main room in the house and Carla had created a mini Costa del Sol. Two large deep-red sofas were decorated with a cornucopia of scatter cushions and throws. Spanish clay pots and colourful wall hangings decorated this vast room. At its centre was a large redwood buffet table, dotted with a range of crackers and nibbles and surrounded by the assembled dinner guests. Ursula knew she wouldn't recognise anyone. Carla was sure to hold at least one party a month and Ursula had yet to meet the same people twice. There was always a mixture of people Carla had met on her recent travels, friends from home whom she would offer to put up for a week or two and they would end up staying for six, plus new members from her flamenco class.

Within half an hour Ursula had been introduced to a pilot and his air stewardess partner from Dublin, two Queen's University lecturers, a housewife with four children under six years of age (popular with the middle-classes according to Carla), three accountants and a pizza-delivery boy. The delivery boy wasn't a guest as such but, having made the fateful mistake of coming to the wrong address, had been pulled by Carla in to the party. He was now supervising the main course of stew and peculiar-looking dumplings as it bubbled and heaved on the hob. Carla's two new flamenco-dancing friends had failed to arrive, much to Ursula's relief.

The air stewardess was the first to take Ursula on as her networking project for the evening. After hurried general introductions, she then launched into the re-telling of every airline story ever crafted. She was always in the thick of this or that potential disaster.

"And then there was the time . . . when was it, darling?"

Her pilot boyfriend was an accomplished sidekick.

"Last summer."

"Yes, last summer. We were on our way to . . . where was it, darling?"

"Jamaica."

"That's it. Last summer on a long haul to Jamaica. I got hit by an . . . sweetheart, what do you call it?"

"Overhead locker."

"That's it, overhead locker."

Ursula began to slouch.

"Then there was the time I had to deal with that irate passenger from . . . where was it?"

"Dubai."

"The bloody fool had forgotten his . . . what do you call that thing with your photo on again?"

Ursula decided that the woman wasn't being dense intentionally, she just wanted to stretch her long-winded stories out even further than their lifespan. Ursula realised that waiting for a natural pause in the conversation wasn't going to happen. Whenever she did manage to squeeze in a contribution here or there, the stewardess would fall about laughing. She was almost bent double with hysterics when

Ursula told her that she'd never travelled to the States. It was important to the stewardess that everyone in the room thought she was the life and soul of the party.

The pilot boyfriend had little to contribute, so Ursula sought safety in speaking to him directly.

"So what's being a pilot like?"

"Well, you do know the difference between God and pilots?"

Unfortunately, Ursula didn't have the nerve to give the response that was bursting to come out of her.

"God doesn't think he's a pilot."

The airstewardess's exaggerated guffaws stopped all conversation in the room. Ursula was losing the will to live. The 'we're having such fun' message was wearing thin, rapidly.

Ursula excused herself by hinting that she wanted to sample some of the canapés on the other side of the buffet table. Rather than reach over, she lifted her drink and walked as far away to the other side as possible. She didn't dare look back, but just as she reached the other side, she heard the mumbled punchline of 'God doesn't think he's a pilot', followed by the familiar cackle of strained laughter. She turned to see the victim, the young pizza boy, with the pilot and the stewardess either side of him. His face was puce.

"Hi, I'm James. This is Eamonn."

Ursula's re-positioning had led her to the two university lecturers. They were both in their late forties and immediately the verses of the children's rhyme, 'Jack Sprat', came leaping out at Ursula. One was tall, redheaded and extremely skinny, to the extent that his skull was visible through his flesh. His friend was small, round, with a shirt pulled so tight around his stomach that circles of white flesh were poking out between each strained button. The round man was amusing himself by playing a game of sneaking the appetisers off the skinny one's plate.

"What's that behind you?"

Ursula looked behind her. Having seen nothing, she turned back and saw that her own plate was now half-empty. As the round one chuckled, pieces of pastry flew out of his mouth and started floating in his glass of red wine.

"You might be able to help us. James and myself were having a bit of a disagreement. In your opinion, between the two, would you say Cheddar or Leicester was the superior cheese?"

Before Ursula could muster a response, Eamonn pointed to a painting in the far corner of the room.

"Is that a Piccasso print?"

Ursula half-turned in order to inspect the painting, but having turned back again, she discovered her plate was now completely empty. The chuckling continued, as the round one, having had his fun, reached over the table and passed a plate over for Ursula to replenish her own. The skinny one dipped down and whispered in Ursula's ear.

"A decent Red Leicester has far superior texture and flavour."

"What is it you two lecture in exactly?"

"Personnel Management."

The skinny one's spectacles kept falling as he spoke and a red welt had formed on the bridge of his nose where he had so frequently kept poking them back up. Dipping down to Ursula's level made them fall even more readily and in the end, frustrated, he took them off and left them dangling from the corner of his mouth.

"No date tonight?"

"Not tonight, no."

Ursula felt like she was being dropped from an aeroplane, with no parachute.

"Lovely girl like you. Don't get stuck with a couple of old farts like us. He'll eat your dinner and I'll bore you rigid."

Ursula looked up at the skinny one with a few new shreds of respect. Even with his stretched skin, his smile was reassuring and friendly.

"We only hang out together so that we don't spoil another couple."

As she chatted with them further, Ursula soon began to realise that in their own ways, both men were humble, endearing and quite charming. Ursula even warmed to the round one as he endeavored to supply her with a full selection of fresh starters and nibbles.

Ursula rebuked herself for judging the books by the covers. But needless to say, she had her fingers crossed that she wouldn't be seated next to either of them over dinner. She was hungry after all and didn't have much to say on the topic of cheese. Her fingers didn't have to stay crossed for too long, before Carla dramatically swayed into the room announcing dinner was ready.

The dinner settings were quickly re-organised as each guest arrived at the dining table. Fourth in line, Ursula found herself plonked between the mother of four, Mona, and an accountant, Brian.

Mona spent most of the meal running to the toilet. The two-pint portions of borscht had really taken their toll on her bladder. Once this starter was finished, Carla ceremoniously ladled out huge rustic bowls of stew and dumplings. With her bowl half empty, Mona made her apologies again and headed off in the direction of the toilet. Ursula was left in the awkward position of having to talk to Brian on a few occasions. To be fair, they had tried a few times to strike up a conversation, but each time his accountant wife, seated on the other side of him, would dig him in the ribs. They were a handsome couple, but she had one of those smiles burnt on with a branding-iron. Ursula was well used to the 'keep off my man' look and she certainly wasn't going to enter into any conversations when Brian's wife was holding a bread knife. With his wife out in the yard having a smoke, Brian finally moved his seat so that he was facing Ursula directly. He was the most handsome man Ursula had met in a long time. His square jaw and Roman nose made his face strong-looking, and ocean-green eyes twinkled with his warm smile. She smiled back and he leaned over to whisper in her ear.

"I'm mad I am."

Oh no, Ursula thought.

"I'm completely mad. You know what I did last year on my holidays in Florida? Bungee jumping."

"Really."

"All my mates say I'm mad too. I'm a right laugh. I sometimes meet clients wearing one blue sock and one green one. Just when they're thinking 'here we go again, another boring accountant', they get a glimpse of my socks. What a laugh! Do you know what they call me at the office?"

A right bollocks, Ursula was thinking, just as Mona returned to her seat. Brian also noticed his wife had finished her cigarette and he sheepishly shifted his seat back again.

32

"Sorry about that Ursula, my bladder's never quite been the same since I had the weeins. Have you any children yourself?"

"No, I haven't."

"Mine are right buggers, every last one of them, but . . ."

"But, I know, you wouldn't do without them."

Mona rolled her eyes and smiled softly. Ursula was starting to feel pleased with the seating arrangements. With the pressure of the two Portaferry flamenco dancers gone and a glass of very full-bodied red wine in her system, she was starting to enjoy her chat with Mona. Very early on in the meal, Ursula had discovered that Mona's husband worked as a solicitor, the same profession as her ex-husband. They had spent the first half-hour slating off the judges they both knew. Mona was about the same age as Ursula, but with her mousy-blonde hair scraped back into a ponytail and loose-fitting denim shirt over a full-length navy skirt, she was very much dressed for practicalities rather than style.

"I love the way you've done your hair, Ursula. I wish I could get mine to look like that."

"Mona, if I had four toddlers running around, I'd be doing my best to get up in the morning, never mind anything else."

"It's true, I suppose. I buy clothes that are as dark as possible so they don't show up any grubby little finger marks, I keep my hair tied back so the wee one doesn't start pulling on it and I keep my nails short so I don't end up scratching the little buggers once they start playing up."

Both women laughed and Ursula topped up Mona's wine glass. As Ursula rarely drank and was driving home, she had offered to take Mona home after the party. Mona didn't

33

need to be asked twice and was now enjoying the very fine wines Carla had on offer. Ursula soaked up the remnants of the Russian stew in her bowl with torn-off chunks of wholemeal bread. At this point, Carla, who had been engaged in deep conversation with the two lecturers, bustled off to the kitchen. She returned with a large cherry and cream gâteau, greeted by welcome gasps from her guests. The men tucked into the dessert with gusto and the women made polite excuses. Except that is, Carla, who helped herself to two portions.

An hour later, at about 11.30, Carla declared it was time for some dancing. Once the meal was over, Mona and Ursula had commandeered one of the big sofas and had slowly, over the course of the evening, sunk into its deep recesses. When Mona volunteered to be Brian's dance partner, it took two men to lever her out. Carla had hijacked the young pizza-delivery boy and the stewardess and pilot made the final couple. Ursula was happy to stay seated, even if this meant enduring the cold harsh stares of Brian's wife seated on the sofa opposite. The Spanish acoustic guitar music began with an explosive opening and quickly shifted into its vibrant rhythm. You could see the stewardess and pilot moving their lips as they counted their steps and Brian and Mona looked like a jumbled-up mess of elbows and knees. Carla started moving slowly and with care and precision indicated the correct moves to her dance partner. Ursula was forced to notice that the pizza boy was an excellent learner. Within minutes he was confident enough with the steps to take his eyes off his feet and look directly into Carla's face. At that point the magic began. Somehow their hips became one and their hands seemed to barely touch as they rotated and curved and arched their backs. The boy couldn't take his eyes off Carla, as she was transformed into her sensual and sexual persona. The long tresses of her hair swayed with the rhythm of the music and kept brushing against the chest of the young apprentice.

Ursula decided that it was time for her to leave. She didn't need to stay, as she knew the plot from now on so well. Carla and the boy would dance for perhaps another hour, they would then go to bed (the details of which Carla would try to share with Ursula over the telephone the next day at which point Ursula would hang up) and then for the next two weeks the boy would become Carla's lover. After two weeks, the boy would go back to his teenage girlfriend, a very much wiser young man, and Carla would move on to the next apprentice. Mona was happy to take up Ursula's offer of the lift home and both women said their farewells. They opened Carla's front door and were immediately doused in the heady scent of the sea combined with faint diesel odours from the marina.

"I could feel Brian's wife's eyes boring into me all the time we were dancing."

"You're lucky, Mona. I felt them all night."

"I'd hardly think me, with all my weeins and a fat arse, would be much of a threat."

"Mona! Don't put yourself down."

"If I had your looks, I wouldn't."

Both inside the silver Ford Puma, Ursula started driving through the town centre, dodging the throngs of teenage drunkards as they poured out from the pubs and made their way to the many nightclubs dotted up High Street. Ursula was careful not to stop the car, otherwise she would have been bombarded with requests for a taxi. Mona rested her slightly inebriated head on the car seat and hoisted one leg up on the dashboard. They continued for about a mile in silence, Ursula happy to concentrate on her driving. After a few minutes they were on the Bangor Ring Road heading towards Groomsport. The structured streetlights were now replaced by sycamores and ash.

"Isn't it great fun, Ursula, going out on your own like, with no bloke? I've met quite a few of Carla's conquests. You must have some fierce craic too."

"Sometimes."

"How long is it since you left your husband?"

"I suppose it's about seven months now. Doesn't time fly!"

"Aye, when you're enjoying yourself. And what did it . . . you know what made you leave him?"

"We were incompatible."

Ursula gave her stock answer. She'd practised it hundreds of times and over the last few weeks it had started to finally sound real to her. Carla, who had been her friend for nearly ten years and a good one to her ex-husband as well, had probed her over and over as to why she had left him. It was hard for her friends and family to understand why she should leave a perfectly loving husband and a perfectly happy five years of marriage. In fact most of her friends and family didn't understand or accept it. How could a woman just up and leave like that? Financially, she had been fortunate to be able to cash in an endowment policy and put down quite a sizeable deposit on her new house. The job at the BBC was enough to pay the bills. At first she had missed the luxuries of her 'previous existence' as she called it: the five-bedroomed house in Holywood, his and her Mercedes, three holidays a year. But she was happy to have broken all ties now and hadn't seen her husband since that day seven months ago when she had walked out.

"Incompatible? I see."

Ursula's stock answer had worked.

"You know, I'm surprised I don't know him, what with all those boring old solicitors' dinners I get dragged to. Richards did you say your name was?"

"I've gone back to my maiden name, yes, Richards. His is Keane."

"Roger Keane?"

At this moment Ursula pulled the car up outside a large suburban five-bedroomed house. Mona quickly fumbled with the latch of the car door. Ursula turned on the courtesy light to help her passenger see better. Mona's face was pure white and her eyelashes were dotted with tiny specks of moisture. Her left hand frantically searched for the car door handle, like a hamster scrambling in its wheel. Ursula reached out and pulled the doorhandle. After a murmured 'thank you' Mona rushed up to a beautifully sculptured bay tree in her front porch, where she threw up.

Poor Mona. Ursula congratulated herself for not letting herself get into that kind of state. She rarely touched alcohol, other than the odd glass of wine at dinner parties. The nearer she drove to her own house, however, the quicker the self-praise was forgotten. As she pulled into her drive, she regretted not leaving the outside light on. Her house was dark. She could see faint flickers of silver and blues through the curtains of the Watsons', as, no doubt with the girls safely tucked up in bed, Christine and Alex were enjoying a late-night movie. The new couple across the road had left their hall light on before going to bed. The strange man next door at Number 8 had also turned out all his lights and it was in complete darkness. This only echoed the loneliness of her own home and the comparison sent a cool chill down her spine. His Golf GTI, as usual, was peculiarly parked on the road, leaving an expanse of empty drive. She shook her head before turning the key in the front-door latch. Another evening done and dusted. Nothing exciting, but then again nothing catastrophic either. She hadn't made a fool of herself by chasing after young boys or throwing up in a herbaceous border. Quite a satisfactory outcome all in all. She entered the front door and pulled it firmly shut behind her.

Once inside Ursula could see the red light on her answerphone flashing. She thought for a moment about leaving it until the morning, but then she changed her mind.

"Ursula darling, it's Carla. I've got some great gossip about Mona and a mystery man. Can't talk now as I'm having sex. Meet me tomorrow for lunch."

Chapter 6

Frances had got a telephone call at about 8.30 the following morning and had hurried out of the house with a quick peck on Fergal's cheek and a succinct 'see you later'. Fergal stretched himself out until he could reach all four corners of the king-sized bed. He woke at around 10.30 in exactly the same position. Including his snooze on the sofa last night, he totalled up his sleep to thirteen hours. The thought that he had been asleep more than he had been awake in the past twenty-four hours motivated him to shower, shave, dress and eat his breakfast all within ten minutes. Swigging down the last of his mug of tea, he was pleased he had made up for some of the lost time.

Looking out of the front window, Fergal could see sparrows hunting for grubs on his front lawn. They dipped their long beaks deep into the soil, with the occasional successful discovery of a plump pink worm. Yesterday's sunshine had been replaced with a blanket of dense silver-white cloud, but his late-night prayer for rain had failed.

The grass was dry enough and if he didn't have both the front and back lawns cut before Frances got back home, he knew there would be hell to pay. Hung up on the garage door was a pair of old bottle-green tracksuit bottoms and a 1994 Winter Olympic's sweatshirt. He changed out of his beige chino trousers into the tracksuit bottoms and pulled the sweatshirt over his grey polo shirt. He then carefully adjusted his collar, until it neatly sat over the neck of his jumper. Fergal then pulled green Wellington boots over his cream silk socks and carried the petrol mower over to the front steps.

As Fergal sat tugging away at three-week-old grass remnants caught between the blades, he heard shouting from across the road. The Lawnmower Man from Number 8 was standing in his rear garden with his back to Fergal. He was obviously involved in a heated discussion with someone who was hidden from view by the over-tall fence. Fergal craned his neck – however, his view was not improved. The conversation suddenly calmed and the Lawnmower Man disappeared around the back of the house. Fergal was intrigued and shifted his mower across to the far corner of his front lawn in order to improve his sight line. There was no improvement and, as he looked back towards his own house, he could see the impression his boots had made in the wet lawn. A series of deep wounds were staggered along the lush grass. Seeing his investigation was proving futile, Fergal retraced his footprints back to the step and set about starting up the mower.

Fergal checked that the fuel tank was full and then yanked hard on the starter motor. After two or three violent spats the mower went silent. He pulled up on the cord with his clenched right hand and jammed his foot against the stubborn implement's side. There was one shudder and then silence again. This time he tightly clasped both hands around the handle and gave out a ferocious roar, which starkly contrasted with the absolute silence of the mower.

"Bugger, bollocks, shite . . ."

"Hello."

He quickly turned round to see the elfin face of the little girl from across the road looking up at him. She was breathing rapidly with her red curls tucked up inside a baseball cap and with slightly rosy cheeks.

"Can't you get it going, mister?"

"No."

"I'm eight now."

"Good for you."

"Is it broken?"

"I don't know."

"Shall I see?"

"No, it's not broken."

"Will I have a go?"

"It's a bit big for little girls. Is that your Ma calling you?"

"No, Mummy's talking to Mr McAllen over there. Go on, give us a go."

As Fergal's temper was starting to bubble, the gorgeous divorcee from up the road pulled up in her silver Ford Puma and rolled down the car window. Her blonde hair was loosely tied back at the nape of her neck with a flowing copper and gold silk scarf. Her make-up was impeccable with bronze lipstick accentuating very full lips and picking out the highlights in her scarf. She was wearing a pale pink linen blouse. As she leant forward Fergal could just about get a glimpse of a very white cotton bra. Fergal was pleased

41

with himself as he stood up and could now see the intricate lace detail around the right cup of the bra.

"I see you've a little helper there, Fergal."

Having momentarily forgotten about the little thorn in his side, he glanced down to see the girl smiling up at him.

"Aye, Ursula, I don't know how I'd manage without a bit of help. The little rascal. Off somewhere nice?"

"I'm meeting up with my friend Carla for lunch. She says she has some hot gossip for me. Any plans yourself?"

'Was this a chat up?' he confidently thought for a very, very brief moment.

"Not really. I'm looking for any excuse to get out of this job to be honest."

He wasn't going to let this opportunity go without a small battle. But before Ursula could reply, Fergal heard a loud thudding followed by a droning roar. His eyes, looking down, were met with the big smiling eyes of the child looking up. Molly had successfully started up the lawnmower and her obvious pleasure more than equalled Fergal's blossoming embarrassment. Ursula waved a farewell and sped off. Fergal was sure he saw her laughing. Molly certainly was as she skipped back over to her own front garden. He was left standing alone with his ego throbbing along at the same pace as the lawnmower. Sitting back down on the step, he looked down at himself. His sweatshirt, with silver grey hairs from his chest peeping out from the neckline, was stretched beyond the call of duty and revealed the outline of two ample shaped breasts.

"Grey hairs and thrupenny bits. For fuck's sake!"

As he looked up again, a police patrol car drove past. The policeman driving the vehicle waved and Fergal returned the greeting. Jesus, he thought to himself, he was waving at the RUC now.

How had this happened to him? When had it happened? Fergal thought back to the photograph in the study. The skinny, grubby Derryman, always the best of craic, who took two days to tell a story. Now he was suburban man, who hadn't told a good story in years and hadn't had a good curse in weeks. Fergal had grown up with four older sisters, all with a predestined future of benefits or jobs in the shirt factories. He had broken the mould and been the first in his family to pass his eleven plus, to go on to grammar school and then, the miracle of all miracles, go to university. He tried to pinpoint the exact moment he turned into the man he was now. Was it when he met Frances in his third year at university or was it when he got his first job and the first time he'd paid income tax? He couldn't pick one moment, one change of events. It had been a slow process. The drip, drip, drip of subtle changes had worn away the boy and left the carcass of the man.

Again he thought back to the photograph and his childhood friend proudly holding the freshly caught salmon in the air. Fergal and his friend Brendan had been poaching all night and at four in the morning Brendan had caught a six-pounder. Fergal never went poaching again. Shortly after catching the salmon they had got back into their boat and paddled out into the middle of the river. The River Fahan was dotted with red flashing specks as the poachers lined along the banks sucked on their cigarettes.

"Fergal, the last time I saw a fish that size was the one caught by yer man . . . you know the one with the dodgy leg."

"Paddy Boyle?"

"Naw, he's Billy's brother. This guy hung about with the Porters."

Brendan squeezed his skull between clenched fingers.

"Wait, I've got it . . . fak it, it's gone. His name's going to drive me mad all morning."

This time Brendan gripped his hands behind his head and clamped his forearms tightly against his temples.

"Fergal, go through the alphabet. Andy, Alan, Aiden, Eamonn."

"Eamonn's not an 'a', he's an 'e'."

"Ambrose."

"Ambrose? How many fakin' Ambroses do you know in the estate?"

"Bobby . . . Brian . . . Blaise."

Fergal was losing patience. He opened and closed his mouth several times, but failed to find the words to express his exasperation.

"What, Fergal? Blaise is a name. Saint Blaise, the patron saint of sore throats."

"You must be joking."

"Sure, there's a patron saint for everything now. A patron saint of TVs, a patron saint of Hopeless Cases . . ."

"Hang on a minute, Brendan. A patron saint of TVs?"

"Stop putting me off. Where was I? B's. Brian, Bernard, Bob . . . bastard, I nearly had it!"

The two men rattled through the rest of the alphabet at great speed, but Brendan began to flag when they came to 's'.

"Steve . . . Stewart . . . Seamus."

"Seamus Devine?"

"Bobby Devine?"

"Bobby Devlin?"

Across the river, one of the other poachers had shouted out 'Noel Devlin'.

"That's it, Fergal – Noel Fakin Devlin. Anyway, he's dead now."

Fergal had been sincerely remorseful, as he'd spent many a school lunch break exchanging empty bullet cartridges with Noel Devlin.

"God, Brendan, that's a real shame. He's only our age."

"Hang on a minute . . . no, he's not dead. That's another fella who's dead. What's his name?"

Fergal had stopped rowing and was about to throw a handful of maggots at his friend when he suddenly heard a rattling sound. Brendan then also heard it. He got out his binoculars and spotted a motorbike on the far side of the river. The cigarette lights were all quickly extinguished. Brendan kept his eye on the motorbike and followed it as it manoeuvred up and down the country road. Suddenly, everything in front of his binoculars went completely black. He abruptly realised that the rattling sound hadn't been the motorbike at all. It had been the sound of a motorboat and standing right in front of the two fishermen was a huge angry bailiff. Brendan and Fergal had all the fishing gear, plus the binoculars, confiscated. Shortly after their adventure Fergal had headed off to Coleraine University. He thought back to the photograph and wondered what his friend was up to these days. 'What happened to you too?' he quietly said to himself.

Fergal made his way back into the house and towards the kitchen. He switched on the kettle and walked over to the bread bin looking for a cake or something nice to eat along with his tea. Stuck to the tin was a yellow Post-it. Fergal quickly recognised the handwriting as his wife's.

Fergal,

Thought this was the best place to get your attention. I'm off to Amsterdam with the volleyball team. I'll ring and fill you in later. See you Sunday night.

Love Frances.

Chapter 7

"Mummy, The Baby's shoved a fridge magnet up her nose."

As Christine slowly opened her eyes, she found she was eyeball to eyeball with the plastic boot of a jolly green giant hanging loosely from her youngest's nose. As The Baby laughed joyously, her sister Molly bounced up and down on the bed, flipping her bare heels in the air. Molly feverishly pushed away the dancing red curls as they tumbled into her eyes. Ruth, the messenger of doom, was crying in frantic spurts. She dramatically flung out her arm and knocked a half-empty glass of water from the bedside cabinet. Tiny bubbles of mucus fell from her nose onto the white linen bedsheet. With her left hand, Christine reached under her pillow and removed a handful of tissues. As she passed one to Ruth, with her right hand she pulled a bronze pin out of her own hair and scooping up Molly's wayward fringe, she jabbed a bunch of curls into a tight coil. She dropped the remaining tissues onto the bedroom carpet and with her right foot carefully mopped the spilt water. Her hands were now free to attempt the removal of the offending magnet. As The Baby continued to laugh, the giant's foot rocked in and out. Carefully monitoring the rhythm, Christine calmly waited for an outward movement, before pinching the boot between her forefinger and thumb. It came out; or rather it came off. With The Baby's head tilted back, a tiny white stump could be seen buried into the back of her nose.

Christine gave Ruth and Molly orders to quickly dress themselves and to wait in the car. She swiftly changed out of her pink cotton nightdress and, lifting The Baby, wrapped her in a woollen cardigan that had been draped over the end of the bed. As Christine pulled the bedroom door behind her, she looked over at Alex. Her husband lay with his face buried in the pillow and his shoulders softly rocking with his pulsating breath. He had not stirred.

Christine had been easily woken, as she was only resting her eyes after a long, sleepless night. Apart from a few courteous comments and a brief 'I'm having an early night', she hadn't spoken to Alex about what she had seen through the window. As she lay in bed last night, she could hear her husband downstairs opening and closing the kitchen cupboards. He had gone to bed at around three o'clock in the morning, and as Christine pretended to sleep, he had fumbled with his clothes before sinking into bed. As Christine now looked down at him with darkened heavy eyes and with The Baby cradled in her arms, she could see that, between eventually coming to bed and now, her husband hadn't moved an inch.

Twenty minutes later, Christine and her three girls were sitting in the casualty department of the Ulster Hospital in Dundonald. Molly was amusing her baby sister by plaiting her hair the way her mummy had shown her countless times. The twelve-year-old Ruth sat reading the public notices pinned to a board behind her. Christine sat with her fingers interlocked on her lap and stared down at the neat folds in her long navy skirt. One was slightly ruffled and she delicately re-positioned the pleat and pressed it down firmly with the palm of her right hand. She couldn't think about Alex right now – the girls needed her. She'd had the night to think of nothing else.

"Mummy, have you got a pen?"

Without lifting her eyes from her lap, Christine reached into her handbag and pulled out a biro, which she mechanically gave to her eldest daughter. Alex was under a lot of pressure at the practice, she thought to herself, with extra hours and paperwork. Maybe he was under stress. Her thoughts raced ahead and then raced back again as her mind drifted to their wedding, nearly fifteen years ago. Painfully shy, Alex had visibly turned grey whenever Christine had explained that the invitation list had grown to nearly 200. As the young couple and their two mothers waded through the list trying to cut the numbers down, Alex had quietly and slowly slid down the leather armchair in his mother-in-law's front room. The three women hadn't noticed that Alex had slumped to the floor, crawled under the coffee table and on hands and knees was making his escape to the door.

"And a wee bit of paper too, please, Mummy."

Rattled from her trance, Christine looked over as Ruth pointed to the telephone number of a Lesbian helpline, advertised on the hospital noticeboard. The notice was jammed between the Multiple Births Society and advice on 'what to do if you get the flu'.

"Mrs Watson?"

"Yes, that's me."

A nurse with over-large breasts and white plimsolls stepped over a slightly inebriated teenager sprawled on the floor and shuffled over to Christine.

"We just need to get some more details before the doctor gets a chance to see your wee girl."

"That's fine."

"What age is she?"

"Two."

"Is she allergic to any medications?"

"No."

"Has she been in casualty before?"

"No."

Christine responded briskly and the nurse, thinking this was an oral challenge, joined in by continuing her rapid-fire questions.

"Can I have your full address, Mrs Watson?"

"Number 5, The Ashbury, Bangor West."

"Your daughter's date of . . ."

"Seventh of the eleventh '97."

"The name of your family doctor?"

Christine had continued to stare at her gently rocking hands throughout the swift exchange. Her feet were tightly crossed and tucked under the blue bucket chair. She carefully tried to moisten her dry lips by running her tongue gently along the outline. Directly in front of her, the morning sun was beaming in through the hospital window. The sunlight revealed a series of grubby handprints smeared onto the glass.

"Mrs Watson? The name of your family doctor?"

"Dr Watson?"

"Oh, a relative?"

"No, he's my husband."

An hour later Christine was driving her three girls back home. Since leaving the waiting room her demeanour had greatly altered. She was agitated and her hands flitted from the steering wheel to her hair, then to her top lip and then back to the wheel. She drove with her mobile telephone in her lap for a few minutes and then rang home. Christine briefly explained to Alex what had happened.

"Why the hell didn't you wake me?"

"I knew she'd need a x-ray anyway."

"How is she?"

"Grand."

"Look, Christine, work's just rung and they want me to go in. There's been a bad road accident and all doctors have been called on duty. I won't be here when you get back."

"How long will you be?"

"Could be hours. Will you be able to manage on your own?"

The words 'manage on your own' echoed in her head as she said her brief farewells to her husband. She turned the family's white Renault Espace off the dual carriageway and drove through a series of roundabouts on the outskirts of Newtownards before taking the Bangor Road. As she waited at the traffic lights, to her left she saw a short, square man clambering up a lamppost on a set of ladders. In his late twenties, he wore a pair of football tracksuit bottoms and a capped-sleeve white T-shirt. Supporting the bottom of the ladders was a primary-school-aged boy, identically dressed, with the same short, square body frame. The man reached into a supermarket plastic bag tucked into his belt and pulled out a Union Jack and an Ulster flag. The flags were tangled and the more the man tried to untangle them, the more they refused to part. The young boy looked over at Christine and gave her a warm, beguiling smile. The traffic lights turned green and Christine drove away.

Within a mile from their home and an hour later, the Watson girls and their mother were still in the car. They were held up in traffic as a result of an Orange Order parade on the outskirts of Bangor. The trauma of the day had left The Baby exhausted and she lay gently snoring in her car seat. Molly and Ruth were becoming agitated.

"One, that's my bag of crisps and two, that's my coke."

"Three, I don't think so."

Christine caught sight of herself in the car's wing mirror. A tiny coil of red hair had escaped from its metal pin at her temple. She didn't re-pin it.

"Four, give it over or else."

"Five, or else what?"

"Six, seven and eight, I'll tell everyone in school that you're adopted, you wee shite."

Both girls glanced over at their mother, but the expected admonishment didn't happen. The tail-enders of the parade turned into a side road and the cars held up in the jam slowly started to move again. Within a few minutes the white Espace pulled onto the driveway of house Number 5. The cul-de-sac was quiet except for Fergal Coyle across the road, who had his garage door open and was awkwardly pulling a green sweatshirt over his head.

As the car came to a sudden stop in the drive, The Baby was prematurely woken and her eldest sister unlocked the car seat and attempted to console her. Christine got out of the car and opened the rear passenger door, which had been secured with a child-lock. When she opened the car door, three girls poured out onto the tarmac; Ruth and Molly at the bottom with their fingers in each other's eyes and then their sobbing younger sister as the cherry on the top.

"Get the fuck up off the ground!"

Christine stood towering over them. Her pupils looked plump as they dilated under a film of tears. Her daughters were silent. A thick wet line was drawn in sweat down the front of Christine's pink cotton blouse. A cascade of auburn ringlets framed her white face, each balancing a tiny drop of salty moisture. Their mother held her stare as the girls remained crumpled and motionless. Suddenly, as Christine's hands trembled, a bunch of car keys crashed to the floor. The three girls burst into uncontrollable tears.

"Who wants to earn a tenner?"

Mr McAllen had been standing in his back garden and at the point of the car keys falling onto the ground he appeared from behind the Watsons' car. The girls' sobs gradually transformed into whimpers.

"Well, I won't ask again!"

All three stopped crying and stared with round pitiful eyes in the direction of this large imposing figure. Christine also turned to face her neighbour. He left traces of soil and grass across his navy shirt with a quick swipe of his strong hands. The debris had formed deep stripes, as if a claw had torn through the cotton fabric. Maurice's cobalt blue eyes maintained their focus beyond the shadow formed by the overhang of his square bronzed brow.

"That's better. This is the deal. Your mission is to take

the wee one inside and make her something nutritional and tasty to eat. Come back in half an hour and I'll give you a tenner."

At this, Maurice pointed to Ruth. She responded by pulling up her baby sister from the ground and carrying her obediently into the Watson house.

"And you."

His neck craned the whole way forward as he peered down at the diminutive Molly still sprawled on the tarmac.

"Go and do two good deeds for your neighbours. Then come back and claim your reward. This mission is top secret."

Molly remained mesmerised, with her mouth slightly ajar and her eyes wide and enquiring. Maurice reached down without bending his knees and scooped the eight-year-old up with his right arm. The child appeared weightless against the stranger's flexed muscular forearm. Brought to her feet, she gently wobbled and then slowly regained her balance.

"Now go!"

Molly jumped to attention, grabbed her doll Suki from the back of the car and headed purposefully across the road.

By enveloping Christine's small, shaking, white hand within his own, Maurice led her into his back garden and out of sight of any passing neighbours. As he guided her, Christine fixed her stare onto her small feet, encased in soft, leather court shoes. His stride was long and deep and she shuffled rhythmically behind. As they reached the step leading to his back door, she pulled her hand away aggressively and thrust her frightened face upwards towards his.

"What the hell did you do all that for? I had everything under control."

"It didn't look like it."

54

"Where do you get off telling complete strangers how to handle their children?"

"That was handling them, was it?"

A burning red had replaced the white of Christine's cheeks and temples and as she angrily bit into her lip a tiny dot of blood pricked the skin. Maurice's composure had not changed and he continued to maintain control and authority. This provoked Christine.

"When you've got three children – one with plastic jammed up her nostril, one with membership of the Ellen Degeneres fan club and the other a would-be mother of three, maybe then I'll listen to you!"

"Mrs Watson, you're being hysterical."

"How dare you!"

"Just listen to yourself."

"Listen to me? What about you, Mr McAllen? You're hardly Charles Ingles, are you? What do you know about raising children?"

"Nothing."

"Or keeping a family together?"

Briefly Maurice lowered his icy eyes and with his forefinger carefully stroked the bridge of his nose. His voice became deep and barely audible.

"Your getting out of control has nothing to do with me. I know I don't really know you, Mrs Watson, but I do know that wasn't the real you I saw over there just now."

"You're right . . . you don't know me."

The exchange had begun in hushed tones but had now grown into a combination of Christine's loud rantings and Maurice's composed forceful responses. Across the road, Maurice caught a glimpse of Fergal Coyle from house

Number 2 peering nosily. He was sure he didn't want that one listening to his business and turned his broad shoulders in order to mask his neighbour's view. Christine misinterpreted the manoeuvre as an approach in her direction and swiftly retreated to the far end of the garden. Maurice took two steps towards her and then stopped abruptly.

"I know you are a good mother, Mrs Watson. In fact you're an excellent mother. I don't know what's going on, but you've got what most people look for all their lives. Don't lose it."

For the first time since the previous evening, since the moment she saw her husband inject himself, Christine felt her racing heartbeat subside. The throbbing within her head, though still present, turned from that of a hammer to a tree tapping a window in the breeze.

"I envy you, Christine."

Maurice had slipped his hands into his corduroy trouser pockets and stood with his long legs shoulder width apart. With the first kind words she had heard all day, the frenzy and turmoil battling within her skull slowly disintegrated. The residue was bitter. What had she said to her girls? Had she really left them trembling in front of her? What had she said to them? Like a deflated circus tent, Christine slumped down onto the grass and burst into tears.

"I'm sorry! I'm so sorry!"

As the tears trickled through her fingers, with one motion of her hand she wiped her eyes and then brushed her hair away from her face. As Maurice motioned to move towards her, Christine held up the palm of her hand.

"Please don't come any closer. I'm so ashamed. Look at me. I'm a mess. My life's a lie, a façade. My husband injects himself. I saw him. He's a drug addict.

56

"Are you sure?"

"Just before we went down to get an X-ray for The Baby; a young lad who had overdosed on heroin was rushed in on a stretcher. His two friends sat either side of me for fifteen minutes, talking across me as if I wasn't there. They had the same glazed look, the same snuffles and jerky movements. The same as Alex."

"Christine, it doesn't mean Alex's the same."

Christine was now having difficulty speaking as her sobs took control. To Maurice she was no longer a school matron, but a frightened young girl. Long slim legs were folded tightly under her chin as she embraced them with her slender arms. The vigorously bitten lips were, as a result, a full ruby red and they delicately tightened and relaxed with each sob. Maurice stepped another few paces towards her, whilst retaining a controlled stance.

"I wanted my children's lives to be everything mine wasn't. Seeing him inject himself last night shocked me. But what shocked me most were the lies and the disappointment."

"Have you spoken to him about this?"

"No."

"Believe me, it's the only way to deal with it."

"Believe me, I can hardly look at Alex right now, let alone talk to him."

Calmed and more composed, Christine looked up at her unlikely confessor. Maurice maintained the rigid stance and harsh glare that she was familiar with from their previous brief exchanges. As he slowly knelt on the grass within two feet of her, however, a soft kindness escaped from his penetrating blue eyes. She was struck by the sharp contrast between

Maurice and her husband. In front of her was a type of man her mother would have definitely called 'bad news'. His mystery and danger had been intimidating, but now as he gently stroked the blades of grass at his heels, there was sadness and loneliness chiselled into his handsome features.

Maurice continued to brush his hand along the grass. He stopped as he caressed a single blade. From halfway up the shaft it was gnarled and twisted. The lawnmower blade had contorted the grass, making it hard and sharp, in strong contrast to the silky smooth blades surrounding it.

"Trust me, you must talk to your husband."

"Look, me blowing up like that, it was a one-off. I can start getting back to my life again now."

Maurice yanked out the gnarled blade of grass and crushed it in his palm.

"Christine, you know that's not possible."

"It's worked before. Don't look at me like that. I've never actually seen Alex inject before, but I've had my suspicions for some time now."

"How long?"

"I started noticing changes in his behaviour about the time I was pregnant with my youngest. Must be nearly three years now."

"For God's sake, Christine. And you've just continued as if everything is normal?"

"You tell me what's normal, Maurice."

Christine could see from the expression on her neighbour's face that she had dealt a painful blow. Her irrationality, petulance and anger she could excuse, but not cruelty.

"I'm sorry. I didn't mean that. As a child all I longed for was to be normal. I longed for a mummy and a daddy who lived together. I longed for birthday parties like everyone else, and I longed for stability."

She carefully removed the hairgrips that had earlier been thrust into her chaotic hair.

"More than anything I longed for bloody straight hair like everybody else."

She gently smiled and for the first time since she had seen her neighbour step out of the small removals van a year ago, she saw him smile too. Her life was a mess, her marriage was a mess and she looked a mess. They both stood up and left behind small dark craters imprinted on the grass.

"Thank you for all your help with the girls. I'm sorry you saw me like this, but a wee bit of mascara and a few more hair clips and everything will be as right as rain."

"Not everything, Christine."

Christine dusted off a few bits of twig and grass from her skirt. She had avoided eye contact for the last few minutes, partly due to embarrassment and partly due to the intensity of Maurice's stare. As they stood close together for the first time, Christine felt frightened by his size. Maurice's vast shadow enveloped her. She just wanted to get away, quickly.

"Thank you again."

She craned her neck to look up at his face, but with the sun directly behind him now, he was a black silhouette. As a farewell gesture, Christine put out her right hand, which he gently shook with his own. Tenderly, Maurice held onto her hand and pulled Christine towards him. With both their hands cushioned within the small of her back, he leant forward and with the gentleness of a breeze, he kissed her.

Chapter 8

With her story of the bloke who boasted of winning thirty-eight 'Harry Ramsden's Challenge Certificates', Frances won the Worst Chat-up Line Competition. He had thought being able to eat the king-size portions of cod fillet, chips, mushy peas, bread and butter, dessert and tea thirty-eight times would impress her. The minibus was about five minutes from Belfast International Airport and their flight to Amsterdam. Back with her old team, Frances was feeling like a fish out of water. It was hard for her to imagine that only an hour ago she was holding Fergal's nose in bed, in a feeble attempt to get him to stop snoring. Now she was with five sleepy-eyed volleyball players, off to seek adventure.

The telephone had rung at eight-thirty that Saturday morning. Fergal had shown no signs of moving, so after several deep sighs, pokes in the ribs and a cruel jab in the neck, Frances had gone down the stairs and answered the telephone herself.

"Frances, it's me, Niamh. Is your passport up to date?"

"Why?"

"We're off to play in a tournament in Amsterdam today, only Deirdre's just rung to say she's done her shoulder in carrying her kitbag down the stairs."

"Finely tuned athletes as ever I see."

"Come on, Frances. It only leaves us five players and you know they won't let us play without the six."

"Niamh, I haven't touched a ball in nearly a year."

"It doesn't matter. The flights are booked, the hotel's booked, we've even got a minibus to take us to the airport. Just pack your kneepads and a bottle of Bacardi and we'll pick you up in half an hour."

Niamh had fought the bit out with Frances for another five minutes.

"Look, I'll even bring the Bacardi and the kneepads – you just shove on your coat."

Frances continued to trot off excuse after excuse. She looked down at her crumpled Betty Boo nightdress and dangling unshaven legs and the sight fuelled her resistance. The blue nail polish she had applied methodically to her toenails only four weeks earlier, was now unsurprisingly chipped and flaking. With her excuse-barrel empty, Frances progressed to suggest three or four other players for Niamh to contact.

"But it's you we want, Franny. It's all the old team. You'll have a ball."

"I can't."

"Why not?"

"I've a stack of washing to do and it looks like it's going to be a great drying day."

There was a moment of deathly silence and then both women laughed.

"What time are you picking me up?"

Frances had dusted off her sports bag, found crammed under the bed, thrown in whatever clothes were washed and ironed and quickly scribbled a note to Fergal.

Niamh also lived in Bangor and arrived to collect Frances first. With her polo shirtcollar starched upright and pressed khaki shorts, Niamh did justice to her schoolteacher profession. Her make-up was impeccable and treacle-black permed hair had seen more than its fair share of rollers that morning. On their way through Holywood, they stopped to pick up sisters Rose and Cathy-Ann. They were perched on the front wall surrounding their ground-floor apartment. As usual they were bickering, this time over who had packed the hairdryer. Rose was the same age as Frances, and Cathy-Ann, a frequently reminded 'accident', was twelve years her junior at 22. Both worked in the restaurant trade, Rose as a manager and Cathy-Ann, her commis chef. Working together and living together was not a happy combination in their apartment. Combined with Cathy-Ann being three stone lighter, six inches taller and a mere twelve years younger than her older sister, the rivalry was always bubbling away. Niamh, always the teacher, immediately split them up by seating Cathy-Ann in the front with her and putting Rose in the back with Frances. Just a few minutes later they were heading along the Sydenham bypass. There was little traffic for a Saturday morning and they were making good progress. Ahead of them on the path, a woman weighted down by a heavy backpack was jogging along at some speed.

"There she goes. I'd recognise that arse anywhere."

Niamh was pointing to their fifth player, Orla, who after

a quick spurt was now checking her time against a stopwatch. The minibus pulled over and the jogger hurled herself on board. Orla's claim to fame was a seventh place in the semi-finals of the 5,000m in the 1984 Olympics. That, plus the fact that she was Miss Butlin's Arm Wrestling Champion, three years running, tended to make up the bulk of any general introductions. For the next ten minutes of the journey the five teammates caught up on all the news and gossip. The conversation was civilised and polite. Frances joined in the discussion, but still felt very much the outsider.

The minibus made steady progress along the M3, before turning off at the roundabout at Duncrue Industrial Estate. Waiting in the lay-by was the last of the team. It was still only half-nine in the morning, but she emerged from the passenger side of the small Peugeot clutching a sleeping bag, a small rucksack and an opened can of Smithwicks. Leaning back through the car window, she lazily kissed the driver and then strolled over to the minibus. Roberta's short bleached-blonde hair was gelled up into nine or ten stiff spikes and her green eyes were circled in thick black eyeliner. Her elf-like face beamed from ear to ear as she swaggered over to the back door of the minibus. As the five women turned to greet their final passenger, Roberta swiftly bent over and mooned through the window of the back door.

Only now that the final cog was complete, did the gear slowly click into place. Abuse, indecency and the artful skill of 'talking shite' briskly replaced the friendly idle chitchat evident at the start of their journey. And now only a few miles from the airport and with a win in the Worst

Chat-up Line Competition, Frances started to wonder if she had made the right decision after all.

Fifteen minutes into the flight, Frances started feeling travel-sick. Rose, Orla and Roberta were seated in the row directly in front and Frances sat between Cathy-Ann at the window and Niamh in the aisle seat. A lethal cocktail of heat, Cathy-Ann's heady Opium perfume and Niamh's schoolroom jokes intensified her nausea. The peach blusher, hurriedly smudged onto her fair cheeks that morning, now grotesquely stood out against her pale green skin. Her hair suddenly felt greasy, so she scooped the neat bob into two tight bunches.

"I feel awful."

"Don't worry, Frances. I'll keep your mind off it with some more jokes. Paddy Scotsman, Paddy . . ."

A chorus of 'no' and 'stop' thudded from the two rows of seats occupied by the team, followed by a louder 'no more' from a row of three elderly men seated behind. Niamh shrugged her shoulders and submerged herself in the health and safety leaflet.

"Cathy-Ann, I must look even worse than I feel."

"You think *you* look bad – I can feel a spot right here on my chin. It's just dying to explode."

Cathy-Ann pointed to a microscopic pink blemish on her beautifully sculptured tanned chin. She wore a cropped white T-shirt and bootleg tight jeans. Long chestnut-brown hair was neatly pulled back into a French plait. Her Italian features starkly contrasted with her sister Rose's red hair and pink freckled complexion. No matter what the conversation, Frances knew, if Cathy-Ann was involved, it would eventually revolve around her. Brief acquaintances quickly tired of Cathy-Ann's insecurities and moved on after a few minutes, happy to re-confirm their stereotypes of the dumb beauty. But her teammates didn't. Frances placed her hand on that of the young woman.

"Cathy-Ann, you look as gorgeous as ever."

"Are you sure?"

"Yes, I'm sure."

At this, Roberta leaned over the middle seat directly in front.

"Jesus, Mary and Joseph – it's the size of a house. Come over here and I'll squeeze it for you."

Niamh and Frances both reached forward with their right arms and shoved Roberta by the face back into her seat. Niamh reached under her seat and pulled out her patent black Chanel handbag. Having pulled down her tray, she emptied out the entire contents of her handbag. She rummaged for a moment through receipts, make-up brushes and loose change, before pulling out a small packet of travel-sickness pills, which she gave to a by now desperate Frances, and a small tube of concealer which Cathy-Ann greedily accepted. With her forearm outstretched, Niamh dragged the contents back into the bag and with it perched on her shoulder, she walked off in the direction of the toilets.

As Cathy-Ann busily applied the concealer, Frances gingerly swallowed the two tiny white pills and cradled her head against the seat. She was starting to feel guilty for abandoning Fergal. There was a time, if the roles had been reversed, she would have hit the roof. But not now – that was before they were married, before they trusted each other. That trust made her feel comfortable. She looked at the bobbing crowns of Rose, Roberta, and Orla in the seats in front. Rose had been married and divorced in her twenties and Roberta and Orla were still single. Frances felt a warm smugness. The self-satisfaction that she was no longer on the 'scene' in her thirties and looking for a man momentarily dulled the nausea. As she looked across to the other row of seats on her right, a small baby was hungrily sucking on the knuckle of her mother's little finger. The baby softly clenched and unclenched her tiny pink hands. Frances's sickness returned and she quickly pressed her eyelids tight together.

"We've a bet on. Do you want in?"

Orla had jammed her muscular backside into the seat briefly vacated by Niamh. Rose and Roberta had perched themselves on their knees and were looking over the back of their seats towards Frances and Cathy-Ann. Orla took the lead to explain further.

"When will Niamh put her black boob-tube on? Rose reckons it'll be when we get ready to go to the tournament disco tonight. I've got my bet on it being straight after the last match and Roberta tips before she gets off the plane."

"What does the winner get?"

"The winner gets to write a forfeit on this bit of paper, mix it with four blank pieces and stick them in this sick bag. We all draw and the loser then has to promise to accomplish the forfeit whilst we're in Amsterdam. I'll hold on to the paper and bag until we have a winner."

"So if we don't enter, we don't have to do a forfeit. Is that it?"

"Yes, but you also miss an opportunity to stitch one of us up."

At this, Roberta reached down to her half-eaten meal-tray and held a small sachet of salad cream up to her chin. As she squeezed the silver packet, a jet of yellow thick cream spurted out of a tiny hole.

"Oh, Cathy-Ann, that makes me feel so much better."

Roberta had hit a nerve and Cathy-Ann quickly entered 'by the last dance tonight' into the bet. Frances, however, was feeling that she had moved on from these silly familiar games. Were these women stuck in a time warp? She was confident that Niamh, who was married with two teenage sons, had at least managed to move on. It was true that in the past Niamh was very much a chameleon. She was famous for using a trip to a volleyball tournament as an opportunity to undertake some serious flirting. But that was all before she became deputy headmistress and her husband got a big job at the bank. Of course she had changed. Niamh had grown up, unlike the rest of them. Confident that the boob-tube had been dumped long ago and, therefore, no one would be the winner and there would be no forfeit, Frances reluctantly joined in with the bet.

As her friends returned to their seats, Frances felt the colour slowly return to her cheeks. The nausea had almost completely subsided. She looked down at her lap and compared the size of her grey tracksuit-clad thighs to those of her slender denimed co-passenger. Frances felt enormous. Cathy-Ann's concave stomach also only served to exaggerate the small mound of Frances's, that was uncomfortably balanced over the top of her seat belt.

"Does this T-shirt make my boobs stick out?"

"Cathy-Ann, they're supposed to stick out. It's when they don't that you get worried. Trust me."

67

Frances had been too busy comparing herself to Cathy-Ann to notice Niamh had returned to her seat. She was transformed. Her jet-black hair had been vigorously backcombed and with little dabs of hair mousse had formed dishevelled, 'just got out of bed' layers. The rose-pink of her lipstick delicately applied that morning had been crudely painted over with a vibrant fuchsia red. With her polo shirt roughly tied around her waist, a skimpy ebony-black boob tube tried vainly to suppress a voluptuous bust.

"Let the party begin."

As she said this, Niamh pulled out a half-litre bottle of Bacardi, expertly stashed in the inside pocket of her bag. She discreetly passed the bottle across to Frances with both arma at the same time crushing together a magnificent cleavage. Frances felt a thud in her stomach.

Following her bizarre, American-chat-show-style makeover, the rest of the team proceeded to ridicule Niamh. She took it all in good humour. Frances felt abandoned by her one comrade-in-arms and she concluded that this was going to be a weekend to endure rather than enjoy. Fergal's 'I told you so' face was looming vividly as she suddenly felt extremely lonely. When informed of the bet, Niamh just burst out laughing and gave the boasting victor, Roberta, a congratulatory kiss on the lips.

Orla methodically gave a blank piece of paper to Roberta and placed four folded pieces into a sick bag. Roberta dutifully scribbled a few sentences on the piece of paper with a red biro. She showed no sign of emotion and conducted the exercise with gravity. Cathy-Ann was the first to draw and with French-polished fingernails, delicately drew out a piece of paper from the top of the bag. It was blank. Rose followed by rummaging through the bag in an attempt to retrieve the very bottom piece. This was also blank. Next was Frances, who in an attempt to hide her nerves, dived straight into the bag and pulled out the first piece of paper that her fingers touched. She was about to unfold it, when an instinctive urge forced her to shove it back into the bag and pull out another piece. As she unfolded the paper, the red ink of Roberta's pen could be seen absorbed like water through a tissue. Frances read out the note.

"The conditions of this forfeit are that it must be delivered in the presence of at least twenty people, in a public place. You are going to streak."

Frances's nausea abruptly returned.

Chapter 9

Carla's detail of her sexual exploits from the night before was making Ursula grimace. She called the waitress over and asked for a coffee refill in an attempt to silence her friend's unwelcome descriptions. Carla looked as if she hadn't had an hour's sleep the previous night. Which would have been about right. Squeezed into a pair of brown leather trousers and a cropped emerald-green woollen jumper, she noisily intermingled her conversation with slurps of expresso coffee.

"The night was wonderful."

"Carla, I've told you. I don't want to know."

"Don't worry. I'm not going to talk about sex. After all, we didn't have any."

"But you've just spent five minutes telling me how nubile and erotic the pizza-boy was."

"Oh, but he was."

"And you didn't make love?"

"I told you already. We didn't have sex."

"Carla, I'm glad to hear it."

Ursula breathed an audible sigh of relief. What she hated even more than hearing her friend's sexual exploits, was the thought that this was the best her friend could do.

"Anal penetration doesn't count as sex, does it?"

Ursula spurted out a mouthful of hot silky coffee, splashing the tablecloth with a milky spray. Carla was easily the most intelligent and knowledgeable person she knew. Her travels had taken her to countries Ursula could only dream of, but her relationships with men, in Ursula's opinion, were foolish.

At 10am on the Saturday morning, the coffee shop was bustling. The Poetshouse, just off Bradbury Place in the centre of Belfast, was a popular spot for BBC staff and foreign university students, who supplied the occasional dash of colour. The décor was rustic, with tables made from re-conditioned railway sleepers and wooden benches for chairs. Outside the temperature was gradually rising and waiters busily set out benches and tables on the pavement in front.

Having skipped breakfast, Ursula had welcomed the hot milky coffee and was ready for the breakfast she had ordered. For the five years she was married, her staple breakfast had been muesli with chopped banana. Her ex-husband was a fitness fanatic and had taken total responsibility for their grocery shopping. At the time, this had been a weight off Ursula's shoulders, as not having to plan their weekly menu had suited her. Roger had also prepared all the day-to-day cooking, much to the envy of Ursula's friends. The lemony dressings he created for salads were divine and he could grill fish to perfection.

The waitress placed the friends' breakfast orders in front of them; a small buttery croissant for Carla and a large doughy soda filled with two dripping fried eggs and several rashers of streaky bacon for Ursula. Ursula stared guiltily at the mammoth meal for a moment . . . and then attacked it with her knife and fork.

"This answerphone message about Mona and another man was just a rouse to get me here, wasn't it? You just couldn't bear not having anyone to talk to about your sordid love life."

"No. I was just getting to that. Well, last night, just after my young lover grabbed . . ."

"Stop it, I don't want to hear any more."

"Just after he grabbed a towel and nipped off for a shower, the telephone rang. It was Mona in floods of tears. I could hardly make out what she was saying. How she didn't wake up that husband and four children of hers, I don't know. Some people could sleep through a hurricane. Did I ever tell you about the time I was caught up in that storm in Peru?"

Ursula was content to let her Spanish friend become sidetracked for a moment. Carla was a great storyteller and Ursula enjoyed being transported to far-off places with the sound of Carla's Spanish accent punctuating her fluent English.

By now there wasn't a free table in the entire coffee shop and the air was filled with the aroma of coffee beans and expensive perfume. Ursula's eyes were drawn to a couple of students who had just sat at the last table by the window. Both girls were in their early twenties and were dressed in a flourish of lilac and cerise chiffon and silks. Ursula made a mental note for a fashion feature she was planning for the

BBC's regional light news programme. The girls looked fresh and carefree and French.

"Where was I? Yes, Mona was blubbering away and what with the drink she'd had and the tears, I'd say it was a good ten minutes before I heard a word of what she was saying."

"And?"

"She was ranting away about some affair or other."

"The last I saw of her last night, she was throwing up with her heels in the air. Do you think it was the drink making her all emotional about some past indiscretion?"

"Ursula, you're such a prude."

"What do you mean?"

"Indiscretion? What kind of word is that?"

"Was the drink just stirring up emotions from the past?"

"I thought that at first, but there's something else. I can't put my finger on it. She said she wanted to come round to my house tonight, so maybe I'll have more biz for you in the morning . . . that's if you can stand talking about 'indiscretions'."

Ursula greedily swallowed the last piece of bacon and began to carefully re-apply her bronze lipstick. She refused to get drawn into yet another conversation with Carla about her 'having no blood in her veins' or being a 'dried-up walnut'. Ursula was confident that she could be every bit as sensual as her Latin-blooded friend . . . when it was appropriate. Carla placed her elbows on the table and, as she leaned towards Ursula, her woollen jumper gaped revealing the strong contoured lines of the bones at the base of her throat. Carla leaned further forward and whispered.

"Sex isn't a dirty word, you know. Look around you, I can see at least half a dozen men who wish they could have sex with you right now on this table."

73

Ursula flippantly scanned the room. She made immediate eye contact with a couple of forty-something businessmen at a table near the door. They smiled warmly. To the left of them sat three students who also looked across at her. They giggled childishly and when the handsome dark one in the middle winked, Ursula turned back to her friend sharply. She felt the heat rise to her cheeks and nervously stroked the back of her neck.

"What you need is a good dusting down."

"Carla!"

"Since you left Roger, how many men have you been with? I've fixed you up with dozens, but how many have you actually slept with?"

"I'm not a one-night-stand type of person, you know that."

"Well, maybe you should be."

The waitress interrupted with two large cocktails decorated with slices of pineapple and kiwi.

"The two men in the suits by the door asked me to send these over."

"Would you please mind sending them back and tell them, thank you, but it's too early in the morning for us," said Ursula.

Carla sat with her mouth agape as Ursula dispatched the visibly irritated waitress. The admirers quickly paid their bill and left sheepishly. Ursula glared at her friend, who for once decided to keep silent and sip the remains of her now cool expresso.

This unsolicited attention had left Ursula feeling uncomfortable. She was familiar with this kind of scrutiny and in the past she would have handled it differently. As she got older, however, she was finding her confidence diminishing; the opposite of what she expected. When Ursula first met her ex-husband Roger, she was at the pinnacle of her confidence. She had joined the local horse-riding club and on her first beginners' night, she had been immediately drawn to this very tall and very handsome beginner who stood grooming a black stallion in the stable yard. Ursula knew he was watching and wanting her and she also knew that by ignoring him, he would want her even more. After half an hour he came over to introduce himself and give her some advice on her sitting position. This had irritated Ursula and she wondered what made him such an authority, being only a novice like herself. Her indifferent manner did not dissuade him and every ten minutes or so he would come over and give her some more riding advice. When the first session was over, Ursula saw him heading towards her and she made a quick beeline for the toilets. Once safely inside a cubicle, she had heard a voice from the other side of the door.

"I see you made a big impression on Roger Keane, the big handsome bloke."

"He just seems to want to share what little he knows about horses."

"I'd say he knows a thing or two – being an Olympic silver medallist."

They were married within three months and Ursula never sat on a horse again.

Girlish laughter by the window drew Ursula's attention back to the present. The French students now had company and as the one on the left tilted her mane of white-blonde hair as she laughed, Ursula saw the smiling face of their companion. 'Walk the Bike' was immersed in conversation, with his chestnut hair, for once, swept away from his face and his large hazel eyes darting between the faces of his beautiful acquaintances. His white T-shirt was untucked at the front and pulled tightly across his wide chest. The girl on the left, the taller of the two, reached forward and gently, with her hand, ruffled 'Walk the Bike's' hair, until it lay in its usual big loose curls across his brow. Still laughing, he pushed her hand away, his broad tanned arm looking like it could snap the girl's with one touch.

Ursula leaned forward on her chair in order to make eye contact with her window cleaner. 'Walk the Bike' did not notice her and continued his animated conversation. When she turned her chair almost 90 degrees in his direction, he still did not look across. Carla had immersed herself in the menu and was considering ordering another croissant. As she lifted her head and looked at her friend, she decided she wasn't going to let Ursula get away with sending the cocktails back after all.

"What did you and Roger do in bed? Play Scrabble?"

She could not have predicted the reaction in a million years. Ursula's honey-toned face dissolved into a stone-cold grey. Her thin long fingers clenched the plastic checked tablecloth so hard her knuckles turned white and the plastic began to tear. With her head fixed forward, there was only a tiny ring of the ocean-grey eyes visible in the blackness.

Then she stood up angrily and rushed out of the coffee shop leaving behind her cardigan, a half-cup of coffee and her bewildered friend. Carla held her stare on the now empty chair of her friend, then as she looked back to where Ursula had so abruptly departed, she saw the rear of 'Walk the Bike's' head as he also ran through the door.

Chapter 10

The yellow Post-it was now grey and tattered. Fergal had read the message from his wife over and over, until it was no longer yellow and no longer sticky. Most men's wives might get up in the morning and decide to go and get their hair done or nip to the shops, but his, she had just upped and gone to Amsterdam. He couldn't decide whether it was the fact that she was away to a foreign country that annoyed him, or that he had just spent two hours cutting the lawn for no reason. Fergal looked down at his grass-stained fingers and two perfectly spherical stains on his trouser knees. He looked over at the house across the road and saw the shape of a woman in the upstairs window of the Lawnmower Man's house. But he was too irritated to even let this unusual occurrence distract him.

Fergal thought for a moment about the implications of being in the house by himself for the weekend. Since marrying Frances and moving from his home in Derry three years ago, he hadn't spent a single night on his own. The moment of contemplation was brief, as he threw off his muddy Wellington boots, rushed over to the kitchen and plunged into the fridge. He took out a bumper pack of chocolate Wagon Wheels and four bottles of Budweiser. With a biscuit jammed between his teeth and a bottle of beer in the process of being opened, he threw himself onto the sofa. Continuing to munch, he searched under the cushion for the remote control. Lunchtime on a Saturday – must be sport, he thought to himself. Fergal was annoyed that the remote wasn't in its usual place and he groped down the sides of the sofa. He was going to have to get up again in order to find it, and this was agitating him even more. He proceeded to search in the magazine rack, behind the curtains, behind the sofa. After three minutes the search then extended to the other rooms in the house.

Half an hour later and the search proving futile, Fergal sat back down on the sofa, reached forward and with his left thumb turned the television on by the main controls. Up came the closing credits for Grandstand. He turned the television off again and stared at the blank screen. He could see half of his face perfectly reflected, tinged with green and black.

"What has become of me?"

As he gazed at the reflection of his own sardonic smile, no answer came back. A tear slowly ran down the face on the screen. The side facing away from the window and away from the sun was in total blackness. There was no tear on this side of his face. He needed to find out what had happened to him and knew where to go to find out. He grabbed a navy blazer hanging on the banister and shoved his house and car keys into its pocket. He was going home.

Within ninety minutes Fergal's car was beginning the steep climb up the Glenshane Pass on the main Derry Road. There was the familiar dense white cloud, which contained the growing heat, set against the lavender furze and rust heathers blanketing the hills. His speed was quickly checked by a tractor and about twenty cars crawling behind. He tried to recall the journey up to this point and couldn't remember any stage of it. It frightened him that he could have driven for this length of time and be oblivious of the road and the countryside around him.

A dead fox lay bloody and mangled at the side of the road. With his mission to return home driving him and frustration at the slow traffic, Fergal became agitated. He brushed the beads of sweat off his brow and wiped them on the passenger car seat. The beige car directly in front had four un-seat-belted children fussing in the back. The one on the driver's side was leaning out of the window, waving his arms at anyone who would notice him. Fergal's anger stepped up a gear. The trail of cars crept up the hill, bumper to bumper, each waiting to lunge as the road approached a dual carriageway.

The sprawling hills dipped into a valley of granite and the muddied fleece of a herd of grazing sheep. A gap momentarily opened up in the clouds and shafts of brilliant sunshine bounced off the car roofs. One by one the cars ahead of Fergal approached the dual carriageway and then shot off past the lumbering tractor. As Fergal's turn approached, he thrust his foot onto the accelerator, then clutched and changed down gear to give him added acceleration. He pulled down the visor to shield his eyes from the intensity of the light glimmering off the quickly departing cars. Fergal shoved the accelerator pedal down the last few inches and then . . . the engine went silent and within a few seconds the car's wheels had almost come to a standstill. As the car lethargically plodded on, the tractor overtook and grunted past.

"Bloody, shite, bastard . . ."

Fergal pulled the car over to the lay-by and yanked up the bonnet of the ailing vehicle. After ten minutes he realised he didn't have a clue what he was actually looking for, and staring at the engine wasn't going to fix it. Ahead, the tractor was a mere blip on the horizon and behind were miles of empty road. The grazing sheep hadn't raised their munching heads and the gap in the clouds was gone.

Fergal knew that the Ponderosa Bar and Grill, the highest pub in Ireland, was near. He began locking up his car, but then realising the futility of this, he set off walking. His step was heavy and within half a mile he could feel his weight becoming a burden and the intensifying heat stifling. A granite boulder at the side of the road ahead began to look soft and welcoming, providing the necessary impetus for him to reach the brow of the hill. He sat with his shirt off, and dusty shoes and saturated socks balanced on the kerb.

As Fergal closed his eyes, his imagination opened onto the image of himself and his friend Brendan hitching to Belfast on the other side of the road. They were seventeen and with the shabby appearance of yobs, their hitchhiking had been a disaster. In four hours they had got only two offers of lifts; the first, a Dutch long-haul truck driver, had looked hopeful. But when he opened the passenger door and they saw the driver was wearing no more than a half-eaten packet of crisps on his lap, the boys had quickly declined. Their second lift had proven more useful, but the elderly farmer was only driving as far as Dungiven. Hungry, cold and dejected, Fergal and Brendan had proceeded to walk the eight or so miles from Dungiven to the top of the Glenshane Pass. For this adventure to a rock festival in Belfast, they had gathered together a few pounds, a bundle of records and a snooker cue. The money was to buy them their dinners and they were hoping to sell the rest to pay their entry into the festival.

"It's because we look like hoods."

"Speak for yourself, Fergal. My Ma knitted this jumper."

It was three in the morning, they had no food, they were miles from anywhere and the last car had gone by half an hour ago. They had sat at the side of the road, just like Fergal did now, but they didn't give up. Fergal had found them a small, warm hidey-hole under some hawthorn bushes and had made a small fire with a few dead twigs and a newspaper they were carrying. He had been proud of his 'man-at-one-with-nature' survival skills, but then Brendan's cigarette lighter had played a vital role too. Brendan was charged with scavenging for some food and within twenty minutes he had come back with three large potatoes found lying at the side of the road, having literally fallen off the back of a lorry.

Fergal, the man, sat with his bare feet brushing against the heather and he could taste those baked black potatoes as if he was still there. It was the most tasty and satisfying meal he had ever had and was likely to ever have again. As the boys cracked open the chargrilled skins, the centres were fluffy and hot, with a steaming sweetness. They had sat smelling the hot vapours for a few minutes before taking huge, ravenous bites.

The Derry-to-Belfast bus flashed past on the other side of the road and as Fergal was shaken from his daydream he saw two young men, both around seventeen years old, give him 'the finger' from the rear of the bus. The memory of the roadside supper made Fergal's stomach groan and he quickly put his damp socks and shoes back on and continued with his walk. Within fifteen minutes he was inside the Ponderosa Bar and Grill and, having telephoned an emergency car-repair service, which would be with him in forty-five minutes, he was standing at the bar ready to order lunch. The place was empty except for one other customer, a young girl in her early twenties, who was eating from a bowl of soup and a plate of sandwiches. When Fergal had entered, she hadn't looked up. The barman, also in his twenties, dried two glasses, placed them on a shelf under the bar and then came over to serve his customer.

"Yes?"

"Are you still serving food?"

"Yes."

"Is there a menu I can look at?"

The barman lifted a menu from the far end of the bar and placed it on the beer mat in front of Fergal. Before ordering, Fergal had to check his wallet for cash.

"Do you accept credit cards?"

Fergal didn't wait for an answer, as he could see from the barman's vacant look that this wasn't likely. His wallet, rather than his appetite, therefore, dictated an order of egg, chips and beans and a pint of lager shandy.

The bar was brightly lit with a mixture of American diner and traditional Irish pub style décor. A large open fire roared at the far end of the bar and a dull film of grey fogged the surrounding wall and ceiling. Three large windows along the right wall were open and the blazing heat from the fire soared out to greet the heat outside.

As he waited for his lunch, Fergal picked up a leaflet from the bar advertising 'Popular Glenshane Hikes'. The barman returned with a knife and fork sandwiched between two napkins.

"Do you know anything about these walks?"

"There's two, a short one and a long one."

"Are these maps?"

"Yes. You leave your name and details with us, just in case you don't come back."

"Has anyone not come back?"

"No."

"That's a relief."

"But then no one's ever gone on them."

It was only then that the loneliness and the desolation of the Ponderosa struck home to Fergal. At least there was one other customer. He looked over at the young woman who, having finished her lunch, was carrying her bowl and plate over to the bar. She then walked around the back of the bar and put a shiny plastic apron around her waist. Without words, the barman then removed his and walked round to the customer side of the bar. He duly ordered and paid for a pint of Guinness from the young woman. Fergal wasn't sure whether he was more amazed that his fellow customer was actually the second bar shift of the day, or the fact the barman had paid for his drink. The concept of the alternating customer and staff amused him.

Fergal ate his piping hot lunch with gusto, and drank his refreshing shandy in two swallows. His hunger forced him to then eat the remaining garnish of lettuce, grated carrot and cucumber. It was over an hour since he had telephoned the local road-recovery company. He telephoned them again and was told they were on their way.

Fergal could feel his pulse-rate racing all over again. The heat, combined with his feeling of helplessness, were clearly visible on the ashen face reflecting back from his empty glass. If only Frances was here to keep him company. Mind you, these days, being with Frances only made him feel even lonelier. At least now he had that little person who lived in his head for conversation, compared to the reality of Frances's disgruntled and disappointed face.

It hadn't always been like this. He thought back to the time he introduced her to the music of Pink Floyd as they stood on the ancient walls of the Grianán Na Aileach fort. It was 1987 and Frances had laughed at him for his out-of-date taste in music. From Fergal's home in Derry, they had driven up to the omnipresent monument on the Donegal border. It was midnight, freezing cold and the sleet was bouncing off their icy faces. From the walls you could see the dusty orange glow of Derry city to the right and, below to the left, small farms peeked through pockets of mist. They had shared Fergal's Walkman, an advanced piece of technology at that time – now stashed away in the attic. Frances had giggled and squirmed as Fergal held her slender arms around her body, like a self-imposed straitjacket. They were both wearing the headsets. She was facing out of the fortress ring and out onto the landscape beyond. The freezing sleet danced on her eyelashes and the hostile wind crashed over the megalithic stones. Beyond there was nothing more than desolate blackness for miles and miles.

Fergal slowly turned up the volume of the music and both stood motionless. He released his captive's arms, but she kept them tight around her. That night was the first time they had cried together. But it was not the last.

Fergal caught his reflection in a glass-framed picture hanging on the wall of the Ponderosa.

His loneliness returned, but his companion inside his head said 'when she's ready, she will return to you'. His reflection faded away as Fergal now saw through it to the picture behind the glass. It wasn't a picture, but a page from The *Belfast Telegraph*. The headline was announcing 'Power to the Ponderosa'. Fergal read the article further, which explained how the Ponderosa Bar and Grill was finally being connected to a mains supply of electricity. The newspaper was dated 1994 and as he tried to imagine how the bar managed before then, he scanned the other news items of the day. In the far right-hand-side corner was a round-up of the daily courtroom dramas. He read through them to himself, until he came to the last.

"Trial began today of RUC Officer arrested on charges of collusion with loyalist paramilitaries. Constable Maurice McAllen faces five counts of bribery and corruption. Trial continues."

Chapter 11

He hadn't had a woman in his bed for nearly four years. Maurice quietly walked down the stairs and into his kitchen. It was only three in the afternoon, but his lover had drifted into a light sleep. The heat of the afternoon had intensified and even after drinking two cans of cola, Maurice's thirst remained unsatisfied. He sat in his living-room armchair sipping on a third can. The curtains were drawn making the room dark and musty with the only light source coming from a sliver of light where the curtains did not meet. The room was spotless with a brown leather sofa and two deep chairs, an oak bookcase and coffee table and large marble fireplace. The fire hadn't been lit since Maurice had bought the house, but its clinical appearance was an irony not appreciated by its owner. The house embodied the mood of a showhouse. Not in style, as there was little evidence of style, but more in the way it was all ready for someone to live in it. Maurice's house was waiting to be occupied. The occupant would be responsible for putting together the finishing touches and for making it their home. The house was waiting to become a home and its present occupier was merely a caretaker.

Maurice's long legs stretched from the sofa to the hearth. He was dressed in a clean pale-blue T-shirt and beige chinos, as he tidied his blond hair by running his hands swiftly through it. He hadn't slept with a woman in four years. The thought raced through his head again and the memories of the last two hours came back to him in no particular order. First came the memory of the point of ejaculation and the intense feeling of vulnerability and lack of control. Then he thought of the feeling of her hair brushing against his chest and stomach. That memory wasn't complete until his mind rushed back to when he had led her by the hand up to his bedroom. Within seconds he was reliving her tender kisses on his cheek and down his neck. The memory of the ejaculation came back again, and again. Maurice heard gentle rustling sounds from his bedroom, followed by soft groans and then silence. He took another sip of his drink.

As the sun moved its position, the intense light from the chink in the curtain also moved until it now cast a sharp stripe of light across Maurice's face. He reached into his back trouser pocket and pulled out his wallet. Squashed between a donor card and a tightly folded wad of ten-pound notes was a small slightly creased photograph. With the dimness of the room, it was impossible for Maurice to see it clearly. He stepped up to the curtains and pushed them swiftly open, inviting the strong sunlight to bathe the room. Little flecks of dust could be seen purposefully spiralling in the air. It took Maurice a moment or two to adjust his eyes before he stared down at the photograph; three large succulent ice-cream cones were being devoured by a woman and two children, boys. She had dark chestnut hair tied back in two pigtails and the boys had white-blond mops of curly hair. Maurice placed his thumb over the image of the woman and stared at the boys' faces. The intensity of his blue eyes returned as he pulled his shoulder blades in tight and gripped the photograph with his strong slender fingers.

The doorbell rang and he could hear his lover stir upstairs. Maurice's first thought was to let the bell ring, but when the second and third rings came, he could hear more unsettled noises in his bedroom. He didn't want to wake her, so he carefully unlocked the bolt and opened the front door.

"Have you seen my mummy?"

The unwelcome caller was Molly. Her frizzy red curls, so like her mother's, were squashed into a baseball cap and her favourite doll was held balanced on her hip.

"No, I haven't."

"Can I have my reward now?"

Maurice looked nervously up the stairs and then crouched down until he was on the same level as his young visitor and in a position to whisper.

"Your what?"

"I did what you told me, two good deeds. First I helped Mr Coyle across the road start up his lawnmower – it was giving him all kinds of bother. Next I pulled out some weeds for Ursula in Number 7."

Molly held up a bedraggled punch of once perfectly healthy marigolds. Maurice pulled out a ten-pound note from his wallet and gave it to the girl.

"Now run along."

"Is my mummy with you?"

Molly's persistence was only matched by Maurice's anxiety and he continued to check his staircase. Suddenly light footsteps could be heard from above.

"You've got your money. Now run along."

"Is that my mummy?"

Before Maurice could answer, naked slender ankles could be seen at the top of the stairs, then long shins followed by tanned knees as the woman gingerly descended the stairs. Maurice tried to close the door, but the weight of the heavy mahogany door and the pressure of his massive shoulders behind it, could not compete against the girl's tiny foot wedged there. He tried to lift it out, but Molly squirmed like an eel, until she now had her entire body perched inside the door and she was looking directly up the stairs.

"Hello, Molly."

"Hi, Ursula. I picked these weeds for you."

Chapter 12

It took several aggressive confrontations with cyclists before Frances realised that she didn't have the right of way. The walk from the hotel to the sports stadium criss-crossed a labyrinth of cycle lanes and Roberta almost came to blows on two occasions. Still, Frances was glad of the walk in the fresh air to clear away the last remnants of travel sickness. She decided to put any thoughts about the streak on the back burner, well – the grill, all right – the hob, she thought to herself. First things first; it was two in the afternoon and in half an hour they were scheduled to play their first match against a local Dutch team. Her focus had to be her first game of volleyball in over a year. The team had already changed into their kits in their hotel rooms and each was now carrying a small holdall with their shower things. They had agreed to shower in the sports hall after their last match and leave getting dressed for their night out until they got back to the hotel. The thought of communal showers had worried Frances, but that thought too was relegated to the back burner until she got this first match out of the way.

The street leading to the stadium was peppered with street cafés and expensive-looking boutiques. Orla had set the pace by jogging on ahead and Cathy-Ann and Niamh kept stopping to browse. But every time they did so, Roberta threatened to break wind if they didn't get a move on. Rose and Frances were backmarkers.

"It's like riding a bike, Frances; it'll all come back to you again."

Considering her recent difficulties with cyclists, Frances didn't appreciate the analogy.

"Rose, I reckon I've put on at least a stone since I last set foot on a court. It's bound to affect my game."

Rose grabbed her own midriff with both hands, forming a soft round cushion of flesh.

"Don't talk to me about weight. You could make another person out of what I've got going spare. I'm worried the referee will complain that we're playing with seven players rather than six."

"Rose, don't be so hard on yourself."

"Don't you be so hard on yourself either. At least you don't have someone like Cathy-Ann at home, reminding you everyday what you would look like if you didn't eat those chunky KitKats."

"No, I've got Fergal, who just has to look at me and I'm annoyed."

The two women could hear a squeal from behind as Roberta delivered her threat on her two loitering teammates.

"Frances, we've hardly heard from you this past year. All

of a sudden you just stopped coming to training. Are you and Fergal having problems?"

"It's not Fergal; it's me. I'm one big oozing problem. I just can't seem to get my act in gear. Just getting dressed in the morning can seem like swimming Lough Neagh in cement shoes at times."

"Well, use this weekend to chill out."

"Maybe I could if I didn't have to squeeze a size fourteen butt into size ten shorts."

"Look, Frances, it's not like you've got to streak or something."

Both women laughed. Frances remembered how much she loved Rose and how much she'd missed her warmth and generous spirit. Rose had been a friend of hers and Fergal's for years, ever since she worked in the university bar. Rose was now manager of the busiest restaurant in Belfast and frequently headhunted to run restaurants all over the world. But North Down was her home, much to her employer's relief. In return she was given a generous salary and clothing allowance, plus they offered to take on her younger sister as a trainee chef.

With the intimacy of an old friendship re-kindled, Frances and Rose continued their walk arm-in-arm. The street veered to the right, cutting across an arched bridge straddling a canal. A cruise barge drifted underneath, laden with camera-draped tourists. As they walked over the brow of the bridge, the women were hit with a torrent of sunflower yellows, rose reds and tulip oranges as a tiny florist's sat nestled on the corner.

Beside the florist's was a brothel. The team were walking along the fringes of the notorious red-light district and this was the last brothel on this side of the city. Red and pink neon lights flashed above a large oblong window. Seated inside was a large North African woman dressed in a white basque and silver stockings. A group of four German businessmen were standing outside, laughing and jeering at each other. The prostitute sat composed and dignified on a tall wooden stool. There was some bargaining going on between the businessmen and the woman, all done by means of sign language. The teammates continued walking past without taking their eyes off the street ahead. Frances alone stopped briefly and looked across, just for one second. As she did so, the prostitute looked over the heads of her potential customers at Frances. Though easily in her early fifties, the prostitute produced the gentle smile of a child. Frances returned the smile and for that second there was an unexplainable connection. The second passed, and the prostitute returned to her negotiations. Frances walked on. The boutiques and cafés were now thinning out and the rest of the team had now caught up with Frances and Rose.

The five women were now silent as they entered the stadium, each carrying their own apprehensions and insecurities. The sports hall throbbed with the sound of an avalanche of bouncing volleyballs from the warming-up teams. The three far courts were dedicated to men's matches and the two ahead of them were for the women. Orla was standing on Court 2, waving frantically at her teammates.

"We're on in fifteen minutes. Hurry up and get stretched."

The fixture list posted at the side of the entrance listed the other teams in their Pool: three were local Dutch teams, there was a junior French one and an English team from Hastings. The sports hall was crammed with players. There

93

were few spectators, apart from male players watching the women's matches and vice-versa. Orla had stripped off her tracksuit and was now limbering up in the team's short black Lycra shorts and red volleyball shirt. There was a loud crackle of the intercom and then a Dutch-sounding commentator announced the next matches in English.

"The next match on Court Number 2 is TDK Rapide Voorburg versus Gwen's Footwear from Belfast. Match starts in ten minutes. Best of three full sets."

Frances had hoped that the team had got a new sponsor since she last played, but 'Gwen's Footwear' was a legacy from their first and only sponsor over five years ago. She took off her tracksuit jacket and trousers, at the same time as pulling her sports shirt out from her shorts and stretching it down over her behind. She then proceeded to pull the legs of her shorts down as far as they could reasonably go. Orla paired Frances with Cathy-Ann for five minutes of general ball-work before the start of the game. This was just what Frances didn't need as she could see a line of Dutch men form behind Cathy-Ann, gasping each time she bent down and picked up the ball. The warm-up turned out to be a waste of time as Cathy-Ann started to make self-conscious unforced errors and Frances was distracted by her too short shorts cutting her in two.

"Am I swinging my arm too fast, Frances?"

Cathy-Ann asking if she was swinging her arm too fast was a bit like a synchronised swimmer asking if her smile was too bright. Frances had her own more personal problems to deal with, but she stifled her irritation.

"Cathy-Ann, you're playing great. You look great and you're playing fine."

These words of encouragement temporarily buoyed up Cathy-Ann's confidence and when the referee blew the whistle to start the match, she raced over to her starting position. Frances's starting position was the middle of the front court. She stood facing the net and looked across at her opponents. She had been so wrapped in her own self-consciousness, she had totally forgotten about TDK Rapide Voorburg. Their front row consisted of three six-foot blondes, no older than twenty. The three on the back row were six foot plus. Frances felt an urgent need to empty her bowels. Orla was standing to her left, eyeballing her opponent. Niamh was standing to her right, shaking hands with hers. Frances looked up at the Amazonian player in front of her and was about to speak when the referee blew the whistle to start. Before she knew it, Cathy-Ann had served the ball and they were in the middle of a rally and then before Frances had a chance to draw breath, the rally was over. Then their opponents had won the first point.

Gwen's Footwear lost the following five points and Frances hadn't even had the opportunity to touch the ball yet. On the seventh serve, the Amazon served the ball directly at Frances, who moved crab-like into position. The serve floated over the net and began to dip at her feet. As Frances stepped forward to pass the ball, Orla's left arm swung in front of her forcing the ball to fly off in the direction of a team of Cathy-Ann's admirers sitting on the sideline. The next seven points followed the same pattern, until Gwen's Footwear were 14 – 0 down and their opponents were serving for the first set. Frances's need to go to the toilet hadn't deteriorated and her stomach-gurgling had now become audible. Roberta gave her a reassuring wink.

The ball was served and Frances pulled off the net ready to attack the ball. Rose set the ball to Cathy-Ann who was drawn opposite the tallest and most gruesome of their opponents. She was no match and the ball ricocheted straight down off the plank-like arms of the Dutch woman, down onto the floor at Cathy-Ann's feet. The whistle blew for the end of the first set and Frances and her teammates scurried over to the other side of the court, with their heads and hearts low. Niamh took it upon herself to try and lift the team's morale.

"The match isn't over yet. Come on, heads up girls! Let's at least get some points this set!"

"We're fucking useless."

Orla didn't have quite the same friendly approach.

"What's up with everyone? Six goldfish could play better than this."

"Am I hitting the ball too hard?"

There was a general groan, as even Cathy-Ann's tolerant teammates didn't have the energy right now to deal with her. Frances stood silent, shifting her head from side to side as each of the players made their own diagnosis. The referee blew her whistle for the second set and the six dejected players took their positions on court. The first six points exactly mirrored the previous set and before they knew it, the team from Belfast were looking at a score of 0-6 down. The Amazon took languid steps up to the service line and reached her right arm up in the air, about to serve the ball.

"Time out, referee, please."

The rest of the players looked in amazement at Frances. The referee looked, confused, at Orla who as captain should make all requests for time outs. Dumbstruck for once, Orla repeated the request for a time out to the referee, who subsequently blew her whistle affording the thirty-second break. Gwen's Footwear stepped off the court and huddled around Frances with their faces blank.

"OK, I haven't played for over a year, but if we're going to play anyway decent, you've all got to stop trying to cover for me. You're all doing it. If you want to play with five players, I'm going home right now. Yes, I'm nervous as hell and yes, I'm frightened of letting you all down, but if we're going to get back into this match we're going to have to trust each other. OK?"

Not that they were likely to, but before anyone could respond, the whistle blew for the match to resume. The Amazon delivered a swerving serve, which thundered over the net directly at Frances. As the ball bounced off her arms, she could feel the sting of hot pain race up her forearms. The pass was by no means perfect, but Rose was able to scramble over and set up a high ball in the middle of the court for Roberta to take a swing at. Roberta jumped with both feet and thumped the ball over the net. Gwen's Footwear watched as one. The ball thudded down on the wooden floor, landing two inches off the sideline, and in court. The six women jumped in the air, with Frances squeezed in the middle. There was a roar of support from Cathy-Ann's admirers, who also ran on the court and joined in the hugging. The referee blew her whistle over and over for the game to resume, but the celebrations wouldn't end.

Three hours later Frances stood in the shower cubicle with her face turned upward facing the torrent of water. She was naked and surrounded by half a dozen youthful slim bodies. But she didn't care. She didn't care what she looked like. They'd still lost the game, but the five points that they won in that set were the sweetest ever. In fact, the only real success of the four pool matches they played that afternoon, was the one set they took off that Dutch team. But what mattered to Frances was her sense of empowerment and the first time in six months that she had taken control, rather than things taking control of her. Frances wanted the moment to last and her face, chest and thighs were red as the high-powered water repeatedly pounded off her.

Roberta had headed back to the hotel for a shower, but Frances could hear the rest of her teammates drying themselves in the changing room. Niamh was singing and the others were joining in the chorus. There were four different versions of the same song all going on at the same time, but to Frances they sounded like angels. The sound of the singing, plus that of the water flooding over her as percussion, generated orchestral music all around Frances' naked body.

The walk back to the hotel had taken about half the time it had taken to get to the stadium that morning. Niamh and Cathy-Ann called into an off-licence and stocked up on Bacardi and beers for everyone, whilst Rose disappeared and said she'd meet them back at the hotel. Orla and Frances walked on ahead, with the task of picking up some snacks on the way. Frances's short fair hair was still wet and had stuck to the back of her neck. Wet drips were evident on the back of her tracksuit top. Her face was still red, but her coffee-brown eyes glistened. The earlier euphoria was slowly starting to fade and her self-consciousness was returning.

"Whatever you're on, Frances, I want a pint of it tonight."

"Sorry, Orla, unfortunately it doesn't have all that much staying power. You get yourself a bloke tonight and that'll be you back on form."

"Men and staying power have the same problem with me too."

Frances had no doubt that Orla could out-stay any sexual encounter. She was as athletic today as she had been in her Olympic competition heyday, the only difference being that she was now 12 years older and had dodgy ankles and knees. Beyond her manly jawbone and masculine-cut short reddish-brown hair, Orla hid femininity and beautiful willow-tree green eyes. Unfortunately, the only men who weren't intimidated by her tended to be body-builders, with whom she had had four long-term relationships. The last had unglamorously fizzled out three years ago.

"When you're finished with Fergal, can I have a turn?"

"Orla, you'd eat him alive. You'd be welcome to him, if I didn't know he wasn't your type. Have you no one on the go at the moment?"

"I did, but it's not really working out. Same old story."

The two women turned off the main road and entered a side street leading to their hotel on the corner. Thoughts of the night ahead started to dart in Frances' head. The rush she had been in getting ready that morning, had meant that when they had arrived she discovered she had brought with her, amongst the jumbled mess, one shoe, a pair of baggy combat trousers and an 'I Love The Algarve' T-shirt. The issue of the streak was also never far from her thoughts. But as they stepped into the lift up to their room, Frances quickly opened up the back burner and shoved her thoughts inside. Her teammate's troubled love life was the priority right now.

"What happened this time?"

"I've been seeing a married man for three years. We'd first met over fifteen years ago when we were both training for the Olympics, but we didn't start seeing each other properly until 1996. I didn't know he was married until I'd been seeing him for eighteen months and by then I was in love."

"Jesus, Orla, have you no sense? A married man!"

"Seems not. He did talk about leaving his wife nearly a year ago and I've been seeing him ever since. On and off."

"And has he left her now?"

"Not yet."

"Does he have any kids?"

"No, he doesn't want any. He's sure about that."

"Excuse me, Orla, but he sounds like a right bollocks."

Frances's honest response frightened even herself and she half expected Orla to turn around and thump her. She had no escape in the lift.

"Frances, you're right. He is. Imagine being married to him."

"I suppose he was one of your typical weightlifter boyfriends. Did he lift weights at the Olympics?"

"No, believe it or not he's a showjumper, won the silver. He was very famous for a week or two when the Games were over. Roger Keane, do you remember him?"

Chapter 13

With her shoe heel firmly jammed into the soil, Christine had been trapped. She had tried to make a dramatic, elegant departure, but the stubborn shoe was having none of it. The memory of the moment was powerful enough to ignite a fresh feeling of embarrassment. As she stood washing lettuce for the evening's dinner, Christine could feel the knot tighten in her stomach again as she thought back to her awkward hurried departure after that kiss. Eventually, in her haste to escape Maurice's grasp, she had abandoned her brown court shoe and hobbled back home. Maurice hadn't called after her.

Christine had spent the afternoon apologising to her girls for her earlier behaviour in the driveway. Her excuse to them was how worried she had been about their trip to casualty. All three of her daughters had continued to look at her with unforgiving eyes and Christine had begun to think that the damage was deeper than anticipated. She knew she was going to have to work hard to fix this one.

"What about if we don't go to Grandma's tomorrow."

She had their attention. The Sunday ritual of visiting Christine's mother in the old people's home was never popular in the Watson household. Her mother had long since lost command of her faculties and to the girls she was a crotchety old woman, who smelt funny and kept pinching them.

"Instead, after church tomorrow, we'll set off on an adventure."

"Where to?"

"That's the adventure. You'll have to wait and see."

The deal was done. The girls spent the rest of the afternoon amusing themselves, while Christine completed three loads of washing, vacuumed the stairs, defrosted the freezer and was now getting dinner ready.

She looked down at her bowl of washed lettuce and saw that while her mind was distracted, she had washed enough to feed the family for a month. With the dinner preparations more or less complete and the house unusually empty, Christine dashed up the stairs and ran piping hot water into the bath. From a tall, slender crystal bottle she poured out three thick drops of bath oil and the rich vapour of lavender and honeysuckle circled the bathroom. As she undressed, she carefully stroked her clothes where Maurice's hands had briefly touched them. When she came to the base of her blouse, where both their hands had been held, Christine abruptly reached over and locked the bathroom door. With her clothes removed, she unpinned her red curls and stepped into the steaming bath. The hot vapours swamped her body and she lay with only her knees, shoulders and breasts bobbing on the water's surface.

As Christine closed her eyes, the image of the silver

needle squeezed into her husband's arm darted aggressively into view. She immediately opened her eyes again and looked across at her pile of clothes neatly folded on the toilet seat. Against the white enamel, the lines of their folds looked severe and harsh. Little pimples of sweat started to appear on Christine's face and shoulders, and delicate trickles began to manoeuvre down her neck.

Within twenty-four hours her simple life had become complicated. She didn't know what to think. She no longer had control over her thoughts as they randomly raced ahead. Thinking about Alex only gave her heartache and thinking about Maurice generated an aching throb in her head. The heat of the water slowly encouraged her nipples to soften and plump up to pale pink mounds. Christine arched her spine back and forth, gently rocking her breasts in and out of the water. Only ten minutes earlier she had been immersed in her day-to-day domestic chores of being a mother, but now contained within the four walls of the lime-green bathroom, Christine's sensuality had taken command. With her big toe, she wiped the steam away from the mixer tap. The curve of the aluminium exaggerated the length of her slender legs and the roundness of her knees sitting like islands in the water. Her body-frame filled the bath, but in her mind's eye she could see the spindly legs of Christine the child. Her frequent mission then had been to jam her toes in the taps. On her twelfth birthday she had succeeded, but unfortunately, had succeeded too well. She lay in the icy bath for over an hour, too embarrassed by her emerging adolescent curves to call her mother. Christine had eventually become so cold her toe had shrunk and with the aid of a now mushy bar of Palmolive soap, she had managed to release herself. The transformation to womanhood had been slow and cumbersome. Her transformation to motherhood had happened within the blink of an eye.

A bright blue toy seal lion, that had been precariously balanced on the edge of the bath, plopped down under the water and emerged with his flippers casually flapping. The seal lion's rotating flippers reluctantly stopped and its assortment of brightly coloured comrades, crammed along the sides of the bath, jealously looked on.

Imagining her hand to be Maurice's, Christine placed it in the small of her naked back. His hand had felt hard and strong and his powerful long fingers had locked tight around Christine's. What was she doing? What had she done already? Through the steam, she drew a line with her finger on the bath tile.

"I've seen my husband and father of my children take drugs."

Christine drew another line against the first on the tile.

"I've been lying to myself for years."

A third line was dragged along the tile.

"I've taken a complete stranger into my confidence."

Christine drew another two lines. The second long and bold.

"I kissed the stranger . . . and I enjoyed that kiss."

Christine briskly lay backwards, thrusting her head into the water until her hair, brow, and ears were all submerged. The underwater world of the bath creaked and gurgled. Swirls of red hair floated on her shoulders and gently tickled her neck. The sound of her breathing was audible above everything else, as she deliberately inhaled deeply and extended the exhalation.

Christine couldn't remember the last time she had taken time for herself; time to concentrate on something so simple as the breath that gave her life. Only yesterday morning when she had bathed, The Baby, Molly and Molly's entourage of dolls had all hijacked her bath. Ruth had also poked her head around the door in the relentless pursuit of a razor to shave her hairless legs. Alex had momentarily popped into the bathroom, with scouring pad held aloft, in his pursuit of dust. He was pleased to discover neglected toilet and sink pedestals and promptly rectified the problem with vigorous swipes. Alex's daily involvement with the sick and diseased had long since been Christine's excuse for his obsessive behaviour. Right now though, she was only irritated. She was irritated by the very idea of him scouring and polishing around her and also irritated now by the thought of him flooding her mind and intruding on this moment.

Christine quickly refocused on her breathing and after a slow inhalation, held her breath for several seconds before releasing it again. Her thoughts were battling within and against her and as she tried to separate them, they swiftly sucked back into a sticky mess. She held her breath again and counted for ten seconds. On the final count, Maurice's large frame, looming down over her, formed in her imagination. With this thought she not only felt the battle in her head, but also in her body. Christine moved her right hand's tight grip from the edge of the bath and rested it a few millimetres off her stomach. She could feel her soft delicate body hair floating in the water like seaweed on the ocean floor. Slowly and precisely she moved her hand up towards her right breast, still maintaining the fraction of distance from her skin. Christine's breath was now shallow and racing and noisily rattled around the chamber of the bath. Delicately she balanced her palm on the tip of her right nipple. Immediately it went erect. Christine was now panting.

"Mummy, Mummy!"

Christine held her breath in order to hear more clearly. The voice was coming from downstairs and was muffled by the sound of the water in her ears.

"Mummy, where are you?"

Quickly, Christine lifted her head out of the water. She heard the front door close and no more. The water had distorted the sound. She could hear the words, but she couldn't be sure who was calling her. Maybe there was a problem. Maybe one of the girls was hurt. Christine stepped out of the bath and pulled a white cotton bathrobe around her dripping body. She tightly coiled a white bath towel around her hair and tried to unlock the bathroom door. The lock was jammed. In the two years the Watsons had lived in Ashbury, the lock had never been used and, feeling quite superfluous, had seized up. In an attempt to loosen its stubbornness, Christine carefully manoeuvred the door handle up and down. With a heavy smearing of expensive shampoo, she then softly massaged the base of the handle. And then with one violent pull, she yanked on the door handle. It came off in her hand.

The lock remained tightly jammed. Christine looked down at the brass handle, now dripping soapy suds onto the floor. Frustrated, she turned to throw it out of the open window and then, on second thoughts, raced over to the window and leaned out. The cul-de-sac was empty. Below the bathroom window was the gently sloping roof of the garage. As Christine reached forward she could touch the burnt-umber slates with the tips of her fingers. The tiles had thirstily absorbed the heat of the afternoon and Christine was forced to pull her fingers swiftly away. At the side of the garage, only four or five feet below, was the black wheelie bin shimmering in the sunlight. Alex was proud of how pristine his wheelie bin was, inside and out. Christine knew she had the agility and the fitness to attempt the escape, but she wasn't sure her dignity could complete the farce. She quickly assessed her options and she knew that if this had happened less than twenty-four hours ago, climbing out of the bathroom window would not be an option. But today, anything was possible.

Christine sat on the bathroom window ledge and hoisted both legs outside. Her left leg easily reached the garage roof and she carefully swung the right one down beside her. She alternated her weight from the left leg to the right as the hot tiles burned the soles of her feet. Christine pushed herself off from the ledge and, separated from her perch, she now felt precariously vulnerable. She could see Molly walking away from their house and over in the direction of Maurice McAllen's.

"Molly, love!"

The girl did not hear her.

"Molly! Over here, Molly!"

Christine's daughter continued to walk in the direction of house Number 8. She was singing to herself and every three paces would skip and the back of her lilac pinafore dress would bob up, revealing long spindly legs. Hanging limply from her right hand was a bunch of bedraggled flowers. Christine froze. Should she still try and make it

107

safely for the bottom or should she aim to pull herself back up into the bathroom window? Which would be quicker? The bathrobe clung to her damp legs and her auburn curls had formed tight ringlets, with tiny water droplets balanced as precariously as she was. Christine slowly tried to edge herself along the garage roof towards the bin. The indignity of the moment combined with the indignity of the day itself was not lost on her. She looked across at her daughter, who had now rung Mr McAllen's doorbell, and was standing fidgeting with the hem of her skirt. Luckily there didn't appear to be any answer from Number 8 and Christine took the opportunity to carefully nudge herself over to the edge of the garage roof. She crouched and stretched her left leg down towards the wheelie bin. Her long slender legs, which she always had difficulty in finding adequate-length trousers for, were in this instance, six inches too short. Christine rolled over onto her stomach and gently tried to lower herself over the edge. Her toes were now only a few inches off their target.

Christine took a deep breath and looked over towards Molly. Number 8's door was now open and Molly was inside. Christine could see the back of the child's head gazing up towards the staircase. She momentarily closed her eyes with relief for the gift of time she had been given to complete her escape. When she opened them again, only a second later, she could see that Molly was still standing inside the doorway. Only this time she could see Maurice McAllen's face towering above her daughter and staring directly at her. His furrowed brow instantly betrayed his confusion and, even at this distance, the cobalt blue of his eyes shone from the darkness of the interior of the doorway. A knot in

Christine's stomach tightened and her pulse raced. With the confused emotions of a schoolgirl, she quickly decided a smile might defuse the awkwardness. As she did so, Ursula Richards from number 7 stepped out from behind Maurice. She looked agitated and Christine wasn't sure if she also saw her farcical predicament. To her own surprise, feelings of embarrassment and vulnerability were entirely overshadowed by those of anger and jealousy.

Chapter 14

The fan belt was replaced in minutes, but the three-hour wait for the vehicle-recovery company in the first place had left Fergal irritated and worn out. He finally arrived in Derry at around 7pm, five hours after he had first set off from Bangor. The New Bridge reflected the lilacs and pinks of the early summer's evening sky and the windsock hung lifelessly. To Fergal's right, as he crossed the bridge, he could see the empty skeleton of a redbrick mansion. On his left, the shell of a grey modern five-bedroomed detached residence, with alabaster pillars and pebbledash façade. Yellow strips of tape, forming crosses on the smudged windows, were the only evidence of colour. Fergal raced through a series of roundabouts before making a left turn into the Galliagh estate. Each time he returned to his home town, he scanned the horizon for glimpses of furze and heather, so much a part of his past, but gradually receding behind a heavy fog of bricks and mortar. On Fergal's last visit home, the newly planted saplings, dotted along the main road into the estate, had looked weak and vulnerable set against the sharp edges of the houses and blasted by wintry drizzle. Was it really six months since he had been home? Some of the saplings were now broken in two and slowly withering, but ironically these seemed to provide a protective barrier for a dozen or so lush green young oaks.

Fergal carefully manoeuvred the car around a large group of young children and toddlers busily dismantling a shopping trolley in the centre of the road. Reluctantly, they stood aside to let the Vauxhall Vectra past, with the girls smiling inquisitively and the older boys making vulgar gestures. Fergal slowly parked in front of a bank of whitewashed terraced houses, divided by an arched alley leading to the rear. He stepped up to the end house, turned the key which was permanently wedged in the keyhole, and entered his home.

"Yes, Fergal."

"Yes, Eilish."

"Two arms the one length as usual."

Fergal's eldest sister Eilish was perched against the electric fire preparing potatoes and carrots for supper. The fact that her baby brother had just arrived unannounced after nearly half a year, wasn't going to distract her from her chores. Aged fifty-five, Eilish was the family matriarch and, having never married, was the only Coyle family member still living in the family home. Maeve and Donna, the twins, were both in their late forties. They had married within a few months of each other, nearly twenty years before and both moved to the Bogside to live. Estelle, Fergal's fourth sister and nearest to him in age had spent the greater part of the past fifteen years of her marriage in dramatic three-month flits between her and her husband's house in Creggan and long spells in Eilish's spare room.

"Is our Estelle here or there?"

"Here."

"How long this time?"

"Four months and three days."

"That's a bit of a record."

"She has my phone bill through the roof. See that white lump of plastic over there with the curly cable sticking out the back."

"The phone?"

"Oh, you do know what one looks like?"

Fergal groaned, relieved to have the mandatory dig at him for not keeping in contact with his family out of the way. He could relax now.

"Any tea going? And something nice to go with it."

Fergal hunted out the *Derry Journal* l, stuffed underneath the seat of the 'TV chair', and plonked himself down. Eilish left the carrot and potato peelings down on the hearth and disappeared into the kitchen. Fergal looked up from his newspaper briefly to see the back of Eilish's head scurrying away. Through her bleached blonde waves of short hair he could see an inch of pure white roots and her once strong firm back had softened and was slightly curved. Eilish wore a pair of practical elastic-waisted cotton trousers and loose denim shirt. Her huge breasts, once the admiration of Fergal's closest friends (only the closest were allowed to discuss them), now seemed to be pulling Eilish forwards and downwards.

As Fergal glanced through the local newspaper, he read out stories to his sister in the kitchen. A competition

112

ensued as to who knew most of the main protagonists. Fergal scored highly on the drunk and disorderly list, but Eilish cleaned up on the births, deaths and marriages.

"Wait till you hear this one, Eilish. There was an old copy of the *Belfast Telegraph* hung in the Ponderosa about a cop on trial for bribery and corruption."

"And the point is?"

"There's a strange sort of fella lives across from us, with the same name."

"Which is what?"

"McAllen."

"You big lump. How many McAllens do you think there are in Ireland?"

When Eilish returned to the living-room five minutes later, carrying a mug of piping hot tea and a plate of buns, the newspaper was quickly cast aside.

"Eilish, you wee honey . . . wheaten scones, gravy rings, turnovers!" His eyes were larger than a child's at a Woolworth's pick 'n' mix. "This is what 'something nice for a cup of tea' means. Frances just doesn't get it."

"Looking at the belly you've on you these days – she must be doing something right."

Fergal decided to let this second barbed comment go . . . for the time being. His current concern was to see how much butter he could smother over the turnover. Eilish returned to her peeling. With an extra mouth to feed for supper, there was more to be done. The discarded mound of peelings was now taking on 'Close Encounter' proportions.

"I wish we still had the Brock-Man."

"The what?"

"Don't tell me you've forgotten about him . . . well, *they* actually. When we lived up in Creggan – the two albino boys who'd come around on their horse and cart and collect everybody's 'brock' buckets? Buckets full of leftovers and peelings, like this lot."

"And what did they do with them?"

"Took them up to the pig farm."

"Your head's cut."

"You were wee at the time, but you must remember them?"

"Are you saying that long before there was any talk of protecting the environment and recycling, the Creggan had its own recycling system going?"

"We did."

"And they happened to be two albinos, on a horse and cart?"

"Exactly."

"Your head's full of sweety mice."

Brother and sister huffed away silently, each smouldering with frustration and irritation. The peelings were starting to get thicker and Eilish had given up on cutting out the eyes and the damaged bits where shovels had cut into the skins.

In the eight years since their mother had passed away from a stroke and the four since their father had died of a blood disorder, Eilish had taken the responsibility of preparing daily for the soup pot. If Estelle was staying with her, or even if she was on her own, there was always a pot of soup to feed an army. She had effortlessly slipped into the role of the head of the Coyle family; whether it was providing a home for the vagrant Estelle, acting as the negotiator in the constant bickering between the twins, the figurehead at family occasions, or a shoulder for her baby brother. As the last peeled potato tumbled out of the pot and onto the duck-egg-blue hearthrug, Eilish turned to Fergal.

"So what's up?"

"What do you mean? Can't I come and visit my big sister when I want to?"

"Is Frances all right?"

"Of course she is. She upped and headed off to Amsterdam this weekend with her mates."

"Is that what's wrong with you? It'll do her good."

"I know that. I'm happy she's gone. Everything's fine and dandy. Where's our Estelle?"

"She went to the off-licence to get a bottle of Black Bush. Our Maeve and Donna are coming over tonight for a card night."

Fergal's face visibly winced. An evening with his four sisters, over a game of cards and a bottle of Bush, instantly brought back memories of his childhood and more so, his adolescence. The script for the evening was so predictable. Stage one, which would involve soup and half a bottle of whiskey, would start with idle chitchat about this or that neighbour. A full bottle and a round of egg and onion sandwiches later in stage two, Fergal would be sent out to buy a few bottles of full-bodied red wine and the raucous laughter would build up around each other's husbands or boyfriends or both. Stage three quickly followed with Maeve and Donna getting into a fight, Estelle disappearing to her room in a huff and Eilish sitting full proud with her bra stuffed with the winnings she had taken off the other three. Stage three took only minutes to complete, but as an awkward, self-conscious and sensitive teenage boy, was best to avoid.

"I might go out tonight."

Big grown men also know when to make themselves scarce. Eilish rolled her large grey eyes, an exact copy of Fergal's in colour and size, but delicately edged in charcoal mascara. She lifted the overflowing pan, squeezed an ill-fitting lid on the top and rested it on her hip. Brother and sister were caught for a moment in the shared recollection of the infant Fergal, who was a permanent fixture on his teenage sister's hip. For a second Fergal was jealous of the dull cast-iron potato pot. Eilish broke the spell by releasing her uncomfortably squashed right breast and resting it on the pan lid. She quickly headed back into the kitchen.

Fergal reached again for the newspaper, but the living-room and its contents caught his eye. Eilish hadn't changed much in the house since their father had died over four years before. The same religious pictures and ornaments held their key positions dotted along the mantelpiece. A print of a very youthful Jesus hung above the television, with the delicate pinks and bluish tones of his skin illuminated by a red neon light. Eilish had replaced the old brown velour sofa with a newer brown velour sofa and there were a few more porcelain ornaments than when Fergal had last visited. The twins Maeve and Donna had eleven children between them, and most of the ornaments looked like children's holiday trinkets. Fergal was particularly impressed by the over-large fluorescent Blackpool Tower, which had managed both to outshine Jesus's neon light and overshadow a plastic turquoise bottle of holy water, marked 'Lourdes' in biro.

"If you go out tonight, where will you go?" Eilish shouted from the kitchen to her brother, barely audible over the sound of running tap water.

Fergal hadn't moved from the 'TV chair' since he'd arrived.

"Dunno. Haven't thought about it."

"Why don't you give Brendan a shout? He's still at his ma's old house."

Fergal had lied. He had been thinking about contacting his old fishing mate ever since he left Bangor. The last time he'd seen his friend was over three years ago at his own wedding and it must be nearly ten years before then that they had actually gone out for a drink together. What would they have to say to each other? Fergal felt and heard a rumble in his stomach. He attempted to stifle the sound by tucking in his green polo shirt, but as this exaggerated the expanse of his stomach, he decided to calm the sound with a sugary gravy ring, swallowed in two bites.

"I haven't seen Brendan in donkeys."

"Don't talk with your mouth full."

Fergal could be accounts executive up in Bangor, but here in Derry he was just a wee lad.

"I said I haven't seen Brendan in ages. We'd have nothing in common."

"Nothing but living in each other's pockets since you were no age. Until you went up to the university, we never saw one of you without the other tagging along. Give him a ring. He'd be over the moon to hear from you."

Fergal waited for the repeat dig about him never telephoning home any more, but when the kitchen remained silent, followed by the gentle gurgle of potatoes in boiling water, he unclenched his fists. Maybe he would just stay in tonight. A Saturday night with his four sisters wouldn't be that much of an ordeal.

Fergal glanced out through the green and white venetian blinds onto the street. The children had tired of trying to remove the far left wheel of his car and had moved, en masse, to surround the 'mobile' down the street. The mobile shop hadn't moved in over fifteen years. A few of the children were getting 'messages' for their mothers, but the others without shopping errands were just loitering in an attempt to irritate a few free sweets out of the young and inexperienced counter girl. But the young girl held her own and didn't appear intimidated by their cheeky banter. A smallish boy, squeezed into an even smaller Manchester United football shirt, came rushing out of the house opposite and the children scurried away. Fergal was relieved to see some evidence of discipline, especially in a boy so young. His mop of dusty brown hair and round cheeks reminded Fergal of his own. Maybe if he had a son, he would look like this small boy.

The girl behind the counter rewarded the boy with a large handful of penny sweets. Fergal looked on proudly as if the youngster was, in fact, fruit of his own loins. But as the boy leapt behind the nearest garden fence and started sharing his prize with the other children who were accomplices in the plot to deceive the girl, Fergal's heart sank. This wasn't his child at all; he was more likely to be Brendan's.

'That's it,' Fergal thought. 'I'm definitely staying in tonight.' Here he was, nearly forty, married, with a staff of twenty working for him at the building society; it was time he started showing everyone at home that he wasn't a wee lad any more.

"Fergal, run over to the mobile for us. I've run out of sanitary towels."

Within a few seconds Fergal was on the telephone

118

keying in Brendan's number. He surprised himself by knowing the number off by heart, even after all these years. As the telephone rang, Fergal perched himself along the top of the sofa, like an elongated cat taking its afternoon nap.

"Brendan. It's me, Fergal."

"Jesus, mucker! What a bolt from the blue. What are you up to? You still owe me a fiver."

Fifteen years rapidly faded away and within minutes the two lost friends were like they'd never been apart. Brendan hadn't changed at all. His humour, love of fishing and big-breasted girls were the same as ever and the deep singing tones of his voice lifted Fergal out of the estate and into the fields and hills of Donegal. Brendan quickly decided they had to meet up that night. Fergal suggested that he would have to check with Eilish, as she was having a family card night. When Brendan laughed so hard he almost choked, Fergal knew his bluff was called.

"Brendan, where do you fancy going? What about the Castle?"

"Nobody goes there these days. Anyways, I'm barred for leaving my Uncle Joe's coffin on the food servery."

Fergal chose not to explore this one.

"What about the Gweedore? Best Guinness in the town."

"Naw, it's too pokey for a hot evening like this. Anyways I'm barred . . ."

"Where then?"

"For a reunion like this . . . needs to be somewhere special."

"A pub where you're not barred sounds pretty special to me, Brendan."

"I've got it. Get a sleeping bag, beer and a packet of fire-

119

lighters and I'll see you up at the old place at eight. Don't be late or I'll tell everyone you kissed Stinky Deirdre on your fifteenth birthday."

The telephone line went dead, as did the colour in Fergal's cheeks. Eilish had overhead the entire conversation, well, half of it anyway. She craned her head around the kitchen doorway, keeping one eye on the boiling soup.

"So where are you off to?"

Fergal reached forward with his left hand and pointed out of the window towards the heavens. Eilish stepped over towards the sofa and carefully looked up past the white pebbledash houses across the road, beyond to the grey pebbledash of Galliagh. Above them were the rolling mountains of Donegal and at the top perched a small mound in the distance, silhouetted by the declining afternoon sun. Grianán Na Aileach, the medieval ring fort, stood majestic, stately and historic, casting a Celtic presence over the cobweb of modern state housing below.

A loud sizzling sound erupted from the kitchen.

"Shite, my soup!"

Chapter 15

The child was a blessing. Molly's persistence with the doorbell had provided Ursula with an unexpected escape route, as she hurriedly said her goodbyes to a bewildered Maurice. She was well aware of her neighbour's passion for driveways and borders and she trampled across both with gusto. She didn't look back and once cocooned inside her own front door she slid in a heap onto the coarse doormat.

Slowly, she picked herself up and headed for the shower. Much hotter than usual, she let the steaming water blast her back and shoulders until they were red raw. Turning to face the spray, she clumsily scrubbed away her make-up and then began methodically rubbing away at her body. Once finished, she smothered herself in a thick film of moisturising body butter. Applied too thickly, the barrier remained in sweeping circles all over her body. She vigorously rubbed her hair dry and pulled it back tight into a tortoiseshell clasp. She was dressed within moments in a large orange baggy T-shirt, usually reserved for clearing out the garage, and a pair of navy tracksuit bottoms. Back downstairs she could see the flicker of her answerphone. She sat curled up in her armchair, staring at the flickering light.

The telephone insistently informed Ursula that she had three messages. She pressed the 'play' button. 'Beep . . . Ursula, it's Carla. I'm sorry I upset you. Please call me.' 'Beep . . . Ursula, sweetheart, it's your big-mouthed, stupid friend. Please ring.' 'Beep . . . Ursula, I'm not sure if I said I was sorry the last time I called. If not, I am, sorry that is. Please call. I'm worried about you. Don't do anything stupid.'

Ursula tightened her crouched position. There was a knock on the door. If she could make herself into an even smaller ball, maybe they'd go away. The knock came back louder. She was conscious of her own booming breath and held it for a few moments to preserve the silence. The sound of her lashes as she blinked noisily combined with the crescendo of a deep swallow. Ursula heard footsteps move away from her front door and slowly dissolve away in the distance. Her unwelcome visitor had certainly not travelled by car. On her hands and knees, with her cordless telephone tucked under her right arm, Ursula crawled along the maple wooden floor of the front room and then onto the Chinese slate of the kitchen. Still on her knees, she gingerly opened the fridge door and was instantly bathed in a pool of bright light. A fresh-cream chocolate gâteau appeared to almost hover above a selection of fresh fruit, vegetables and bio yogurts. With her legs now crossed, Ursula balanced the dessert on her lap and plunged her left index finger between the moist sponges and deep into the ice-cold fresh cream. Pulling her finger carefully out again, she delicately placed the cream into her slightly gaping mouth. The telephone rang and she answered it.

"Ursula? It's Carla. Are you all right? I've been worried sick. What are you doing?"

"Right now, I've my head in the fridge and I'm about to suffocate on carbohydrates and fat."

"Look, sweetheart, I'm sorry about what I said. Just me ranting about something I know nothing about. Please don't commit calorie suicide on my account."

"What you said, Carla, that's the least of my worries. What about sleeping with the neighbour?"

Within fifteen minutes Carla was sitting in Ursula's dining-room. The half-eaten cake sat deflowered between the two friends.

"You left the café in such a temper. I'd never seen you like that."

"You touched a raw nerve, that's all."

The scene was a mirror image of their earlier meeting in the café; both women facing each other over a dining-table. This time, however, both were leaning towards each other, with their arms pressed against the table edge. This time their conversation was hushed in a gentle conspiracy. Looking at her make-up-less friend, Carla was struck by Ursula's true beauty and with her hair still severely scraped back into a clasp, the delicate contours of her cheeks and jaw belied her 34 years.

"I'm sorry, Ursula."

"When you asked if all Roger and myself did in bed was play Scrabble, you didn't know how right you were."

For once, Carla's assessment of the situation was appropriate and she remained unusually silent.

"It wasn't Roger's fault. It was mine. We were married so quickly after we met, and with me still living at home, we hadn't really much opportunity to make love before that. But once we were married, it quickly became clear that I just wasn't interested."

"Ursula, same happened to me, honest."

Ursula looked unconvinced.

"Remember the Malaysian student I was seeing a couple of years ago? After a few months the sex started to get a bit dull. So I suggested we try combining oral sex with the pleasure of food and we agreed to both bring along something we love to eat. Of course, my contribution that night was fresh cream and chocolate sauce. Smothering his firm slender body and licking it all off again was sensational. When it was his turn, Ping-Pong, or whatever he was called, grabbed his knapsack and pulled out a carton of sweet and sour noodles."

Ursula grimaced.

"I was discovering noodles in my knickers for days afterwards. The lesson is: don't be afraid to experiment and let yourself go."

"I tried, but the once-a-week chore rapidly became a once-a-month duty until by the end we simply didn't pretend any more and I moved into the spare room."

"That must have been tough for both of you. Was there no help you could get?"

"Four years down the line and I was getting daily hormone injections and psychotherapy."

"Ursula, I meant help for both of you."

"It wasn't Roger's fault. It was me."

Ursula tore a large piece out of the remnants of the cake and Carla snatched at the remainder.

"It all came to a head one evening when we both

returned from some horsy gala or other. He'd been asked to make a presentation at it. He'd come into my bedroom and made love to me. But this time as he lay all hot and heavy across my body, thrusting and rocking as I held tightly onto the edge of the mattress, I finally realised we weren't making love. Roger was having sex with me. And at that moment, I also realised that my emotions in the whole event counted for nothing. Roger was nothing more to me than a punter is to a prostitute. Prostitution was the price of my nice home, clothes and car. And the worst part of it all was that Roger liked it that way. The next day I packed my bags and left.

"Jesus!"

Carla's Irish accent was progressing nicely and her 'Jesus' had the correct weight and resonance of a local. There was far more to this visit than she had anticipated. And they hadn't even got to the nitty-gritty detail of the sexual liaison with the neighbour yet.

There was a knock at the front door and they remained motionless. Ursula whispered. "Don't answer it. I think it's him. He was here half an hour ago and I wouldn't go to the door."

There wasn't a second knock and footsteps could be heard moving away from the door. Carla began soaking up the remaining crumbs of the gâteau with her moistened right index finger. The heat in the house had forced Carla to tug down the zip on her red and black panelled dress, revealing the delicate trim of her maroon bra. Her long black hair was swept over to one side and she started to suck on a strand which had accidentally fallen into her mouth. She didn't want to probe her friend too much, or too fast. She knew that she had already intruded into an arena of Ursula's life that had been stifled for years. Ursula stared at the now empty white porcelain plate. With great inner turmoil, Carla tried to suffocate the many questions bombarding her mind.

"What about the neighbour, Ursula?"

Carla was Latin-blooded after all.

"That was a big mistake."

When Carla first arrived, Ursula had refused to turn any house lights on and as the day's sun had retired behind a thin veil of smoky grey cloud, the kitchen was lit with the fluorescence of the opened fridge. Carla thought she was going to explode with anticipation. She started to slowly rock on the back legs of her chair. The pace increased with her impatience and the chair squeaked like a lover's bed.

"What happened? Please, Ursula."

"I stupidly stormed off and left you in the café. That's what happened. And as I was getting into my car, I nervously dropped my purse and he picked it up.

"The neighbour?"

"No – 'Walk the Bike'. He said he'd seen me upset in the café and was worried about me."

"What did you say?"

"Nothing. I didn't get a chance. He then put his hand on my cheek and stroked it."

"The dirty brute. Did you slap him one?"

"No."

"What then?"

"As his finger stroked my lips, I kissed his hand."

Carla's chair rocked too far. As her three-inch black stilettos, one with a piece of chewing-gum stuck to the heel, rose to the top of the table, she was just in time to stop herself from falling backwards. As if nothing had happened, she regained composure and was quickly back on the case.

"I thought it was a neighbour you slept with?"

"Oh, nothing happened between 'Walk the Bike' and me. I was so embarrassed I jumped into the car and raced off back here. All the way home I kept thinking about what I'd done and what a fool I was, but at the same time I was thinking about what you thought of me – some frigid, old, dried-up walnut."

Carla tried to protest, but Ursula now had the momentum of a falling rock.

"When I got back here the house seemed as shrivelled up as I was and I just had to get out. I saw Maurice McAllen's car, parked on the road. He never . . ."

"Parks in his drive. I know."

Carla was keen for Ursula not to become distracted. Not now.

"I went round to his house and made some excuse or other about running out of light bulbs. As he stood in the doorway I felt like a mouse in the shadow of a cat. His shoulders filled the doorframe and his piercing blue, blue eyes bore through me and through my clothes. I'd seen him looking at me like that a few times before, but up close, he was terrifying . . . and we ended up sleeping together."

Carla felt greatly cheated.

"Hang on a minute. There's some detail missing, isn't there?"

"Not really. To be honest I think 'Walk the Bike' had done all the foreplay with that touch of his on my face. Maurice just did the easy bit."

"And?"

127

"And what?"

"Was it worth the wait?"

"I lay curled in a ball afterwards pretending to sleep and he went downstairs. It could have been Roger I heard pulling on his shirt and trousers and tiptoeing out of the room. Everything was exactly as I remembered it, the same empty feeling inside, the same disappointment and the familiar sense of being outside the whole experience. What's wrong with me? Why can't I be normal?"

Ursula sobbed into her hands and Carla leapt up and stood behind her with her arms cradling her friend's shoulders. As she looked down, Carla's black hair fell over Ursula's baby-blonde locks. It was like oil seeping over the soft feathers of a swan. Carla's thirst for the details of her closest friend's inner trauma swamped her with guilt. This unusual emotion made her feel uncomfortable and equally wretched.

The knock on the door returned, only this time more forceful.

"Don't open it, Carla! It'll only be him. I couldn't bear to see his face again. I'll never forget that look as we were making love. It was so vacant, as if he was . . . I don't know, thinking of someone else."

Carla had slowly edged her way over to the front window and had carefully lifted the edge of the heavy cream velvet curtains.

"Ursula, it's not who you think it is."

Ursula was too absorbed in her own introspection to pay heed to Carla. The knocking was now heavy enough to rattle the mahogany doorframe.

"That was it. All the time he was making love to me he

was thinking about someone else . . . another woman. Can you imagine how that feels? All the time he was touching me, he was imagining someone else."

"Ursula, it's that woman with all the kids from across the road. Christine Watson, isn't it?"

Ursula instantly stopped her ranting. Her ashen face abruptly turned towards the shaking door.

"Let her in."

Chapter 16

The door swung open with little resistance. As Orla continued to walk on to her own hotel room, down the dimly lit corridor, Frances stepped inside. She walked across the nylon carpet to the pine wardrobe and felt a wave of static electricity crawl up her body. Her hand brushed against the wardrobe's brass handle and a spark shot up her arm, forcing her to leap towards the window. It was six-thirty on the Saturday evening and the shops facing the hotel across the canal were busily clearing away the day. The worker in the pastry shop was washing down empty shelves and the florist was dragging huge buckets of Crayola-coloured flowers back into the store. She cast the occasional tulip into the canal and their wilting blooms bobbed and then disappeared under the blackening water.

The shopkeepers' day was at an end and Frances felt that hers was just beginning. Out of her holdall, which she had hurriedly stuffed under the bed when she arrived, she pulled her outfit for the evening. In an attempt to loosen a few stubborn creases, she hung a burnt-orange velvet blouse on the window latch. Her jeans were quickly unfolded and laid flat on her bed. Frances looked in disappointment at their wide hips and old-fashioned stitching, but reassured herself, partly, with the fashionable bootleg shape.

A pocket-sized make-up bag was placed on her bedside cabinet and Frances began to arrange an assortment of brown and beige eye shadows, dusty pink lipsticks and an all-in-one tube of foundation and face powder. She lined them up in order of their intended application and moved an oblong mirror, balanced in the corner of the small room, up onto the cabinet. The mirror was slightly cracked in the top right-hand corner and as Frances positioned it and then stared at her reflection, she good-humouredly saw her right nostril stretched up over her forehead and the delicate fine hairs on her top lip magnified into Freddie Mercury proportions. She laughed aloud at her hideous metamorphosis. As she bent her knees and looked at herself full length in the undamaged centre of the mirror, she quickly ceased smiling and abruptly exhaled a thick cloud of mist onto the mirror. Her reflection was now smothered.

With the gracefulness of a bag of parsnips, Frances sat down on the edge of her bed and removed her sports shoes. As she massaged her aching feet, the aches in her knees and lower back began to tighten. She hadn't touched a volleyball in nearly a year and here she was, forcing her out-of-practice body beyond its capabilities. While removing her slightly damp socks, Frances spotted a blackening toenail and, when hit with the fresh air, it throbbed enthusiastically. What on earth was she doing here? Trying to recapture something that belonged to her past? She flung herself onto the mattress and let her weary legs dangle weightlessly off the end. Closing her brown eyes, she imagined she was swinging in a calico hammock with tanned, sexy legs and draped in a thin veil of silks and chiffon. Mel Gibson was walking over to her, with a cocktail in each hand.

"Not now, Mel. I'm relaxing."

The half-awake part of Frances fought an internal battle with the sleeping beauty on the beach.

"No, no, come back! I didn't mean it."

Too late. He was away. The battle between the conscious and sub-conscious became bloody and Frances fought bitterly to control who and what happened in her dream. She was winning the battle. Mel Gibson returned and as he leant towards her, his handsome face brushed against her cheek and she felt the soft caress of his bristles. Frances hungrily parted her lips and, as she did so, the face leaning to kiss her instantly transformed from Mel Gibson to that of her husband, Fergal.

"Shit!"

Startled out of her slumber, Frances jumped forwards and found that she was surrounded by Orla, Niamh and Roberta. They looked like they were paying their last respects to a corpse. Suddenly Orla grabbed hold of Frances's arms. Niamh forced her wriggling legs down firmly and after a few seconds of resistance, Frances lay still like a day-old loaf. Roberta, who was clearly in charge of the assault, stared down with her heavily made-up eyes and held Frances's head between her palms.

"Frances, you are charged with the serious crime of desertion. Count one, is the charge of abandoning your teammates at the end of the season, leaving them all alone to face the might of the Ballymoney Blockers. Count two, you proceeded to make yourself unavailable for the following season, including league matches, cup competition and Niamh's monthly coffee mornings."

Niamh clenched tightly on Frances's ankle and nodded her head in approval.

"Count three. Orla spotted you on the 6th day of June, leaving the Castle Court Shopping Centre wearing paisley-patterned leggings. On count one, how do you plead, guilty or not guilty?"

"Guilty."

"Count two, guilty or not?"

"Guilty."

"Count three . . . ?"

"Not guilty. They had buttons and a wide waistband, and, therefore, were not technically leggings . . . as such."

Roberta quietened Frances by placing her hand over her mouth.

"Friends and jury, please give your verdict."

A hushed chorus of 'guilty' followed.

"The jury has decided a unanimous verdict of guilty and it is my duty to pass sentence on your poor, depraved, unfortunate soul. Orla, could you please administer the punishment."

From behind the bed, Orla produced a two-litre bottle of duty-free Bacardi. She tilted Frances's neck forward and like a mother feeding her fledgling, she poured a measure into the opened mouth. The heat of the alcohol raced over Frances's tongue and singed her gums. For several seconds she was not capable of swallowing, but when she did, she gagged and balked.

"Happens to me too, every time I swallow."

133

As Roberta spoke, she leant forward and kissed her still suffering friend on the cheek. Orla followed suit, followed by Niamh wagging her wedding-ring-free finger. Finally released, Frances leapt up and inspected her tongue in the mirror. It had turned a fuzzy white and her teeth felt rough and sticky.

Cathy-Ann and her sister Rose now entered the room. Frances turned away from the mirror and found that her bedroom had been invaded and taken over by an array of lingerie, hairdryers, perfumes and make-up pallets. Niamh, the ever-organised teacher, opened her large Antler bag and pulled out eyebrow curlers, hair tongs, a French manicure kit, followed by gin, tonic and a jar of olives. Frances's orange blouse had now been relegated to the windowsill and her jeans had disappeared under a sea of animal-print skirts and black Lycra T-shirts. Frances's sanctuary had now become the team's 'getting ready to go out on the town' room. Thirty-something professional women had suddenly been transformed into the Pink Ladies. The hotel room swelled with the commotion of make-up exchanges and hair-style advice. Niamh's eyelash curlers proved to be very popular and there followed a hum of hairdryers in action. The very beautiful Cathy-Ann had secured herself a quiet corner near the door and she professionally applied her make-up without distraction. With an effortless wisp of gold eye shadow and a dust of rosy pink on her cheekbones, she instantly looked stunning. Roberta mischievously nudged Cathy-Ann's elbow as she tried to apply a faint charcoal line to her upper eyelid. The result was a heavy smudge drawn from her eye to her ear. Cathy-Ann's eyes swelled with tears as she surveyed herself in her compact mirror and drew her long elegant finger along the imperfection. Niamh came to the rescue and with cotton wool and eye-make-up remover, delicately returned the imperfect to the perfect. Niamh then stripped down to her pale pink matching bra and knickers and began carefully applying a maroon line around her own pouting lips. A slightly stretch-marked stomach pushed against her knicker-line.

Rose returned to the battle of curling her poker-straight hair. She reluctantly settled for a couple of kinks in her fringe. Roberta's make-up was applied in minutes and, forever the nuisance, she was starting to feel at a loose end.

"For a million pounds, who would shag that wee squirt who referees our home matches?"

Roberta's unprovoked question created a general sense of 'here we go again'. Whilst massaging body oil into her large athletic biceps, Orla was the first to answer.

"I would. Aye, for a million, I would."

"What about the wee squirt's granda?"

"I'd need to have a look at him."

"OK, if you had to choose – who would you sleep with, Cindy Crawford or Jimmy Hill?"

"Cindy Crawford."

"You must be gay then."

"How do you work that one out, Roberta? I think it says more about how bucking unattractive Jimmy Bloody Hill is actually."

"OK, Orla, what if the choice was, let's say, Cindy Crawford and Rose."

"Easy, our Rose. She's lovely."

Rose gave her teammate a warm smile.

"See, Orla. You are queer."

135

"Roberta, it means nothing of the kind."

"Yes, it does. You're able to discriminate between which women you would sleep with. OK, girls, if you all had to choose between Jimmy Hill and a donkey, who would you shag?"

A chorus of 'donkey' momentarily silenced Roberta. Seconds later and she was bombarded with a barrage of lipsticks and damp sports socks. When Cathy-Ann took revenge by throwing an ashtray, the floodgates were fully open and there was a general agreement to throw anything in Roberta's direction that wasn't nailed to the floor. She made her escape, under fire, to the ensuite bathroom.

With their mischievous friend out of the way, the team enjoyed a period of calm and continued dressing. Frances was the slowest as she took a moment to observe the transformation of her friends. Cathy-Ann was dressed in a fake-zebra-skin, knee-length skirt, with long patent black boots and a tight black silk blouse. She was now sitting on the windowsill, using the natural light to apply her Moroccan Poppy lipstick with a pencil-thin brush. As she crossed her legs in order to balance her elbow, her tight skirt slightly rose up and her blouse delicately gaped open as she leaned forward. She pulled at Frances's now discarded blouse from beneath her, as it was making her seating uncomfortable.

"Some old doll left this in the room."

She held the now well-crumpled blouse aloft.

"It's mine. I'm wearing it tonight."

Frances's teammates faced her in unison. They had each been so busy with their own preparations, they hadn't noticed Frances huddled in the corner applying her beige eye-shadow and pale pink lipstick. Niamh was the first to check her teammate.

"Jesus, Frances. Get thee to a nunnery. We're in Amsterdam, for heaven's sake. It's Saturday night, you're in the company of five horny women and you're getting ready to go to Mass."

"It's all right for you girls. You've all kept your figures. Look at me. I've kept my Da's."

Immediately, Rose stood up and lifted the straps on her bra, revealing her heavy and downward-facing breasts. Niamh, likewise, stood up and turning, pointed to a crawling blue vein protruding from the back of her knee. Roberta, waving a white piece of toilet roll as a truce gesture, poked her head from the ensuite and, lifting her bleached blonde fringe, unveiled a line of red angry spots. Orla followed by lifting her skirt, clenching her buttocks, and showing a thin veil of dimpled cellulite on her once muscular thighs. Cathy-Ann was the last to contribute. She eagerly looked at her body from various angles in a pitiful search for a suitable fault. Genuinely embarrassed, she started to fluster, before her face illuminated with relief.

"Look at my hands. There's an ugly big freckle right there above my knuckle."

The women appreciated the gesture and, for the first time this weekend, Frances felt the familiar sense of belonging and comradeship. For the past six months, she had been very much an isolated figure and to some extent had accepted it as her future. But maybe she wasn't alone and here were people who could possibly be brought back into her confidence. She had kept the lid on her worries so tightly over the past months, she didn't think a bulldozer could open it. But was she starting to feel the gentle friction as the lid was opening?

137

"We're not going out with you looking like that!"

The lid stopped moving. Roberta yanked the offending blouse from Cathy-Ann's hands and threw it out of the window. The headless and legless figure danced downwards towards the pavement and then sharply hit a cyclist on the back of the head. Within seconds a new outfit was assembled comprising Niamh's black velvet trousers, Orla's ruby-red halter-neck blouse and Cathy-Ann's stilettos. Frances was pleased that at least her gorgeous teammate and herself had their shoe size in common. Once re-dressed, Roberta pulled back Frances' fair hair into a French twist. With a blob of hair wax, she sculptured the ends into spikes and tipped them with silver specks of glitter. As a restaurant manager, Rose was always immaculately made-up when on work duty and there was a general murmur of agreement when she was volunteered to improve on Frances' first dull attempt at make-up. A coat of ruby lipstick immediately complemented the borrowed blouse and, with a dash of mauve and charcoal eye-shadows, Frances stared at her transformation in the mirror.

The women were pleased with the result of their project. As they scurried around her, the differences and the similarities of her friends struck Frances. Roberta was illuminated with the glow of being centre of attention. Niamh the teacher, and expert on all playground humour, giggled as she re-told jokes for the second and third times this weekend. Though Rose and Cathy-Ann enjoyed telling everyone how much they didn't get on, Frances could clearly see the very special way the two sisters fixed each other's hemline or brushed away wayward flecks of mascara.

Orla threw back her head and fell into a bout of

infectious giggles. Her physique was strong and powerful, but with her head and hair thrust backwards as she laughed, she was a child once again, without a care in the world. On Orla's earlier revelation of the name of her long-term lover, Frances had decided not to admit that, not only had she heard of him, but she was also a neighbour of Roger Keane's ex-wife, Ursula. She was glad that for this evening anyway, Orla was leaving her troubles behind.

The six women stood coven-like in an embrace. They struggled to control their laughter as Niamh naively took this as a compliment to her schoolyard jokes.

Frances imagined she was looking from the outside in. No one could say the friends were anything other than stunning. Tonight these friends were the most beautiful women in the world and she was one of them.

"Right girls, I'm ready to get naked."

Frances could not believe what she had just said or what she was about to do.

Chapter 17

The only way to keep going through the day, Maurice decided, was not to analyse it too much. By three o'clock that afternoon he'd managed to get involved in a domestic battle between a mother and her three daughters, he'd then kissed her and an hour later was taking another neighbour up to his bedroom. His policy of keeping as low a profile as possible was in tatters. Ursula's hasty departure had eased the situation slightly, but whenever he tried to analyse what had actually happened to him that day, his head hurt. The pain was also compounded by the sight of Christine walking past his front window in the direction of Ursula's house. When he saw her walking back home again a few minutes later, the pain eased slightly. Half an hour passed by and Christine walked past his window a second time. As he sat studying these trips through the seclusion of his vertical blinds, he gradually began to feel the pressure of the living-room walls squeezing in on him.

Maurice knew he had to get out of the house. This

feeling of forced imprisonment was familiar and uncomfortable. He grabbed his car keys and wallet from the sofa. The memories of the afternoon came hurtling back to him as he picked up his sweater, shoes and socks. All of which had been hurled around the room as he and Ursula had hurriedly undressed an hour earlier. When dressed, Maurice made one more security check through his front window. For a third time, Christine was walking over towards Ursula's house. Maurice pulled back from the blinds and decided to wait for her return home again. The minute wait turned into two, then four. After ten minutes, Maurice craned his neck to look down towards Ursula's front door, but Christine was nowhere to be seen. What was going on? He decided not to dwell on his predicament too hard and to use the opportunity to make an escape. Pulling his front door gently behind him, Maurice then, for the first time since he'd moved into the Ashbury Development, ran across his drive and lunged into his car.

As Maurice sped out of the cul-de-sac, he kept his eyes facing forward. His priority right now was to create some distance between himself and his neighbours. It was time he regained his composure and self-discipline and to do that he needed to get away. But as he drove past Ursula's house, he struggled to maintain self-discipline and he couldn't resist a sideways glance. Through Ursula's front window he could see the silhouettes of three figures; the one in the centre was bent over and the other two appeared to be shouting at each other. Involuntarily, he slowed down his car and as he did so all three figures looked directly out of the window and in his direction. Maurice thrust his foot down on the accelerator pedal and scurried away.

As Maurice approached the main road, he had to choose between turning right and heading into Bangor town centre or turning left and driving along the main Belfast road. The decision was made for him as his car appeared to automatically turn in the familiar direction of Belfast and onto the journey Maurice had made every day since moving into the development.

Within fifteen minutes he was on the Belfast outer ring road. The traffic lights appeared to be held on red forever. He didn't like this idle time, as he found himself drifting back to the incidents of the day. He lifted both his hands from the steering wheel and rested them on the back of his head. His blond hair felt so rough and coarse compared to that of Christine's or that of Ursula's. He moved his hands downward onto his wide powerful neck. This too seemed vulgar and heavy compared to the women's. He was tantalised by the memories of the day, but the emotions he felt most were those of guilt and betrayal.

A car horn beeped from behind him and as he quickly heeded the now-green light and changed into first gear, Maurice was abruptly halted by an RUC officer. The tall willowy frame in the green uniform stood arm extended directly in front of him. Maurice nervously looked down towards the car's glove compartment, but blind panic froze him and his hand remained glued to the gear stick. The policeman stared at Maurice, but his intention was not evident. There was a flicker of recognition on the officer's face, but before he could make a connection, the reason for his presence revealed itself. An Orange Order parade turned out of a side road and began marching directly along the outer ring road in Maurice's direction. The round red faces of the Lambeg drummers led the marchers, with the capillary veins on their cheeks throbbing with the beat. A sea of bowler hats and white gloves followed, with stern faces contrasting sharply with the cheerful youngsters diving in and out of the parading legs.

Maurice directed his gaze downwards towards his lap with intermittent glances towards the glove box. Wherever he turned he was trapped. The last two years of trying to get his life back together, and the drive to regain control and regain anonymity, felt shattered and crushed. Within twelve hours he had managed to destroy it all. Maurice pulled his knees together with a force that would crush a child. The blond hairs on his burnished arms stood erect against his taut forearms, and his shoulders hunched firmly in towards his neck. The battle to fight or flee took hold of him, with the conflict keeping him frozen in his seat.

The last of the paraders, a group of mothers, toddlers and pushchairs passed by. The RUC officer turned back towards Maurice and walked towards him. He was peering through the windscreen as if trying to convince himself he knew the driver. As he got closer, Maurice sat rigid, tightened his whole body frame and held his breath. The policeman walked around the front of the car and towards the driver's window. As he tilted his hat up and away from his face and began to bend his knees, in order to stare through the window, an impatient driver sounded his car horn behind. Angered, the officer abruptly turned in the direction of the offending driver and waved Maurice's car onwards. The smoke gushing out of the exhaust was nothing compared to that bursting out of Maurice's lungs.

The roads were full of early-evening Saturday shoppers,

returning home. The declining sun's rays bounced off the shop windows and a warm pink glow radiated from the red-brick houses on the right side of the road. As Maurice drove through the city centre and towards Shaftesbury Square, the traffic became less and less and as he began his familiar drive up the Lisburn Road, the only other traffic was the occasional bus or taxi. After driving for a further mile, he turned off into a side road and pulled up alongside a majestic sycamore tree casting a massive shadow across the street. Inch by inch, Maurice edged the car along the kerb, until he had the car positioned precisely where he intended. Without getting out of the car, he then awkwardly shifted across to the passenger front seat. His long legs brushed against the handbrake and his hair bristled along the rear-view mirror. Once firmly seated, he wound down the window and re-positioned the side mirror. A three-storey town house was now centred in the mirror. A bedraggled-looking Russian vine stretched across a green-glossed front door, and obviously once-adored rose bushes looked slightly mildewed and neglected against the ivory paint-work.

Maurice laid his head back against the headrest and turned his eyes towards the mirror. The headrest was speckled with blond hairs where his head had been many times before. He removed his boots, stretched out his toes on the floor mat and slowly pulsated his feet by clenching and relaxing his toes like a cat. He felt like a child burdened by the bulk frame of a large man. The real Maurice was way deep inside, somewhere in the middle of his heaving chest. The child was no longer strong enough to manoeuvre the heavy arms and long legs of this Trojan horse. Even the head felt lead-like and monstrous.

Maurice opened the glove compartment and checked the safety catch on his gun. He then placed it on his lap and covered it with a tattered road-map. With his hands now securely on top of that, he rested his head once again. For the first time that day, Maurice felt the beginnings of an inner calm and, as he slowly closed his eyes, he focussed on the steady falling of the microbes under his eyelids. Within ten seconds Maurice was asleep.

"For God's sake! Will you leave us alone!"

Maurice was sharply awoken by a ferocious tapping on his window. A tall, elegant woman was roaring at him with blazing eyes and tight lips. She clenched her hands tightly around her slender waist. Through the gaps created between her arms and her body, two small boys cowered.

"Why can't you just face it? We don't want you! It's over."

The gun in Maurice's lap suddenly felt ice-cold and heavy.

Chapter 18

Against the evening sky, Grianán Na Aileach looked like a massive sleeping dinosaur. The winding road leading up to it, only one car wide, kept dipping and rising and with each rise more and more of the dinosaur came into view. Fergal knew he should turn back. But he didn't. Burt Chapel, built as a replica of the fort before its demise into ruin, sat nestled at the bottom of the hill. The grazing sheep, dotted along the road, cared little for their majestic view of Lough Swilly and the Inisowen Peninsula.

Fergal parked in the small car park at the bottom of the rocky path leading to the fort. The ancient builders of Griánan would have been impressed with the car park's uniform construction and conformity of European-funded proportions. Fergal awkwardly dodged between the granite rocks and the purple heathers. The cast-iron gate leading to the belly of the fort was wedged ajar. The entrance floor was worn away by the footprints of centuries of visitors, leaving a pool of rainwater, which being sheltered from the sun, never dried away. Fergal leapt across the puddle, but his right heel did not quite make it, resulting in a splash of muddy brown water on the back of his trouser leg. Inside the stone circle, Brendan was sitting cross-legged throwing clumps of turf onto a small open fire. He was dwarfed by the twenty-foot-high stone walls leading up to the open sky.

"Yes, Mucker."

"Yes, Brendan."

With the formalities over, the two friends shook hands, before Brendan pulled Fergal towards him and gave him a firm hug. With their sleeping bags rolled up into cushions, they then huddled around the fire and opened a couple of cans of Guinness. It was eight o'clock in the evening, but still very bright. The far end of the inner circle, where a hole led into the innards of the stone circle, was half in shadow and very black.

Fergal stared into Brendan's face, which began to glow with the heat of the flames. There was very little difference between him now and nearly twenty years ago. His hair was still pulled into a short ponytail. His wire-rimmed glasses still balanced at an angle and his clothes still resembled the rocker of bygone years. Brendan's red-and-hazel-speckled moustache completely hid his top row of teeth, but the occasional grey wiry hair was the only difference Fergal could spot. He immediately envied the way his friend looked. Compared to Fergal, he looked youthful and fresh. The years had indeed been kind to Brendan.

"I see the checkpoint is all boarded up."

"Aye. Shortly after the ceasefires, no-man's-land became every-man's-land. It hardly looks the same place. It seems strange going across the border now. Smuggling sheep is no fun any more."

Both men laughed as they recounted the story of the trolley Brendan had constructed for sneaking past the window of the customs and excise hut. If you rolled it down the road and lay completely flat, luge-style, you could smuggle all kinds of stuff right under the guards' noses. The bleating sheep, held tight across the two boys' chests as they raced along at twenty miles an hour, was the pinnacle of their poaching career.

"What happened to that sheep?"

"Nothing, Fergal. Nobody was up to the final deed, so my Ma donated it to the chapel for their nativity play."

"How's the Ma doing?"

"The best. I'm the only one left in the house now."

"And what are you working at?"

"You name it; I'm doing it. Poaching's still going well. I've got my own boat now. I badgered Mickey One Eye to trade it for a dinner table and four chairs. I had to meet him in the middle of the night at the old City Dairy. The night was pitch black and deadly silent. Next thing I heard this noise, squeaky squeak, squeaky squeak. Round the corner pokes Mickey One Eye with this bloody great boat balanced across an old, beat-out, Silver Cross pram. The weight of the boat was causing the squeaky squeak. God knows how far he'd walked with that bloody noise.

Fergal's envy raged as he compared Brendan's simple life with his own. Again he questioned as to how it had all happened to him. His friend had totally escaped the ravages of time and sitting now, directly in front of him, was the mirror of the twenty-year-old photograph in Fergal's study.

"Jesus, Mucker, drink up. We've all these to get through yet."

Brendan pulled a blanket away from a case of assorted beers. Fergal decided not to ask where he had got them all from.

"Brendan, I can't handle drink any more. Three beers and I'm on my ear."

"Down at the Metro last night I had five Smithwicks, a half bottle of vodka and two pina coladas. And still had room for a curry chip."

The two cocktails surprised Fergal, but the amount Brendan could drink without falling unconscious did not. He forced himself to drink the remainder of his can as Brendan opened him a second and passed it over to him. This was an English wheat beer with the aroma of an ashtray. But after the second mouthful, the smell improved and left a warm yeasty taste in his throat.

A couple of Dutch-looking tourists poked their heads through the gate. They saw the two men, muttered something quickly, and hastily departed. Brendan and Fergal climbed the stone steps up to the top of the walls and saw the rapidly departing backs of the terrified tourists. They were back in their hire car and down the hill within minutes. As the men stood upright, their faces were blasted with a warm southerly wind. Below there wasn't a breath of air, but this wind at the top was a permanent resident of Griánan and had been there ever since they first visited the old fort as young boys. From the top was a view of Derry and Burt. Across the lough was Inch Island, sheltered by the mountains. As the evening approached, the soft twinkling lights of Derry could been seen dancing in the distance, with the occasional chapel spire bursting into the dimming sky.

The water colour view filled Fergal's heart – topping up

the cavities that had begun to appear in recent months. The two men stood bathed in that silence, only understood and accepted by true friends. Fergal had thought he had built up quite a wide circle of friends in Bangor and he got on well with his new neighbours. But at this moment, he realised, his real friends came from his past. As he thought more deeply, Fergal decided that everything he truly cared about came from his past. He didn't like what he had become and thoughts of the present and the future sickened him.

Brendan audibly inhaled as the fresh wind circled them, filling his lungs with the scent of the mountain. Fergal did the same, but unfortunately inhaled too much and exploded into a ferocious coughing bout. Brendan assisted his friend, now bent double, back down to the open fire and passed him a bottle of American lager to clear his throat. After several sips, Fergal recovered and sat on his sleeping-bag with his chin resting on his chest, his hands on his stomach and his feet perched on a case of beer.

"Do you know what your problem is, Fergal? You've lost your stomach for the hard stuff. Get this one down your neck."

Brendan threw over a cheap-looking bottle of Czech beer to Fergal. Fergal didn't have the energy to muster an argument and accepted the challenge unenthusiastically. As Fergal quietly sipped from the bottle, his friend recounted stories of fishing trips and drinking games. Fergal could have recounted tales of the big account he secured last month from a pharmaceutical company, or the story about the four executives from an oil distribution company he had wined and dined at £40 for a brandy shot. Or maybe about the patio doors he was planning for the family room. But he thought not.

The centre of the fort was now smothered in total shadow, as the evening sun finally fell behind the granite walls. Fergal's grey eyes turned muddy and his round body tightened against the sudden light chill. Brendan had been unable to continue with his last poaching story due to a fit of consuming giggles. Brendan had always enjoyed his own company. In between his laughter bouts, a word or two escaped, but he was quickly overcome again. Eventually, he gave up on the story and resumed drinking.

The fire greedily accepted a few more mounds of turf and sparked and roared with satisfaction. Red circles began to form on the cheeks of the two friends. Brendan's only added to his already mottled complexion, but Fergal's usual grey pallor was illuminated and iridescent. The grey returned to his eyes. Brendan continued to be invigorated by the alcohol racing through his veins.

"Do you remember the bombs we used to make when we were weeins? We'd nick a whole load of stuff from Johnny Doyle's and squeeze it into old lemonade bottles. Anything we thought might be explosive would do. You must remember? The one you made with the Harpic, baby milk and HP sauce was magic. We shook it up, threw it against the wall and . . ."

"Nothing happened."

"It did. It exploded like a fireball."

"Now, Brendan, don't start believing your own stories now. I was there, remember. It didn't go off."

As the alcohol energised and lifted Brendan's spirits, it did exactly the opposite to his friend. Brendan was only momentarily deflated, before his spirits surged again.

"Here's me doing all the talking. How's the missus? Still playing basketball?"

"Volleyball. She hasn't played for the past while. But she's away playing this weekend in Amsterdam."

"And you let her go?"

"Why wouldn't I?"

Brendan made a feeble attempt at a sexual mime, by gyrating his hips and groin. The resulting image was that of a canary masturbating against a perch. Fergal knew this image would still be with him tomorrow.

"It'll do her good."

"Jesus, I thought you two had split up or something. You've hardly talked about her all evening. Last time we met it was Frances this, Frances bloody that . . ."

"We've had a difficult few months, that's all."

Fergal could have shared with his friend all that had happened over the past few months. How this date, six months previously, had changed his life for ever. How it had destroyed Frances. His anxiety, frustration and loneliness, they could have all been shared.

But before he could continue talking, Brendan thrust another bottle of Eastern European beer in his direction. Brendan regretted opening an obviously tender wound. His solution was to quickly share yet another poaching story. The two friends relaxed in the comfort of their banal conversation. Fergal was relieved and thought to himself how comforting tedium can be. Surely only true friends could be this comfortable with monotony?

The evening had raced on with great speed and as both men unfurled their sleeping bags and lay facing the clear sky, they discovered they were encircled by a cloak of stars and constellations. Brendan's countless evenings in his fishing boat had made him an authority on all that was heavenly.

"I'd say by looking at the North Star in relation to the moon . . . it's just gone midnight."

Fergal checked his watch. It was ten minutes past twelve. It was Sunday the 1st of July. The 1st of July echoed in his head and its importance pulsated with the rhythmic force of a marathon runner's feet. He knew, without doubt, right now Frances was feeling the same unending pulse. Not that she would admit this to him. They didn't talk any more. Not about real stuff. Over the past six months, they too had become comfortable with each other's tedium and the monotony of day-to-day living.

Both men saw a shooting star dart across the sky. Neither made a wish.

Behind Fergal's sleeping bag was a small well that he had made by shovelling out a few handfuls of dry dusty soil. Into which, every few minutes, he poured beer from his bottle. With his stomach churning with six pints of beer, Fergal had given up trying to drink alongside his friend and had turned to subterfuge. Obliviously, Brendan continued to drink and was now sucking on a skinny home-made cigarette, speckled with tiny dots of marihuana.

"Want a smoke?"

Fergal declined, pointing to his half-empty bottle.

"Don't want to interfere with my drinking."

"Good thinking."

Both men began to feel the chill of the evening and curled themselves up inside their sleeping bags. Fergal had come home to Derry to find answers to the many questions crushing his thoughts. But as the moon now hid behind a doily of wafer-thin cloud, Fergal realised there would be no answers tonight. Again, he looked on his friend with envy, as he lay pathetically forming smoke circles with his face staring up at the sky and the stars reflected in his pupils. How come he had lost all that Brendan still had? What had he gained in return? A couple of stone around the waistline, a house in suburbia, a wife who didn't talk to him any more, a suit and tie, satellite TV? What had he become?

Fergal hadn't noticed, but he had in fact been talking aloud. He stopped and saw Brendan staring at him in total amazement.

"You've turned into a Protestant."

"Fak away off."

"That's what's happened to you, Fergal. Suburbia has drained every last Hail Mary out of you. Go on. Admit it. You've started doing your shopping in Ballymena."

Fergal threw his hands up in disbelief.

"Answer this one then. I bet you've now got mates in the RUC."

"Have not."

"Bet you have."

"I haven't. I know a fella in the Reserves, but that's not the same."

"Aye, it is. Who else?"

"No one. Well, there's this weird neighbour of mine, Maurice McAllen. I read an old newspaper article in the Ponderosa on my way up about a cop on trial. You never know, it might be the same fella."

"Jesus, aye, I remember that case. It was famous at the time."

"Was it? The article said he was on trial for passing on names and addresses to the UVF or one of those organisations."

"Aye, Fergal, it was all over the news. One of the

addresses he passed on was all wrong and two little uns and their Ma were gunned down in their beds. You must remember it? It was on TV. The news opened with shots of two wee coffins draped in white lilies and the next shot was this huge six-foot-plus fella being led into the court with a mop of blond hair and ice-cold blue eyes. He was scary-looking."

The clouds thickened over the moon and it went into total blackness.

"And he's your neighbour?"

Chapter 19

She looked a mess. Christine thought she had never seen Ursula without her make-up complete and clothes immaculately presented. Standing before her, in baggy track suit bottoms and loose T-shirt, with her hair almost, but not quite, showing signs of grease, Christine wondered what kind of day Ursula was having.

Christine entered the house and was swiftly introduced to Ursula's friend, Carla. Christine guessed by the friend's accent that she was Spanish or Portuguese. On first impressions, she also felt the foreigner was dressed a little cheaply. She assumed the ex-wife of an Olympic show-jumper would socialise with friends of a certain class and appearance. The friend had unzipped her dress until it was almost at the navel, with her bra exposed. Christine wondered for whose benefit she dressed in the morning. A bedraggled strip of jet-black hair also limply clung to her cheek and Christine wondered whether or not it had just fallen into her dinner by mistake. Christine made her mind up about the character of this friend within those first few minutes. She was probably a student, hanging around Ursula for an opportunity to meet some rich and successful local men. Christine was confident that Ursula could teach this hanger-on a thing or two about the opposite sex.

After a few cordial pleasantries, Christine was invited to sit down and the Spanish friend appeared relieved to be given the task of making coffee.

"Christine, how are you keeping? How are the girls?"

"The girls are fine, thanks. How's your work going?"

"Fine, fine. Busy, you know, but fine."

"Good."

"And Alex? Is he working today?"

"Yes. He wasn't supposed to be, but he got called in at the last minute. You know how these things are."

"Yes."

Christine wondered why her neighbour just didn't come straight out and ask her why she had called. She knew the onus was on her to make her purpose known, but she was quite enjoying Ursula's obvious discomfort at playing the host. Throughout their introductions, Ursula had remained seated, with her legs hunched underneath. Christine noted her neighbour's body language and countered it by stretching out her own long legs over the maple floor and languidly dangling her arms over the sides of the chair arms.

"Your room's lovely. Have you decorated again?"

"No."

"Maybe new lighting?"

"Yes, that'll be it."

"Lovely."

The two neighbours' houses were exactly the same in

157

design and layout. Christine noted how Ursula's style of interior design was far more minimalist than her own. She had ice-blue walls with three ivory-white rectangle insets carved out of the plaster. Set within each inset, a single white vase was illuminated by a recessed halogen light. There was lots of glass furniture and shelving. Ursula's maple wood floor was unblemished. Christine imagined her three girls smudging their sticky fingers on the glass tables, throwing bean bags at the vases and dragging their heels along the polished floor. She was tempted herself to scrape the heel of her beige court shoe along the wood, as she stretched out even further. But even in her current peculiar mood, she recognised this would be purely vindictive.

Carla re-entered the living-room, carrying a tray. Christine and Ursula both said, 'Coffee, lovely' at the same time and with rather more enthusiasm than was appropriate. Ursula's friend looked at the two of them and then made a hasty retreat into the kitchen. On the tray were three olive and mustard-coloured Denby mugs, with a matching side plate of assorted soft fruits, including strawberries and peaches. This re-confirmed Christine's opinion of her neighbour and she was not surprised to discover that Ursula wasn't the type of woman to have either biscuits or cakes on the premises.

Ursula busily sliced the peaches and removed a handful of grapes from their stem. Like her friend, she also appeared to Christine to be relieved to have a task to complete. Christine recognised that her own pleasure in the awkwardness of the encounter was both irrational and out of character. But then, today was her day to be anybody other than herself. Already this weekend she had been bad-tempered with her children, foolish with Maurice, adolescent-like in the bathroom and now manipulative with her neighbour. But the sense of liberation was exhilarating. The Presbyterian doctor's wife and mother of three had been let out of the suburban box this weekend and she wasn't ready to go back.

The Spanish-looking woman returned carrying a Denby milk-jug. When she offered milk, both Ursula and Christine graciously declined.

"So, Christine, is it?" asked the friend.

"Yes, Carla. Have I got that right?"

"Yes. Was that you knocking on the door earlier?"

Ursula visibly blushed. Christine was impressed by the friend's directness. The game's momentum had shifted slightly.

"Yes, it was."

"Must be important then, Christine. What do you want?"

The game had swung full circle and now Christine was starting to feel ill at ease. Ursula appeared to absolve all responsibility for her friend and for the situation. She casually dissolved into the back of her chair. When faced with the direct question, Christine's expediency diminished and she struggled to formulate her concerns into coherent sentences. She wanted to know if Maurice had confided to Ursula their intimate liaison earlier that afternoon. Had they been amused at her expense? How important was Christine's embrace to Maurice? Had Ursula also seen her stranded from the bathroom window? In fact, above all, she wanted to know exactly what Ursula was doing inside Maurice's home in the first place. No one, other than Maurice, had ever been seen entering or leaving his home.

But how could Christine get answers to all these questions without exposing herself and losing the upper hand?

"I was thinking of asking Mr McAllen to advise me on a new lawn. Do you think that would be a good idea?"

What was she saying? Christine couldn't believe she had just asked the most banal, inappropriate and pointless question. The question had no relation to what she intended and was totally superficial. She pulled her long legs back tight against the chair and crossed her arms firmly across her stomach. In contrast, Ursula confidently unfurled from her crouched position and lifted her legs until they were comfortably balanced on the glass coffee table.

"Are you asking me if I would recommend Mr McAllen for seed planting?"

The Spanish friend exploded into laughter, turned her head away and was forced to stuff her mouth with her fist in an effort to suffocate a further outburst. Ursula now leaned forward, with the size of her presence increasing by the second.

"Is that what you're asking me, Christine?"

Christine felt totally out-matched and out-manoeuvered. This was not how she had planned things would go.

As Ursula repeated the question, her friend this time had to bend over in order to suppress her laughter. Ursula was now standing upright and towering over Christine. Inexperienced in confrontation, Christine thought her best defence was to mirror the posture of her adversary and she, likewise, stood up and attempted to inflate her presence. Carla became dwarfed by the two figures.

"Yes, that's what I'm asking."

"You tell me, Mrs Christine Watson."

Both women now towered with Amazonian proportions,

expanded by aggression and hormones. Before either could continue with the drama, a car driving past the front window caught their attention. The driver, Maurice McAllen, peered in for a moment, before hastily departing. His face looked stricken. Frozen in Christine's mind was the cartoon picture of herself and the two other women. What would the caption read underneath? And what was going through Maurice McAllen's mind that very moment?

Chapter 20

She looked a mess. Ursula had never seen Christine without her schoolteacher-like pristine appearance. Her usual calf-length skirt was replaced by a tight-fitting, navy, corduroy one, which only just reached her knees. On her top half, Christine was wearing a burgundy camisole that hadn't been tucked in at the back. Her usual tightly sweptback hair was loosely pulled together at the neck, leaving a cascade of red curls surrounding her face. Ursula wondered what kind of day her neighbour was having.

"Hi, my name's Carla – I'm a friend of Ursula."

"Hello, Carla, I'm Christine. A neighbour."

"I don't think we've met before."

"No, we haven't."

"Come on in. We're just about to make coffee, aren't we, Ursula?"

Ursula looked at her friend with confusion, as this had not been the plan at all. But Carla, recognising her own weakness for hijacking situations, had herself decided that

162

the best place for her was out in the kitchen. With Carla busy preparing refreshments, Ursula and Christine briefly attempted everyday chitchat. Ursula began to feel extremely agitated. Why had this woman been pestering her all afternoon and why wouldn't she just come straight out and ask her what she wanted? If it was a game Christine was playing, she wouldn't find a competitor with Ursula. The complicated events of the day had left her feeling emotionally drained and physically weak. Ursula considered that, maybe, if she just sat quietly her neighbour would drink her coffee and eventually move on.

When the coffee arrived, Ursula regretted her earlier over-indulgence with the chocolate gâteau. She herself hated drinking coffee without something sticky and calorific to dunk into it. But she was glad her friend had arrived back in the living-room. Surely Carla could help diffuse the overly pleasant conversation? But Carla disappeared two seconds later on a quest to find milk. Ursula was feeling increasingly uncomfortable and she started to feel intruded upon in her home. Why was it taking Carla so long to find the milk?

After the decoration and the lighting had been discussed, Ursula wondered to what level they could sustain these forced pleasantries. She wasn't sure if Christine's compliments were genuine or not. Having strolled past her neighbour's house countless times, she knew her and Christine's interior design styles were very different. Christine's home was always scrubbed and pristine. In fact, it was generally accepted in the cul-de-sac that Christine's home was a germ-free zone. They had all seen the husband vacuuming the driveway and disinfecting the window frames and knew that dust mites didn't stand a chance. Even with three children, Christine's living-room always had showhouse standards of tidiness. The multicoloured, washable soft furnishings and the absence of anything ornamental within the potential reach of a young child, revealed the practicality of the room's design. Ursula recognized that her own tastes were far more simplistic and modern.

But even in the mood she was in, Ursula had to admit to herself that she often walked past Christine's house envying the softness and warmth she sensed within.

Carla returned with a brimming smile and a brimming milk jug. At last, Carla would be able to start talking about all the different countries she'd been to.

"Must be important then, Christine. What do you want?"

Ursula was appalled by the directness of her friend. But as she reclined further into her chair, she inwardly thought to herself 'Yes, exactly what do you want?' Her neighbour was coming into her home, making her feel intimidated and under pressure. But when Christine asked if Maurice McAllen could be recommended for planting a new lawn, Ursula felt a shock of anger throughout her body. Raging daggers straightened in her spine and she abruptly sat upright. Her earlier suspicions were verified. Christine was indeed the other woman Maurice was thinking about as they made love. This self-righteous, prim and proper housewife was coming into her home and playing some sort of mind-game with her. She couldn't believe the nerve of this woman. Christine was having an affair, for God knows how long, and she had the audacity to come pestering and prying into Ursula's life. This was the woman Ursula had hitherto positioned as a earth-mother figure, who dedicated her life to raising her family and being a dutiful wife to her doctor husband. She was the one who would come running over with a recipe for Beef Wellington or would go door-to-door raising money for the latest famine appeal. Christine's husband was a church elder and she even helped with the church floral arrangements. And yet all this time there was another side to her. Ursula concluded that, perhaps, the most innocent are often the most guilty. Carla leant forward with the milk and exposed an expanse of her bra.

Ursula then began to examine her own sexual encounter with Maurice that afternoon. Was she just the result of a lovers' tiff between him and Christine? Was the courage she had taken to try and banish her sexual hang-ups and insecurities simply wasted on some bitter revenge battle between her two neighbours?

When Ursula challenged Maurice's mistress, she could immediately see Christine's earlier confidence and defiance evaporate. Ursula had been bullied throughout her marriage and she wasn't going to let it happen in her own home.

As she waited for an answer, Ursula suddenly became aware of Maurice's car outside her window. For that moment her anger at Christine was transferred to the driver. What fun he must be having at all their expense! And what exactly was going through his mind right now?

Chapter 21

Stiletto heels were not designed for stumpy feet or blackened toenails, decided a slightly disgruntled Frances. Having agreed to walk to the tournament party, a few of her team were also suffering. Their initial swagger had been replaced with a few limps and groans. On the street map, Bergenstrasse looked like a short walk from their hotel. In reality, having now been walking for thirty minutes, they discovered why they shouldn't have taken the crow's route as their guide.

The team was now in the core of Amsterdam, amid the hustle and bustle of city life. Before them was the criss-cross of cyclists and trams. The street cafés were filling up, and sophisticated women with ebony-framed glasses and red lipstick shared conversation with elegant men in black leather jackets and polo-neck sweaters. Parents with brightly dressed youngsters stopped and watched the assortment of street entertainers dotted along the pavements and squares. The athletic Orla and sisterly Rose busily studied the street map as they walked, stopping every few paces to realign the map. For once, the mischievous Roberta was quietened by ill-fitting shoes and Niamh was helping her to walk. Cathy-Ann appeared to be the only one not suffering any discomfort as she sauntered in knee-high boots, totally oblivious of the sea of admirers as she passed. Frances momentarily forgot about her own discomfort as a cyclist pulled up beside her and gave an admiring wink. The rest of the team hadn't noticed and, to Frances, this devalued the gesture.

After five more minutes of forced marching, at Orla's instigation, the team's squadron leader eventually pointed to the street sign 'Bergenstrasse'. The tournament party was being held on the top floor of Hotel Van Goor. A dimly lit staircase ran up the side of the hotel to the disco area, so that partygoers were kept completely separate from hotel guests. At the foot of the stairs sat two huge Dutchmen behind a Formica counter. The team-mates recognised them as volleyball players from the host team. Their heads were completely bald, making their faces look plump and shiny. They appeared to be still wearing their orange playing shirts and together, perched on the table, they looked like genetically modified satsumas. Niamh had collected entrance tickets for her team during the day and passed the bundle to the doormen. They in turn stamped a yellow smiley face on the wrists of the women. The smaller of the two men, only actually smaller in appearance because his skull was flat, rather than conical, murmured something in Dutch to his friend and the two laughed. It was obvious from their stare that the joke was the women's appearance.

"Cheeky buggers. Did you see the state of those two and they had the nerve to look us up and down."

Roberta had taken her shoes off for the last few minutes of the journey and had regained her spirits. But Frances also felt annoyed, especially with her recently renewed confidence. Double doors decorated with silver clouds and stars led the way to the top floor. Little puffs of disco smoke were oozing out of the bottom of the door like Dr Frankenstein's laboratory. Roberta opened the doors onto a swirl of thick smoke, with the only glimmer of light coming from a silver glitter ball dangling from the ceiling and four or five laser machines. A burst of smoke had just been emitted and gradually a sea of dancing arms could be seen wafting it away.

The white smoke, with its heavy scent, gradually lifted and sat like rain clouds above the revellers. Only then did Frances and her team discover the reason behind the doormen's sneers. Before them was an ocean of pale pink bald heads and swirls of orange linen and cotton. Over the sound of the drumming garage music was the thud of cowbells and tambourines. With the thud of an anvil, the team as one shuddered with the sudden realisation that this was a fancy dress party and the theme was Hare Krishna. The six women from Northern Ireland, dressed to kill, were the ones who felt self-conscious and out of place, as they were swarmed over by two hundred leaping bald heads with blobs of toothpaste dabbed on their foreheads.

"We need a drink."

Orla seized control and spotted a table near the gents' toilet. Whilst the rest of the team lunged at the anonymity the table afforded, Orla went to the bar and ordered three pitchers of Dutch beer.

"Niamh, you big eejit! Did you not read the tickets?"

Roberta was never one to let a mistake go unpunished.

"I did read them, but the writing was all foreign. I read the words 'Hare Krishna', but thought that maybe they were sponsoring the 'do'."

"God help the next generation, if all the other teachers in your school are as daft as you are."

The three pitchers arrived just in time. Six pints were poured and drunk within a minute. A second round was poured and the women sat back in their chairs. Frances could not believe her bad luck. The first time in ages that she was feeling remotely sexy and she was forced to stick herself next to the gents' in order to avoid embarrassment.

The second pints speedily disappeared and Rose, this time, went to the bar for a repeat order. Cathy-Ann joined her sister to lend a hand. Niamh and Roberta had forgotten their disagreement and had jointly decided that they weren't going to let anything spoil their evening. Niamh wagged her wedding-ring-less finger and she and Roberta left the table, disappearing into the dancing mass. Having spent the previous day organising lifts for her eldest son to his computer club, freezing home-made quiches and lasagne for the family's dinners over the weekend, plus drying three washing loads, Niamh was going to be difficult to hold back.

"It's going to take another few pints before I lift my arse off this chair."

Frances agreed with Orla. They were the only two left from the team still seated. Rose and Cathy-Ann stood at the bar with their drinks order before them. A pack of Hare Krishna men had gathered around them and the group looked to be deep in conversation. Unbeknownst to Rose or

Cathy-Ann, Orla slid up beside them, lifted all three pitchers and returned to Frances at the table. Two pints were poured and thirstily received.

"Cheers, Frances."

"Bottoms up and all that. Fancy anyone, Orla?"

"Aye, take your pick. Anyone with a bald head and wrapped in a bedsheet will do."

"What a disaster, Orla."

"Could be worse."

"How?"

"I dunno."

A Dutch women's team, wearing bathing caps covered in tangerine face paint, encircled the two friends. Above their heads, in their Dutch accents, they chanted 'Hare, Hare Rama, Hare Krishna', over and over and over again. Frances threw a guilder at them, but they wouldn't move on. Orla was less diplomatic.

"Will you'se fuck off!"

Their understanding of the English language was sufficient and they made a hasty retreat to the next table, where the group's chants received a more gracious welcome.

"Orla, I should have worn my orange shirt after all."

"Aye, you get a lot of Hare Krishna's in velvet maternity blouses."

Frances took a giant swig of beer, leaving a frothy, creamy moustache on her top lip.

"Slow down, Frances. You'll make yourself sick."

As Orla spoke, the theme tune from 'Hawaii 5-0' blasted out of the speakers and two hundred Hare Krishnas plunged onto the floor and began rowing their imaginary canoes. In the centre of the orange mass were the two colourful figures of Roberta and Niamh. Both had their skirts pulled up to their thighs, providing the occasional flash of pink and white lingerie, whenever they paddled too enthusiastically.

Rose and Cathy-Ann were still pinned to the bar by a group of six or more men. Rose was working hard and was having some success in making a couple of the men laugh. The rest of their company were, in turn, struggling to bring a smile to Cathy-Ann's sullen face.

"How come if I had a face on me like that, everyone would say 'look at that miserable bitch'?"

"Frances, it's fashionable with young ones these days to pout and look moody. It's the French look. Try it."

Frances turned down the corners of her mouth until her bottom lip totally smothered her top one. She rested her face on her hand and remained motionless in deep contemplation. As she did so, two handsome men from the group surrounding Rose and Cathy-Ann approached the table. Both men strangely suited their bald heads. The taller, more athletic of the two, leaned over to Orla and asked her if she wanted to dance. She accepted and joined the dance floor just as a Jive Bunny compilation hit the turntable. The second one, smaller and with kind eyes, continued walking, straight into the gents' toilet behind.

Frances took another large gulp from her pint. She was tired of all the knocks and setbacks. Whenever she felt she was getting herself back together, another blow cruelly shattered her confidence. She was tired of it. She pulled the grip out from her hair, releasing the French plait and letting her fair hair fall to her shoulders. She then kicked off the stiletto implements of torture and gave freedom to her throbbing, injured toe. In a few hours it was going to be the

1st of July, and she was going to face the day as herself and not what others thought she should be.

A stream of arms forming the shapes of Y, M, C, and A in the still smoky air replaced Jive Bunny. Niamh was enjoying the Y's as her raised arms forced her short skirt to jump even shorter. A man dancing beside her, who at just over five foot high was unusually short for a Dutch player, likewise enjoyed his view. Roberta had secured herself a fan club of players, who surrounded her dancing figure chanting 'Roberta, Roberta'. Quite a few of the crowd had formed intimate pairs and had sneaked off to quiet corners of the room. The costumes of the remaining dancers started to look unsafe and quite a few safety pins were strained by the swirls of sheets. The tangerine face make-up was also starting to slide and form ugly patterns. The dancers were starting to look like unlucky rejects. Even with the quality of the competition diminishing, Frances didn't expect a sideways glance in her direction.

The tempo of the music changed and, as the beat slowed down, there was a general exodus from the dance floor. Niamh remained, firmly entwined with her short admirer. Roberta continued to dance without a partner, but surrounded by her newly acquired fan club. They copied each extravagant move she made, with their own Dutch interpretation.

Frances glanced across at Rose and Niamh and the circle of men had reduced down to only two. Where had the rest gone?

"Do you mind if I join you?"

Towering above Frances was the Dutch man with the kind eyes, who had only a few minutes ago walked past her in the direction of the gents'.

"Sure."

She cleared her aching feet from the seat next to her and, pulling her legs under her chair, she rested her left foot on top of the blackened toenail.

"My name's Klaus and you are?"

"Frances."

"I had to give up wearing my high heels. They were killing me too."

Frances looked down at Klaus's feet. "Jesus sandals are far more attractive anyway."

"We Hare Krishnas know how to dress. Your friends over there told us you guys didn't know tonight was a fancy dress party."

"We did know. It's just that as we're already Hare Krishnas, we decided to come as middle-aged women from Northern Ireland."

"Well, it suits you. Very much."

Frances was unsure if this was a compliment. Either his accent, or her lack of practice, confused the issue. His face seemed genuine enough, but then he had just spent the best part of the evening trying it on with Cathy-Ann. But, however hard she tried, she couldn't quite force herself to dislike Klaus. He smiled easily and when he did, his kind hazel eyes looked directly at her. Frances guessed he was in his late twenties, but his manner had the maturity of a much older man.

"How are you girls getting on in the tournament?"

"We're not. What about yourselves?"

"We're through to the semi-finals tomorrow morning. Well, saying we, I really mean, they are. My contribution is to keep the bench warm and be number one water-carrier."

He was honest too. But he was sure to be stingy.

173

"Frances, can I get you a drink? They do great cocktails here."

"No thanks. I've still two pitchers to go."

All right, so he isn't mean. Then Frances remembered where Klaus had spent the entire first half of the night.

"Did Cathy-Ann not want a drink?"

For the first time, the smile from Klaus' face was absent. His eyes were still kind, but confused.

"How do you guys stand her company?"

"What do you mean?"

"She's the most self-centred, vain egotist that I have ever met."

"Oh, that."

"You think so too?"

"Sure, we all do."

"And you still hang out with her?"

"We wouldn't hear a bad word against Cathy-Ann."

Klaus leant back in his chair and was now even more confused than earlier.

"Look, Klaus, she's young and she'll grow out of it. She has to, or she'll end up very lonely. Who's she talking to now?"

Both looked up and saw Cathy-Ann standing alone by the bar, with her sullen expression casting a dark shadow around her.

"Happens every time we go out. Guys are attracted at first, of course. But it doesn't take them long to realise she's maybe gorgeous outside, but there's not much going on inside. She always ends up on her own."

"That's very sad."

"But, Klaus, look at the rest of us – you couldn't get a more dysfunctional bunch of women."

Klaus glanced over in Rose's direction. She was mid-through telling a story that had the two male listeners totally enthralled.

"There. Rose seems happy."

"Rose is the most complicated woman I know. Growing up alongside Cathy-Ann has been tough on our Rose. As soon as the baby sister came along, both of Rose's parents gave up on their first-born altogether. As a teenager, you never met a more introverted and self-conscious character. She's got a fantastic job now, managing the most stylish restaurant in Belfast, but she has to work at it every day."

"But she looks to be enjoying working at it now."

"Sure, but every year or so, our Rose just shuts down. She decides to stop working at it and collapses into deep depression."

As Frances said this, Rose finished her story and her two admirers burst out of laughing. Rose smiled warmly, but didn't laugh with them.

Frances had Klaus's full attention. Unlike most men she knew, Klaus appeared genuinely fascinated by the inner workings of women. She felt she was almost talking to another woman. Frances had never before spoken to a total stranger this way; so indiscreetly. Was it something about her listener, or something about the day itself, or maybe, just the alcohol? Klaus leant forward again and Frances followed suit. Their faces were close enough for her to feel the whisper of his breath. The distance was tantalising, but Klaus held back from leaning any closer. Frances poured herself another pint of beer and a second for her new companion. The pitcher was now completely drained and the third was only two-thirds full.

"What about your teammate with the short guy's hand on her behind? She's having a good time."

"Niamh's married, you know."

"She doesn't look very married."

"And she's totally faithful. Every time we go out anywhere, the hair comes down and the boob-tube comes on. But all the years I've known Niamh, she's always come home with us at the end of the night."

"That guy's going to be very disappointed."

Niamh had just disappeared off the dance floor in the direction of the ladies' toilet. The short guy was standing waiting right outside the toilet door, nervous that his territory might be invaded.

"Do you think she'd be searching for all this attention if it was available at home? Now Niamh's kids are grown up and doing their own thing, she's doing hers."

"What does her husband think?"

"As long as he's got a glamorous wife on his arm for all his corporate dinners, he's like a pig in shite."

Halfway through saying 'shite' Frances regretted it. She tried to change the word to 'muck', but it was out too far. Her only hope was that Klaus's English wasn't as accomplished as it had been thus far.

"But the woman with the muscles, she's not married."

"No, but she's been having an affair with a married man for three years in the hope that she could be. But I know he split up with his wife over a year ago and he hasn't told Orla."

Klaus was entranced. The intensity of his stare slightly unnerved Frances, but she was in no doubt that he was genuine. But was it just what she was saying that intrigued him, or the storyteller herself? Regardless, Frances rested her left hand on her own right forearm and the touch made the tiny hairs on her arms dance. Her skin felt softer than usual and highly sensitive. With her little finger she gently massaged the fine bones on her wrist.

Frances had stopped counting at five, but guessed she had drunk more than seven pints. Her loaded bladder was signalling the same, but she was afraid of moving and not being able to recapture this intimacy on her return.

"She's very fit-looking. Is Orla an athlete?"

"She used to be. But her fitness has become a bit of an addiction now. Her lover is an ex-Olympian, who wouldn't appreciate it if she let her standards down."

"I'm not getting a very good impression of men from Northern Ireland. Surely your friend dancing on the table doesn't have problems with men?"

A round, teak-coloured table in the centre of the dance floor was graced with the stomping heavy shoes of Roberta. Her version of Irish dancing was unique and bore little resemblance to the original art form. She kept banging her ankles together and accidentally kicking her left knee on a back flick. Her legs also moved at twice the pace of the music.

"No, you're right, Klaus. Roberta doesn't have problems with men. She's gay."

Before Klaus could respond, Frances answered his deeply confused expression.

"Yes, gay in every sense of the word. She just hasn't come to terms with it herself. But when she does, we'll all be there for her."

"So, she hasn't come out yet?"

"No, not to anyone. Not even herself. You need to see where Roberta grew up to understand her. She's from a strict Baptist family and the only daughter in a family of four boys. They know how she carries on when she's out, but if they thought for one minute that their precious little daughter was anything other than one hundred per cent heterosexual, she would be thrown out of the family altogether.

"That's shite!"

Klaus understood her language better than she thought. From rubbing her wrist, Frances had moved along her hand and was now gently stroking her knuckles. She pushed her knees together and as she did so, she softly brushed them against those of Klaus. He didn't move, but let them rest that way. Frances's borrowed halter-neck top began to cling to her body as she mildly perspired. The alcohol made her veins pulsate rapidly, causing her skin to glow and her heartbeat to race. She had this handsome man in the palm of her hand, which in turn made her feel sensual, young and reckless. Without touching her, Klaus leant full forward and whispered in her ear with a voice that was sexy and gentle at the same time.

"And you, Frances, my beautiful friend? What are your problems?"

"I don't have any. Not a care in the world."

The music on the dance floor stopped and the DJ announced that it was midnight and time to slow the music down again. Frances glanced at her own watch and the small date box signalled July 1 in fine gold filigree. Today was to have been the start of a different life for her and Fergal. But their hopes and dreams had been snatched away. Stolen.

"Klaus, that's not entirely true. There's one problem I have to unburden."

178

For the first time since he had joined Frances's company, Klaus touched her. He pulled her right hand into his own and held it tightly to his own broad chest.

"Frances, please tell me."

"I have to do this."

Pulling away from Klaus's embrace, Frances abruptly stood upright. She placed her hands around her back, undid the buttons, and her trousers fell to the floor. Now crossing her arms in front and lifting the hem of her top, Frances yanked the halter-neck swiftly off her body and threw it onto the table. The lilac bra was removed with the ease of a gigolo and the matching lace knickers, once wriggled down across her hips, were off seconds later.

The last Klaus saw of his new companion that night was the sight of Frances's naked body dashing across the dance floor, in the direction of the exit sign.

Chapter 22

With the car engine started up again, the noise of the woman was marginally overpowered. She continued to roar 'leave us alone' until her throat began to strain. The two boys remained silent and sheltered themselves behind their mother's back. The younger of the two made a few attempts to leave the sanctuary of the woman, but the elder boy kept pulling him back by his grey sweater. A few of the neighbours had overheard the commotion and were standing in their own doorways. But no one stepped any closer.

"What will it take for you to realise that we don't want you any more?"

The woman succeeded in being audible, even above the engine noise, so Maurice then turned on his car radio. The newscaster was hosting an interview with a group of astronomers and historians about the lunar eclipse expected tomorrow evening. For the first time in over three years, the prediction was a blood moon where, once the sun had cast the shadow of the earth across the moon's face, a red glow would cover the surface. The radio discussion was about how ancient man would have interpreted this natural phenomenon.

Maurice couldn't hear the final analysis, as the woman began beating her hands against the passenger-side window. Maurice turned up the radio volume, but he still couldn't smother the sounds from outside. The younger boy eventually managed to escape the clutches of his brother and ran around to the front of the car. His body was long and gangly and his walk awkward with long strides. The boy's blond, thick hair made him feminine-looking, but together with his serious blue eyes, his expression was a mirror image of the man in the car facing him. His young, still undeveloped, voice was not powerful enough to compete with the radio. But Maurice could easily lip-read the seven-year-old's words.

"Daddy, please go!"

He communicated above and beyond any decibels. Maurice nudged the gear stick into reverse, drove backward ten yards and then did a three-point turn back down the street. As he steered the car back out onto the Lisburn Road, Maurice glanced through his rear-view mirror. The woman was hugging the small boy, who struggled to free himself. The older boy had gathered pebbles and small stones from his front garden and was throwing them in the direction of the car. There was no chance any would have succeeded in reaching the rapidly departing vehicle, but he continued to throw them anyway.

Teenagers and students were leaping out of taxis and rushing into the many bars dotted along the Lisburn Road. Naked legs, midriffs and plunging necklines were pressed against the short-sleeved football shirts and tight multi-coloured vests of their male companions. A queue had formed outside a cash machine, where a few disappointed rejected faces pressed buttons over and over again. A hen party was gathered outside an Italian restaurant, with the hen adorned in black satin lingerie, with water-filled condoms pinned to the bodice. One of the party, a woman with bleached white hair and silver-and-gold-speckled mascara, was trying to commandeer any single men as they walked past and force them to kiss the bride-to-be. But it was still too early in the evening for the girl to accept their offers and, with the innocence of a virgin, she politely declined. If any of the young men were still interested, the woman with the bleached hair was happy to oblige with a heavy, deep kiss. At the intersection with Shaftesbury Square, a few single young men paced purposefully underneath the neon signs waiting for their dates.

Instead of continuing in the direction of home, Maurice turned the car right into the tree-lined Elmwood Avenue, right into University Avenue and then right again, back towards the Lisburn Road. The streets were still relatively tranquil, so he was able to drive back to where he had just come from and crawl to the junction. Looking back down the road, he saw that the woman and the two boys were no longer there. All was as it had been when he had first arrived, except for a few stones scattered along the tarmac. Maurice turned into the road. He didn't park in his usual place, but chose to drive another hundred or so yards up the road. He stopped outside a house similar to the woman's. The empty drive, the lights off and a dried-out Yucca plant visible in the window signified to Maurice that the owners were away on their summer holidays. He wound his window down a third, so that he could smell the scents of the summer evening. This time he remained seated in the driver's side and through his mirror he could just about see the wrought-iron gate to the woman's house. It hadn't been closed correctly and swung gently with the evening breeze.

The gun was still on Maurice's lap, but the map had fallen slightly with the motion of the car. The matt-black tip of the gun peeked out.

He closed his eyes and, in his imagination, saw the wrought-iron gate rattle as a football kept bouncing off it and back into the garden. Maurice had Lewis, his younger boy, sitting on his shoulders, as the two of them were trying to kick the ball past Matthew, the goalkeeper. In this daydream, Matthew was about six and, with the stubbornness of his mother, refused to accept any tackle as anything other than a foul.

"Keeper's ball."

Matthew mimicked the goalkeepers he had seen on the television and waved his arms frantically. He mouthed made-up words, as he wasn't yet old enough to decipher the curses and blaspheming of the players he saw on *Grandstand*. Like his brother, he had his father's thick blond hair and long limbs, but his eyes were a coffee brown, with tiny speckles of jade green. His eyes were exact replicas of the woman cheering in the background. Maggie, Maurice's wife, was trying to mow the lawn for the first time after the winter. The obstacles the football match had created burdened the chore and the result was a zigzag of short grass with intermittent long bits. Maggie would stop every few minutes and cheer on whoever was losing at the time. Her long chestnut-brown hair kept falling on her face as she leant over to empty the lawnmower, but rather than tie it back, she let it fall loosely, the way her husband liked it. Maggie loved her garden and though Maurice's shift pattern didn't give him much time to give her a hand, when he could he would also help out. But today he was busy playing with his boys. It was spring and the immaculate rose bushes leading to the front door were bursting to explode with colour. But the morning frosts still held them back. Maurice had painted the front door an emerald green the previous weekend and its shine reflected the image of the football as it soared through the air before calls for yet another foul.

The daydream had now changed into a dream, as the comforting images had seduced Maurice into a heavy sleep. Without control of his thought patterns, his subconscious now suddenly switched to an autumn. The boys were a little taller and stronger-looking, still playing football outside and using the wrought-iron gate as goal posts. Matthew was insisting on yet another foul. Maggie was mowing the lawn for the last time before the winter. The lawnmower was that bit older and much harder to push around. She was having to use all her weight to get enough momentum to start it off and she was starting to feel the pains of her labour in her lower back. The decaying rose heads had been ripped off the bushes and lay rotting in the compost heap, in the far corner of the garden.

The boys got a glimpse of their father in the upstairs bedroom.

"Please, Daddy, come down! You can be keeper if you want to!"

Expressionless, Maurice looked down upon his sons

through the thick glass of the Regency-style windowpane. He was unshaven and his hair was lank and greasy. Maggie looked at the boys waving and then looked up at Maurice. She gave him a warm welcoming smile, with a sense of hope in her otherwise quite sad eyes. Maurice didn't react and tuned away into the darkness of the interior.

As Maurice wakened and opened his eyes, he immediately caught sight of himself in the rear-view mirror. Beneath a thick film of moisture blanketing his eyes was the familiar piercing steel blue. He tried not to blink in case that would then free the water to form a tear. He couldn't remember the last time he had cried. Forcing his eyelids to stay open only made them smart and so, after thirty seconds, he reluctantly blinked. The tears fell and lay like raindrops on a windowpane; the weight of the water dragging its own path down his cheeks. Maurice didn't wipe them away, but let the salty water sting his eyes and prick his skin. As they fell into his slightly open mouth, he let them slide onto the tip of his tongue and then back out again onto his bottom lip. A sob tried to force its way up his throat, but Maurice remained calmly silent.

Maurice stared at the rear-view mirror again, but this time a band of blood-red surrounded his blue eyes. His blond eyelashes held tiny drops and as he blinked they fell like water off a closing umbrella.

Maurice re-focused and his face became a fuzzy blur as his vision was now focused on the background. The iron gate had stopped swinging. Someone had gone into the house and fastened it correctly. Either that or someone had left the house. Maurice frantically looked down and across the street. It was empty. The evening light was now dim, with the only brightness coming from the occasional streetlight and between drawn curtains in the front rooms of the terraced houses. Maybe it was just somebody visiting the house. But it was past ten o'clock in the evening and who would be visiting his family at this time of night? Was it a man? A man visiting his wife? Maurice suddenly heard the sound of scurrying footsteps.

"Who is it?"

Maurice turned on the car's ignition and changed the gear into first in order to turn the car back round and in the direction of his wife's house. The turmoil of his emotions caused him to accidentally change into third gear and the car shuddered and hopped forward a few feet. This time Maurice grabbed the gearstick with his whole huge palm and yanked into position, watching the gearstick intensely to ensure he did not make the same mistake twice. The car withstood the force, but creaked and groaned with disgust.

Once reassured that the gearstick now knew its place, Maurice looked back up at the road ahead. There, the young boy who had been throwing stones earlier stood with his arms held straight in front of him. They quivered slightly and in his hands, pointing directly at Maurice, he held a handgun. Maurice immediately looked down at his own lap and lifted the road-map away. His gun was missing and was now in the hands of his son.

Chapter 23

"Sweetheart, the moon is made out of cheese."

Molly looked at her mother sympathetically.

"No it isn't, Mummy. It's made out of rock and rotates on an axis, much the same as Earth."

Their discussion over dinner had begun with the lunar eclipse forecast for the following evening. But as Christine tried to explain to her daughters what would be happening, she found she was getting more and more confused herself. She decided to opt for the fairytale version, which Ruth her eldest was happy to accept, but the recently turned eight-year-old was having none of it.

Christine then tried to recreate the positions of the planets using the hard-boiled egg and two vine-ripened tomatoes on her plate of salad. She had them reasonably positioned when The Baby reached over from her high chair and stole one of the tomatoes. Within seconds, half was in her mouth and the other in bloody splashes down the front of her bib.

"Does that explain why it's called a blood moon?"

Christine couldn't quite work out if Ruth was just being difficult, or whether or not her eldest daughter really did have a learning difficulty.

"Not really, Ruth."

"Why then, Mummy?"

"Just. That's why."

Christine knew she had given in to her last-resort answer far too early in the conversation, but considering the day she was having, it would do.

Once Maurice had been spotted in front of Ursula's house, the entire heat from the two women's afternoon battle appeared to evaporate. Neither women had the strength or the desire to continue it and Christine had scurried out of the house like an uninvited fieldmouse. When she had got back to her own home, she found that Ruth and Molly had decided to fix their own dinner. The Baby appeared to be quite enjoying the meal of Weetabix, cheese slices and brown sauce. But within ten minutes Christine had them cleaned up and seated for their evening meal of home-made tomato and lentil soup followed by egg and ham salad.

"Why's Daddy not eating with us?"

"Daddy's still at work, Ruth. He left a message on the answer machine saying he has to stay on call tonight. He'll see us tomorrow."

"Will he be back in time to come on the adventure with us?"

"We'll have to wait and see. Now eat up, if you want your dessert."

The Baby announced that she was 'all done' in a language that only a mother could translate and subsequently confirmed her announcement by placing the empty bowl on top of her head. Molly and Ruth copied their baby sister and the three sat like the Stooges waiting for their ice cream and pear halves. The girls were taken totally by surprise when their mother, rather than scold them as usual, balanced her own empty plate precariously on top of her head. The Baby began laughing, with a chuckle from deep within her stomach and the other two followed with the abandon and expression exclusive to children. Christine then lifted three strips of spring onion and gave herself two eyebrows and a moustache. The three girls laughed even harder, so hard that recently swallowed apple and blackcurrant juice shot up Molly's throat and out of her nose.

"Yuk! That's gross."

Even though her younger sister revolted Ruth, the incident just intensified everyone's good humour.

Christine would usually then clear away the dinner table and stack the dishwasher. This evening, she decided to leave things as they were and after a quick wipe with the corner of a tea towel over The Baby's entire face, hair and body, all three girls and their mother abandoned the dinner table in favour of the living-room. With the cushions from the sofa, a stage area was created, framed by the Laura Ashley window curtains. Ruth opened the show with gymnastics, almost knocking out the ceiling light with a cartwheel. The Baby mimicked her big sister with her own version of a roly-poly, which simply involved putting her forehead, hands and feet on the floor. Unfortunately, the rapturous applause she received on the first attempt only spurred the two-year-old on to continue for the next fifteen minutes. Her two sisters had long since lost interest in her

189

efforts, but her mother was as enthusiastic on the twentieth as she was on the first attempt. The climax of Ruth's performance was the splits. This wasn't quite the full splits, but enough to make Christine wince.

Next up came Molly, who chose to sing a nursery rhyme. Her mother was surprised at how angelic her daughter sounded, until the song's lyrics were transformed into a crude playground version. A few of the words were shocking, but Christine gauged from both Molly's and Ruth's reaction, that neither girls fully understood their true meaning. Molly finished with a series of dramatic curtsies and it was only Ruth, throwing a cushion at her head, that forced her to eventually stop.

The Baby was encouraged to dance and as her head bobbed to the rhythm beating in her head, her feet chose another. A combination of the bobbing and spiralling around caused her to feel light-headed and after a few minutes of frantic dancing, she rolled over on top of a busy Lizzie. The Baby lay on the floor with her loose, red locks entangled in the lime-green leaves of the plant and looking like an infant Medusa. She loved being the centre of attention and refused to get up again. No amount of coaxing could encourage her, so the family left her sprawled in the corner like a living ornament.

With the show now complete, Ruth and Molly began to clear away the cushions. Christine stopped them, insisting on her own performance. The two older sisters were stopped in their tracks. Even The Baby sat upright and open-mouthed. Christine delved deep into her personal archive of childhood memories. From somewhere, long since thought forgotten, Christine remembered a tap-dancing routine she had learnt from the television many years before. The routine was a birthday present for her mother, but unfortunately her mother had had to work overtime that night and the sixteen-year-old baby-sitter plus her spotty boyfriend became Christine's audience. As she hummed the tune to 'The Good Ship Lollipop', she launched into her routine. Without tap shoes, some of the effect was lost, but the mere fact their mother was clipping her heels and stomping her feet was enough for the girls. Caught up in the hysteria, Molly and Ruth joined in with the routine and as The Baby began clapping, she set the beat for the three woeful dancers. Christine caught sight of their three flashing figures in the reflection from the front window. The sight of a thirty-six-year-old, imitating Shirley Temple, was hilarious. She also discovered she wasn't the only witness to their escapade. Two figures were walking past the front of her house, but they scurried away when they, likewise, discovered they had been spotted.

Half an hour later, The Baby was sleeping soundly in her cot with pieces of ham salad and leaves still wedged in her hair and sprinkled on her pillow. Christine tried to remove them as her youngest slept, but then decided not to disturb her. The other two were supposed to be reading each other stories in their bedroom. In between overly loud extracts from *The Wind in the Willows*, however, Christine could hear Ruth telling rude jokes to her young sister. Christine felt reassured by the silence of Molly's response, which suggested, as in the case of the earlier crude words, she hadn't a clue what they meant.

Christine turned down the dimmer switch on the upstairs landing light and went back downstairs. She could hardly open the door to the living-room, for all the cushions and toys scattered across the floor. She tiptoed over an assortment of stuffed toys, dolls' clothes and Lego bricks. The armchair looked like it was elevated above the turmoil and beckoned her towards it. With two giant leaps, Christine cleared the obstacles and was secure within the soft furnishings of the powder-pink armchair, with only a Sindy doll's shoes jammed between her toes.

Her usual routine for this time of night would be to finish clearing the kitchen and then begin stacking the children's toys into their appropriate boxes, which were then stored under the staircase. If possible, when her husband was working late, she liked to have all evidence of the children removed and catalogued, before Alex returned home. Regardless, he would also patrol the house looking for stray toys or splashes of dinner that may have escaped Christine's notice and found refuge on the ceiling. She couldn't quite equate the man who wanted the house so neat and tidy, with the man who then wanted to be the first up in the morning when the girls awoke. At the weekends, he would sit for hours with them, telling them stories and creating magical make-believe worlds.

Once the evening patrol was complete, Christine and her husband would turn on the television and begin watching the first ten minutes of either the news or a natural world documentary. By the time the headlines were over, or the baby giraffe had been conceived, both would be fast asleep. Christine would eventually stir at about eleven o'clock, but Alex would usually be wide-awake again and full of energy. She knew now where the energy came from and she supposed he had been re-injecting himself as she slept on the sofa. Where did he do it? In the kitchen? In the bathroom? Or did he just fire the needle into himself right here in the living-room, in her presence?

Christine lifted her legs and rested them on a stuffed elephant, affectionately known as Thunder. After two years of hugs and squeezes, Thunder wasn't as firm as he used to be, but he did the trick. She looked down at her hands resting on the arms of the chair and didn't recognise them for a moment. They looked so much older than the last time she had looked. Faint purple veins stretched along the surface and previously unnoticed light-brown freckles dotted her knuckles. She pinched the flesh and it slowly fell back into place. With neither the time to bite or cut her nails, they were at various lengths and shapes though kept scrupulously clean with a nailbrush.

Immediately, she visualised Ursula's carefully manicured talons and dashed into the kitchen to hunt through the medicine cupboard. Squashed into an old biscuit tin was a bottle of Calpol, crepe bandages and Vaseline, plus a bottle of pearl-white nail-polish. Christine dated it to pre-The Baby days, when she had bought it for herself in the January sales. She guessed the tiny bottle was at least four years old, but being unopened she hoped it would have remained fresh. She also discovered a small pair of scissors and a tatty-looking emery board, which looked like the last user had been Alex removing hard skin from his feet. Back in the comfort of her armchair, Christine began to cut her nails and file them. They were thicker than she had anticipated, but she surprised herself by being able to create a reasonably consistent shape. The nail-polish was then applied in thick coats and she was pleased with translucency of the colour.

As the paint began to dry she held her hands in front of her.

"They belong to a transvestite."

But she wasn't deterred and moved on to shaping and polishing her toenails. This was the second time today that Christine was spending time on herself. Was it becoming a habit? She doubted her mother ever had time to herself. Working long hours with overtime gave her little personal time, never mind time with her family. Christine's one goal in life was to give all her time to her children. But as she tried to stop her middle two toes embracing and smudging the polish, she began to consider the time she spent with her family in more detail. Sure she was a full-time housewife and dedicated to raising her girls, but how much time did she actually spend with them? Tonight's relaxed meal and after-dinner show was exceptional. Most of her day was spent either doing school runs, cleaning and tidying, preparing meals or the general up-keep of their home. It was only from spending time on herself that she began to realise how little time she actually spent enjoying her children.

Christine thought briefly about the time she spent with Alex, but was still too angry with him to allow him much thought. By the time her mother had raised her family and was in a position to stop work, she had begun to fall ill. When the grandchildren came along, she was confined to an old people's home, where on her bad days she was barely able to recognise her own reflection. Her daughter still cared for her, but felt uncomfortable with sickness, and her grandchildren considered any visits to be a monumental chore.

Christine realised how neglectful she had been of her mother over the past while. She rifled through a pile of books and comics and found the telephone hiding on the coffee table.

"Hi, sorry, it's late, but is Mrs Doyle still up?"

"Who's speaking?"

"Tell her it's Chrissie, her daughter."

There was silence and then a clatter of teacups and saucers in the background. A slightly out-of-breath, gentle voice came to the telephone.

"Chrissie? I was just going up to bed. Anything wrong?"

"No. Nothing. Just wanted to know how you were doing."

"Grand. The old biddy in the next room keeps drinking my tea though. How's Robert?"

At seventy-one, Mrs Doyle still considered herself anything other than old-aged. She had also been forgetting the name of her son-in-law for the past few years. Christine didn't get a chance to reply.

"But sure, Chrissie, I can fill you in when you call tomorrow."

The guilty pang shot right across Christine's heart. She had forgotten she had promised her girls that they wouldn't be visiting. She imagined her mother sitting there now in her nightdress and dressinggown. If the hairdresser had been for her usual Saturday appointment, her mother's dyed black hair would be ironed straight and pulled into a short ponytail. But, if the hairdresser had a wedding on that day, her hair would be frizzy, with grey dappled auburn roots making their escape.

"Sorry, Mummy, something else has cropped up with the girls."

"That's OK. I've plans for tomorrow myself. Give both of them a big hug from me."

The guilty pang tightened and disabled Christine's breathing. Her mother knew exactly what to say in order to cripple her daughter with guilt. No matter how many times Christine reminded her mother she had a third daughter, events that had occurred over the past couple of years were a blur to her. And yet, she could remember exactly what she ate for Christmas dinner in 1972.

Christine had spent so little time with her mother as a child that the bond that should have formed between mother and only daughter had never really taken hold. As an adult, Christine felt guilt, responsibility and respect, but no love. When she met Alex she first discovered that she was actually capable of love and as she fell in love with each of her children, the emptiness she felt for her own mother was only exaggerated.

"I'll be up as soon as I can."

"Right you be."

"Goodnight, Mummy."

"Goodnight."

Christine's mother hadn't repositioned the telephone on the hook correctly and she could hear her wheezy voice slowly fade into the distance. A faint voice shouting 'Get off my tea' could be heard, before someone noticed the dangling phone cable and the line went dead.

Christine's toenails were now completely dry. She mostly wore court shoes and knew that she would probably be the only one to know they were painted. She didn't imagine Alex would notice. Who would? She walked over to the window and began drawing the vertical blinds to a close. The couple across the road, Fergal and Frances must be away together for the weekend. There were no signs of life.

Without children they had the freedom to do whatever they wanted and she was sure they would be away somewhere having a romantic weekend. She could just about see that Ursula was still at home and her foreign friend's car was still parked outside. They were probably having a good laugh about her own visit to them this afternoon. But Christine didn't care. As she craned her neck that bit further, she could see car headlights heading towards Maurice's house. It was him. He slowed down and parked on his driveway. But he doesn't park there. She could see the silhouette of his huge body filling the car seat and as he leaned back and stretched, his arm span reached almost across the full width of the car. Even in the darkness of the evening, Maurice's blond hair glistened with the rays of the car's courtesy light and as he turned his head, the profile of his strong face and heavy brow sat jet-black against the light's rays. Once parked, he dived out of his car and within three long strides on his lawn he was inside his home. But he doesn't walk on his lawn, thought Christine.

Christine's house was silent. All three girls were fast asleep. But she was far from sleepy. She placed her pale-blue cashmere cardigan over her shoulders and stepping out of her front door, she quietly closed it behind her.

Chapter 24

On discovering he was living next door to a bent cop, Fergal's first thought Sunday morning was to go straight home.

"But why, Fergal? Sure Frances isn't back until tonight."

Brendan was right. Fergal didn't fancy being in the house on his own now anyway, especially with the Lawnmower Man just a few doors away. But it was four in the morning and he was restless. Brendan had woken Fergal and himself up with a loud blast of flatulence and now neither could get back to sleep. The light morning dew had settled on the two grub-like sleeping bags and all that was left of their turf fire were tiny red dots glowing on the end of charcoal-black sticks. Fergal's body felt like toast, but his face was blanketed in dew. He buried his head deep inside the sleeping bag, but he was unable to tolerate the smell. He had slept in his clothes and the stale stench was only bearable for a few seconds. Brendan didn't have too much difficulty in this area, but the massive amounts of alcohol he had consumed the night before had left him feeling dehydrated.

"I'm dying with drouth, Fergal. Did you bring orange or coke or anything?"

"Sorry. I might have a scone in my coat pocket. No butter though."

"Jesus, man. The way I'm feeling, that'll be like salt to a slug. A cup of tea and something nice to go with it would do me just right."

Both men snuggled back into their cocoons, with only their pink noses visible. Above them the colours of the sky were somewhere caught between night and day. Any moment dawn would break and the two agitated friends, alongside the ever-patient mother nature, waited expectantly. Both men pretended to sleep, but their stony silence gave them away.

"Are you sleeping, Brendan?"

"Naw. Are you?"

The men returned to another few minutes of silence.

"Are you sleeping now?"

Fergal threw an empty beer can in his aggravating friend's direction. The can hit Brendan perfectly on the back of the head and then bounced back down onto the grass. There was a huge dent in its side. Brendan called out a muffled 'ouch', but didn't stir.

A light mist was beginning to clear from the mountain and along with the now clear morning sky, came the first glimmers of the rising sun. A tiny sparrow jumped down from the thirteen-foot-wide walls and began pecking the grass around the motionless men. He stretched out his wings and, as he shook them, he effortlessly gave out a small shrill.

With the morning now officially declared, Fergal and Brendan both jumped up out of their sleeping bags, scaring the sparrow in the process. When they had both feebly brushed away their wrinkles, rolled up their sleeping bags and cleared away the empty bottles and cans from the night before, they stood looking at each other.

"What'll we do now, Brendan? It's only just gone four in the morning. Nowhere will be open yet."

"Come with me. I've got a plan."

With just grounds, Fergal was fearful of Brendan's plans. After all, last night's camping under the stars didn't exactly turn out as he'd expected. Fergal had hoped to find a few answers and instead he just felt middle-aged, boring and now was suffering from a painful crick in his neck. But he decided to go along and just see what Brendan's plan was. The men left the fort and began to stroll back down the stone path to the car park. Miraculously, Brendan managed to skip along, like a man who had just had eight hours' sleep. By comparison, Fergal scurried behind with his step made heavy by two hours' sleep and a heavy hangover. He tripped over the very same rocks that had hindered him only hours earlier.

When they reached Brendan's car, Fergal was halted in his tracks. Fergal hadn't noticed anything remarkable about his friend's car when he had arrived the night before. Literally in the cold light of day, he could see that it was a miracle that it hadn't rolled over and collapsed in the night. Fergal guessed that it was held together with Blu-tack and rubber bands. The thirty-plus-year-old Volkswagen Beetle had sky-blue wings, a scarlet bonnet and a navy-blue roof. This was discounting the masses of orange rust splashes which held the whole heap together. The road tax disc was a poor photocopy and stuck beside it on the windscreen was a used envelope, scribbled with the simple message;

On route to scrapyard.

"This is 'Merlin'. I'm restoring him."

"To what? A shopping trolley?"

"I know he looks a bit rough, but he's structurally sound as a pound."

Brendan opened the bonnet. There were lumps of turf and clay wedged at the back, where grass seeds were starting to germinate.

"Jesus, Brendan. You've got vegetables growing in here."

The rust at the front of the bonnet was so bad that the gravel tarmac could be seen through it.

"It's like the Anthill Mob's car. Can you see your legs running along inside when it's going?"

"This is a classic car."

"And how long have you been restoring it, Brendan?"

"A while."

"How long's a while?"

"Five years."

The similarities between Brendan and his car were massive, but Fergal didn't have the energy to put them together. Brendan wasn't deterred by his friend's contempt for his beloved vehicle and rummaged through old blankets and boxes in the bonnet. He pulled out a varied selection of fishing-rod pieces.

"My best rods are down with the boat in my Ma's back hall. But I reckon I've got bits and pieces of at least half a dozen here in the car."

Brendan began to assemble the rods like an infant with

an old familiar jigsaw puzzle. He had the same satisfaction when he managed to complete his task, albeit with a few of the awkward corners cut out to make them fit.

"Brendan, I haven't fished since we were lads."

"It's like riding a bike. Mind you, you didn't learn to ride yours until we were at secondary school."

"Thanks for reminding me. It's taken me years of therapy to get over it."

From Fergal's blank expression, Brendan wasn't sure if this was the truth or not. To assure his friend that he was only joking, Fergal produced a nervous twitch with his right eye. Brendan was still unsure.

"If we're going fishing, Brendan, we're going in my car. I'm not setting foot in that deathtrap."

Brendan looked across at Fergal's pristine Vauxhall Vectra and gagged as if he'd just swallowed a hairball.

"But if anyone spots me in that up the town, they'll think I've been lifted by the cops. I've my image to think of."

Fergal had the fishing rods, a box of flies and a net in the back of his car before Brendan had time to protest further. The Vectra pulled out of the car park and left the ancient fort to return to its solitude and tranquility. As Fergal slowed down at the T-junction at the foot of the mountain, he glanced back up towards Grianan. This Celtic fort had given birth to countless battles, had withstood the elements of rural Donegal and escaped industrialisation and modernisation. Now, thousands of years later, it kept company with sparrows, hawks and fieldmice, a rusty heap of bald tyres, vanilla car-freshener and zebra-skin seat covers.

With directions to drive to Mount Errigle, Fergal headed

off into the heart of Donegal. The River Owenea was their final destination, but Brendan was keeping the actual location of his proposed fishing site close to his chest. There was little road traffic, except for the occasional tractor or very drunk-looking cyclist. As the sun was rising, the rural landscape of Burt and Letterkenny transformed to rugged rocks and gorse with large slashes of recently cut turf.

Fergal's passenger had fallen asleep midway through retelling the story about the eighteen-pound salmon he had caught on the Owenea. Fergal hadn't reminded his friend that he had heard the story at least five times before and each time the story was retold, the poor fish gained a pound or two. Fergal could also have explained to his friend that he was actually with him the day the fish was caught and that proof of the catch, in the form of a photograph, was still proudly displayed in his study. But Fergal was beginning to believe that Brendan was actually starting to believe his own stories. By the time the story developed into the battle between fish, rod and man, Brendan had fallen asleep. This was confirmed by the various noises escaping from his dozing body and the tiny dribble of spittle falling on his collar.

The road had begun to follow the voluptuous contours of the landscape, with tight bends and downwards sweeps only punctuated by sharp corners. Around the very next serpentine corner, Fergal came within inches of a stone wall, recently painted with black and white checks and a sign saying: *Accident Black Spot*.

The area around the wall was serene and calm and a small bunch of mildewed irises was pinned below the sign. Fergal found it hard to accept that for a few minutes, maybe even seconds, there had been extreme violence and power here. A vehicle had been ripped apart or contorted into a crumpled mess by its own force and weight. He expected the energy of that accident to be still visible or present. But it wasn't. The energy had been expended and dissipated. Maybe it had been transferred to another hazardous corner further up the road, where maybe in a few years Fergal would discover another newly painted black-and-white-checked wall.

Brendan's head rocked gently with the motion of the car, with the delicate filament of dribble falling from his collar to his shirt. Fergal again found himself envying the simplicity of his friend's temperament and the life he had created for himself. These days Fergal couldn't eat his dinner without feelings of remorse, fasten his coat without regret or turn a corner without having black thoughts. Here he was trying to recapture something of his past, in order to accept his present. Why couldn't he be like Brendan? What had happened to the excitement in his life?

After half an hour or so, Fergal approached the first straight stretch of road he had seen in ages. The road for half a mile was lined with sycamores leaning towards the centre of the road. Their summer foliage was so dense that the trees created a tunnel. Fergal took the opportunity the straight road afforded and increased his speed. Unbeknown to him, however, hidden by the canopy of leaves, there was a slight dip in the road immediately succeeded by a large ramp. Both passenger and driver were separated from their seats for a split second.

"What the . . . !" Brendan was immediately awake. "Did we hit something?"

"Naw, Brendan, but I might smack you one in a minute.

You're supposed to be navigating. I haven't been down this road in ten years."

"Oops, was that O'Casey's bump?"

Recovering from the shock and allowing for his stomach to come back down from his neck, Fergal had reduced his speed so drastically that he could have been driving Miss Daisy.

"You mean the ramp's so well known it's got its own name? And you didn't let me know it was coming up?"

"Jesus, Fergal, I only thought I'd nod off for ten minutes. Sure we're nearly there."

"I know."

Brendan ruffled his own hair in an attempt to revive himself and nonchalantly wiped away the spittle from his jacket. A brown and white sign signalling the Owenea River came into view and Brendan delivered a complicated list of directions to his driver. Fergal's dramatically reduced speed did not go unnoticed.

"Right one hundred. Full. Left fifty. Rise. Caution."

The men were now an hour into their journey and Fergal was in no mood for his friend's banter. Absolutely nothing was turning out as planned.

"Stop, Fergal. We're here. The best fishing spot this side of over there."

The car was parked and the two men, laden with an assortment of fishing tackle, strolled off along the river. The river banks looked very uninviting, protected by thick nettles and marshy pools. Brendan took the lead and ducked down under a thick briar hedge barricading the footpath from the river. As they emerged back into the light of early morning, Fergal found himself in a fisherman's oasis. The river bank, dotted with maroon and copper stones, gently led down to the crystal clear water. A massive willow overhung the glade and the sun's rays were starting to burn through the leaves and dapple the water. Dotted in the river were half a dozen 'eddies' where the rocks turned the water, leaving still pools.

"Heaven, Fergal?"

"Heaven on a fucking stick, Brendan."

"And we're only a mile from Jackie Doran's. I'll run over when they open and get us some supplies."

A fishermen's nest was subsequently arranged with rocks and clumps of dry grass for seats. The two men removed their shoes and socks. It was now five in the morning and the cloudless sky allowed the sun to gently warm the rocks and stones. Dragonflies skipped and pond-skaters scurried along, creating a slight dimple of tension on the water's surface.

Brendan studied Fergal's first few attempts to assemble his fishing rod, but then his exasperation became uncontrollable and he snatched the rod away. Five minutes later, he gave the rod back to Fergal with the orders that all he had to do was hold it.

"Yippee, Brendan, I get to hold the rod!"

"Aye, but if you get a bite, let me bring it in."

At first, Fergal thought his friend's lack of confidence in him was mildly humorous. But the light-heartedness was rapidly replaced by irritation.

"I haven't forgotten everything I know about fishing."

"So why've you left your shoes so close to the bank?"

Fergal's chocolate brogues were soaked as the gentle swell of the river splashed against them. He threw his fishing rod onto the bank and jumped out of the water.

"If I were here on my own, Brendan, I'd be grand. It'd all come back to me. It's you. You're putting me off."

"What have I done?"

You're still you, thought a sullen and damp Fergal to himself. With his shoes and socks drying on an upturned log, Fergal regained his fishing position, two feet from the riverbank, alongside his friend. Brendan had lit up a cigarette and let it idly rest on his lips.

"I just need to get back into my old stride, that's all. It'll come back to me."

"Come to think of it, Fergal. You were never any good at fishing, even in the old days.

Fergal was having difficulty coming to terms with being a shell of his former self, but to be told that this former self wasn't up to much either was a bitter blow.

"Fuck off."

"You used to talk incessantly and make too much of a splash when you were casting. You had no finesse."

A second, painful blow.

"You didn't complain about finesse when I was throwing stones at the army."

"You didn't throw them. Your job was to gather them up from all the old grannies' gardens and pass them on to the rest of us."

"Bollocks!"

"Sure, you were no good at throwing. Breaking your collarbone in P7 meant you only had a girlie left-handed throw for nearly a year after."

"What about the bin lid I threw at the Saracen?"

"But it bounced off, Fergal, and hit you back on the head."

207

"The Provos said I was a hero."

"No. Your Ma said that the Provos said you were a hero. That's different."

Fergal felt the memories of his youth fade through his body and out into the river. He had nothing to retaliate with. Well, almost nothing.

"You never caught an eighteen-pound salmon, Brendan. I've a photo and it was only about six, if that."

A swarm of midges with their bodies warmed by the sun had gathered around Fergal. He batted them away vigorously, but they were relentless in their pursuit of pasty white skin.

"And that's why a decent fisherman smokes."

A midge-free Brendan held his slow burning cigarette in the air and in the direction of his friend. When he saw a reconnaissance party of flying insects leave Fergal's group and head in his direction, Brendan quickly returned it to his mouth. He then sulkily dropped his head down onto his chest and stared pathetically at his wet feet.

The comment about the alleged size of the salmon had cut Brendan to the quick. Fergal was also bruised by Brendan's assault and decided he had the claim on any sulking. When he fought with Frances he knew that she, being female, always had right of way as regards sulks. After all, she always had tears as a backup strategy. But in man-to-man combat, Fergal reckoned he'd give it ago. Both men remained silent, refusing to look in each other's direction. The only sounds were the occasional coughing splutter from Brendan, or the sound of slapping as Fergal battled with the persistent midges.

With Brendan's back turned away, Fergal confirmed his thoughts that even from behind, Brendan was a mirror image of himself twenty years ago. There were no love-handles, rounded shoulders, or even heavier legs. From his pigtail to his turned-up jeans, he was as he had always been. For the first time on his trip back home, Fergal didn't feel envious, but sensed something peculiar in that. Something didn't seem quite right, but he couldn't fathom what.

But what Fergal was sure of, was that this was one sulking battle he was determined to win. He'd lost too many to Frances to let another man break his silence.

"I didn't have a girlie throw. Even underhand, I could lob a brick further than you could."

Restraint wasn't one of Fergal's strong points.

"In your dreams, Fergal."

"And I was as good a poacher as the rest of you."

"You're not having much luck now, are you?"

"We're not poaching. You've a permit, don't you?"

"Don't be daft."

"Jesus, Fergal, I can't be caught poaching. I've got . . . I've got responsibilities."

It was out before he could do anything about it. Everything that he'd known about himself, but refused to accept. He'd become a man with responsibilities.

"But, Fergal, you always had responsibilities."

Probably for the first time since he'd met up with Brendan yesterday, Fergal's friend was speaking the truth and as he spoke, his wide honest expression frightened Fergal.

The sixth hour of the morning was greeted by a swan landing on the water, only a few metres away from the fishermen. His lifetime mate was nowhere to be seen. After the energy of the descent, he bobbed effortlessly and preened himself, taking care not to jar the silver fishing gut tangled in his wing. As Fergal stared at the swan, he tried to gather his thoughts and make sense of what Brendan had said. Was Brendan suggesting the unthinkable, that Fergal as he was now, wasn't that much different from what he was like in his past?

Fergal glanced around him and discovered that he was alone. Brendan had disappeared. His fishing rod, box of flies, shoes and socks were also gone. All that remained as evidence that Brendan had actually been there at all was an empty tobacco tin. Fergal picked it up and saw his own face reflected in the lid. The midges had left a plague of red dots. Fergal was only alone for a moment. As he held the tin closer to his face for further inspection, he also saw the reflection of a man behind him. The stranger was stocky, broad and held up an identity badge indicating 'Bailiff'.

Chapter 25

8 The Ashbury
Bangor, Co Down

Sunday 1 July 2000

Dear Matthew,

You stopped breathing two days before your first birthday. One minute you were crawling after the cat and the next you were lifeless. For one second your mummy and I stopped breathing too, but from somewhere I'll never fully understand, we discovered a mighty inner power. Your mummy rushed to telephone an ambulance and I began to give you mouth-to-mouth resuscitation. You were so small and soft, I felt I could crush you with each breath. Your blue mischievous eyes had turned back in their sockets and your cheeks were like alabaster. I held your tiny palm in mine, but it wouldn't curl around my finger as normal. So I curled it for you and held it tightly.

After making the call, Mummy raced back to join us. As she

counted I breathed. Calm would be the wrong word to use here, perhaps – composed and controlled would be better. We were a team, that's for sure. It was not long before your baby chest starting rising by itself. The ambulance crew had great difficulty in prising you away from our arms. They then had even more difficulty in unfurling your tiny hand clasped around my finger. But as they did, both your mummy and I wept. The inner power that had flitted into our lives had evaporated just as abruptly, leaving exhaustion and fear.

The doctors monitored you in the hospital for a few days and then sent you home saying it was a one-off incident and would never happen again. Unknown to anyone else, not even Mummy, I sat by your bedside every night for the next three weeks. I never fell asleep, but would just stare at the rising and falling of the cotton blanket around you. For a further three months, I would wake up four or five times a night and visit your room and wait for the blanket to move before returning.

That was the father I was. And the father I want to be again.

Then, I knew how many beats your heart would make per minute, now I don't even know what football team you support or what you like for breakfast. You are twelve now and becoming a man. You showed me that last night when you did the right thing and dropped the gun and ran back inside the house. I know I have done little over the past few years to show you that I want to be your father again. I've done bad things and behaved badly to you, your brother and your mummy. But it'll all change. I promise.

Your Mummy and I were a team once and we will be again.

I only wait outside your house for a chance glimpse of you and Lewis. Sometimes I catch you guys playing football in the garden. When I do and I hear you laughing or sometimes *quarrelling, I close my eyes and imagine I'm there with you. For those few stolen minutes I'm back with my family. In a week, I maybe capture five minutes of imaginary time, but it's like oxygen through my veins.*

Matthew, please don't be cross with me. I know I have dealt with an awful situation badly. But we will be together again, somehow. Please be patient. I promise.

Love always
Daddy

Placing the pen back down on the table beside the armchair, Maurice slotted the letter in an unmarked envelope. He was still wearing his jacket and placed the envelope in his outside pocket, but then moved it to the inside one, nearest his chest. Maurice got up and repositioned his armchair until it was facing the front window directly. It was still the early hours of Sunday morning and the moon was fully framed by the window. He sat back down in the chair and turned it 180 degrees until he was now facing an empty glass cabinet, pushed up tight against the far wall. He adjusted his position slightly, so that the reflection of the moon was now dead centre of the glass.

As Maurice leant back in the chair, his movement gently rocked the letter in his pocket. As did the handgun beside it. He removed the gun and from his trouser pocket lifted out a bullet. He clicked the bullet into place in the gun's chamber and watched it swirl round as he gently rotated the barrel. The gun looked like it could melt in Maurice's mighty hands, which were so flexed and taut that every vein and sinew were visible. His eyelids were heavy and cloaked the cobalt-blue pupils into a charcoal grey. The brown leather jacket had bunched into honey-coloured folds, but its softness only emphasised the hard, military mass within it.

Maurice rotated the barrel a tenth time. He then reached again into his trouser pocket and lifted out a further three bullets. These were inserted into the gun's chamber, making a total of four.

Chapter 26

The sound of the applause was deafening. All the players in the sports hall stopped whatever they were doing and faced Frances as she walked in with her team. A banner had been erected over the centre court with a large pink bottom painted and a shamrock on each cheek. Frances could hear the stifled chuckles of her teammates around her. The support they said they would offer over breakfast that morning had the tenacity of tissue paper.

Frances scuttled over to Court 4, where the team was scheduled to play their knockout match at ten-thirty that morning. A sea of hollering and clapping players parted to let Frances pass through. Their opponents for the morning were already warmed up and waiting on the far side of the court. The six players hadn't been caught up in the furore and Frances guessed they were too busy focused on the game in hand. This was until they turned around in unison and revealed six large plastic, naked, bottoms that had been stitched to the back of their shorts. Frances did not believe that the laughter could get any louder, but it did. Her five so-called friends also added to it.

Frances' only defence against the humiliation was an ironed-on smile and a feeling of being there in body, but not in spirit. This sensation had been generously provided by a raging hangover.

The referees blew the whistles for the start of the ten-thirty matches and the players returned to their warm-ups. A few players from teams who had played earlier came over and patted her on the back, but the ironed-on smile was starting to crease and they quickly moved on.

The match was over before it began. By the time Frances had re-tied her shoelace the first set was over, 25-3 to their opponents. The second set was going the same way until Roberta landed awkwardly on the floor and sprained a wrist. Without a substitute to replace her, the match was forfeited. Their opponents congratulated themselves on making it through to the next round, whilst Frances and her team congratulated Roberta on giving them the excuse for a speedy exit from the tournament.

The women eagerly retired to the balcony café, which looked directly down onto the volleyball courts below. A bag of frozen peas was found for Roberta and she sat with her arm elevated and drips of defrosting ice falling to the floor.

"Does that mean we're not in the final?"

Roberta wasn't going to let her throbbing wrist dampen her spirits.

"I think another few points and we would have had them."

Orla poked Roberta's wrist.

216

"Jesus, what's that for, Orla?"

"Nothing."

Niamh and Rose brought over six milky coffees and six Danish pastries. Orla nudged Roberta's share along the table, until they were a few inches beyond her reach.

"You lot are mean to me. Well, is nobody going to ask then?"

"Ask what Roberta?"

Niamh's mothering instinct couldn't let her see her friend suffer any further and she pushed the coffee and pastry over towards Roberta.

"Is nobody going to ask Frances what it's like to be caught buck-naked by a Dutch policeman? And cautioned for civil disturbance? The cop was only a wee lad too. He didn't know where to look."

Frances's cheeks reddened instantly. Her teammates must have guessed that she would be mortified by last night's performance. They had hardly mentioned the incident all morning. To Frances it was all just a murky nightmare now. After she had run across the dance floor, she just didn't stop running; down the stairs, out of the hotel, down the Bergenstrasse and probably Forest Gump style forever, if she hadn't bumped headfirst into the chest of a police officer. Roberta was right, he was probably only in his early twenties. When Frances first ran into him, she was still too overcome with alcohol and exhilaration to notice much at all. But after the long escorted walk back to the hotel where they were staying, with only the policeman's jacket around her, she became very much aware of what was going on. She was aware that the jacket was half-an-inch too short at the back for dignity and the hat held tightly to her front was half an inch too narrow for self-respect. The rest of her team had caught up with her by the time she got to her bedroom. Even Niamh's short admirer had made the journey and was found curled up asleep on the corridor the next morning.

Roberta wasn't deterred by the lack of response from the rest of the team.

"Anyway, Frances has got balls, more than the rest of us. Except for you, Orla."

Frances was relieved that Orla's athletic build and subsequent manliness had deflected the attention away from herself. Before Orla could physically respond to Roberta's banter, a commotion on centre court attracted their attention. A men's match had been interrupted by a player in the process of yanking the whistle from a referee's neck. There was obviously some disagreement regarding a line call. The agitated player, much smaller than his teammates, was cursing at the terrified referee. By comparison with his fellow players, his legs were short and hairy and their restricted size made it difficult for him to reach the intended victim. His fellow teammates struggled to pull him away but as they did the half-strangled referee pulled a red card from his top pocket. His vocal chords were bruised, but he mustered the strength to whisper, "Disqualified". As the disgruntled player was dragged off, there was a general panic to find a substitute. The team's bench was empty and the players began to search frantically for their substitute before they would be forced to forfeit the game.

In the far corner of the hall, a figure scurried, laden down with two large plastic water containers. His team spotted him and shouted him over to the court.

"Klaus, Klaus. You're on."

Frances's teammates all looked at her, each

the ill-prepared player as Frances's companion fro.

night before. The match re-started and once again t.

attention was transferred to Frances. She decided to pre-

empt any personal attacks by speaking first herself.

"Now we're out of the tournament, there's no point hanging around here. Why don't we see a bit of Amsterdam before our flight this afternoon?"

"Why not? Amsterdam's seen a lot of you."

Roberta was the only one to laugh at her own bad joke. Niamh instantly began organising everyone's itinerary. It was agreed that she and Orla would go and thank the organisers, whilst Cathy-Ann and Roberta chose to stay and watch some of the finals. Frances and Rose decided to head off into the city centre and they'd all meet up for lunch at the Rijksmuseum. There followed a general agreement that as they had hardly broken sweat during their match, getting changed out of their sportswear was hardly worth the bother. Once they'd finished their drinks, therefore, the team went their separate ways.

There was a welcome silence to the pounding sound of volleyballs as Frances and Rose closed the sports hall door behind them. Frances was also glad of some private time with Rose. Over the weekend they had had little time together and they had a lot of catching up to do.

At 11.30 in the morning, the seventeenth century streets were busy with Sunday tourists. The churches and museums were popular, as were the hundreds of cafés. Late breakfasts were being enjoyed and the aroma of ham and fresh pastries mingled with those of lemon tea and

219

cappuccinos. The flap of opening and closing newspapers and cups clashing with saucers peppered the pavements. Frances was glad of her sports-shirt as the sun was starting to blaze above the rows of terraced buildings. But it wasn't much of a fashion statement compared to the very chic and sophisticated tourists around her. A bunch of girls had perched themselves on the stone steps of the Oude Kerk and were sharing a large baguette with brie. All four had the sullen expression so perfected by Cathy-Ann. They too looked elegant and moody and the baguette looked honoured at being torn apart by the tanned slender fingers of its attackers.

"Looking at those girls over there, Rose, how does it make you feel?"

"Makes me feel bloody hungry. Let's get something to eat."

"Doesn't make you feel frumpy and old-fashioned?"

"I've had a lifetime of feeling like that. But right now I just want to eat."

Frances and Rose debated the merits of a snack on a canal barge, versus a pavement café, versus the Stedelijk Modern Art Museum. The ten-minute discussion was going round and round in circles, until Rose had a brainwave.

"What about a coffee shop? A nice frothy cup of coffee, a croissant and a joint."

"Jesus, Rose, I've had enough excitement already this weekend to last me until I'm a pensioner."

"Yes, but I haven't."

Rose was suddenly very matter-of-fact and something in her manner made Frances nervous of disagreeing with her. The two friends turned off from the main tourist area and took a slim side street. The street was lined with an array of coffee shops. They were much smaller and dingier than the cafés on the main streets, plus there were no seating areas outside. Hand-painted marijuana leaves and smoking pipes were scratched on the frosted windows and Frances discovered where all the plastic multicoloured door strips retired to after the 70s.

Rose picked a coffee shop with a painted marihuana leaf resembling a shamrock on the door and a row of bar stools dimly visible within. Inside, they walked up to a counter in the far corner and ordered two caffé lattes and two huge chocolate-filled croissants. The waiter was a young student type with wisps of unshaven hair desperately trying to imitate a beard and moustache. From a menu on the blackboard behind him, Rose selected an eighth of an ounce of Lebanese Gold and then asked for tobacco and cigarette paper. Frances was all the while silent, trying desperately to look like she did this kind of thing all the time.

The coffee shop had half a dozen other customers, ranging in age from late teens to a pair of elderly women with a chihuahua. Frances chose a bar stool next to them, as she reckoned at least they would be more old-fashioned than she would be. Rose began rolling a cigarette.

"Where did you learn to do that?"

"I used to smoke until about ten years ago."

"What dope?"

"No, Frances, tobacco. But I smoked a few spliffs at Uni. Didn't you?"

"No way. The girls I hung about with thought cider in your Ribena was pushing things too far."

Once lit, Rose gave the fat cigarette over to Frances. She gingerly sucked in and dramatically blew out.

"You're not inhaling, Frances."

"I am."

"Give it here."

Rose sucked on the cigarette with the ease of an experienced smoker. She had ten years of prohibition to fill her lungs with.

"Rose, you even hold the thing like a seasoned pro."

"You were trying to hold it like an old man in a bookie's. Try again."

Frances attempted to mimic her friend and tried again to inhale from the now slightly damp cigarette. Nothing happened. She couldn't even taste the marihuana over the strong flavour of her coffee.

"Frances, that's good money wasted on you. Suck it right into your lungs."

"I did it that time. Jesus, what a buzz. I can feel my head spinning."

Frances could feel nothing of the kind, but she was tired of looking like a Protestant at Mass.

The cigarette was passed back to her friend and Frances could now enjoy demolishing her croissant. After the first bite, the large airy pastry collapsed into a million flaking pieces, most of which found sanctuary on Frances's top lip. The old women beside the two friends had also chosen croissants for their brunch and delicately sliced sections off with sharp silver knives, before swallowing the pieces cleanly.

"Even old biddies here eat more gracefully than I do."

"You need to stop pulling yourself down, Frances. You never used to be so neurotic."

"Am I neurotic?"

"Is the Pope a Catholic? Stop beating yourself up. That's what happens when you stop playing volleyball. You were never like this before."

"What was I like?"

"You were the one who used to sort the shit out for the rest of us."

Frances hadn't thought about herself in the past for a long time. Her life at present had become far too stressful. Each day had become a battle with her confidence and self-esteem. She was a failure and no one on the outside, not even Fergal, could understand her.

"I think you're depressed, Frances."

"Too bloody right."

"Seriously, Frances. I think you are suffering from clinical depression."

Frances yanked the half-smoked cigarette from Rose's hand and sucked greedily on the heady smoke. Again she wasn't able to inhale, but the charade of doing so gave her something to hide behind. Rose took the cigarette back, reclined on the stool and poised herself like a compressed Marlene Dietrich. Her short legs and even shorter body restricted her from being anything other than a potted version of the original.

"OK, therapist, what are my symptoms?"

"Tell me, Frances, do you feel tired all the time? Are you unable to sleep? Do you have racing thoughts? Do you feel valueless?"

"Stop."

Surely she wasn't a depressive? Frances was just miserable. Not the same thing at all. Frances decided she didn't want to continue with the conversation any more and she would make light of it in order to show what a fun person she could be.

"Well, doctor, will it be a course of Prozac or electric shock therapy?"

"No, Frances, the Prozac's for people like me. I've had a lifetime of hitting rock bottom. You need to discuss your problems and whatever trauma has affected you this way."

Frances instantly felt like a selfish idiot for making fun of something that she knew had impacted on Rose's life since she was a child. She closed her brown almond eyes and wished herself away. How could she be so self-centred and self-absorbed? Frances was a failure, even to her friends.

"I'm sorry, Rose. But maybe you're projecting a wee bit."

"Maybe I am. Are you telling me nothing terrible has happened to you over the past six months? You've had no bad experience?

The air-conditioning began to kick in, which involved a fan hanging from the ceiling with photographs of Bob Marley glued to each propeller. At first the fan was uncomfortably noisy, but as it gathered momentum the noise turned to a constant hum and Bob Marley's face transformed into a revolving blur.

The cigarette was now a tightly wrapped stump and barely visible in Rose's slender fingers. Her long fingers and hands were disproportionate to her short body and as Frances studied them, she began to notice that in isolation, Rose looked slightly grotesque.

The old women beside the two friends had finished slicing their croissant and in one unified action, lit up two smoking pipes carved from red cedar. Within this surreal moment in time, Frances felt the ambiguity of her own reality. She had spent the last six months in an isolated haze. She had been isolated from her family, from her husband, from her friends and even from herself.

The two old women sucking on pipes, the revolving image of Bob Marley, the distorted proportions of her best friend and the heady smell of dope and coffee, all combined to create a surreal atmosphere. This was an atmosphere where Frances could feel open and honest.

"When I was a weein, Rose, my gran taught us that on the first day of a new month, the first thing you should do when you open your eyes in the morning is chant 'white rabbit, white rabbit, bring me good luck'. Well, today's the 1st of July and do you know what I said first thing this morning?"

Rose remained silent, rolling a second cigarette. She knew that if she made eye contact or spoke, Frances would become self-conscious again.

"Fuck you, rabbit!"

In the coffee shop, in Amsterdam, time stood still for Frances. And whilst the past, present and future were arrested, she was ready to unburden her soul. Frances was ready to be truthful.

Chapter 27

The tips of the ladder rattled against her bedroom window. Ursula was in a half-sleeping state, where she felt that her eyes were open and her mind wide awake, but she couldn't get her drowsy body to move. She tried to scream to alert her neighbours, but her voice was cruelly silent. Two or three times she managed to move her limbs and convince herself that she was fully awake, only to find herself back motionless in bed, still unconscious. The ladders rattled further with the ascending weight of whomever was climbing them. Ursula managed to move her left arm and pull back the damask duvet. With it she awkwardly pulled her legs down from the bed, onto the carpet. A man's hand could be seen reaching up to the top of the ladder, pulling himself up. Panic-stricken, Ursula attempted to run to her bedroom door, but her legs were limp and lifeless. With a heavy thud she fell to the floor. Ursula opened her eyes and she was back in bed, in the same position she had been the other four times when she had thought she had managed to wake herself.

"God help me!"

This time Ursula was awake. It took half a minute for her to convince herself that she was no longer dreaming and she lay motionless staring at the delicate lemon fleur de lys on her bedroom wallpaper. During the nightmare Ursula must have been thrashing all over the bed. She found that her head was now at the foot of the bed, with her heavy cream quilt lying on the floor.

When she had gone to bed the night before, Ursula had abandoned her usual cleanse, tone and moisturise routine, followed by dressing in either a silk or lace camisole with French knickers. This particular morning her mascara had left spider marks on her cheeks and pillow and she was wearing the same baggy T-shirt she had worn yesterday. She was naked from the waist down and with the duvet now on the floor, she was feeling chilly. She hadn't even pulled the curtains together and the sun's strong rays informed her that she had slept in unusually late.

She was reluctant to move. She turned over to scoop the duvet off the floor and provide some warmth to her chilled lower body. As she did so, she saw that the ladder in her nightmare had actually been a reality. Propped against her bedroom window was a wooden ladder. For a few seconds it rattled and then a man's hand grabbed hold of the top runner. Frozen, Ursula then saw the top of the head of the frightening stranger. All that was visible was chestnut-brown hair. The second hand reached up to the top, this one was carrying a blue bucket and a sqeedgee. Ursula instantly recognised these as the tools of the trade belonging to 'Walk the Bike'.

Just as 'Walk the Bike's' forehead, smothered in curls,

was about to peer over the window frame, Ursula heard his deep voice.

"Shit. Where's my sponge?"

The head and both the hands disappeared from view. As Ursula promised herself never to go to bed without closing the curtains, she grabbed a dressinggown from the corner of her brass bed and rushed downstairs.

With a piping hot mug of water with a lemon slice floating on top in front of her, Ursula composed herself at the kitchen table. She could hear 'Walk the Bike' manoeuvering around the house, with the sound of squeakily clean windows and the ladder clashing against the walls as it was positioned and re-positioned.

The debris of the chocolate gâteau from the night before sat before Ursula. After Christine's hasty departure, Carla had stayed with her friend for a while and tried to comfort her. Coffee and more coffee didn't seem to work, so eventually they went for a walk through the development. The sight of Christine playing happy families with her children in her front room, unfortunately, only added to the tension and they returned back after only ten minutes.

"She has a brass neck, Carla."

"She's a terrible dancer too. Tell her to come to my flamenco classes."

Carla had an appointment with her friend Mona to keep, followed by a rendezvous with a lover. So she had reluctantly announced that she had to part company with Ursula.

"Carla, please don't be phoning me in the morning with details of Mona's affair. I don't want to know about your sexual antics either."

As Ursula thought back to Carla's friend, whom she had

228

briefly met at the Russian dinner party on Friday night, she decided her confidence in married women with children was diminishing by the hour.

"Really, Carla. No gory details. I don't want to see, hear or have notions about sex for the next thirty years."

Carla had, as usual, kissed her friend on both cheeks as she left and, as usual, tutted at the poker-like feel to Ursula's embrace.

Unfortunately, the ten-minute walk had not counteracted the umpteen cups of coffee Ursula had consumed that evening. Her inability to sleep and subsequent nightmare were punishments for her caffeine overdose.

The hot water was half-drunk and Ursula began removing the uncomfortable T-shirt from under her dressing-gown, without actually removing the gown. Years of changing out of soggy swimsuits as a child on Ballyholme Beach, surrounded only by a handtowel, had made Ursula a professional. As a teenager, she had also perfected the art of removing her bra from under jumpers, blouses, even tight-fitting T-shirts. This was due to a sensation of constraint, rather than liberation. As a grown woman she soon realised why she had been so popular with pubescent boys, especially during the winter months.

Ursula could also put her bra on again with equal skill. As a teenager this was important when she returned back home. As a married woman the skill was utilised whenever her husband would climb into bed beside her. Before Roger knew it, she would barricade herself behind heavy-duty underwear, in the knowledge that he wouldn't want to try too hard to satisfy himself.

With the T-shirt artfully removed, Ursula re-secured the

belt to the magnolia-coloured dressing-gown. She could hear 'Walk the Bike' laying the ladder on the driveway and beginning to clean the downstairs window, starting with the front of the house and the living-room. The morning sun shone directly into Ursula's kitchen. The smudges of chocolate and spilt coffee looked three-dimensional on the kitchen table as they reflected the direct light. But Ursula noticed that her windows were surprisingly clean. Apart from the occasional decomposing suicidal greenfly, they sparkled dust-free in the sun's rays.

Ursula licked her fingertip and dragged it under her eyes, lifting charcoal traces of mascara and eyeliner. She then pulled her long blonde hair back and tied it in a knot. The utility room led to the backdoor, which Ursula unlocked. As it opened, she was swamped by searing sunlight.

The lawn at the rear of the garden was surrounded by Castlewellan Golds, punched by four tubs of geraniums. Several of the trees had failed to establish themselves in the sandy soil and through the perimeter gaps, Ursula had an open view of the cul-de-sac and her neighbours' homes. She waited patiently for a few moments. 'Walk the Bike' came around the corner of the house and strolled towards her. He looked surprised, but pleased. His familiar white T-shirt had been stripped off and he had it stuck into his belt strap, the weight of which slightly tugged on his jeans making them rest just below a line of dark hair running down from his belly button. Big chestnut curls framed his face and his friendly smile widened as he came nearer to Ursula.

"Lovely morning."

"Weren't you here less than two weeks ago? They only need cleaning once a month, you know."

'Walk the Bike's' smile dissolved. Ursula's first instinct was to hug him and tell him not to worry. But her head told her to be strong. She was safe being an ice-maiden and that was how she intended to live her life in the future.

"Come to think of it, you must have cleaned these windows half a dozen times in the last two months. Are you planing to hit me with some exorbitant bill or something?"

"I haven't asked you for any money."

"Not yet you haven't."

'Walk the Bike' looked down at his feet and crossed his strong arms across his chest. As he lowered his head, a cascade of curls fell into his eyes. The burning sun transformed the brown into a rich gold and he looked almost Roman. The gentleness of his actions overpowered Ursula and she longed to reach over and gently stroke his hair, his face and rest her fingers in the small hollow of his neck. 'Walk the Bike' still clung to a blue sponge in his fist. Soapy water began to drip from it and fall onto the grey flagstone. The dichotomy of this man's masculinity and his gentle manner unsettled Ursula. It was unfamiliar and, therefore, frightening. Her ex-husband's whole persona was led by testosterone and even her recent acquaintance with her neighbour had only confirmed Ursula's experience of men as physical and powerful. But deep inside men were all the same, weren't they?

"Are you conning anyone else around here?"

"I'm not conning you."

"Then who are your other customers? I'll go and ask them."

"There are no others."

"So, I'm the only one you're ripping off."

"I'm not ripping off anybody. You're my only customer."

Ursula could feel her body tingle at the sound of his soft voice. She could sense her nipples erect against the silk of her dressinggown and could feel it clinging to the small of her back. She was still standing in the doorway of her home, but found herself involuntarily taking a step down onto the concrete slab.

"You don't clean any of my neighbours' windows?"

"I don't clean any windows. Anywhere. I'm not a window cleaner."

Ursula's icy guard melted away and was replaced by utter confusion. She could feel the knot in her hair loosen and softly fall down her back and the tight muscles in her shoulders suddenly relax.

"I don't understand. Why are you here then?"

Chapter 28

"I could really do with something nice to have with that. I'm half starved."

Eilish buttered a couple of cherry scones and served them to her brother alongside his piping hot tea.

"And did the bailiff do nothing but caution you, Fergal?"

"Only after he'd had a good laugh at the fishing rod Brendan had put together for me. The fact I hadn't caught any fish also went in my favour. He said if I had caught any with that rod, he'd have given up his job and become an accountant. Eilish, I was mortified. I felt like a wee lad again being ticked off for nicking ten pence out of my Ma's purse."

"And Brendan just left you?"

"The bastard must have seen the bailiff coming and just legged it. I don't know how he's going to get back to Griánan to pick up that wreck of a car of his. I didn't hang around after him."

When Fergal had arrived back home at around nine-thirty in the morning, the streets of Gallaigh were deserted.

Eilish and his youngest sister Estelle were also both still in their beds. The late-night card school had, it seemed, run its usual course and whilst Estelle was nursing hurt feelings, Eilish nursed a pile of pound coins and 50 pences stacked on the mantelpiece.

Fergal had let himself into the house with the key still in the door from the day before. Eilish had heard Fergal fumbling in the kitchen trying to find tea bags and sugar, so had reluctantly pulled a lilac flannel bathrobe around her and come down to meet him.

The vertical blinds in the front window were still drawn from the night before and the brother and sister sat in the half-light comforted by the hot tea and floury scones.

"But, Fergal. It wasn't a total disaster surely. How did the night camping up at the fort go?"

Fergal couldn't find an immediate answer. His memories of the evening were bizarre and difficult to articulate. He was also still annoyed at being abandoned to the mercy of the bailiff.

"The old fort was as magical as I remember it."

"And Brendan. What kind of form was he in?"

"The same as ever."

There was his answer. Brendan was the same as he ever was. Brendan's appearance had been the same, his manner and his whole attitude to life. He even had the same old fishing and drinking stories, except for a few generous embellishments added for the sake of a good yarn.

Fergal impatiently scanned the living-room, looking for anything to distract him. Only now, he noticed a white bedsheet pinned up against the back of the door.

"What's that up there for?"

"Estelle had dug out some old cine-film from the good old days. So we had a bit of a screening last night. We got a lend of a beat-up projector from her Mickey. Most of the films weren't up to much, to be honest, either over or under-exposed or bucking scratched. But there's a good bit of all of us up at the old house."

'Her Mickey', Estelle's part-time husband, was a hoarder. He kept everything and anything. Rusting empty paint tins, stuffed with nails, screws and washers, were his specialty. If anyone needed anything, they visited Mickey first. His most frequently told anecdote was the one about the boy who arrived with a blade asking if Mickey had a razor that would fit it.

"And am I in the film?"

"Shove it on and have a look."

The rusty old projector was hidden in the corner of the room, under a box of scrambled cine-film. Eilish pulled out a nest of formica side tables and selected the middle one. She positioned it exactly where she knew it had to be, in order to get any picture at all on the home-made screen. She riffled through the dusty box and pulled out one film reel and began threading it through the projector. Fergal closed the window blinds and the door to the kitchen.

At first, the light from the projector was just a blaring circle on the sheet, highlighting a few stains and pulled threads. But after a few seconds, there was Fergal's old home in full colour. The colours were largely faded and muted and the occasional scratch cut across the frame, but there it was.

"Now, Fergal. Don't expect any sound."

Fergal didn't care. He was mesmerised, especially as one by one his family took it in turns to pose for the camera.

235

Each stood motionless, challenging the notion of 'moving' pictures. They all looked young and fresh and carefree. Their only irritation was a tiny figure, who kept trying to jump up and get in each shot. Fergal recognised this boy as himself.

Fergal's father was the first to be filmed. He was short and stocky, with wirerimmed, cock-eyed glasses. They were either ill-fitting, or he had one ear higher than the other. His beaming, motionless smile revealed an assortment of broken and missing teeth.

"The Da was a looker in his day."

Next on duty was Fergal's mother. Obviously camera-shy, she was shoved over besides her husband by a mystery arm. She too was short, but slim, with a curvaceous figure that belied the fact that she had borne five children. Both parents looked totally embarrassed at being forced to pose together and giggled like teenagers. Tiny hands could be seen trying to clamber up. Mildly irritated, they both attempted to encourage the little glory-seeker away.

When it was Eilish's turn and the by now familiar two hands could be seen grasping at her jumper, she reached down, lifted the toddler up and introduced him to the camera. The boy was wedged between two ample breasts, forcing them apart. Her beehive hairstyle and heavily made-up eyes didn't hide the fact that she was truly stunning. Her face had the symmetry and flawlessness of classic beauty. Even the dull colours of this dated film could not muddy the emerald flecks in her wide eyes. Why had she never married was Fergal's first reaction to her image and his second was how similar the two faces of brother and sister were in shape and fullness.

"I was a cute wee lad."

"Aye, but look what happened to you."

"Look what happened to you more like!" Fergal suddenly felt the guilt of his spiteful comment. He backtracked awkwardly. "You're still gorgeous but . . ."

The teenage Eilish tickled the boy under the chin and then delicately kissed him on the cheek. The film cut to the twins, Maeve and Donna. They were as motionless as their parents before them; only they didn't even have the nerve to blink. You could see their eyes water as each attempted to hold the fixed smile for as long as possible. That was until a tiny head bobbed up in front of them and they took it in turns to take vicious swipes, before the film cut to the last member of the family, Estelle. She smiled with her mouth firmly closed, hiding the gap where two front teeth had recently fallen out. The grimacing child used her fist to forcible remove her clambering baby brother, who had changed his tactics to pouncing from behind and grabbing his sister's neck.

The camera quickly cut away for a few seconds, to Fergal, in tears on the bottom step.

"No wonder I was always so bloody miserable."

The next camera shot was of a precession of neighbours walking past the house and waving at the camera. Fergal recognised faces, but not names. At the end of the parade was Estelle's Mickey, prancing along, obviously in an attempt to impress his new girlfriend. As he sauntered past the camera, he used his left hand to coif his very prominent sixties quiff. With his right hand, he shoved a tiny boy, walking alongside him, abruptly into the box hedge.

"Hang on a minute. Wind that back a bit."

"What for?"

"I've a point to prove."

Eilish wound the film back a dozen or so frames. The tiny boy was Fergal, yet again the victim of contempt.

"What was it with you people in those days? Was it a free-for-all?"

"Hang on, Fergal. Let me rewind that back again."

"Want a second look at your baby brother getting the shit beat out of him, do you?"

"No, I've a point to prove too."

Eilish rewound the film back to exactly the same spot. Fergal grimaced in anticipation of his undignified removal from the shot. Eilish froze the film at exactly the point where Mickey's hand was inches away from Fergal's tiny head.

"Look, there. I told you so."

Behind the two figures in the foreground, was the haze of the background. But even with the blur, it was still clear to distinguish a cart travelling on the road, laden with heavy-looking buckets and being pulled by a dappled grey horse. Seated at the front of the cart were two men, both with shocking white hair.

"The Brock Man, Fergal!"

Eilish moved the film on slowly, frame by frame. The white-haired figures flickered across the screen and disappeared at the point where Fergal also made his hasty departure into the evergreens. Their presence on the film was ghost-like and Fergal felt a cold chill.

The film's location made an abrupt leap to the outside of a chapel. Parades of miniature brides, on their way to First Communion, filtered past. The camera zoomed onto

Estelle, whose friend has goaded her into smiling. Still hiding the gap created by the absence of teeth, she grimaced at the camera. The shot then panned away to an Elvis Presley look-alike, who was ordering the girls into a crocodile-walking pattern. His heavily Brylcreemed hair glistened from the dull opaque colours on the screen and when he turned to face the camera directly, the white of his priest's collar shone out further.

"Isn't that Father McLaverty? Wasn't he thrown out?"

Eilish didn't like discussing anything untoward about the priesthood. Especially not with her younger brother, a lapsed Catholic.

"No, he wasn't. He was sent away to a mission, that's all."

Fergal often found his sister's blind faith irritating, but today he couldn't muster the energy to be provoked into another one of their heated debates.

The next scene was hard to make out, as large burning welts had formed on the surface of the film. In and out of the damaged images, Fergal just about recognised scenic shots of the beach at Fahan. A medley of snippets of blue skies, turquoise sea and caramel sand filled the sheet.

"Why does it seem like the sun was always shining when we were young?"

"Because it was."

After a few more frames, the damaged film looked to be rudely spliced and sellotaped to the next segment, which was back to the Coyles' old house. This time the family was assembled in the back garden. Again the sun was shining and the girls were dressed in sleeveless mini-dresses and the men in tight black suits. A small boy wearing a sweater two sizes too small came hurtling into the frame on a tricycle. He stood up and began an imaginary flight around the garden with his arms outstretched. As he dipped and took a sharp left turn, he came whizzing headlong towards the camera. At about two feet from the lens, an arm came into view, pushing the unfortunate soul over. The weeping boy was next seen being lifted by Eilish and carried away.

"Look. Another clout."

"You were a right wee show-off."

"So?"

"You used to annoy folk."

"That's great. Thanks for the confidence boost. I was only a wee lad, for God's sake."

"You were spoilt."

"Aye, it looks like it."

"You were."

"By who?"

"Me."

The bright light of the projector against the screen and the whirring of the end of film as it whizzed around, indicated that the film was over. Both Fergal and Eilish sat for a moment staring at the blank sheet and indulging in the repetitive, soothing hum of the spinning film. Fergal felt comforted by it somehow.

"Eilish, are there any more films in that box?"

"Aye, but they're all too damaged. Mickey reckons they're for binning."

"I'll take them home with me."

Fergal couldn't bear the thought of all those ancient memories ending up in a skip somewhere, even if they were damaged beyond repair. Maybe some time in the future, they'd invent a way to repair old film, whenever they've discovered how to freeze bodies and bring them back to life. He knew his hopes were remote, if not ridiculous, but Fergal didn't care, as he carefully rewound straggly bits of film and dusted off stubborn flecks of dust.

To date, Fergal's memories of his past had been stored in black and white and were motionless, like old photographs. To see his parents in the prime of their lives, enjoying full health, in full colour and moving, transformed his recollections. His voyage of self-discovery had taken an unexpected twist, but what it told him, he didn't know.

As Fergal sat mesmerised by the shreds of film, Eilish began dismantling the projector and opening the window blinds again. The rays of daylight broke Fergal's spell and he searched for, and found, his cup of now cold tea.

Eilish could sense sadness in her brother's mood, but was unsure as to how to comfort him. The days of rocking him on her hip were long gone. She studied him dipping a buttery scone into his tea and found herself remembering her one and only trip away from home when she was eighteen. Eilish had gone to London to find work and as she walked through Piccadilly, she put her hand in her pocket and discovered one of Fergal's dummies. Discovered in floods of tears by a passing traffic warden, Eilish was then taken to the nearest train station. She was back in Derry the next day. The furthest Eilish had been in the twenty-eighty years since, was to Belfast to see 'Disney on Ice'.

What could Eilish do now to help her obviously hurting brother?

"*The Journal* came in this morning. Do you want to go through the births, deaths and marriages?"

"No, thanks."

"What about a visit to the Ma and Da?"

A trip to the cemetery wasn't much of a development on Eilish's original suggestion. But Fergal, in his mood of self-analysis, thought carefully for a split second and accepted his sister's suggestion.

Eilish was washed and dressed within fifteen minutes, time enough for Fergal to enjoy a second and third buttered scone. She came back downstairs, in her Sunday best – a navy blazer pulled tightly across her chest and a cream pleated skirt that was raised slightly at the back. Before they left, she checked herself in the mirror above the fireplace and pressed down her hair with a damp comb. By 10.30 in the morning they were on the road to the City Cemetery.

"Do you always drive like this?"

Fergal was in fact a careful driver, but Eilish, unfortunately, was a nervous passenger.

Outside the cemetery gates were a number of flower sellers with assorted carnations and lilies, kept cool in green and yellow plastic mop buckets. The sellers were enjoying busy Sunday trade and the flowers were looking slightly picked over. Eilish bought a small bunch of yellow carnations and Fergal chose three bunches of unopened lilies. Back in the car, Fergal drove slowly up the hill past the eighteenth century family tombs dotted along the bottom, with prime views of the Brandywell football ground. Hooded crows sat sunning themselves on the warm stones, occasionally lifting their tail feathers and excreting. The road weaved up the hill and as the tombs ended, they were replaced by granite gravestones, stone crosses and unmarked plots. Three-quarters of the way up the hill,

Fergal pulled over to one side. They walked past the mammoth monument belonging to the Republican plot. There had recently been a memorial service and an abundance of fresh flowers and wreaths were strewn across the 'volunteers" graves. Fergal and Eilish's family gravestone was huddled in the row behind them.

The family footstone said 'Coyle', barely visible through an attack of moss. The marble white headstone was dedicated in silver script to Fergal and Eilish's parents and their grandfather. Two of their mother's stillborn babies were also buried here, but their presence was unmarked. Eilish removed a few half-dead roses left by the last visitors and lay her own, and Fergal's, directly at the foot of the headstone.

"You've got to admit it, Fergal; they've a nice view."

The family plot had a prime view of the River Foyle and, across the valley, the city walls.

"Even the Bogside looks half-decent at this distance. Do you want a place here or up in Bangor?"

"What are you trying to tell me, Eilish? Do I look ill or something? Of course I want in there."

"You'd need to run that by Frances. She might have other plans for you and her."

"I don't think Frances would fancy being cooped up with me for eternity. Trust me."

"Surely things aren't that bad between you two at the moment?"

"Want to bet?"

"But you've been through so much together these past months."

"No, Eilish. I've been through my problems and she's been through hers. There's no 'together' about it. You know

243

what day it is today. And where is she? Wouldn't you think that we should be together today?"

"Maybe she needed to get away."

"Away from me?"

"That's not what I meant, Fergal."

"We should have been away together. The Ma wouldn't have left the Da. They had true love. Maybe Frances and me don't."

Eilish didn't respond. She bent over and lifted a few of the stray flowers from the Republican plot and placed them on an unmarked grave beside them.

"Fergal, you shouldn't compare yourselves with the Ma and Da."

"I know."

Fergal used the underside of his clenched fist to rub away at the footstone. Tiny flecks of moss skidded off leaving their green stain on his hand. Two elderly men strolled past them, nodded and then walked down the hill. Both were dressed for the winter with dark suits over woollen jumpers. Watched by Fergal and Eilish, the men stopped beside a grave in an old section of the cemetery.

"Just think, Eilish. Those old codgers are probably the last people with living memories of whoever is buried in that plot. What happens when they die?"

"You really are morose today."

"You bring me to a cemetery and complain that I'm morose?"

"Since you got here yesterday, Fergal, you've hardly been yourself."

"That's my problem. Don't you see? I'm not myself any more. I've become this suburban junkie. Seeing Brendan after all these years just made me green with envy. Everything about him is the same."

"And you think that's good?"

"Jesus, aye. Not a care in the world, days spent fishing and hunting, nights spent in the bar with your mates. Not a responsibility anywhere."

"Brendan's thirty-five, like yourself. Don't you think it's time he did have responsibilities?"

"Why?"

"It's called growing up. He's thirty-five and still lives with his Ma, for heaven's sake."

Eilish was unusually sharp with Fergal and tightened her arms around her chest. Just like his mother used to.

"Is he still getting thrown out of bars?" she asked.

"Yes."

"Does he still tell the story of the fifteen-pound salmon?"

"It's eighteen now."

"You've moved on with your life. There's nothing abnormal in that, Fergal."

"But I used to have much more spunk about me. I was never this – this conventional."

"I think your memories of your youth are the same as they are of the Ma and Da."

Fergal tried to argue back, but he couldn't find the words, stuttering awkwardly. Eilish stepped along the side of the grave and ran her fingers over the outline of her parents' names etched into the gravestone.

"Of course they loved each other. But the Ma and Da could fight the bit out."

"Eilish, that's a lie. They were the most affectionate and loving couple I've ever known. They never had arguments."

"No, never. They just used their fists instead. They used to beat the hell out of each other."

"How can you say such lies, when they're laid there in front of you? I never saw any fights."

"That's because they only happened when they both came home drunk at the weekends. You were always in your bed. I was baby-sitting, remember?"

This was the second time this weekend that Fergal had been told that his recollections of his past were seriously flawed. But he couldn't accept them. His current unhappiness with his future had been protected by his memories of his past. If his past wasn't all that great either, Fergal didn't know where to turn. There was something comforting in being able to say to himself 'I didn't use to be like this'.

Fergal turned away from his sister and started walking back to the car. On the next row from his family's was an open grave, with recently dug out soil heaped and baking in the sun. The chapel bells rang and Fergal could see the darkly dressed congregation pouring out onto the road leading up the hill. Eilish crossed herself in front of her parents' grave and followed her brother back to the car. In stony silence they both drove back down the hill. The hooded crows remained perched on the splattered tombs.

When the car reached the bottom of the hill, the cascade of mourners parted to let the car pass by. As they turned left out of the cemetery and onto the Lone Moor Road, Fergal glanced through his side mirror and saw a small white coffin being carried by a man, about the same age and build as himself.

Back in Galliagh, Fergal didn't get out of the car, but made his excuses to head back to Bangor.

"Come on in, Fergal. Have a cup of tea and something nice before you go."

"No. I've a presentation to prepare for work in the morning. And I want to get back before Frances does."

"The Ma and Da did love each other, you know."

"I know."

"I only told you that, to show you that everyone has their problems. I've got mine, Brendan's got his and you've got yours. Go home and talk to Frances. You need each other."

Fergal had kept the car engine running, which muffled his hurried farewells to his sister. She stood at the garden gate, waving as he turned the car around. The boy he had seen yesterday with the mobile shop scam came hurtling down the passageway, brushing past Eilish as he did so. She gave him a clip on the ear and then walked up the path back into her own home.

Fergal's journey back to Bangor seemed to fly by. When he reached the Glenshane Pass again, he couldn't remember passing Dungiven or any of the usual milestones of his journey. As he drove passed the Ponderosa Bar and Grill he breathed a sigh of relief when his car didn't decide to repeat itself and break down. He also remembered the article he had read about his neighbour and was shaken from his daydream back into the reality of his life. This lasted only a few moments and once the bar was a faint outline in the distance, Fergal returned to his dazed world.

As Fergal turned the key to his front door, he again realised that he had missed most of the journey back. This frightened him, but his current numb state softened the blow. Piled on the doormat were a number of letter and flyers. He scooped them up and headed up the stairs. Once inside his study, he closed the door and rested in his black leather desk chair. So much had happened this weekend to overturn all that he thought was true. He was a greater emotional mess than when he had set out. Looking down at his stomach squashed against the edge of the table, he also decided his physical wellbeing had suffered as a result.

Fergal looked across from his desk, through the study window and saw Christine Watson, her girls, Ursula Richards and a man in his twenties racing across Ursula's lawn. He was intrigued and leaned across the desk in order to get a better view. The pile of letters crumpled under his hand and as he looked down, the top letter attracted his attention. There was nothing unusual about the envelope – a plain brown one with a small clear Cellophane window. It was addressed to Mrs Frances Coyle and the postmark was the regional health trust.

The commotion on the street was instantly forgotten, as were all the problems of the day. Though it was addressed to his wife, Fergal opened the tiny brown letter.

Chapter 29

"Why are you here then?"

Ursula repeated her question in response to 'Walk the Bike's' disclosure that he wasn't a window-cleaner. As he nervously hesitated and struggled to give an answer, the sound of running feet could be heard along the side of Ursula's house. The first steps were heavy and sharp like a woman's shoe, followed by a series of lighter and softer steps.

Christine Watson was the first to appear from behind the corner, swiftly followed by her three children. Their expressions portrayed varying degrees of agitation and concern. Christine was dressed in her usual style of cotton trousers and blouse, but she had let her auburn curls fall loose on her shoulders and rather than buttoned all the way to the top, she had left three buttons unfastened on her blouse. Christine wasn't used to exercise and she struggled to find her breath after her run.

"I think something terrible has happened to Maurice McAllen at Number 8."

Ursula's first thoughts were to look at the innocent faces of Christine's children huddled beside their distraught mother. She wanted to scold Christine for bringing her back into their illicit affair, but the girls' presence held her tongue. 'Walk the Bike' was the first to respond.

"What's the problem?"

"He's sitting in his front living-room, motionless. All I can see is the top of his head and his left hand resting on the arm of the chair. He won't even answer the door."

"Maybe he's just taking a nap."

"But I saw him through the window in exactly the same position late last night. It's nearly twelve hours later and he hasn't moved an inch."

Ursula's concern for Maurice was overshadowed by questions such as, what was Christine doing round at his house last night in the first place? And what was she doing round there this morning? But again the sight of the girls' trusting, innocent faces stopped her from sharing her thoughts.

"What makes you think that this man's behaviour is anything but normal? I've dozed off like that myself," said 'Walk the Bike'.

"You'd need to see him every day to know why I'm worried . . . sorry, I didn't catch your name."

"Sam. I'm a . . . I clean Ursula's windows."

"Nice to meet you, Sam. I'm Christine from Number 5. I know I maybe sound slightly paranoid, but this really isn't like him."

Sam, Sam. Ursula was surprised by the name. 'Walk the Bike' was no longer; now he was a real person. He also knew her name, which surprised her even more.

"Ursula would agree with me, Sam. Maurice McAllen's not like any normal neighbour."

Ursula frantically checked Christine's expression for any innuendo or sound of malice. But there was none. She was genuinely distressed. Christine began to regain her breath and Sam led her by the hand and seated her on the step.

"For a start, Sam, he's left his car parked on his driveway. In the two years that he has lived here, I've never seen his car on the drive. He never ever sleeps in late. I've been up as early as six with one of the girls and I've seen Maurice up and about. He's usually pottering about in the garden or in his garage. This fella's not normal; he's an enigma."

"Do you want us to call the police, Christine?"

"I'd hate to get the police out and discover that he's maybe just been drinking or something." Drugs also came into Christine's mind, but she didn't say that.

"Well, maybe, Christine, that is exactly what he's been doing."

"No. There's something not right. I can feel it."

Ursula remained silently dissecting the situation. Christine was right. There was something very odd about Maurice's behaviour. But then Christine was his lover and obviously hiding something. Ursula's first instinct was to call the police and step away from the problem, but the inquisitive, feline element of her nature wanted to pursue the mystery further. Sam was being more cautious and was the stable factor in the situation. As he questioned Christine, who was still seated on the bottom step, Ursula caught him briefly glancing up at her and turning away with embarrassment when their eyes connected. He managed to combine the control of a man with the nervousness of a boy. This tantalised Ursula.

251

"Look, Christine, before we do anything drastic, let me go round and try and attract his attention through his front window," said Sam.

Christine agreed and Sam politely held her hand, providing balance as she stood up. Ursula was instantly jealous, and angry with herself for being so.

The three adults and three children hurried across the American-style open lawns towards house Number 8. Ursula walked directly behind Sam, in the cooling shadow created by his large rugby-player build. Christine was forced to stop every few paces and yank the heel of her court shoe out of the lawns as they walked over. After getting stuck three times, she took the shoes off and threw them onto the pavement and continued barefoot. The soft leather on the shoe uppers scraped and scuffed as they bounced.

Once re-grouped on Maurice's front lawn, there was a moment of calm, generated in advance of the anticipated storm. Like planets around the sun, they all stood at various distances from the house. The girls stood the furthest away on the pavement, with Christine just in front of them. Ursula was the next nearest, also barefoot and tiptoeing on the dry grass.

As the group stood still, a green Vauxhall Vectra drove slowly into the cul-de-sac. Fergal Coyle in Number 2 had returned home, but he appeared oblivious to the commotion as he drove past with his head facing straight forward. Whatever was distracting him led him out of the car, up his garden path and into his house with his front door pulled tight behind him, before anyone had a chance to attract his attention.

Sam stepped up to the window and began gently

knocking on it. The knocks got more frequent and then louder until he was almost thumping the glass with both fists.

"Mr McAllen! Mr McAllen!"

The women knew from his blank expression, when he turned away from the window, that he had received no response. The posse re-congregated in the driveway. Sam continued to take charge of the situation.

"What do you want to do now?"

Christine was driven by her new sense of adventure; Ursula by her desire to stay in the presence of Sam for as long as possible. They both looked across at Sam's ladder lying in Ursula's driveway. Christine was the first to put what both women were thinking into words.

"I went around the side of Maurice's house earlier to see if I could get his attention through the back door. I couldn't. I tried opening it, but it was locked. As was the front. But I noticed he'd left the window on the upstairs landing open."

Sam looked at the women's faces, searching for reason and rationality. Agreeing for the first time that weekend, both women nodded at Sam to continue. Christine's girls ran back to the side of the house, now excited by the drama unfolding.

"Mummy, this is the best adventure ever!"

This was not how Christine had planned to keep her promise to her children.

Chapter 30

There was a loud clunk and then a puff of smoke as the propellers of the fan gave up on their battle against the heat. Slowly the face of Bob Marley came back into view. The young man behind the counter brought a stool over to the centre of the room and, once he'd stood on it, began to poke away at the mechanism with a blunt knife. Frances was no expert on health and safety matters, but she guessed live electric wires and a metal knife didn't go together. But the counter assistant survived his ordeal and after a few pokes and prods in the correct places, the whirring of the fan started up again. Frances guessed that the breakdown of the air-conditioning system was a regular occurrence in the coffee house.

The battle between machine and man had distracted Frances and Rose momentarily. But Rose was eager for this to be only a temporary setback.

"Frances, why is today such a significant day for you?"

As she spoke, puffs of white smoke escaped from her

mouth and nostrils. Frances breathed them in deeply. Since she was having no luck inhaling the marijuana directly herself, she thought she'd try passive smoking instead. For a second or two she did feel slightly light-headed, but she couldn't discount hyperventilation as she breathed in and out again in rapid succession.

"Rose, you probably don't remember me phoning you last autumn to say I couldn't make training that night. I had some excuse about having to work late or something."

Rose nodded her head in agreement.

"I was actually ringing you from the public toilets in Tesco. I couldn't train that night because I reckoned I should be taking it easy. As I spoke to you I was still squatting on the toilet with a positive pregnancy test in my hands. The pink positive dot was glaring back at me the size of Australia. I was only a few days overdue with my period, but I just couldn't wait to get home and do the test. I think I did it more to confirm to myself that I wasn't pregnant, so that I could put it out of my mind."

"Didn't you want to be pregnant?"

"More than anything in the world. The ten or more tests I'd done in the months previously, where no pink dot appeared, were testimony to that. I just wanted to get what I expected to be the familiar disappointment over with. When the test turned out positive, I was surprised, overwhelmed, excited, frightened, you name it. So much so that I couldn't shift myself out of the loo."

For the first time that afternoon, Frances smiled at the memory of that moment.

"I had a whole big surprise planned in order to tell Fergal the news when he got home from work. But I just couldn't wait, and hit him with it as soon as he came in through the door. The two of us sat staring at the little plastic tester splashed with my pee – lovingly as if it was the baby itself. Fergal then wanted to know if I had any cravings and did I want to put my feet up. He hadn't really grasped what was involved at this stage."

"And is that why you didn't come back to training?"

"I just couldn't risk it, Rose. I'd wanted this baby for so long. I became super-paranoid about everything."

"But why didn't you tell us? We're your mates."

"I know, Rose. And I don't know why. But you should have seen Fergal and me during those first few months. We were nauseatingly sloppy. Every day Fergal would come home from work with something for the baby or me; a silver picture frame, vitamin supplements, breast pads. Of course I lapped it up completely. You know in the olden days when women used to faint and swoon. That was me. A complete drama queen. I was wearing maternity knickers at only twelve weeks and I didn't even have a bump yet."

Rose scrubbed out the last few embers of her cigarette in the ashtray and leant forward on her stool, until her face was only a few feet from her friend's.

"Frances, what happened to that baby?"

A small crowd had gathered on the side street directly in front of the coffee shop. There was some sort of procession marching down the street, as the sound of chanting and drumming could be heard getting louder and louder. The street wasn't very wide and the small gathering had to push their backs against the assorted boutiques and coffee shops. Then a parade appeared in the form of a group of men dressed in sports clothing and carrying home-made drums, created out of upturned buckets and biscuit tins. Held on the shoulders of three of them was another man who was obviously been ceremoniously paraded around the city. He nearly fell a couple of times as his leg slipped off the shiny Lycra shoulders of his bearers. The small crowd clapped and cheered, adding to the young man's exuberance. The mini-parade was now only yards from Frances and Rose. The young man nearly fell again as one of the bearers tripped over. He awkwardly corrected himself and as he was swung back into the air, Frances instantly recognised the man as her companion from the previous night. The glazed glass of the coffee-shop window and its dark interior protected Frances from being discovered. It was obvious from the way Klaus stared at himself in the window's reflection, fixing his hair and shirt, that he was unaware that there was anybody inside at all.

"Frances, isn't that the fella you were talking to last night?"

In his left hand, Klaus lifted a garish pewter trophy into the air and swung it victoriously.

"His team must have won the tournament. Don't they belong to you, Frances?"

With his right hand, Klaus paraded a lilac lace bra and pair of matching lilac knickers. Like a knight's colours given to him by his loved one before battle, he swung his flag through the air. All Frances could focus on was the tiny cotton threads hanging from the knickers, a combined result of overuse and excessive boil washes. The parade's pause outside the coffee house was brief and they quickly continued with their celebration down the street. The small crowd dispersed again.

"You didn't leave your underwear at the party?"

"My underwear, Niamh's trousers, Orla's blouse and Cathy-Ann's shoes. I totally forgot about them."

The disappointment of losing her clothes was minor to that of realising that she had been a bad judge of character. Frances had chosen a poor sort as her friend and confidant last night. Something else she couldn't get right.

"I never was a good judge of men."

"You did all right picking Fergal."

"I thought so too, until . . ."

Rose carefully manipulated her friend back again to their earlier conversation. As she did so, she began rolling a third cigarette, licking the tissue-thin paper to make a seal.

"When I was nearly three months pregnant, myself and Fergal went to the maternity hospital for our first scan. The Jubilee was fighting a battle against closure and the place was buzzing with talks of demonstrations and appeals. I felt like a granny when I looked around and saw all the other mums waiting for their scans: teenage girls, either with their mums or spotty-looking boyfriends in football shirts and trainers. On our way into the hospital, we passed two girls who looked like they were going to have their babies any minute. They were puffing on cigarettes like their lives depended on it. Fergal was going to say something to them, until I yanked him by the arm and dragged him in."

"Were there no other women our age?"

"I suppose there must have been."

"Maybe after trying for a baby for so long, you're blinkered now into remembering only those you assumed didn't deserve to be there."

"Thank you, Dr Freud. What's your hourly rate again?"

"I'm sorry, Frances. Please don't stop."

"No, you're right. Over the past months that resentment has only grown and grown. If a pregnant woman walks past me now eating a burger, I think she should be chastised for not eating the proper food for her baby. Before the scan, the midwife took us through all the usual booking-in procedure. Everything she asked me, like was I eating the right foods, did I smoke, did I drink, everything was as it should be. I smugly sat there as if I was sitting the Eleven Plus all over again. She then went through my family's medical history and even on that I reckoned I scored an A plus. She quickly checked through Fergal's family history, but with his Ma dying of a stroke and his Da dying young from a blood disorder, she suggested I should have picked better genes. She didn't know how right she was.

Frances attracted the attention of the waiter and asked for another two caffé lattes. On his way back to the counter, the fan again gave a loud thud and gushed a puff of smoke. The repair procedure was completed yet again, and the coffees brought over.

"With the usual questions and then urine and blood tests done with, we were both taken into another room where all the scanning was done. I had been told that you get the best scan pictures if your bladder is full to bursting, so with a litre of diluted orange cordial inside me, I was a walking beach ball. I remember the room as being very dark and dismal, with the curtains drawn so that the monitor on the scanner could be seen better. There was just me, Fergal and two midwives. Next to the scanning bed was a tatty poster advertising a rally to save the hospital. It was two months old. Next to that was a giant full-colour poster detailing the various stages of foetal development."

Frances wiped a frothy moustache away from her top lip.

"They slap some freezing gel onto your stomach and then begin searching your abdomen with the scanner. The scanner monitor was facing us directly and the first thing the midwife came across was my bloated bladder, which I was quite pleased with. They then moved the scanner around to my womb."

Frances sipped a mouthful of hot coffee, which was fractionally cooled by one of her tears falling into it.

"All I remember now is the blackness of it. The monitor was just black."

Frances took another sip of coffee and then another.

"Both midwives went totally silent. The older of the two asked the other to fetch a consultant and she disappeared in seconds. The silent time that Fergal, the midwife, the scanner and me waited must have only been seconds, but it felt like hours."

"Oh, Frances, did you lose the baby?"

"No. There was no baby there in the first place. Well, there were a few cells in the first few weeks. But I had a blighted ovum, which meant that even though my placenta was growing, there was no baby there for it to grow for. I suppose they needed the scanning room for all the appointments so myself and Fergal were taken back through the main waiting-room and through to a smaller room to discuss what was going to happen. The most vivid memory I have is walking through that room past all those pregnant women and their proud partners and the tears gushing from me."

Rose leant forward and hugged her friend. Frances gave into the hug completely and stifled her sobs in the warm embrace.

"You lost a baby, Frances. You need to mourn that loss."

"No, I lost a dream. There was no baby, but I lost the dream of one."

"You mustn't have wanted to tell anyone that you were pregnant, because deep down, you knew that something was wrong."

"Maybe."

"But, Frances, you can't go through something like that and not share it. The days when a woman just got on with these things are long gone. That's the days belonging to our mothers' generation. Sure my Ma still calls a miscarriage, 'a miss'. Why in God's name would anybody want to abbreviate such a word? So you and Fergal went through this all by yourselves?"

Rose could feel Frances's body tighten in her embrace. The sobbing stopped and the anger and frustration manifested itself through her muscles and joints.

"No, I went through it by myself. There was no Fergal to go through it with."

"He wasn't there to help you?"

"He was there in body all right. But that's the whole problem you see. I doubt that he ever actually cared for that baby, or for me come to think of it."

The anger Frances felt had suffocated the tears and she was now able to recompose herself. Rose kept her arm by Frances's side for her to lean against, but her friend chose not to accept the support. Frances's face betrayed a red splash of blotches and a dripping nose, so easily ignored by the movies. Rose began to gently wipe Frances's face for her with a soft napkin, but her friend quickly snatched it away and used it to violently blow her nose.

"Frances, how can you just brush Fergal away like that?"

"Because Fergal cried when his pet hamster died. He sobbed when Lassie came home and he even shed a tear when he accidentally reversed into a lamppost on the day he got his new car."

"And? So what?"

"After all we've been through, Fergal hasn't cried once. My baby was due today, the 1st of July, and during the six months since this happened, he hasn't even wiped his eye. He just continues as if nothing has happened. You see, Rose, I haven't just lost a dream; I've lost a husband. And I don't think I want to find him again."

Chapter 31

When the heavy sobbing had calmed, Fergal began to control his breathing again. Only then did he slowly take his head out of his hands. They were drenched in tears and mucus and his cheeks were imprinted on his palm where they had been so tightly held. Fergal thought that his tears would have dried up by now, but even after all these months, they came upon him in convulsions. He wasn't sure what time Frances would be home today, but he was sure that she mustn't see him like this. He was supposed to be the rock. Fergal opened out the letter and read it for the second time:

Dear Mrs Coyle,

Congratulations! Our records show us that your baby is due about now. We want to take this opportunity to wish you well and tell you something about the healthcare support that is available to you.

The letter progressed to detail a series of support services including health checks and local mother-and-toddler groups.

We also have a recently formed breast feeding support group in your borough, which we are sure will be of benefit.

Fergal stopped reading and tore the letter into pieces. He then methodically took each piece and shredded it further into even tinier fragments. The paper became congealed by the fluid mixture in Fergal's hands and formed a tight ball. He threw it up and caught it in the same hand a few times, before rushing back down the stairs and telephoning the regional health trust.

"I don't care if it's a Sunday. Get me somebody in authority."

The receptionist hadn't quite muffled her receiver and after Fergal had explained the letter to her, Fergal could hear her panicked voice on the other end. A few minutes later a man's voice spoke on the other end.

"Mr Coyle. The receptionist has explained to me what has happened. I can only apologise for what is a system error. Your wife's name is still on our files and, unfortunately, at present we don't have the system to match the information from the maternity hospitals with our own services."

"Can you possibly imagine what would have happened if my wife, rather than myself, had read this letter. Do you know what damage it would have caused? She's only just getting over the miscarriage. She doesn't want to be reminded of it all over again!"

"I do sympathise, Mr Coyle. Please accept my apologies. As soon as the team is back in the office tomorrow, I'll make sure that our records on your wife are updated."

"It's not just my wife you should be thinking about. You should get your team in tomorrow and make sure that all your records are accurate."

"You're absolutely right, Mr Coyle. We'll do that."

Fergal could sense an artificial appeasement and he began to question the seniority of the person at the other end of the line.

"I will take this further personally tomorrow. Goodbye."

Fergal slammed the receiver down. He'd always wanted to, but up until now had never really had call to do so.

Back upstairs, in his study, he picked up the matted paper ball and threw it against the wall. It bounced off a shelf and landed at the foot of his chrome storage cabinet, beside Frances's bottom drawer. Fergal had only cleared a few of her stray belongings into it yesterday morning. He bent down on crouched knees and opened it up. The top was crammed with scraps of paper, old trophies and the white porcelain doll's head that he had picked up yesterday. The next layer was a selection of health and beauty magazines. Underneath these he found a 'baby's names' book, very used, with bent-over corners on every other page. Underneath this was a dozen or so plastic pregnancy tests, with the one partially wrapped in cotton wool. This was the only one with two pink rings marked. He grasped the positive tester in his fist and took it back over to his desk.

Holding the tester brought back instant memories of the day he was first shown it but, as quickly as these images came back to him, they disappeared and he remembered the day he found Frances in the bath. This was a few days after she had come out of hospital having had a D and C or 'evacuation' as the consultant called it. 'Evacuation', what kind of word is that anyway? You evacuate your bowels after a hot curry, not a baby. Frances must have been in the bath for hours, as it was ice cold. Her naked body was pure white and her lips blue. After Fergal had managed to warm her up again, they had sat on the bottom step of the stairs for two hours, just holding each other. When eventually he had managed to coax Frances into sharing how she was feeling, her first descriptions had been that of anger and a feeling of pent-up aggression. She wanted to smash something. Fergal had led her by the hand out into the garden and then brought out a box containing half a dozen eggs. As she threw the eggs one by one at the brick wall and saw the yellow yolks ooze along the lines of cement, the significance of the destroyed embryos was obvious to both of them.

After the egg-throwing incident, Frances retreated into herself. Fergal focused his energies on trying to live life as normal. He tried to create a protected environment for Frances, where she need never think about the baby again. He found this difficult at times and there was many a time on his way home from work he'd find himself in floods of tears in the car. His tears could have been triggered by a pedestrian pushing a pram or an article on the radio. He often had to take the longer route home in order to compose himself before he arrived home and faced Frances.

As he twirled the tester between his fingers, Fergal thought deeply about how their marriage seemed to be faltering at the moment. Emotionally they were miles apart, but he couldn't understand why.

Fergal lifted the framed picture of himself and Brendan from the windowsill. He usually would stare at the figure of Brendan and reminisce about his old fishing friend. This time he looked closely at himself. At eighteen, he had a short close-cropped hairstyle, not that much different from now. Compared to Brendan, who was dressed in the height of fashion for the day, Fergal thought his own appearance quite old-fashioned, even for those days. He was wearing brown canvas trousers and over the top of a tightly pulled brown-leather belt, he could see a round stomach resting.

Brendan was right; there really wasn't much difference between Fergal then and now. He really wasn't the skinny adolescent that he thought he was. Fergal was always slightly heftier than his mates were. The first to be selected for shot putt and the hammer and never for high jump and the sprints. He really didn't like going out when all the riots were happening during Motor Man. He was happiest surrounded by books and comics and proud of his neat and tidy bedroom with its filing system for *The Marvel*, with the cross-reference catalogue he'd invented.

This self-realization was a blow to Fergal, but he didn't know what to do with this newly acquired self-knowledge. If he was the same character that he'd always been, did that make him even sadder than he thought he was?

The midday sun was now blazing down through his window and into his eyes. He reached over to pull the lime-green Roman blind down in order to block out the hot rays. Ursula Richards, Christine Watson and her girls and the mysterious man he had seen earlier were now congregated around Maurice McAllen's front garden. The stranger was carrying a large wooden ladder, which he then stood up against the side of the house. With his boot on the first rung of the ladder, Fergal was engulfed by an instant inner danger signal. What were they doing? Didn't they know that the house belonged to a convicted terrorist? Their neighbour was dangerous and going by his unusual behaviour and late-night mysterious trips, he could still be involved in violence and terror. Fergal raced down his stairs and out through his front door.

"Stop! Stop what you're doing!"

Chapter 32

Sam hauled the wooden ladder onto his left shoulder with one shove and used his right to balance it. The screws on the ladder had turned red hot in the scorching midday sun, instantly turning Sam's naked shoulder pink. But his expression remained steady.

Christine's girls were now exhilarated by the expedition. Ruth had taken a particular shine to Sam and refused to move more than a few steps from his side. Reassured that her twelve-year-old did like the opposite sex after all, Christine did not hold her eldest daughter back. Molly, with a doll under each arm, was much more reticent and stayed close to her mother. The Baby chose to charge around at random, making the most of the freedom to run across the neighbours' carefully manicured lawns.

The group walked back over to Maurice McAllen's house and assembled at the side, just below the open landing window. As he leant the ladder up against the wall, Sam again searched for any last glimmers of reason.

"Now the easiest thing for us to do, would be to call the police. Are you sure you want me to do this?"

Christine looked to Ursula, who had said very little thus far. Ursula was uncharacteristically enjoying the drama and at the same time intrigued by Sam; who he was and how he was dealing with the situation. But the level-headed side of her nature, usually by far the stronger, was telling her to reconsider. Who was Sam? If he wasn't a window cleaner, what was his real job? Was he a stalker? Did he just happen to be in the café yesterday by chance? Or was he following her? In a courtroom, Sam would have been sentenced long ago, but there was something about his manner that was genuine and honest. Ursula was totally intrigued. She was also intrigued by the drama surrounding Maurice. The fact that she was probably the last person to see him yesterday and that had been to have sex, drew her into the mystery further. Her plans for a simple life with no passion or excitement, so carefully crafted during her restless night, were summed up here, in this one decision. If they called the police, Sam would go and she could retreat back into the sanctuary of her home. Then she could stick to her master plan.

Ursula glanced across at Christine. The last thing she wanted to do was side with her. She hadn't forgotten Christine's brazen visit to her house yesterday. Ursula knew that Christine saw her as a rival, which she clearly wasn't. Absolutely no way did she want to be dragged further into the mire. All the arguments favoured backing out of the situation.

"Maybe, we should just phone the police."

Sam was relieved by Ursula's return to reality.

"That's the right decision, Ursula. You don't really know this man. Neither of you."

Ursula blushed. Christine didn't.

Sam shoved his shoulder back under the ladder and began to remove it. The girls' faces betrayed their bitter disappointment.

"Stop! Stop what you're doing!"

Fergal Coyle came running from across the road, startling the posse. His clothes looked slept in, his face smothered in red spots and his hair was squashed flat on the one side.

"What are you doing?"

Sam wondered whether this man hurtling towards them thought there was some kind of burglary going on. He thought, as the stranger here, that he'd better explain himself.

"Christine was worried about your neighbour here – Maurice McAllen. You can see him seated in his front room, but he won't budge. Christine reckons he was like this last night too. The general feeling is that maybe he's passed out with drink."

"But you can't go in there."

"We're not going to."

But Fergal was too hurried to hear Sam's reply.

"Just call the police. Trust me."

Ursula had never seen her neighbour so agitated. The only contact she had with Fergal was the occasional conversation about shrubs and borders. He seemed like a nice sort, a sweet and generally calm person. Sam again tried to reply.

"Don't worry. We've decided to call the police."

But again Fergal rambled on.

"I don't want to go into any details, but this man has a dangerous past."

Now Fergal had the full attention of the assembled group. Even Sam stopped trying to interrupt his ranting.

"You really should call the police. He was involved in something in the past that could very much be still something he's involved in now. I don't know the full details, but I know a young mother and her child were killed as a result."

Ursula felt sick. She immediately thought back to Maurice's peculiar idiosyncrasies; his secrecy, the mysterious trips in the night, the fact that he didn't appear to have a job. The signs were there. He had a life that he didn't want anyone to know about. When she thought back to his handsome strong physique, she recoiled at the memory of his touch.

Sam had given up on trying to converse with the agitated Fergal. He hauled the ladder back down from the wall and pulled a mobile phone from his back pocket. As he waited to find a transmission signal, Ursula looked over at Christine. She had said nothing and her face was pure white. She had pulled her three daughters towards her and was making them feel uncomfortable in her tight grasp.

"Mummy, that's sore." Molly was struggling with her mother's embrace.

"I'm taking the girls back home. I don't want them here."

Ursula was astonished at Christine's transformation. The earlier exuberance and sparkle had faded and her eyes looked heavy and dark. But of course, she's just found out her lover had a dark past and was possibly a child killer. She mustn't have known about Maurice's past. Ursula wanted to remain angry with Christine, but she couldn't stifle the sympathy that she now felt.

Christine pushed her hair tight behind her ears and ran over to pick up her abandoned shoes. She then swept her daughters under the safety of her arms and scurried back home.

Fergal, Sam and Ursula remained by the side of Maurice McAllen's house. The light indicators on Sam's telephone surged up to maximum and a beep signalled its full power. As Sam pressed the first nine on the keypad, a loud slamming of a house door was heard. They all looked across at Christine and her daughters. She hadn't reached her front door yet, but she'd also been alerted by the sound. Seconds later they saw the retreating back of Maurice McAllen as he marched across his lawn and into his car. He looked straight forward, apparently conscious of neither the group at the side of his house, or Christine and her girls. The car engine was started and the wheels screamed as he turned the sharp left onto the road and drove away.

Chapter 33

Rose was stoned. As soon as she breathed in a gulp of fresh air, her head felt like it would explode. Within the confines of the coffee house, she hadn't really felt the full effects of the marijuana, but the combination of ten years' smoking abstinence and the warm air diving into her lungs walloped her off her feet. Frances was transfixed by the dramatic change in her friend's composure. The sudden shift startled her out of her own personal melancholic state and she felt herself fall into the caring role she previously adopted on the team's trips away.

"Can you walk, Rose?"

Frances soon realised she was being optimistic.

"Can you stand even?"

Rose stared her friend straight in the eye and then turned to walk back down the street in the direction of the main shopping area. The sight of a grown woman pretending she was stone-cold sober, but tripping and swaying as she gingerly swaggered, fooled no one. Frances ran after her and supported Rose's flimsy body with her own.

"Rose, we're already over an hour late to meet the girls. Will I see if I can get us a taxi to the Rijksmuseum?"

"No. It's a beautiful day. Let's walk."

Frances was conscious that, as Rose swayed and rocked, she also was sucked into the pendulous motion and one of them looked as spaced out as the other. But for once Frances had given up attempting to blend with the sophisticated crowd and walked confidently as she supported her friend. As they strolled arm in arm, Rose kept pointing out the simplest of objects and insisting they were the most beautiful things in the world.

"Look at the colour of that coat button in the window. So ethereal and translucent. I feel like I could just reach out and dip my finger into its tortoiseshell centre."

"It's a button."

"It's magical."

Frances hadn't solved any of her problems by baring her soul to Rose, but she did feel different. Rose had been right. But the vote was still out on whether this was a good thing.

"Frances, did you ever see anything as delicate and precious as that piece of paper down there?"

A silver foil top discarded from a drinks bottle skipped along the pavement at their feet. The warm currents rising from the air vents lifted it and made it swirl before crashing back down again. A bicycle wheel passed over and flattened it. Its dancing days were over.

"You bastard! Look what you've done!" Rose shouted after the disappearing cyclist. Luckily, with the busy hum of tourists and shoppers on the main street, Rose's voice was lost in the babble. She bent down to pick up the crumpled disc. It took her a few attempts to co-ordinate hand and eye, but once she had it, Rose gave it a healing kiss.

"Can you believe it, Frances? Some people have no respect for art."

Neither did Rose, when they eventually arrived at the foyer of the palace-like Rijksmuseum. The art gallery had a temporary exhibition of contemporary visual art mounted in its huge entrance hall. The thirty-minute journey had been a rollercoaster of moods for Rose and once her exuberance had subsided, paranoia had taken a turn and now she had fallen into nausea. The purple swirls and multi-coloured polka-dots on the walls ahead of them made Rose's head spin even more and, wherever she looked, she was confronted by yet another orange square or a collage of brown hexagonal shapes.

The rest of Frances's team were waiting for them in the foyer. Niamh was the first to spot the swaying figures in the doorway.

"Frances! Rose! We're over here. We'd almost given up on you. Rose, are you all right?"

"It was bothering nobody. And some bloody idiot just squashed it, for no reason at all. It was barbaric. I'm hungry. Anyone any chocolate?"

Rose's ranting had totally confused her friends, but it didn't take Roberta too long to diagnose the symptoms.

"She's stoned. Our Rose has been smoking joints. Some sightseeing trip that was. It's a trip of a different kind they've been on. Frances, you're a dark horse. Is there anything you won't do these days?"

"I wasn't smoking anything. Well, I was, just a wee bit. But it was Rose's idea."

Frances felt like she'd been caught smoking behind the school bike shed. Niamh gave Frances her best teacher-to-pupil scowl.

"Anyways, we're all going to have to hotfoot it now if we're going to make this flight. I'll deal with you two later."

The team suddenly became a jumbled swirl of sports bags and rucksacks as the six women marched out of the gallery. In the rush, they found they were temporarily jammed between the revolving doors, causing a few passing tourists to consider the mass of arms and legs to be a modern art installation.

An hour and a half later, Frances and her team were the last to be seated aboard the BAE 146 to Belfast International Airport. A rapidly sobering Rose greeted her window seat with a welcome sigh and Niamh helped her fasten her seat-belt and even removed her shoes. Cathy-Ann then took the aisle seat next to Niamh. Roberta chose the window seat behind Rose, followed by Orla and then Frances next to the aisle. Niamh hadn't given either Rose or Frances the promised ticking off yet, so Frances was happy to be seated on a separate row.

A great deal had happened to Frances this weekend, most of which was difficult for her to think about. The air stewardess bumped Frances's elbow with the drinks' trolley, breaking her mesmerised trance. Frances accepted a glass of orange juice from the immaculately presented stewardess. Perfectly polished red nails then passed her a tiny packet of peanuts. Frances looked up into the heavy mascara'd eyes of the stewardess and her first thoughts were 'Who'd have time to go to all that bother? Frances surprised herself. Ordinarily she would feel deep envy for the glamorous life of anyone around her, other than herself. But this time she didn't. In the past twelve hours she'd not only been through the emotional mill of discussing her miscarriage, but also half of Amsterdam had seen her buck-naked. The image she had of herself, and of other people, suddenly didn't seem to matter.

The stewardess moved further up the cabin and Frances caught sight of her lily-white neck when her heavily made-up face leaned forward to hear a quietly spoken passenger's order. In the row in front Niamh stood up and, with her huge handbag, awkwardly squeezed past the drinks' trolley and along towards the toilet. Everyone on Frances's team, except Orla and herself, had dozed off.

"Well, Frances, are you glad you came with us?"

"I don't know. Ask me tomorrow."

"You certainly gave us a good laugh."

"Aye, but was it at me or with me?"

"Good question."

Orla sat rotating her taut ankles and flexing her chiselled calves. She didn't want to miss an exercise opportunity.

"One thing's for sure, Frances. I've made my own mind up about a few things this weekend. I'm sick of hanging around waiting for that fella of mine to do the honorable thing."

"Good for you, Orla."

"If Roger won't tell that wife of his what's been going on these past years, I will. It's time Ursula Keane and myself met face to face."

Buoyed by her decision, Orla jumped out of her seat, gently jogged down to the far end of the aeroplane and began stretching her shoulders and biceps against the

277

emergency exit. Luckily Orla didn't look back, otherwise, she would have seen Frances with her mouth wide open and unable to blink. Frances was angry with herself. Why hadn't she told Orla, when she first heard the name Roger Keane, that she was a neighbour of his wife, or rather ex-wife? She hadn't confessed at the time, because she was afraid of hurting her friend. Not that there was much to choose between the hurt of thinking your lover of four years can't leave his wife, and knowing that your lover of four years got divorced over a year ago and hadn't told you. What kind of man was this Roger Keane anyway? What must it have been like to have been married to him? Again Frances noticed a change in her own perceptions and reactions. Any chance meetings she had with Ursula on the street, or in the local shop, she always came away feeling dowdy and dull. But, even with all her glamour, Ursula too had her problems. These racing thoughts dragged Frances back to the difficulties she had to face in her own home when she got back. Could she face Fergal's cheerfulness today of all days? No.

"Penny for them?"

Niamh had returned from the toilet and squeezed past Frances to take Orla's vacant seat. She was dressed back in her schoolteacher conservative clothes, with her make-up reapplied in softer, paler tones. Her ebony hair with its soft perm was rolled tightly into a neat bun, held in place by two silver grips decorated with sapphire butterflies.

"You'd need more than a penny, Niamh."

"Let me guess?"

"You haven't a hope in hell."

"You're wondering how you can get through the day. How you can cope with tomorrow and all the tomorrows to come."

278

Frances lifted her eyes from the Marlborough Man on page four of the in-flight magazine and looked straight at Niamh. The return gaze was that of a friend, a teammate, a teacher and most of all a mother. When Niamh went anywhere with her team, once the handbag was dragged to the toilets, she became a single woman out to have a good time. They all forgot what a fantastic mother she actually was, with two grown-up sons, who would do any parent proud. Frances and Niamh were the same age, but right now, Frances would have given anything to have been her daughter.

"How do you know?"

"Rose let a few things slip before take-off, about three minutes in fact before plunging into unconsciousness."

Niamh gave her friend a gentle maternal scowl of the 'don't think I haven't forgotten to discipline you' kind. Which warmed Frances even more.

"Before my boys, I lost a baby girl at eighteen weeks. I went into premature labour and there was nothing anybody could do."

"I'm so sorry, Niamh. I didn't know."

"Oh, it was long before I started hanging out with you guys. I was in bits for a long time afterwards."

"I know you're going to try and cheer me up by saying you're over it now."

"No, I'm not."

Niamh's gentle gaze stiffened and she crossed her arms tightly across her stomach.

"You never 'get over it', as you put it. But you learn a great deal and it is these experiences in life that mould you and strengthen you. I thought I was the only person in the whole world to have suffered what I suffered and I kept the entire thing a complete secret. But after a while, I decided it wasn't fair on the people I cared about to hide such an important part of my life. You'd share with your family and friends what you got up to on holiday, or what new blouse you bought, so why not share something that was making me feel miserable and alone?"

"And did that help you get over it?"

Niamh tightened her arms even further and pulled her shoulders tight against the seat.

"No, Frances, it didn't. But what it did show me is how many other women out there have been through this. There was almost this secret club, which you needed to lose a baby to join. I think it's time we expanded the membership. It shouldn't be a secret. You feel shit. Let everyone know."

"I don't think I'm ready to stand up and announce 'I'm Frances Coyle. I've had a miscarriage."

"It's not Alcoholics Anonymous. It's just being honest with people who are important. And that includes yourself."

"Will I get over it then?"

"Frances if you say that one more time I'm going to flatten you. You don't get over something like this. But the future will get brighter. I promise you. When I held my two boys in my arms for the very first time and the tears of joy were tripping me, I didn't think, 'I'm over it'."

A gentle smile illuminated Niamh's serious expression and the arms across her stomach relaxed.

"I thought, 'I'm the luckiest person alive'."

They smiled at each other. The society had gained a new member.

"Frances, producing life is like life itself; it's like standing up in a hammock."

"Cabin crew, ten minutes to landing."

The pilot's announcement sounded more Arabic than English, over the muffled interference on the intercom.

"Passengers, please return to your seats and fasten your seatbelts. Due to low cloud cover, we may experience some turbulence as we descend. Please remain seated."

Orla quickly returned to her seat in the fastest sprint she'd done in ages. As hers was taken, she lunged into Niamh's vacant one in the row in front. The aeroplane bumped and rolled as it dived in and out of thick cloud. The air stewardess stumbled up the aisle as she feverishly tried to return the drinks trolley to the galley. A chorus of 'ouch' and 'watch it' followed as shoulders and heads were bashed by the silver trolley, looking way too heavy for its four tiny black castors.

The passengers were divided into those who closed their eyes and bit their lips, to those who craned their necks to watch the aeroplane wings rise and dip above and below the horizon line. Frances alone stared ahead at the upturned table and the tiny button for hanging jackets directly in front of her. As the aeroplane continued to dip and swerve, Frances thought of Fergal. Did she still love him? Did she want him supporting her in the hammock, leaving his crumbs? Was her husband's balance good enough?

The grating sound of the landing gear as it hit the tarmac was greeted with a rapturous applause. The intercom cackle returned again, accompanied by the Arabic tones of the pilot.

"Yahoo! We made it!"

Chapter 34

It took the exhaust fumes from Maurice McAllen's retreating car a good few minutes to disperse, before Fergal could speak. Ursula and her male companion were also speechless. Christine Watson, likewise, stared after the rapidly disappearing car, before disappearing herself through her front door. Ursula's friend was the first to break the silence.

"So, he's alive after all."

"Is that a good thing?"

Fergal was less charitable.

"I don't know if we want a fella like that living next door to us. Who are you anyway? Sorry, that sounds rude. I didn't mean it that way. I also didn't mean to include you in the same breath as yer man. It just came out that way . . ."

Sam was quick to offer an olive branch as Fergal vigorously dug a deep hole for himself.

"It's OK. I'm Sam. I was cleaning Ursula's windows when your neighbour Christine came over, worried about Mr McAllen."

"Nice to meet you. I'm Fergal. I live across the road. If you're looking for any more business, the fella I have at the minute doesn't do the corners. I'm looking for a new window cleaner."

Fergal was surprised at how long it took Sam to respond. In the end, he didn't. Ursula spoke for him.

"He only cleans mine."

Sam and Ursula gave each other a look that made Fergal feel like a nun in a brothel. But Ursula was the first to break the stare and turn again to face Fergal. Maybe Fergal hadn't lost the charm after all. But then, did he have it in the first place? Before he could inspect his navel any further, Ursula leant towards him and placed her soft hand on his arm.

"But you're right, Fergal. Do we want somebody like this living next door? What do you know about him?"

Fergal suddenly felt empowered by the threads of information he had that nobody else knew. He wasn't going to give the story away too easily. After all, the telling of the story was often better than the story itself.

"Let's put it this way. I believe there's a connection between our man at Number 2 and the Loyalist paramilitaries. That's all I can say."

"Why?"

Sam's direct response slightly took Fergal off guard. He turned his head left and then right, as if searching for eavesdroppers, before whispering, "He was also a member of the RUC."

"And you know this for fact?"

Sam wasn't playing the game and Fergal was starting to resent this.

"As much as a newspaper article about a police officer on

283

trial for collusion, the name Maurice McAllen, and a pretty accurate description from an eyewitness."

Brendan hadn't really been an eyewitness as such. Well, not at all. But Fergal allowed himself this slight embellishment.

"So, Fergal, it was in the newspaper, was it?"

"In black and white."

Sam and Ursula again looked at each other, and Fergal again was instantly envious. Ursula was looking to her window cleaner for guidance. How could she, with Fergal standing there, much more senior and . . . a new account executive for Belfast's busiest building society to boot. No mean feat.

"It's all true."

This time, as Fergal emphasised his point, Ursula didn't look at him at all. This was getting beyond a joke. Even when she then started speaking, she didn't look in Fergal's direction once.

"We need to find out a bit more, Sam. Don't we?"

"I'm with you, Ursula. Look, the Central Library is having a special open day in Belfast. Why don't I go down to Belfast and have a look through their old newspaper copies? They're all kept on microfiche."

"I'll drive you."

Hang on a minute. This fella from out of nowhere was going to sweep off with Ursula and steal Fergal's thunder. He'll probably uncover the whole ghastly story and become the hero of the development. They'll probably name the next cul-de-sac they build after him.

"I'd better come too then. I can't quite remember the year, or the paper I saw the article in. It'll come to me on the way. Anyway, three heads are better than two."

Fergal instantly sensed the disappointment on both

Ursula's and Sam's faces. They were definitely in favour of two heads. But Fergal had already weighed up the alternative of staying at home and waiting for Frances. He wasn't ready to face her yet and the more he did to forget what day it was, the better.

Ursula either had a change of heart or was just being polite, but she again grabbed hold of Fergal's arm and stared back into his eyes.

"Thanks, Fergal. That would be a good help."

Of course she wasn't just being polite. Ursula ran back into her own house and grabbed her bag and car keys. Fergal and Sam sauntered back over to her silver Ford Puma parked in her driveway. The saunter then turned into a race as both men realised, at the same time, that there was only one seat going spare in the front of the car. Fergal was pleased with his leap over a fuchsia border, which landed him directly at the door of the front passenger seat. Sam may have been younger and more athletically built, but Fergal still had all the moves.

"So, are you interested in any more window-cleaning business?"

Fergal also didn't like to miss an opportunity.

Again, Ursula stopped Sam from responding, this time by arriving back with her car keys held aloft.

"Sorry. I thought I'd lost them. Are we ready to go?"

Both men nodded and then gazed at Ursula's face as she crouched into the car. Not only had she collected her keys, Ursula had also combed her hair and applied a thin coat of make-up. Fergal couldn't work out whether it was eye-shadow, or lipstick or powder. But whatever she had done, a few splashes of colour had enhanced her natural beauty considerably. Fergal was still staring at her, trying to work out how she had achieved this transformation when he was seated in the car. Ursula caught him staring and blushed slightly. Fergal saw her catch Sam's attention too through the rear view mirror. She blushed considerably more.

The journey to Belfast lasted less than half an hour. A few heavy-looking clouds had started to congregate and the baking afternoon sun was intermittently cooled. The occasional blast through the clouds of strong sunlight forced Fergal to pull down his sun visor. But, as he did so, the small compact mirror on it only served to magnify the pulsating red spots left on his face from the midges earlier. The late Sunday afternoon traffic was light and the city centre was deserted. Fergal was satisfied with Sam's silence, as Ursula and he chatted easily about their houses and the problems they both shared with dodgy plumbing and noisy valves.

Once they arrived at the library, parking was not a problem. The assorted offices, straddled around the mammoth Victorian municipal building of the library, were empty. By chance, Fergal remembered the date of the newspaper cutting he had seen, just as they were walking up the main steps to the library.

Microfiche tapes of the *Belfast Telegraph* for the second half of 1994 were requested from a funky-looking librarian. She guided them along a darkly lit corridor into a small room containing a microfiche projector, a wonky table and a few mismatched chairs.

"I'll be back in a few mo's."

When she said this, she blew a bubble with her chewing-gum, noisily popped it and smiled a heavily braced smile at Sam as she closed the door behind her.

Ursula had also noticed the smile and turned her attention to Fergal. He didn't quite fancy being the reserve, but not enough to turn down the opportunity to glimpse Ursula's delicately laced bra as she leant forward.

The librarian's 'mo' turned out to be literally only one minute. She was slightly out of breath and obviously had pulled out all the stops on this one.

"Here's July to August 1994. I'll have to get back to you guys with the other months."

Another pop of her bubble gum and she disappeared again. Sam set up the machine and the July tape, like he was very familiar with this kind of technology. In less than thirty seconds, the front page of the July 1st edition was staring down at them from the screen. Meticulously they scrolled down the pages, looking for the slightest reference. But there was nothing. July 2nd and 3rd were equally meticulously scrutinised, but again there were no references to a Maurice McAllen. The following weeks' editions were followed in less detail and by the last week in July, only the first six pages of each day were given attention.

The August copies had been stored the wrong way round and began with the last page – sports. The headline was 'Keane Jumps for Silver'. A very handsome show jumper was photographed in the centre of the page, with his neck surrounded by gold and silver medals. On one side was a beautiful stallion adorned with an assortment of rosettes. On his other side was his wife, plainly dressed in a simple straight black dress and black wide-brimmed hat. Her hair was also jet black, the colour of the stallion's mane. Sam recognised the figure instantly.

"Is that you, Ursula?"

"Black was the new black in those days."

"You look so different. I didn't know you were married to *the* Roger Keane.

"We're all full of secrets, aren't we?"

Fergal thought Ursula's response was a bit gruff for such an innocent comment. He hadn't recognised her at all with the black hair, and being her neighbour, he knew her a lot better than Sam. For the first time that afternoon, Fergal found himself sympathising with the young lad. He wasn't really a bad sort. All three stared at the photograph for a moment. In the background were a few out-of-focus supporters. The one on the far right-hand side was noticeable, because she was built like a tank and her broad shoulders and flexed biceps mirrored those of the horse itself.

"Jesus, look at yer woman! You wouldn't want to bump into her in a dark alley."

Fergal's subtlety was not appreciated by the other two. Another out-of-focus figure on the left-hand side of the photograph was also noticeable as she wore a peculiar over-the-top veiled hat, that would have looked more at place on Ladies' Day at Ascot. Ursula touched the woman's veiled face and wiped the screen in a useless attempt to re-focus the figure.

"Do you know when you recognise something about someone, but you don't know where from?"

Ursula again wiped the screen and twiddled with the focussing button. But what they had in front of them was the best they were going to get.

"No matter. Let's find our villain."

Sam quickly scanned to the main news items on the

front pages. And there it was, in the same edition as Ursula's husband celebrating yet another victory, the article on Maurice McAllen. It was a copy of the very same edition Fergal had first discovered in the Ponderosa. In the far bottom right-hand corner of page seven was a round-up of the daily courtroom dramas. As Ursula and Sam read through the first few paragraphs, Fergal pointed to the screen, straight at the article he remembered, and read aloud: -

"The trial began today of RUC Officer arrested on charges of collusion with Loyalist paramilitaries. Constable Maurice McAllen faces five counts of bribery and corruption. The trial continues."

Sam promptly scanned the copy from the 2nd of August. He found what he was looking for, this time on page five.

"Day two of the trial of the RUC officer arrested on charges of collusion with Loyalist paramilitaries continued today. Security chiefs are linking the death of a mother and her two small children to that of information passed on by Officer Maurice McAllen to Loyalist terrorist organisations. Mr McAllen was arrested when officers raided a house off the Lisburn Road as part of a co-ordinated raid across Belfast. Case continues tomorrow."

The copy from August 3rd was vigorously scanned and, this time on page three, Sam discovered a quarter-page article covering the case. Heading the piece was a photograph of the deceased mother and two small toddlers. Fergal recognised the Portstewart promenade where they were sitting eating their ice creams. Fergal took his turn to read the article aloud.

"Police Deny Paramilitary Collusion. A senior security

source today denied that the RUC had any involvement with allegations of exchanging information with Loyalist paramilitaries. 'This is not to say Mr McAllen isn't involved, but is acting as an individual'. This statement follows growing concern as the trial of RUC Officer Maurice McAllen enters its third day at Belfast Crown Court. The accused is due to take to the stand tomorrow."

There then followed a couple of paragraphs discussing the family background of the young mother and her children. Neither Fergal, Sam nor Ursula could bear to read on. Before scanning for the 4th August, Sam turned to Ursula, who now had buried her head in her hands.

"Ursula, we've still no hard evidence that the accused is the Maurice McAllen that lives next door to you."

Sam looked to Fergal for back-up. But there was none available and he was forced to continue himself. "McAllen is a common enough name. Let's not make any rash judgements just yet. Right, Fergal?"

"Sure."

Fergal really wasn't that convinced – after all, Brendan's description had been pretty spot-on. But Ursula seemed to be taking it all particularly badly. Maybe they shouldn't jump to any conclusions. With far less speed, Sam continued to scan the 4th August edition. Pages seven to three contained little of interest, apart from a quarter-page advertisement for conservatories, which caught Fergal's eye. The last to be scanned was the front page. All three read the headline.

"Are These the Eyes of Evil?"

Below the bold caption was a head-on photograph of the accused, Maurice McAllen. The photograph was in full colour, illuminated by the subject's vibrant thick gold hair and cobalt-blue eyes. Ursula jumped to her feet and pushed out the door. Both men waited a fraction of a second before following after her.

Ursula was found leaning against the back of her car on the main street. Fergal could see that she was desperately trying to hold back tears, which she achieved at the expense of a quivering lip and gentle, involuntary sobbing sounds. Fergal was the first to reach her and put his arm around her shoulders. Sam was a few paces behind, as he hadn't managed to frog-jump the exit barrier as effectively as Fergal. As soon as Fergal touched Ursula's shoulder another delicate sob escaped. He was surprised at how rigid Ursula felt in his arm.

"Ursula, don't worry. I know he lives right next door to you, but all of us in the cul-de-sac are involved in this."

Fergal felt that maybe Ursula was taking the whole drama a little too personally. But she had no reason to.

"Come on home. We'll work something out together. Let me drive."

Ursula was grateful for Fergal's offer.

"Thank you, Fergal. I really don't feel up to driving back."

"No problem. Just sit there and relax."

"In fact, if you don't mind, I'll sit at the back, where I can stretch out that bit more."

Ursula subsequently jumped into the back, alongside Sam.

One minute Fergal was the chief comforter and now he was the taxi-driver. He wasn't the least bit pleased. As he pulled the car away, he re-positioned his rear-view mirror so that he could see both his passengers. Ursula was staring out of the window and Sam was looking directly at the back of her head. It had better stay like that, Fergal thought to himself.

It was now early evening and while Fergal, Sam and Ursula had been buried in the library, a heavy build-up of cloud had formed. The cloud served as a blanket for holding in the heat from the baking hot day and the air felt sticky and warm. Fergal decided to break the deadlock of silence.

"Supposed to be a lunar eclipse tonight. Doesn't look like we'll get much chance to see anything though."

As soon as he had spoken, Fergal felt like he was in fact a taxi-driver. He could seal it now with 'Going anywhere nice, love' and he'd get his licence. Luckily neither Ursula nor Sam appeared to hear him.

Fergal was now on the outskirts of Belfast, about to turn onto the Sydenham bypass, in the direction of Bangor. The traffic lights turned red at the junction and he cautiously decreased his speed. It was a dual carriageway and on the lane outside Fergal he heard the screech of wheels as a car was forced to push heavily on its brakes. The screech stopped and the speeding car pulled up alongside Ursula's car. Fergal looked sideways with the intention of giving the reckless driver a punishing wag of his finger.

"Jesus, it's yer man. It's him. The Lawnmower Man."

Maurice McAllen hadn't noticed the open-mouthed audience in the lane beside him. His focus was very definitely on the road stretching before him. His usual composure and large stature appeared to have diminished and Fergal was surprised at how insignificant and small he now appeared. Maurice sat motionless, just staring and willing the traffic-light to change. Which it did. As the lights changed from amber to red, Maurice's car pulled away with a mighty roar.

Fergal was now shaking. But before he knew what he was

doing, he had his foot pressed firmly on the accelerator and was chasing after the red Golf GTI.

"What are you doing?"

"Look, Sam, if we want to get this fella out of the development, we're going to need some hard evidence. I say we follow him for a wee while."

"Fergal, if that guy is who we think he is, I don't think we should be harassing him."

"There's no 'if' about it," said Fergal.

Ursula gave a painful shriek.

"Don't worry, Ursula. I'll keep a safe distance. I've watched enough police movies to know what to do."

Fergal thought for a moment that he'd caught his two passengers rolling their eyes in disapproval but then, at the speed he was now going, he couldn't be sure what he saw. The red Golf continued in its direction towards Bangor. Luckily the traffic lights remained green and there was no need for either the pursuer or the pursued to slow down.

"Maybe he's on a rendezvous with fellow bent cops, or maybe meeting up with some of the thugs. I'll keep my distance. We'll call the police and that'll be it. Sorted."

But Fergal became increasingly disappointed when Maurice's route became all too familiar to him. This was verified when he took the expected right turn into the Ashbury development and slowly pulled up in his own driveway. As promised, Fergal cautiously kept his distance and pulled into Ursula's driveway five minutes later.

Fergal's house looked as empty as before and right now he couldn't bear to think of himself in there alone, again.

"Why don't you'se come on in for a cuppa? Calm the old nerves."

Fergal was pleased with Ursula's acceptance. Not so much with Sam's. Once back inside, Fergal busied himself in the kitchen, calling out once in a while. 'Who's for sugar?', 'Milk?' and 'Sorry, I've nothing nice to go with it'. The kettle noisily boiled, but Fergal was still able to secretly listen in on the conversation in his living-room.

"Are you OK now, Ursula?"

"I'm not sure. Seeing a picture of my ex didn't exactly lift my spirits either."

"He was a terrific showjumper."

"I know."

"Maybe not such a terrific husband?"

Fergal caught a glimpse of the couple through the crack in the door. Both looked like some boundary had been overstepped. Serves the horny wee sod a lesson, thought Fergal.

"I think that maybe I wasn't such a terrific wife."

"I find that impossible to imagine."

"Believe me, Sam, there's things about me that you wouldn't like. No man would."

"But we're all full of secrets. Aren't we?"

Fergal put a stop to the conversation by bustling in with two mugs of coffee and a mug of tea for himself. Ursula and Sam had seated themselves on the sofa, with their knees a hair's-breadth away from touching. Sam had moved his long curly fringe away from his face and, for the first time, Fergal could see the full round shape of his face. Fergal, still holding the handle, passed the hot cup to Sam, who was forced to hold on to the piping hot enamel. The quick move to pass the cup to his left hand forced Sam to jerk and the fringe fell back into his eyes. Fergal gave Ursula the handle to hold on her cup.

The sound of slurping, mainly from Fergal, filled the silence. Fergal was pleased at himself for leaving the living-room reasonably tidy. There were a few old newspapers and empty tea-mugs strewn across the floor, but that was all. In the far corner of the room he could see the flashing light on the top of his answerphone.

"Do you mind if I get this message? It might be from Frances. I'm expecting her back from Amsterdam any minute now."

"Not at all."

Fergal carried his hot cup of tea over to the corner table and rested it beside the answer machine. He then pressed the message button.

"Beep. It's me, Eilish. Just checking you got back from Derry OK. You are OK, aren't you? Ring me . . . Beep."

"That's my sister. You know what sisters are like."

Sam and Ursula were trying to be polite and show that they hadn't been listening.

"Right. Your sister."

The beep for the next message then followed.

"Beep . . . Hi, mucker, it's me, Brendan. Sorry for legging it like that. Couldn't afford to get caught again. I'm phoning from some pub in the middle of Donegal. Oops, my ten pence is nearly up. Hope you got off all right. No prison sentence –"

The call went dead as Brendan's time ran out. Fergal knew that the message sounded worse than it was and quickly looked across at Sam and Ursula to reassure them. But they were busy looking towards the door leading to the stairs. Fergal followed their gaze, which led directly to Frances.

"Frances, honey, you're back."

"He hopes you got off what, Fergal?"

Frances's stern expression was an exact replica of that he had seen just before she left for Amsterdam. Nothing had changed then. It hadn't done her, or them, any good. Her appearance was slightly different, he had to give her that. But, in the same way he didn't know how Ursula had managed to transform herself with a few blobs of makeup, he couldn't quite work out what was different about his wife.

Fergal tried to come up with a snappy answer, that wouldn't make him look a total fool in front of Frances and his visitors. Before he could answer, the answerphone beeped again for the final message.

"Beep . . . Frances, *goedemiddag*. It's Klaus here. Hope you don't mind me calling you at home, but Roberta from your team gave me your number. It's just I need your address. I want to know where I can return your trousers . . ."

Frances winced slightly.

" . . . your blouse, shoes and . . ."

This time there was no doubt that Frances winced.

" . . . your bra and pants. I'll try and catch you later. Bye. Oh, by the way, we won. Bye again."

Chapter 35

"But, Mummy."

"No buts. We're going to see your grandma and that's it."

"But what about our adventure?"

"You've all had enough adventure today."

"But . . ."

"Next one to say 'but' will know all about it."

Christine bundled her three unenthusiastic daughters into the family Espace. As she secured the wriggling Baby into her car seat, she could hear the ringing sound of her telephone. Christine waited a brief moment, deciding whether or not to answer it.

"Mummy, the phone."

Rushing back into the house, Christine was confident that the caller would hang up but, as she picked up the receiver, she heard the familiar sound of her husband's voice.

"Hi, Christine."

"Alex, we're just on our way out."

"Sorry about all this. We've had a few bad road accidents and a family's just come in with a whole heap of gunshot wounds. Everyone's leave has been suspended."

"When will you be home?"

"I'll try and get back in time to see the blood moon. Keep the girls up for me."

"We're just off to visit my mother. They'll probably be wrecked by the time we get back. It'll be hard to keep them awake."

"Please, Christine. I haven't seen them all weekend."

There was a brief pause in which Christine had a premonition that her husband was going to add 'I miss them and I miss you too'. But he didn't.

"How's the lawn holding up with all that sun today?"

"Fine."

"After I've defrosted the freezer tonight, I'm going to check the internet for the best way to take care of the grass during a heat wave."

"Fine."

"Must go. My beeper's off again. See you all tonight."

The telephone receiver was slowly replaced and Christine strolled back over to the car. Before starting the ignition, she checked herself in the rear-view mirror. She had needed more hair-pins than usual to pull her independent curls back to their usual controlled position and she had buttoned her blouse all the way up to her neck. That morning she had applied a thin coat of blackcurrant-tinged lipstick, but all that remained now was a faint pencil-line around her lips.

Christine started the engine and pulled out of her driveway. As she did so, she saw the retreating shape of Ursula's car turning into the main road. She thought she could make out three figures inside the car. But, by the time Christine had changed to second gear, Ursula's car had disappeared.

Before turning her own car into the main road, Christine checked her rear-view mirror before indicating. As she did so, she caught sight of The Baby licking her fingers and spreading the frothy saliva up and down the window. Ruth and Molly were continuing a heated debate, obviously started earlier in the day.

"They're just like us, Molly."

"No, they're not."

"Who says they're not?"

"Me."

"So, what are they like then, smarty-pants?"

"They're smelly and eat rats."

"Molly, that's boys you're thinking of, not Catholics."

Christine's gear change went into second rather than fourth. Her eldest daughter was still showing evidence of contempt for the opposite sex and her middle child was a bigot.

"Molly, who told you that?"

"Nobody. They're not like us, are they, Mummy?"

"Mr and Mrs Coyle at Number 2 are Catholics. Are they smelly?"

"No."

"Have you ever seen them eat rats?"

"No. But I've seen the man eat a donut in one go."

Christine decided it was time her girls got involved in more integrated activities.

"Who fancies having a go at Irish dancing next school term? Molly?"

"Yes, me. What is it?"

Ruth rushed in with her own answer.

"It's like *Riverdance*. And *Lord of the Rings*."

"Mummy?"

"Yes, Molly?"

"Do you have to wear a sparkly thing across your forehead and be really, really suntanned?"

"It's not compulsory."

"Because if you do . . . I'd like to try it. Can I?"

"Mummy?"

"Yes, Ruth?"

"I'll do it if I don't have to wear a girly frock and I can shave my head."

Christine was in no mood to discuss Ruth's ambiguous sexuality this afternoon, so she decided to fall back on an old favourite tool for subduing her girls. She turned on the radio and tuned the station from Radio Four, which her husband always selected, to Radio One. A song from the current record chart came blasting out of the speakers. All three girls sang along with the lyrics, each with their own personal version of the words. Even The Baby had her own interpretation. The sound of three different lyrics, tempos and octaves filled the car.

The journey so far had taken them through Newtownards and down along the Peninsula in the direction of Portaferry. The water in the Lough was a mottled, translucent grey, where the build-up of cloud let the rays of the sun through in occasional bright spurts. Where this light hit the water, there was a vivid white glitter off a breaking wave or a rock. Under Christine's seat, a maraca belonging to The Baby noisily rolled with each turn of the car. This would have driven Alex mad and had he been with them they would have had to stop the car and search for the offending noise long before now. His wife just let it rattle.

This was the first time in years that, rather than it being a duty, Christine actually felt a need to visit her mother. She didn't have anything particular to say or to do, but from the moment that she discovered Maurice McAllen's chequered history she wanted to visit her. This weekend she had been forced to question her own roles as a mother, as a wife and also, for the first time in ages, as a woman. The only thing she was completely sure of was that the balance in her life was distinctly warped. In fact, she had no balance at all. Her relationship with her husband was not only a lie, but had been a lie for many years. As a mother she was slowly discovering a side to herself that was beyond cleaning, cooking and packing school-bags. And her greatest discovery was that of herself as a woman. Maurice had ignited a sensuality long since lying dormant. Rekindling it had led her to feel foolish, envious, spontaneous and now dangerous. After all these years, it had taken a man who had been responsible for the death of a mother and her children to stir Christine's emotions.

"Mummy?"

"Yes, Ruth?"

"What does horny mean?"

"Excuse me?"

"The women in that song were singing 'I'm so horny . . . horny, horny, horny'."

"No, they weren't, Ruth. It was 'I'm bony'," said Molly.

As Ruth and Molly continued their battle over interpretation, The Baby quietly sang "I'm a horsy . . . horsy,

301

horsy, horsy', followed by her own contribution of neighing and horses' hooves galloping.

"Mummy, tell her. It's bony."

"Well, Ruth, pop stars are very skinny these days. Maybe Molly's right."

Christine could almost hear the cogs rotate in her eldest daughter's brain as she tried to calculate if her mother was serious or not. But the debate rapidly evaporated as another familiar song came on the radio and the chorus of three different versions accompanied it.

Further down the road, Christine passed the long grey wall surrounding the grounds of Mount Stewart. The brick wall curved and swooped with the shape of the road, which shape itself was dictated by the contours of the Lough on its other side. The solid wall turning away from the road marked the boundary of the estate. Their journey now took them through the tranquil village of Greyabbey, or 'Grebby' to the locals. A few craft shops were busy selling ice creams and the occasional item of Belleek pottery to American-looking tourists with 35mm cameras and checked trousers.

A few small private houses followed on the outskirts of the village and then the short driveway leading to Christine's mother's residential home. A cream pebbledash exterior only slightly hid the building's nineteenth century turrets and gables. The windows were still leaded and Gothic pillars framed the heavy wooden doorway. Christine parked the car on the gravel driveway, alongside six or seven other parked vehicles. The girls refused to leave their seats, until the tune they had been singing along to had finished. Christine humoured them slightly, as she knew how much they didn't like visiting the home. But the second the song had finished, she yanked them out alongside her on the driveway.

As their mother repositioned one of the stray pins in her hair, Ruth and Molly followed suit by trying to constrain their own rebellious red curls with dabs of saliva. Even The Baby had a go, and wiped her tiny wet hand across her auburn fringe, down her nose and across her chin.

Christine and her daughters sauntered across the gravel in the direction of the Gothic doorway. But the sound of voices and teacups could be clearly heard from the back of the building.

"Girls, it sounds like they're all out the back. Now I want you all to be on your best behavior. Remember, Molly, it's rude to mention any unpleasant smells and, Ruth, its ruder still to ask if old people still have sex."

"The Baby had better not stick her finger in Grandma's eyes either."

"She's only two, Molly, so we'll give her a bit more slack."

A row of grey cement slabs ran alongside the old building and brought Christine and her girls to the large rectangle of lawn at the back. An assortment of high-backed chairs and footstools are strewn along the lawn and in the centre was a tea-trolley filled with teapots, cups and saucers and a large plate of plain biscuits.

Assembled were residents and visitors, with uniformed staff flitting between them with offers of coffee and tea. Christine's mother was sitting in the far corner of the lawn, facing out to a small orchard. She spotted her daughter and granddaughters as soon as they turned the corner of the building and began conversing with them immediately.

"Christine, aren't the trees lovely? It reminds me of ours back home."

Christine's family garden had been entirely concreted, as her mother didn't have the time for gardening. Other than a few weeds peeping through cement cracks, there was never anything growing in their backyard.

"And look at those apples! I could make a demon apple crumble with those."

She had also never had the time to bake and the only dessert her daughter could remember was tinned peaches and ice cream. Christine's girls ran over and gave their grandmother a warm hug. Christine knew how difficult that was for them and felt an inner glow of pride. The moment the hugs were finished, they all ran off into the orchard and joined other visiting grandchildren in a search for fallen fruit.

"How are you keeping, Mummy? We managed to make it after all."

"Sure, I've been expecting you. Got my hair done especially."

The hairdresser must have had a wedding-free day after all. Christine's mother's roots were dyed jet black, ironed straight and pulled into a short ponytail. Her hair was heavily set and as her mother moved her head, the smell of pungent hair lacquer wafted into the open air.

"It looks lovely, Mummy. Really suits you."

"I noticed a few of the old boys over there giving me a few admiring looks. But I'm not interested. Geriatrics, the lot of them."

Christine's mother's raised voice attracted one of the members of staff, who carried over two cups of tea.

"Thank you, dear. This is my daughter Chrissie."

"Nice to meet you. Your mother's always talking about you and your family."

"She's married to a doctor, you now. William. A shy fella. Quiet type."

One of the residents was embroiled in a fight over a cup of tea near the back door, so the staff nurse apologised and quickly went to the rescue.

"That's your woman who keeps trying to nick my tea. She's trouble. Cover your cup with your hand like this. She won't see it then."

Christine's mother sat as if she was hiding her exam work from the cheat next to her. Having spent most of her life focussed on working long hours and keeping the wolves from the door, she now had to protect herself from marauding tea-thieves.

"How is Richard anyway?"

"Alex's fine. He had to work today – otherwise, he would have loved to have come and seen you."

"No, he wouldn't."

Christine was taken aback by her mother's bluntness.

"I scare the bejesus out of him. First time you brought him round to our house he wouldn't let go of the door handle."

"That was a long time ago, Mummy."

"I've never been to another wedding yet where the groom does his speech over the intercom in the hall."

"That was all a long time ago. He's not like that any more."

The mother's long-term memory was as accurate as ever, much to her daughter's chagrin.

Ten or so children were running in and out of the orchard, engulfed in a chorus of mighty screeches. Behind them was an elderly gentleman, with a waxed moustache, chasing them with his false teeth glued to a stick.

"Alex's much more confident now. How could he not be with a house full of women?"

"But, Chrissie, does he still get you to change the TV channels when a love scene comes on?"

This time, out of the orchard ran the elderly gentleman, quickly pursued by ten children carrying dog-faeces-clad sticks.

"No, he doesn't."

He did, but Christine was losing patience.

"Anyway, Mummy, did you sleep well last night?"

"Always do. I've a lovely big bed. Like the one at home."

"Sure, you were always in with me. You said your own one was like sleeping on a bed of nails."

"Did I? Can't really remember. The memory's not so good these days."

Christine knew her mother's long-term memory was impeccable. How could she not remember that?

"Chrissie, I remember reading you *The Hobbit* every night. You loved it. We used to read it snuggled under the duvet with a torch."

"Did we?"

Something in what her mother said lit a fuse in Christine's memory, but she extinguished it quickly with the thought that she and her mother had obviously existed in parallel universes.

Molly came running out of the trees and clung on to her mother's legs.

"Mummy, I found this. Can I eat it?"

Molly lifted a bruised crab-apple up to her mother's nose. The tail of a tiny grub could be seen burrowing in through its skin.

"I don't think so, sweetheart. It'd make you sick. If you're hungry go and grab one of those biscuits over there."

An elderly woman in a wheelchair blocked her with a remarkably swift turn of the chair, abruptly hampering Molly's excursion to the biscuit plate. The woman complimented Molly on her beautiful hair and then pulled out a pack of fun-size Mars bars from the side of her chair. Molly looked across at her mother before accepting. But with the only alternative being dry biscuits, softened by the sun, Christine nodded her approval. Molly remained chatting for a few minutes and then started pushing the woman in her chair around the lawn.

"Chrissie, don't tell me you've forgotten the Bay City Roller outfit I made you too?"

Christine had, but her mother had succeeded in dredging up a hidden memory.

"Did it have tartan wrapping paper glued around the hem?"

"And 'Woody' written across the back of the jacket. The letters were made out of foil milk-tops."

The embarrassing memory of being the only one in the school Fancy Dress not wearing a shop-bought costume came flooding back. As did the even more remote memory of the hours her mother had spent gluing and pinning the whole outfit together. Sewing wasn't a skill her mother possessed and any outfits she made usually only lasted until the walk home. This one in particular managed to survive just about

307

until Christine left the party and then tiny pinpricks and seams becoming unstuck heralded the outfit's demise.

"Sweetheart, go steady!"

Molly's gentle excursion with her newfound elderly friend had turned into a rally with two other wheelchair-bound residents, with the wheelchair equivalent of a handbrake turn changing their direction towards the orchard.

"Careful, Molly!"

But the laughter and hollering drowned out Christine's voice. Christine turned back towards her mother, who amidst all the commotion had fallen asleep. Her creases and wrinkles appeared to fade away and Christine felt that she could have been looking down on any of her daughters as they drifted into sleep. The only true evidence of her age were the grey eyelashes and eyebrows surrounding deep-set eye sockets and sharp lines biting into her lips.

Molly continued to rally around the lawn. The Baby and Ruth were still heavily involved in the chase around the orchard and Christine leant over and placed her mother's hand in her own.

The drive back to Bangor was much calmer than the outbound journey. The Baby and Molly were both exhausted by their exercise and were asleep by the time the car had left the driveway. Ruth had discovered a forgotten, favourite magazine stuffed down the side of her seat and was discovering it all over again.

Christine was feeling subdued herself. She had remained holding her mother's hand for nearly half an hour. She hadn't wanted to leave until her mother had woken again. One of the male residents had spilt hot coffee down his shirtfront and as he was in the process of changing it, a chorus of female wolf-whistles and 'ooh's' and 'aah's' had startled everyone, including Christine's mother. As they said their farewells, again Christine's children had served her proud, by burying their small heads in their grandmother's arms and saying 'I love you'. It was said with such innocent ease. Christine just parted with a 'See you next week'.

The Lough was now deep grey as the evening light had diminished behind a now dense cover of cloud. The light was so poor that even at 7.30 on a summer's evening, Christine was forced to turn the car's sidelights on. The girls had a few schooldays left before the summer holidays, so Christine was keen to get them back in time for their usual Sunday night bedtime routine. Her husband's suggestion of keeping the girls up was ludicrous and she wasn't going to disturb her regular pattern. Anyway there was little chance that any eclipse was going to be visible tonight.

The craft shops in Greyabbey were now secured behind wrought-iron shutters. The only evidence of today's trade were a few abandoned ice-cream cones on the pavement, a welcome feast for passing seagulls.

Christine felt confused about her visit to her mother. Mixed up with the confusion surrounding their shared past histories, she'd learnt a few truths. Though the time with her mother as a child had been rare, it had been full. Was her own fixation with being the perfect mother, because of rather than in spite of her mother? This was a frightening option. Especially alongside the realisation that she had been trying to be perfect in everything she did; a woman who always coped. But this weekend she had come to see that she wasn't coping at all. And maybe that was OK.

As the road turned into Newtownards, the looming

presence of Scrabo Tower stood ominous against the increasingly thickening clouds. Christine remembered the tales of the two spinster sisters who lived in the Tower, dedicating their lives to baking scones for passing visitors. On the hill below she could see the lights of Scrabo Golf Club, a different world entirely.

"Mummy?"

"Yes, Ruth?"

"I'm worried about Daddy."

Christine's mouth went dry.

"Why, love?"

"We haven't seen him all weekend."

"That's what being a doctor is all about."

"And I think he looks poorly. Doctors should make themselves better, shouldn't they?"

"Maybe he just looks a wee bit tired."

"Yeah."

Her twelve-year-old daughter's perception was frightening. This coming from a girl who only last week was asking what 'cubic' hair was. Christine felt as if the suburban cage she had built around her was crumbling and the balls she was juggling in the air were crashing around her.

Ruth appeared temporarily satisfied with her mother's response and turned the page of her magazine so that she could fully see the centre-fold of the latest boy band. Christine could hear her daughter picking at the staples that ran directly in front of the pin-up's unbuttoned trouser flies.

On the outskirts of Bangor, Christine was forced to turn her lights on to main beam and by the time she was driving into Ashbury Development, a late mist was settling on the rooftops. Ursula Richards' and Maurice McAllen's driveways were still empty. Christine lifted the still sleeping Baby out of her car seat and carried her up to bed. She was undressed and had her face washed without a flicker of her closed eyelids. Her mother had perfected this skill to include brushing her sleeping daughter's teeth, but tonight she missed that one out.

Molly had awoken as they pulled into the driveway and she was now in the process of undressing for her Sunday-night bath. Ruth had recently taken to showering by herself and had scurried off to her parents' en-suite shower room with a Barbie bottle of shampoo.

Seated on the rim of the bath, Christine supervised her eight-year-old, encouraging her to wash between her toes and behind her ears. As she did so, she tidied up the towels and the bath toys. Molly wound up the plastic sea lion that had been Christine's bath companion only yesterday. As it flapped along the water, bashing into the side, Christine was instantly reminded of her own foolish experience hanging out of the window. She covered the splashing gadget with a flannel and it continued its water dance muffled.

With all her creased bits and pieces appropriately dried under the guidance of her mother, Molly rapidly dressed in her dusty pink nighty and scurried to bed. As Ruth read her a bedtime story, Christine pulled the bedroom door behind her and went downstairs. When she reached the bottom, she stood for a moment and then turned back again and retraced her steps to Molly's bedroom.

"I just wanted to say how proud I was of you girls today. You really made your Grandma's day."

"We had great fun."

311

"So there'll be no whingeing when we go again next Sunday?"

"Mummy . . . do we have to?"

Christine leaned over and gave both girls a kiss. As she closed the bedroom door a second time, she could hear them titter. Back downstairs, in the kitchen, She began to clear away the dishes, but halfway through she pulled an ice-cold bottle of white wine out of the fridge, took a recently rinsed glass from the drying-rack and made her way to the living-room. The toys and dolls from the night before were still scattered, with the addition of a few tea towels and jumpers wrapped around them as blankets.

The first glass of wine was swallowed swiftly to satisfy her thirst. Christine then sipped gently on the second. She then stood to close the curtains and saw Maurice McAllen's car pull into his driveway. A few minutes later, Ursula's car pulled into her own. As Fergal Coyle, rather than Ursula, climbed out of the driver's seat, Christine's growing curiosity heightened. When she saw all three walk over to Fergal's house, her mind was made up as to her next course of action.

Christine waited until all three of her daughters were asleep and then tiptoed out of her front door and off to house Number 2. Just as she lifted her finger to the doorbell, the door abruptly swung open. Fergal himself greeted her. His manner was exceedingly cheerful, if not bordering on hysterical.

"Christine. Good to see you. We've a bit of a party going in here."

Christine peeked behind Fergal, but the atmosphere was far from jolly. Sam and Ursula sat huddled on the sofa, each

312

squeezing the life out of mugs of piping hot coffee. Frances was standing behind Fergal, almost pinning herself against the wall.

"Please, come on in, Christine. Let's have a few drinks to celebrate tonight's lunar eclipse."

"But looking at the clouds, Fergal, I think you're going to be disappointed."

"Disappointed? How could I be disappointed? Now, if I'd just found out that half of Amsterdam saw my wife bollock-naked and that some weird geezer had my wife's underwear as a souvenir, that would be disappointing . . ."

The coffee cups Sam and Ursula were holding accidentally chinked together, only marginally quieter than Frances' inward gasp. Fergal's familiar cheery expression was replaced by a sour tightening of his lips and enraged widening of his grey eyes. He barely stopped for breath.

"You must come in, Christine. We're just having a neighbourly get-together."

As Fergal spoke the clouds behind Christine appeared to dissolve into thin wisps and through them a full moon was just about visible. The first stage of the eclipse had begun and a tiny slice of the moon's iridescent surface was in total blackness.

Chapter 36

When Ursula accidentally clinked her coffee mug with Sam's, a tiny splash had escaped and scalded her hand.

"Frances, do you mind if I just get some cold water? My hand's stinging."

"Come with me, I've cream for that sort of thing in the kitchen."

The two women scurried away, whilst Fergal poured large brandies for Sam and the newly arrived Christine. As Frances opened the wall cabinet, an assortment of creams and bottles fell out. She picked out the appropriate tube and began closing the cabinet door again. As she slowly pressed it shut, she kept feeding the fallen items back in until the door was about a centimetre wide and she squeezed in the last packet of plasters. As the door was rammed shut, Frances waited for a moment to see if the door would fly open again. When it didn't, she seemed pleased with herself.

"This stuff's great for hot water scalds. Feel any better?"

"Much."

"Have a beer. You'll feel better still."

Frances was seated on the kitchen top and, without getting down, she reached down into a small heavily disguised fridge and pulled out two bottles of Budweiser. Again without leaving her seat, she reached across the kitchen top and lifted Ursula a glass from the draining-board. With the ebb of the burning sensation, Ursula felt much more comfortable here in the kitchen and she too jumped up on the worktop beside her neighbour.

"Not much of a party is it, Ursula? Sorry about the mood Fergal's in."

"Don't worry. We're all having a bit of a bad-hair day. You don't know about Maurice McAllen across the road."

"The Lawnmower Man?"

"He's a bit more than that."

As Ursula recounted the whole story, she was surprised how little it appeared to faze Frances. Her neighbour remained composed, with a confidence about her that Ursula had never seen before.

"Aren't you shocked, Frances?"

"It's terrible yes, but I kind of half-expected there was something peculiar about him."

"We all did."

"He's a good-looking guy and all, but you wouldn't touch him with a barge pole, would you?"

Ursula stumbled for words. She was physically and emotionally drained and too tired to continue her ice-maiden act. What the hell, she thought to herself.

"You wouldn't, would you, Ursula?"

"Yes, I did. Yesterday in fact. Before all this about the paramilitaries came out."

The response Ursula expected from the woman she only occasionally exchanged pleasantries with was not as expected. Ursula almost wanted to be punished and scolded for what she had done.

"Good on you. You're a single woman. Why not?"

"You and my friend Carla should get together some time. I think you'd get on."

"But what's your problem? He was single, you're single. Two virile . . ."

"It wasn't like that at all. I'm not like that."

Ursula had fended off hundreds of questions about her sex life from Carla over the years. Most of which, if she was honest with herself, were for Carla's titillation. But there was something in Frances's manner, something she hadn't noticed before, that made her appear accepting and understanding. Ursula was offered a second beer, which this time she chose to drink directly from the bottle.

"Frances, I'm a dried-up old hag and that's all there is to it."

"You have every guy on this estate drooling after you, including my husband and the murderer across the road, and you still dare to say that?"

"The make-up, hair-dos and expensive clothes are all for show. Inside I'm shrivelled up."

"Ursula, if you keep going on like this you're going to make me angry."

"I don't like sex."

That was it. She'd said it.

"Frances, can you imagine what it must be like to be married to someone like me?"

"You don't need me to tell you that there are two sides to every marriage."

316

"Not mine. He was a saint to put up with me as long as he did."

"You don't mean that."

"Yes, I do."

Frances swallowed a quarter of the beer she was holding and began picking at the red, white and blue label. Ursula sensed there was something on her mind.

"What is it, Frances?"

"Do you still love him, Ursula?"

"No."

"Are you sure?"

"Absolutely."

"What if you found out that he'd been having an affair when you were married and . . ."

Ursula felt sick.

"What if you knew that he was still seeing that woman, but was leading her on by saying he was still married to you. Would you give him saint status then? If he's your only experience of a relationship with a man, I'd say you needn't be too hard on yourself."

Ursula slumped back on the kitchen top, banging her head against the glass cabinet behind her. It didn't hurt.

"Frances, how do you know all this?"

"The woman is a friend of mine on the volleyball team. I only made the connection myself this weekend."

"What does she look like?"

"*She* doesn't matter. It's him you should be angry with."

"I just need to know. What does she look like?"

"Well, I guess you'd describe her as about my height and colouring, but not my build. She's very athletic. A bit like a female weightlifter actually."

The microfiche photograph came instantly into Ursula's mind. She was there, his lover, watching him compete. She was literally in the background all that time. As Ursula recollected the photograph, the nausea drained the colour totally from her face. The secret had been hidden in the photograph and she hadn't seen it. And what else did the photograph hide? Ursula unceremoniously jumped down off the kitchen top and her shoe heels clicked against the Chinese-slate-tiled floor.

"Can I use the phone?"

"There's one behind you. But please don't be hasty. Don't call your husband. I've my friend to think of."

Ursula didn't hear Frances, as she busily dialled the familiar number into the telephone keypad. As she waited for the ringing tone, Ursula could feel her hand tremble and see the damp impressions left by her fingerprints on the black plastic buttons. The ringing tone halted after a few seconds and a deep husky voice replied.

"Carla, it's me."

"Ursula, I've been trying to get you all day, darling. How are you doing?"

"Did you make your appointments last night?"

The breathing of the voice could be heard, but she didn't speak.

"How was it? Did the earth move? Was it full sex, or maybe just a bit of oral to tide you over? Did you do it doggy-style? Did you hear me, Carla? Did my ex-husband take you from behind?"

Ursula growled down the telephone, silencing the conversation between Sam, Fergal and Christine in the living-room.

"Please, Ursula, let me explain. Did Mona tell you?"

"Ah, that's that little puzzle solved. You thought you'd meet her and get off on Mona's own sordid secret, when in fact it was Mona who'd put two and two together herself, that night, in your house."

"So, you haven't been speaking to her?"

"Now I know, I realise that you must have been seeing him all the time we were married. You were always there, getting lifts home, meeting him for lunch, travelling abroad the same times that he was supposed to be travelling to some tournament or other."

"Please, Ursula . . ."

"And all these years, I thought I was the one with the sex problem. No wonder my ex had no interest in me or my needs, he was busy fucking half of Ireland."

"What does that mean?"

"Oh, sorry to burst your bubble, darling. But the only reason I got smart to you was when I found out he's also been seeing someone else all these years. So we've both been duped."

"You're just saying that to get back at me."

"No, if you want the evidence, it's on the back page of the *Belfast Telegraph*, August the 1st, 1994. We were all there that day. And God knows who else."

"That's not true, Ursula. Roger really cares about me!"

"We're just gold medals. Go and shine yourself up and maybe if he's bored, he'll wear you around his neck again tonight."

Ursula hung up the telephone, but as her hand still trembled, the receiver bounced off the hook again and bungee-jumped up and down besides the kitchen cabinet.

319

The whirring dialling tone drifted in and out as the cable twisted and spun. Frances jumped down off the kitchen top and hugged Ursula tight. Ursula's neighbour felt warm and comforting. Almost motherly.

The conversation in the living-room remained silenced. The two women held the embrace for a few minutes.

"Ursula, how did you know your friend was also one of your ex's lovers?"

"Because, I'd seen a photograph today, with the woman you described in the background. I immediately thought of all the deception that photo hid: the 'happy' husband and wife, the charming Olympian, the mistress in the background. And then I remembered the other figure in the picture. She was hidden by a huge, veiled hat and was either very out-of-fashion, or she was trying to hide from somebody she knew. I guess my senses were so intensified by what you had told me, Frances, that suddenly I recognised her as my friend, Carla. Why didn't she let me know she was there? What was her role in this montage of deceit? And then just as quickly, everything just fell into place."

After a few more minutes of silent embraces, Christine Watson tilted her head around the kitchen doorway. Her expression mirrored the accepting and understanding one of Frances.

"Ursula, we all heard. I'm very sorry. Can I do anything?"

Ursula pulled away from Frances's arms and stone-faced glared at the intruder. This acceptance and understanding was unwelcome.

"Frances, this is an interesting turn-up for the books, isn't it?"

"What do you mean, Ursula?"

320

"When I told you about sleeping with Maurice McAllen yesterday . . ."

Ursula heard Fergal cough embarrassingly in the living-room. Sam was silent.

" . . . I forgot to tell you about the other little sordid affair I've discovered this weekend. Isn't that right, Christine? Please tell us all how Mr McAllen keeps your garden seeded and watered these hot nights?"

Chapter 37

Fergal coughed again. But the conversation was flowing full steam ahead in the kitchen and he realised he wasn't going to stop it with his pathetic little noises. Sam looked crestfallen and he hadn't taken a drop of his brandy. Fergal was taken aback by Ursula's revelations, but the macho part of him was more distracted by the thought, 'I could show her a thing or two. She wouldn't be frigid after a night with me'. But as he looked across at Sam's strong arms and tight chest and compared his youthful physique with his own inverted 'v' shape, his inner thoughts dissipated.

Fergal shifted position to the armchair nearest the kitchen door. The acoustics in the kitchen were ample, but he wanted to improve his sight line. The Christine Watson and Maurice McAllen climax to this evening's impromptu gathering was not to be missed.

"You've got it all wrong, Ursula. I haven't been having an affair."

"Don't lie. I've had enough of lies today."

"I'm not."

"So why did you come round to my home yesterday like a cat on heat? Were you trying to sniff out what my interest was in our mystery neighbour?"

"No."

"I've no time for this, Christine."

Ursula had left her seat on the kitchen top and moved off towards the sink. This was better. Fergal could now see the two women's faces full on. Both women looked haggard. He couldn't see Frances at all from this position, but then his wife was just a spear-carrier in this act.

"I admit, I had schoolgirl feelings for him."

"Nothing else?"

"I wouldn't even have had them, if it wasn't . . ."

Christine turned her back to Fergal and this muffled her voice. He wanted to shout 'speak up', but luckily he didn't have to.

"Christine, I didn't hear what you said."

"I said, I wouldn't even have had them, if I didn't have such big grown-up problems at home."

Christine turned back to face Fergal. That was much better. Audio and visual synchronised. But the next person to speak was not one of the main protagonists; it was Frances, who he still could not see.

"Whatever your difficulties, Christine, you've three lovely daughters and an utterly devoted husband at home. Some people only dream of that."

Fergal didn't quite like his wife's tone. Frances continued.

"And for what it's worth, Christine, I'd be one of those people."

He definitely didn't like that. Fergal wriggled in his chair. He looked to Sam for support, but he still sat staring at his full glass of brandy, like an alcoholic on the verge of temptation. Fergal crossed his fingers on his stomach and rotated his thumbs around each other. They got faster and faster in tempo with his racing thoughts. His thumbs stopped moving as Christine spoke again.

"I've three beautiful daughters, I know. But I've been a pretty useless mother."

"Christine, that's just ridiculous. Those girls are the best turned out in the whole of Ashbury."

Much to Fergal's annoyance, the spear-carrier was again trying to increase her lines.

"Frances, the immaculately pressed dresses, trips to the ballet, French classes, they're nothing compared to time spent with them doing nothing but silly things. Those are the things they'll remember. If I didn't try being such a bloody perfect housewife, I would be a more perfect person all round. That includes being a better wife."

"But you have a husband who adores you. At least he gives you his support."

That's it, Fergal had heard enough. He pulled himself out of the armchair and thrust himself into the kitchen doorway. So he wasn't the man he used to be, or maybe he wasn't the man he'd never been. But one thing was for sure, he wasn't going to be insulted in his own home any more.

"OK, Flashing Frances. Make your point. What in God's name is wrong with me? Don't support you enough, is that it? Because if you don't think I'm here for you, I'd like to know why. Would you prefer it if I was like that bastard across the road?" Fergal pointed across towards Maurice

McAllen's house. He could feel the blood vessels in his neck pulsate and his top lip and brow sweat. "Come on, Mrs Moon, say your piece."

"Fergal, this isn't the time."

"I think it is."

"OK. You eat too much, Fergal. Too much junk food, that is. You tell boring stories, over and over again. You fancy yourself and have this made-up bachelor history that has you as some kind of stud in your youth. You're lazy about the house. You wear boring clothes and boring colours. You're grey inside and out . . ."

Once the top was unscrewed, there was no stopping Frances. Each verbal blow pierced Fergal deeply.

"You tuck your work shirt in your underpants. You leer at women with low necklines. You eat donuts in one mouthful . . ."

Fergal was starting to sense a reaction to the torrent of abuse from Ursula and Christine, and it wasn't in his favour.

" . . . And worst of all, your wife had a miscarriage and you didn't even shed a tear. Not one. You just didn't care. My husband's a heartless bastard."

Ursula joined in.

"Mine was a deceitful philanderer, with a peanut for a penis."

Followed by Christine.

"Mine's an obsessive . . . and a drug addict."

All in the kitchen, even Fergal, were silenced by this latest revelation. So the doctor is a drug addict. Sam joined a dumbstruck Fergal in the kitchen doorway.

"I'm not a window cleaner either. I run my own IT company in Belfast. I employ mostly graduates and students

325

part-time during their holidays. I've a staff of about fifty at the moment. I just happened to be passing Ursula's house one day on an errand to fix a friend's TV aerial. I met Ursula and was totally smitten. I guess you could say it was love at first sight. I've been too shy to say anything, but being able to clean her windows meant that I could be there near her and look out for her whenever I could.

The doorbell rang and Fergal, still half-dazed and shell-shocked, left the kitchen and opened the front door. As he opened it, the frame was totally filled with the body of Maurice McAllen. The only light that was visible in the darkness was that from the full moon behind Maurice's head. The lunar surface was pure red.

"Fergal, can I come in a minute?"

Chapter 38

Being left out of things wasn't Maurice McAllen's concern. He was well used to that. But he was suspicious. His lifestyle had taught him to be suspicious and up until this weekend he had managed to be cautious and in control. Maurice had seen his neighbours congregate over in Mr & Mrs Coyle's house. A social drink between neighbours wouldn't have made him curious, but this wasn't usual in the development. On the whole, everyone kept to themselves and that was part of the attraction for Maurice when he moved to Bangor. But as he sat now with his house lights off and looking directly across at house Number 2, he didn't sense that there was a party within. He had seen Christine Watson, as the last to walk across, and he had waited half an hour deciding what he should do.

Maurice knew he shouldn't do anything too drastic, especially in his current state of mind. He had turned back from the post box last night and had sat in his living-room for four hours wondering what he should do with the letter to his son, before finally falling asleep at around six that morning. By then, he was so tired, he just fell comatose into a deep sleep. When he eventually awoke, the intensity of his dreams had left Maurice convinced that posting the letter was, in fact, the right thing to do. He was so reassured that he decided to post the letter through his son's letter box himself and had spent the day on the familiar cycle of waiting and wondering outside his family's home. Just as his stakeout for the day was complete, Maurice eventually posted the letter. Afterwards, he had driven home in a trance, wondering who would read it and what the reaction would be. But as he sat now glaring at the neighbourly gathering across the road, he wondered just to what extent he had exposed himself this weekend. Maurice felt incredibly vulnerable and this petrified him.

The gun remained in his jacket pocket, as Maurice now felt that he needed to be conscious of its presence beside him, at all times. When he had got home this evening, he hadn't even bothered to take his leather jacket off.

Maurice had found a packet of bacon rashers, one day past their sell-by date, at the bottom of fridge and grilled the whole pack, eating them hungrily between thick slices of white bread. A whole carton of orange juice accompanied the quick meal.

Half an hour later and Christine Watson was still inside house Number 2. Maurice could see Fergal and another man, whom he didn't recognise, seated in the Coyles' front living-room. The atmosphere between these two men looked solemn. But as Maurice wiped away the bacon fat from his chin, he saw Fergal abruptly stand and march towards the kitchen. Fergal appeared to be shouting, but at the point when he angrily pointed across in Maurice's direction, Maurice's decision was made for him. His anonymity was crucial and, if this was being compromised in some way, Maurice knew he had to deal with it.

As Maurice left his house and walked across the cul-de-sac, the blackness of the evening was instantly illuminated by a gap in the clouds, allowing the bright rays from the moon to seep through. Moon shadows were cast around him and his own stretched the full distance to the front door of Number 2. As he looked behind him and saw the blood-moon in all its glory, he was struck by its beauty and its purity.

Maurice rang the doorbell and, following a hush within, Fergal Coyle opened the door. As he stood looking his neighbour straight in the eye, Maurice felt momentarily unprepared. He hadn't rehearsed anything and suddenly felt more vulnerable than ever.

"Fergal, can I come in a minute?"

As Maurice spoke, he saw the red angry lines around Fergal's mouth turn pure white. This instantly reassured Maurice that he was right to have his suspicions.

"Maurice?"

"You look surprised, Fergal."

"No. Well, yes. A bit. No. Come in."

From out of the kitchen came a sheepish parade, led firstly by Ursula Richards from Number 7, with Fergal's wife Frances following and then Christine Watson from Number 5. The unfamiliar man he had seen from across the road was the last to emerge. Fergal nervously introduced him.

"This is Sam. I don't think you two have met. He's Ursula's window . . . er friend . . . he's in IT."

Maurice reached out his hand to greet the stranger. Sam's hand was as big as his own was and he held the handshake with equal force. Sam then sat down on the sofa beside Ursula. Her light flowery perfume had wafted past Maurice, as the hem of her skirt had brushed against him as she passed from the kitchen towards the sofa. Tantalising memories of yesterday afternoon came flooding back, but he sensed that she was refusing to share them with him as she kept her gaze firmly turned away in the opposite direction. Christine walked the longest route to the armchair by the window, avoiding any physical contact whatsoever. He caught her eye for a brief moment, but he felt that this was a stolen exchange, rather than one given voluntarily. Frances was the only female in the room who appeared not intimidated by his presence. She walked directly past him, brushing his arm as she went and sat on the arm of the chair now occupied by Christine. Fergal continued his nervous hospitality.

"We're just having a drink to celebrate the eclipse. Did you see it, Maurice?"

"Yes, very well."

"Would have invited you too, but you know . . . thought you were out. Didn't we?"

The grunted 'yeses' weren't very convincing.

"Would you like a drink?"

The strain of the forced hospitality was showing on Fergal and his face reddened until he looked as if he was approaching boiling point.

"No, thank you, Fergal. I won't be staying."

"Oh, right."

"I just get the feeling everyone's a bit on edge and I just

wanted to make sure that it didn't have anything to do with me."

"Oh, right."

"That's all, Fergal. Is there anything bothering any of you? Anything about me?"

Cowardly faces remained turned down towards their feet. Everyone's except for Sam.

"We know about your past history, Mr McAllen. And frankly your neighbours don't like what they hear."

Even though he had his suspicions, being confronted by the gravity of it hit Maurice like a blow to the throat. While his neighbours sat huddled to each other for support, he felt alone, massive, awkward and alone. He was as vulnerable as a newborn baby.

"And, Sam, what exactly would that history be?"

"Your career with the RUC, the liaisons with the Loyalist paramilitaries, the court case."

"I see."

Maurice could see Frances grip onto Christine's hand as she then spoke.

"You can understand that those of us with families and even those of us without, are very concerned."

"Yes, Frances, I can see why you would be concerned. But I'm intrigued as to where you found out about all this 'history'?"

"My husband saw a newspaper clipping and some scanning through past copies of the *Belfast Telegraph* revealed the full details of the court case."

"And that's it, Frances?"

"What else is there to know? Were you involved in other crimes as well?"

Maurice slumped down on the sofa besides Ursula. He could feel her body recoil as he did so. His legs felt like mighty redwoods against her slender saplings. He rested his head against the brown leather and could feel the tight knots in his neck instantly relax. He reached into the inside pocket of his leather jacket and pulled out the gun. As he did so, Sam pulled Ursula towards him, until she was almost seated on his knee and Fergal leapt over with dramatic chivalry and stood with his arms around Frances and Christine.

"Do you have any idea why I carry this around with me? Why I'm forced to carry a gun every day of my life. It's in case I meet ignorant people like you. But maybe next time it won't be pathetic tittle-tattlers from some suburban neighbourhood – it might be someone with a gun themselves. Tell me, Fergal, I hope you don't mind me asking you directly, since you appear to be the instigator here, but at what point of my career did you finish this enlightening research into my history?"

Singling Fergal out was unfortunate for Fergal, but Maurice had a point to make.

"About the fourth day of your trial."

"The day the *Telegraph* printed a full-colour front-page mug-shot of my big ugly face?"

"Yes."

"Why didn't you bother with days five, six, seven?"

"We didn't like what we were reading. We'd heard enough."

"Well, that's a shame, Fergal. Because if you'd had the wit to read on, you would have finally got to day nine, when guess what . . . I was acquitted of all charges. I was given a full apology for what I had been put through, which proved to be a tissue of lies, orchestrated to protect some other informer from coming to trial. But, day nine didn't make the front page. Do you know why? Because it wasn't as dramatic. It wasn't as gruesome a story. You people, like thousands of others out there, wouldn't have bothered to read what went on page fifteen, far right column, middle paragraph, titled 'Officer Acquitted'."

Chapter 39

Like everyone else in the room, Ursula stopped looking at her shoes and stared across at Maurice McAllen. He appeared both massive and tiny at the same time. But right now it was the small gentleness to his presence that encouraged her to leave the protective clutches of Sam and put her hand on Maurice's shoulder. Even though they had made love yesterday, this was the first moment of contact where she felt she had a true connection with this big mysterious man.

"But, Maurice, do you really need the gun?" said Ursula.

Maurice dropped the gun onto the floor and stared as if it was the first time he had ever seen it.

"Ever since the trial, my life and all those around me have been under threat from the Loyalist paramilitaries for one. In order to take the heat from the real informer, they wanted me to 'confess'. I didn't and they've long memories. There's also RUC officers who still believe there's no smoke without fire and then republicans and vigilantes, who didn't bother to read past day four either."

Ursula felt her cheeks and neck redden.

"I carry a gun for self-defence."

No one challenged Maurice's integrity or honesty. There was no need.

The living room was now a hive of activity. Fergal poured Maurice an extra large brandy, whilst Frances was getting beers for everyone else. Christine had left the armchair by the window and now sat on the coffee table just a few feet from Maurice. Ursula could still feel the harbour of Sam's warm soft fingers, entwined in her own. She let them stay that way. Throughout the evening all that she had sensed from Sam was his support. She had confessed to being frigid, had falsely accused one neighbour of being an adulterer and having sex with another, but at no time did she feel admonished by Sam or sense his disappointment. Ursula could see from the corner of her eye that Sam was now staring at her. He had brushed his curls away from his eyes and his focus was only her. She daren't return the look. He too had exposed his innermost feelings to not only her, but a group of people he barely knew. Either side of Ursula now sat large, athletic men, both so very different and both vulnerable in their own separate ways. Ursula had never experienced this in the opposite sex before.

"Please accept my apology, Maurice. And I'm sure I speak for everyone here. We shouldn't have jumped to conclusions. We're sorry. It's just you keep your life so private, so . . ." said Ursula.

"Secret?"

"Yes."

"Ursula, it's my only protection."

"Hiding away from everything and everyone is no protection. Maurice. Don't you have any family?"

"Once."

Maurice's cast-iron exterior was melting away by the second. Ursula kept her hand on his arm and the sinews and muscles continued to soften. Her ex-husband's had never.

Fergal poured a second extra large brandy for himself and then he joined Christine on the coffee table. Frances returned with five bottles of beer and a giant packet of ready salted crisps. Her husband gave his wife the look of 'where were you hiding them?'. But she ignored him and sat down on the carpet beside the fire.

Ursula suddenly felt secure in this inner sanctum. Neighbours who had hitherto exchanged recipes or cures for marauding buttercups now knew so much and so many secrets about each other's lives. The five of them, all suburban residents of a middle-class development, in the heart of middle-class Bangor, with their worlds entwined. Within the fleeting span of a weekend, they had found themselves crashing against each other like balls on a billiard table. The manicured lawns, the Saturday morning car-wash and the barbecues, were all flimsy facades. The vertical blinds and heavy lined velvet curtains were nothing but veils.

As a consequence, Ursula had even discovered an unexpected connection outside of this cul-de-sac. That belonging to Sam, her one-time window cleaner. His disclosure to her had at first been unsettling and she had immediately stored it at the back of her mind as something to be dissected later. But now, as she sat between the two men, she decided not to leave it for her brain to analyse, but to let her feelings act as her judgement. Never before had Ursula let her heart rule her head. She felt excited and exhilarated.

Only yesterday she had felt oppressed and used by Maurice, but as he sat before them all, cornered like a frightened deer, her recollections were under fresh scrutiny. Maurice's giant hands rested on each of his knees and his eyes just stared out of the window. Ursula could see the red moon's reflection in them.

"Have you children, Maurice?"

"Two boys. They're twelve and seven now."

"And do you see them?"

"From a distance of fifty yards if I'm lucky. I suffered from severe depression after the trial and though my wife stuck by me throughout, twelve months of my paranoia and mood-swings finally took its toll. My family went through hell and it was inevitable that they would eventually be lost to me. You can't expect people to put up with what they did indefinitely."

"But how do you get by? I don't mean just from the financial side."

"The finances are the least of my worries. I've been living off a redundancy-and-compensation package. I don't spend much. That's easy, living the life I do. But I miss my family. I miss having my wife beside me. I don't really live . . . I exist."

Ursula knew that what she was about to say would never have previously been spoken in a million years. But then this weekend had been that once in a million experience.

"When we made love yesterday, Maurice . . . I hope you don't mind me asking this, but I sensed that it was someone else you were thinking of. Was it your wife?"

"I'm sorry, Ursula."

Ursula tightened her grip on his arm with her left hand and with her right, twisted her fingers gently in the palm of

Sam's. She looked across at Christine and, without speaking, there was a mutual understanding and acceptance. Christine then leant forward on the coffee table, putting herself directly in between Maurice and the window. Ursula instantly saw the reflection of the moon disappear. Christine then put her own hand on top of Maurice's and spoke softly.

"You can't keep yourself in isolation. And do you know why? You have too much to give. If I hadn't got the comfort and support that you gave me yesterday, God knows where me and my girls would be right now. What I needed was someone to take control for me and you did that. You did that, Maurice. You even made an old-fashioned fuddy-duddy like me feel like a woman again."

For the first time that evening, everyone smiled, Maurice included. It was so rare that he smiled that Ursula was struck by his handsome, strong features and the faint sparkle in his blue eyes. She again found herself drawn to him.

"Maurice, this has been a hell of a weekend for all of us. I guess we've just scratched the surface and we've still got as much hidden away as we've exposed. But if there's anything I can do . . ."

Maurice turned to face her and then leant forward and placed a delicate kiss on her cheek. Unlike their hurried, harsh embraces yesterday, Ursula felt like a child had just kissed her. Could she be in the presence of men and still be herself? Could she be hugged without recoiling?

Before she could say any more, the doorbell rang again. Fergal stepped over to the window and craned his neck to see who was at the front door.

"It's a police officer. There's another one over at your house, Maurice . . . he's now walking across here too."

Everyone in the room looked at Maurice, who nervously put the gun back in his pocket.

"They must have tracked me down. Maybe my wife's put in a complaint. I can't afford anyone to know where I am."

Ursula could feel Maurice tremble and could see him fidget nervously.

"It's OK, Maurice. We're here. You're not on your own."

Frances nodded to Fergal, who then opened the front door, just as the doorbell was pressed a second time.

"Good evening, sir. Sorry to bother you at this time of night. But we've been trying to track down one of your neighbours and I was wondering if you could help me?"

Fergal turned his back so that the entrance to the living-room was shielded and so that the police officers' view of the interior was blocked.

"We've been phoning all afternoon and now there appears to be no one at home. We've tried a few of the other houses, but there's nobody about. Have you any idea where we could contact Mrs Watson from Number 5?"

Chapter 40

"Sam, would you like to come back for coffee?"

"Oh, yes."

The gathering in Fergal and Frances Coyle's house had dissipated rapidly. Christine had left with the police officers and Maurice McAllen had followed after her. The atmosphere between the Coyles was still icy and Ursula was relieved to leave. As she stood outside her front door, with her key in her hand and Sam beside her, Ursula felt as if her whole world had been turned upside down. Usually, at times like this, Carla would have been the first person she would have called. Who could she rely on now?

As Ursula opened the front door, Sam politely kept his distance behind her. When she went to boil the kettle in the kitchen, he stayed in the living-room. Around her, Ursula could see reminders of her weekend, rudely dragging flashback memories: her old T-shirt, thrown over the back of the chair, an empty plate where a chocolate gâteau had once been and two coffee mugs, once shared between two friends. Ursula blankly stared at the kettle for a good few minutes, before realising she had forgotten to switch the power on. She then rifled through her cupboards looking for coffee and sugar, as if this was the first time she'd ever been in this kitchen.

She was surprised as to how quickly the extreme anger she felt when first discovering her ex-husband's adulterous past had dissolved into a dull thud. She now felt numb, as if she was looking at herself from the outside. In her mind's eye, she imagined a woman waiting at home for her husband to return from some competition or other. He was tired, but still looking for sexual gratification of some kind. The woman felt like no matter what she tried, she was unable to give it to him. Both were relieved when the sex was over in a few minutes and she rolled over and stared at the patterns on the wallpaper. The man was asleep in thirty seconds, the woman was still awake two hours later. The pattern on the wall repeating itself over and over.

The steam from the kettle filled the kitchen and tiny drops of condensation dripped off the extractor hood. Ursula stood staring at the boiling kettle. She lost herself in the spray of steam and its constant rhythm. She forced herself to visualise her ex-husband in bed with Carla and any other of his conquests. It was painful, but Ursula felt that this psychological rubbing of her tongue against an aching tooth was important for some reason. All the sexual exploits Carla had forced her to listen to, she imagined had all been with Roger. Alongside these images, Ursula then slotted her actual memories of times spent with her friend, discussing her own marriage and her problems. The recollections of Carla's advice were the most difficult to bear, but instead of avoiding these, Ursula played them over and over again. She was intentionally making herself suffer. This, she knew, was her warped approach to healing herself.

She wanted to visualise every hurtful element of the whole sordid experience, in the hope that she couldn't be hurt again. She wanted to push that tooth until the pain was unbearable.

She would have stood there indefinitely, if Sam hadn't walked in and turned the kettle off at the socket. Without speaking, he took hold of her hand and led her into the living room. As she walked behind him, the shape of his wide shoulders was clearly visible through his T-shirt. His hands were huge compared to her own, but felt soft and yielding. Once inside the living-room, he turned her towards him. His face was inches from hers; so close she could smell his fresh scent.

"Ursula, I'm going now. I think it's best."

Whatever trance Ursula was in earlier, it was now shattered completely. She immediately stopped staring at the past and was pulled into the present. She looked up into his eyes and leant slightly forward, his smell now tantalisingly stronger. He pulled back slightly. He let go of her hand and used both of his own to push his chestnut hair clear away from his face. He kept his hands up and locked behind his head. Ursula was gutted. She felt rejected all over again. He had pulled away from her and was distancing himself by the second. She felt more enraged now than at any time during her traumatic weekend, and there'd been quite a catalogue of rage-inducing events over the past two days: Carla probing too deeply with personal questions in the café, her disappointing sexual liaison with Maurice McAllen,

Christine Watson's prying visit and the discovery of an affair between her ex-husband and her best friend. Ursula could not understand why her anger was greater now than ever before. She could feel her heart race and her thoughts become erratic and disjointed.

"Ursula, you should be on your own."

Sam turned to go. Surely he wouldn't leave her now? But without looking back, he let himself out of the front door and began strolling down the path towards his bicycle. 'He will look back,' Ursula thought to herself, 'and then he'll know what's for.' But he didn't. Ursula pulled her long blonde hair to her mouth and began sucking nervously at the ends. Instantly remembering that Carla also had this habit, she stopped sucking and began biting her bottom lip. Her lips transformed from pale pink to ox-blood red, but the physical pain was preferable to the emotional pain she was feeling right now.

"Go ahead! Go!" she shouted. "It's clear to see that sex is all that you're interested in. Put you off, have I?"

Her intention had been to remain composed and uninterested, but now that she had given free rein to her heart over her head, she felt out of control. Sam aggressively lifted the bicycle over his shoulder and stormed over to Ursula. He was now standing a foot below her on the path, making them equals in height.

"Is that how little you think of me, Ursula?"

"Yes. You're all the same."

"Do you possibly have any idea how insulting that is?"

"Am I being insulting, or just honest?"

"Would I have hung about all these months, pretending to be something I'm not, just for an opportunity to see you, to be near you, if all I was interested in was having sex with you? What do you take me for?"

"A man."

"You can't go around judging every man by your ex-husband's standards. Why don't you judge all women by the standards of your so-called friend? Because if you did, Ursula, you'd be very lonely. Lonely and bitter."

The anger in Sam's expression exploded. He belligerently threw his bicycle down on the grass, buckling the front wheel and sending the pedals spinning frantically.

"Damn you, Ursula Richards! It's exactly because I don't want you to think I'm just like your ex-husband that I'm leaving now. The easiest thing for me to have done in there was to take advantage of your vulnerability, to tell you I'd make everything better."

"You didn't want to leave me?"

Ursula felt her weak voice tremble beside the bellowing of the man before her. At eye level, she could see the unrestrained anger in Sam's eyes, but also an expression of hurt and disappointment.

"I want you so bad, Ursula. When I walked out that door I knew it was a gamble. I risked spending one magical night with you, for the chance of sharing a lifetime."

Sam was breathing deeply, but the aggression faded from his eyes. Ursula was stunned. Sam's proximity to her and the fact that she couldn't reach out and hold him, tortured her. She was enticed by the conflict between Sam's usual tranquil manner and this new exhibition of frustration and fury. Ursula could feel his rapid breathing against her eyelashes, forcing her to blink. He was close enough for her to breathe in as he exhaled, filling her lungs and coaxing

344

her further. Ursula no longer wanted to protect herself behind a barrier of being aloof and indifferent. She felt compelled and driven to give herself completely.

"I want you too, Sam."

Up until now, Sam's rage had caused his whole body to rock and his gaze to flit sporadically from Ursula's face, to the house, to the floor and even up to the heavens. He now was motionless and stared intensely and directly at Ursula. It was obvious from his expression that what he heard pleased him, but he was still unsure of its sincerity. Ursula was fully aware of the power she now had and knew exactly what she now had to say.

"Sam, I want you now, in the morning, tomorrow and all the tomorrows."

As Ursula spoke, her own stare darted between Sam's eyes and his mouth. When she'd finished, she saw a brightness cascade down his face, as a broad smile illuminated it totally. He looked at his feet, momentarily embarrassed, but then stared straight forward. He was now the one empowered.

"Why didn't you say that earlier?"

Sam lifted Ursula and carried her back into the house. He stopped at the foot of the stairs, putting Ursula back down on the second stair up. He remained at the bottom and held Ursula firmly around the waist. She ran her long fingers through his curls, down his cheek and, tilting forwards, she kissed him. She could barely breathe as tight knots formed in her chest and stomach. His lips were soft and moist, generously allowing her the freedom to explore his mouth with her own. Sam tenderly kissed her lips, then her cheek and then her neck. When he kissed the soft dent at the base of her neck, Ursula thought she would explode.

They both sank to the floor, Ursula with her back lying on the stairs and Sam on top of her. His strong, toned arms kept his weight from her and though she sensed his entire body above hers, the only contact between their bodies were the delicate touches of his lips and his tongue over her face and neck. Ursula arched her back, forcing a contact between her pelvis and Sam's. Instantly she felt the hardness of Sam's erect penis and a rush of sensation raced across her. She dipped and arched her pelvis again and again, enjoying the racing sensation and the pleasure of teasing her lover. Sam smiled at her, but when she attempted to do this a further time, he caught the base of her back in his right arm and held her tight. Ursula laughed and he released her. With the stairs still at her back, she crawled up a couple of steps. Sam crawled after her. Ursula speeded up and Sam followed suit. When Ursula reached the top steps of the stairs, Sam held back, resting on his arms, four paces down.

Ursula had never before felt this kind of control. The fun of the tease and the power of knowing how much he wanted her, was all new. She undid the buttons on her blouse, starting at the top and working downwards. Her entire sensory powers were heightened. Even the small pearl buttons felt smooth and seductive to her touch. As each slid out of their tiny holes and revealed more of her breasts, the buttons' creamy sheen and delicate curvature aroused her. Now and again, as she undid another, Ursula accidentally brushed her finger against her own naked flesh. Her skin reacted instantly by forming tiny goose pimples. With each button, Sam slowly moved towards her. He was consumed by the impatience of a hungry predator. As the last came undone, Sam had her in his arms, their bodies and lips totally interlaced.

He began tracing the outline of her bra with his fingers, before slipping his hand under and against her warm flesh. Ursula shuddered and used her own right hand to gently massage Sam's hand against her breast. With her left hand she gently reached under his T-shirt and followed the steep curve of his back. She began in the deep arch of his shoulders and slowly followed his spine down until she reached the top of his jeans. Sam's skin felt fiery as he responded to each touch and as she now ran her fingers tenderly along the inside of his waistband, she could feel tiny erect hairs brushing against her fingertips.

Sam continued to hungrily squeeze Ursula's breast, then he cupped it and his mouth smothered the nipple. At first she looked down and studied his head as she felt his thick curls brush against her skin. But then she closed her eyes and bathed in the intensity of the sensation. Her entire body was given over to the experience. Ursula felt totally uninhibited. The more greedily he explored and enjoyed her body, the more erotic the sensation for her.

She opened her eyes and he pulled away from her for a moment, removing his T-shirt and throwing it down the stairs. Within a second his bare chest was back down on top of hers and as their flesh touched, it heightened all feeling to another level. Sam slipped his left hand down along Ursula's stomach and began to unfasten the zip of her trousers. He delicately caressed the lace around the top of her panties and then moved his fingers down to the lace around the leg. Ursula coiled herself in his touch, trying to manoeuvre his movements. But Sam continued to play with the fabric and the lace. Every now and then she sensed that he was going to move his hand inside, but just then, he would pull back and run his fingers along her thigh or stomach.

Ursula responded to the game by rubbing her own hand across the front of Sam's jeans. His groin felt solid and the bulge swelled further each time she caressed it.

Ursula's tactics were successful and the arousal led to Sam suddenly plunging his fingers fully inside her panties. Ursula groaned with anticipation and then, with pleasure. His hand massaged and caressed with delicate strokes. Uncontrollable, Ursula found herself rocking and increasing the pace herself with the thrust of her hips. Her lover's response was immediate and the pressure and tempo of the caress increased. As she pointed her toes and clenched her fingers tightly on Sam's back, the spasm stretched along her entire body. Her physique and mind were engulfed for a few moments before intensifying into a pulsating vibration between her legs.

Ursula closed her eyes again and smiled in the knowledge that, aged thirty-four, she'd just had her first ever orgasm. She had her second on the stair landing and her third on the bedroom carpet.

The lovers finally made it to the bed at around four in the morning. Spoon-like, Sam lay with his arms surrounding Ursula. She cradled herself in his warmth and softness and listened to his restful breath. Her body and mind were consumed by a sense of satisfaction and contentment.

She looked ahead for the first time this weekend and wondered what her future held. Of course it was too early to know if Sam would be there in the picture. She hoped so. But if not, Ursula had discovered something about herself that no one could take away. She could be loved and she could love back. She could also be sensual and, in this area, Ursula knew she was just starting out. What fun she was going to have exploring this one.

She turned to face Sam, whilst keeping his arms tenderly around her. She reached her left arm around his neck and her right around his waist. The embrace entwined their naked bodies completely.

Sam briefly opened his eyes and whispered to Ursula, "Could we stay like this forever?"

Carla was so wrong. Ursula could be hugged and she knew how to hug back.

Chapter 41

The police had little more information to give Christine, other than the road accident had been serious and her husband had been taken to the intensive care unit of the Ulster Hospital. When she got back to her house, she immediately went on automatic and set about organising and planning. But what she thought was organisation turned out to be rambling and agitation. One of the police officers had to force her to sit down and take a breath. Maurice McAllen had come across with her and sat besides her as she began to calm down.

"Don't worry about the girls, Christine. I'll stay here and listen out for them. You get yourself off to hospital and ring me if you need anything."

"Thank you, Maurice. I don't deserve this. After all you . . ."

"Please let me do this."

"Well, it's gone eleven and the girls are zonked. You shouldn't hear a peep out of them."

"Even if I do, it'll be all right. I'm a parent too, remember."

Christine reached forward and kissed Maurice. This time she knew that it was as a friend. A very good friend.

Halfway along the road to the Ulster Hospital, Christine noticed the fuel gauge flash empty. It flashed just the once.

"Please, car, not now."

She looked through her rear-view mirror and observed how black and empty the car looked. With no girls arguing, no pop music blaring and no passenger asking her what the rocking noise was under his seat, the car was silent. The girls' body impressions were still visible on their seats. In the shelf by the wheel, Christine could see an assortment of her husband's classical music CDs, plus a half-eaten packet of his favourite wine gums. The petrol-gauge light flashed again. Christine knew that she wouldn't pass another twenty-four-hour petrol station again before the hospital. She also knew she was closer to where she was going than where she had been.

"Please, not now. Come on, car."

The light now flashed continuously.

"If you get me to the hospital, I promise you, wee car, I'll never, ever trade you in. Don't let me down."

The hospital signpost, signalling the turnoff in 200 metres, lifted Christine's spirits. She pulled the Espace into the Accident and Emergency car park and, as she did, the fuel gave up its battle and she used the car's momentum to steer it into the nearest parking space. When fully stopped, she kissed the steering wheel.

"That's as a friend too. So don't get any ideas."

Christine ignored the path and chose the shorter route across the front lawn to the main entrance. As she ran, her left court-shoe heel got stuck in the turf. Now totally frustrated with them, she pulled both shoes off and abandoned them in a hedge.

This was Christine's second trip to casualty in twenty-four hours, so she knew exactly where to go. Unlike yesterday, it was quiet, except for a drunk she recognised from the day before, this time with a bloody slash across his cheek. Two nurses were huddled behind the reception desk, chatting through whispers and sign language, so as not to attract the attention of the Sister.

"I'm here to see Alex Watson. Dr Alex Watson. He was brought in earlier this evening. I'm his wife."

The one with the semi-proficient sign language guided Christine out of the Accident and Emergency wing and down to Intensive Care. They passed sleeping patients and dozing porters. A nurse broke the eerie silence by rushing past them with a bedpan.

In the Intensive Care ward there were four occupied beds, separated from each other by an assortment of machines and tubes. Besides each bed, a nurse was either seated or was twiddling with this or that machine-knob. The walls were magnolia and bare. The nurse nearest the doorway greeted Christine with a genial smile.

"I'm looking for my husband, Alex Watson."

"Mr Watson was in here for an hour or so earlier. But he's stable now and they moved him down to the general ward – Ward 2."

The nurse from the Accident and Emergency Unit pointed Christine in the right direction. The giant floppy doors to Ward 2 were only a few yards down the dimly lit corridor. A male nurse greeted her this time.

"Are you Christine?"

"Yes."

"I'm so glad to see you. Your husband's been flitting in and out of sleep, but whenever he's with us, all he's been doing is asking for you."

"And how is he?"

"He's fine. Bruised and battered, but he's going to be fine. The consultant's amazed at how well he's come on. He asked me to let him know when you came in as he wants to speak to you himself. It really is good to see you. It'll mean the world to your husband."

Initially, Christine felt frightened at being left by the nurse, surrounded by sleeping patients, drips and curtains. That was all she could see. But a second later she scanned behind the equipment and saw the frail outline of her husband in the far corner of the ward. As she walked closer, the other patients vanished from her view and all that she saw was the father of her children. He was sleeping. Christine took the seat beside him and, as with her mother earlier, she lifted his hand and held it tight in her own. His right leg and left arm were both bound in casts and elevated. His head was bandaged, partly covering his right ear. Bruises and tiny cuts splattered his face, but he looked peaceful and content. Christine even thought she could see a faint smile on his lips.

"Mrs Watson? I'm Dr Armstrong. Pleased to meet you."

Christine warmed to Dr Armstrong instantly. She warmed to his firm handshake and the dusting of yellow pollen on his nose – acquired earlier when smelling one of his patient's orchids.

"How is he?"

"As you can see, Alex's broken his arm and leg and he's

needed a few stitches in his scalp. But his recovery is quite remarkable. We'll keep him here for a few days, just to monitor him really. But we should have him home soon."

"Thank you. Thank you."

"Don't thank me. Your husband's a wonderful doctor. I've worked with him on call countless times over the years. It was an honour to be able to fix him up."

"Do you know how the accident happened?"

"A load of oil drums accidentally fell off a lorry. Alex swerved to miss them, but hit a tree instead. He's lucky to be alive. Alex's a very strong fella, considering . . ."

"Yes?"

"The reason I wanted to speak to you myself. When I was preparing Alex for his drip, I noticed needle marks in his arms."

Christine recoiled, but she knew that the days of deceit and camouflage were over. She stood up and faced the doctor at an equal height.

"He's a drug addict, doctor. Please don't tell me he was drugged up when he got here." A second, more sinister realisation hit her. "He was coming from work."

"No, no, Mrs Watson. Of course I had to take some samples, but they all came up clear. He hadn't been driving or working under the influence, that's for sure. But you don't need me to tell you how serious this is."

Christine closed her eyes and nodded.

"He's going to have to get help, Mrs Watson. We've had a good chat and together we've filled in some forms for a rehab clinic in Dublin. But before sending them in, he's going to need to talk to you. He can't kick this on his own."

Christine nodded again, acknowledging what the doctor had to say, whilst remaining non-committal herself.

"Christine, Christine?"

Christine turned towards her husband's voice and the doctor drew the flowery curtains around them before quietly disappearing back through the floppy doors. She returned to her seat, but this time she didn't hold her husband's hand.

"Christine, I was just trying to get back in time to see the eclipse."

Christine held her index finger to her lips, encouraging her husband to whisper.

"How are you feeling?"

"Awful."

His eyes were completely red and sugar-pink veins surrounded the sockets.

"The consultant hopes to have you home in a day or two. You're best to rest."

"You're not going to leave me, are you?"

Christine hesitated.

"I mean now, Christine. You're not going to leave me here?"

"No, don't be daft. I just got here."

Alex closed his eyes, but he battled to keep awake. They opened and closed several times as his head bobbed up and down with the heavy weight of exhaustion. Every negative thought that Christine had assembled around her husband over the past few days, appeared to fluctuate with the same beat as each nod of Alex's weary head.

"I'm going to be pretty useless about the house with these casts for a while. Who's going to mow the lawn?"

Christine toyed with the idea of falling into the security and familiarity of their usual domestic chitchat. They could spend hours discussing the best formulae for removing stubborn grass-stains or the attributes of alfalfa in their diet. But this moment past swiftly.

"Fuck the lawn."

Alex's blood-shot eyes widened.

"Mrs Watson, do the church elders know what a foul tongue you have?"

Christine knew her husband's humour enough by now, to know when there was hidden intention. Here it was obvious – disappointment. But Christine was in no mood to be criticised. Not by her husband at least. The easy option would have been to continue playing out the dutiful doctor's wife scenario, the same way she had over the past few years. Maybe if the accident had happened before the weekend, she might have. But not now. Even with her husband lying defenceless and weak before her, Christine couldn't keep the charade going any longer.

"Mr Watson, do your patients know you're a drug addict?"

Alex's bloody eyes closed tight and, this time, he didn't attempt to open them again. Christine felt that she too was being closed out.

"Why, Alex? Are we not good enough? Am I not good enough for you?"

"Christine, you are perfect. I'm the one not good enough."

His eyes were still closed, but he turned his face away from his wife, alienating her even further.

"When did it start? When we had the girls?"

There was no answer.

"Before then? Please don't shut me out now."

She felt as pitiful as the injured patient before her. She held her temples in her hands and rubbed the tips of her fingers in and out of the dense curls. Christine could feel her skull tight against her skin and then hear the crisp ruffles of her hair follicles as they were being rhythmically massaged. She was desperate for an answer.

"We're hanging on a thread here, Alex. Help me out."

"On our wedding day."

"Jesus."

"I started to take tranquillisers on our wedding day."

Alex turned back to face his wife. Any signs of drowsiness had disappeared.

"I was a nervous wreck. All those people, most of whom I didn't even know. And you and me in the centre of them all."

The memory of the moment was visible in Alex's austere eyes.

"The drugs provided an escape, I suppose. For the first time in my life I felt I was able to cope with crowds and with people. Kind of important when you're a doctor."

The patient in the next bed began to cough and Alex reduced his raised voice to a whisper.

"I guess over the years the drugs became a substitute for my inadequacies."

He held his hand up over his wife's mouth as she attempted a reply.

"I know, Christine. I have many. But the drugs started to help get me through the day."

"Didn't you ever try and give them up?"

"Hundreds of times, but always at the back of my mind I thought that if I went back to that shy nervous fool, I might lose you, Christine."

"You took drugs to keep me?"

357

"I guess so."

"Did you go to work that way?"

"No, never. Only at home."

"Jesus, Alex, that sounds even worse. You had to take drugs to be with me."

"No, I took drugs so that I wouldn't be me. So I could be normal."

"So being an addict is normal, is it? I suppose being an obsessive is normal too. Scouring the inside of the cooker at two in the morning is normal? Disinfecting the driveway is normal?"

"I was just trying to be in control. Christine, I wanted to be like you."

"I created you, is that it?"

"No."

Christine imagined for a moment that she was Frankenstein and her husband the monster she'd created. Neither of them came off too well in her analogy.

The rapid quick-fire of their conversation halted and both Christine and Alex grabbed the moment to gather their thoughts and re-evaluate their opinions. Christine stopped rubbing her head and, with her hands still cradling her forehead, she looked through her fingers towards her husband. He stared back at her through the imaginary jail bars. His eyes were full of confusion and anxiety. This Christine shared and understood. But she could also see, in his stern expression, admiration and total respect.

"I'm not perfect, Alex. I'm not what you think I am. I'm just a mother and a wife trying my best. Sometimes my best is short of the mark, but I have to learn to cope with that. And so do you."

Christine pulled her hands away from her face. For the first time in years she felt an honesty between them.

"Don't forget the man I fell in love with. The same man who wouldn't kiss me until we'd been seeing each other for over a month."

"I wanted to kiss you. And a lot more besides."

Alex smiled broadly, which pulled at his stitches and made him wince. Even with his injuries, he now looked years younger, as if a burden had been lifted from him. As earlier, when he had been sleeping, Christine reached for her husband's hand. He took hers and squeezed it tightly.

Christine thought back immediately to their Young Farmers days and the early months of their courtship. She recalled the first meal he had cooked for her in his mother's old farmhouse kitchen. The huge red Aga bubbled away, surrounded by floral print chairs with grubby marks, where the father and son had rested their hands muddied from the fields. The father and mother had excused themselves to another part of the house, in order to allow the 'young couple' time to 'get to know' each other. Christine had been given a series of old photograph albums to study, whilst Alex busied himself in front of the heaving stove. When the meat had been cooked, Alex had then prepared and cooked the potatoes and with these finally ready, he set about peeling and boiling the vegetables. The result of his sequential technique was a plate of both over-cooked and under-cooked food, and a combination of hot and cold temperatures. It had taken her a good few years to teach her husband how to do more than one thing at once. Did she want to start all over again with somebody else? No. But she needed and deserved some reassurances.

Christine released her hand from her husband's tight grip. Without being conscious of it, she brought the hand up to her lips. She kissed his palm and then each of his fingers. When she came to the index finger, she opened her mouth wide and began to run her tongue up and down it. Now she was totally aware of what she was doing. In the past, she would have been inhibited and conservative with any open expressions of affection. But this weekend she had stood at the edge and been enticed by the promise of passion looming from below. And this, she was sure, was definitely something she wanted in her life.

"Mrs Watson, do the church elders know what you get up to?"

This time, there was no hidden barbed tone in Alex's voice. He dipped his fingers provocatively in and out of his wife's mouth, groaning each time she licked the fingertip.

"And you a married woman! Taking advantage of a man who can barely move."

"Just think what I could get up to if, when you get out of here, we went away on our own for a few days."

"Without the girls?"

"Why not? Without the lawnmower, the bleach and the rubber gloves."

Alex gave another wide painful smile. He grabbed Christine's hand from his face and playfully twisted it.

"OK, I submit. Maybe you can bring the gloves."

Christine felt Alex let go of her hand, as a wave of gravity glided across his face.

"But, Christine, there's a trip I'm going to have to do all by myself first."

"I know."

"I'm considering a visit to a drug rehab clinic in Dublin. It's supposed to be the best in Ireland. This year's going to be a tough one."

"We'll handle it."

"Are you sure, Christine?"

"We've too much going for us, for us not to."

"And if we fail?"

"We'll just try again."

"Mrs Watson, have I told you lately that I love you?"

Christine stood up, cautiously reclined over her husband and kissed him delicately on the lips. He kissed back, mingling groans of pleasure with 'ouch'. Alex's eyes were slowly closing, as the fatigue and exhaustion caught up with him again.

"How are my girls?"

"The best, Alex. They've missed you. Sleep now. I'll be here when you wake up."

"Did you see the blood moon, Christine?"

"Yes, it was perfect."

Chapter 42

At a minute past midnight, Maurice's baby-sitting shift was complete. Christine had come home looking exhausted and drained, but radiant at the same time. Her first thought had been to rush upstairs to her children and she appeared overly keen to encourage him to leave. She mumbled something about 'don't rush things' and 'good luck' as she raced along the stair landing.

Maurice reluctantly left the warmth of house Number 5 and set off for his own home. As usual, it lay in complete darkness – even the landscapers had decided it best not to put a streetlamp anywhere near his front door. His heart was buoyed by the fact he was able to help Christine, but saddened by his own emptiness and loneliness.

He stepped across from Christine's driveway onto his own lawn. He could feel the tender shoots crush under his weight. The dense clouds had now recaptured the moon and the night was pitch black.

"Hello, Maurice."

A woman's hushed voice greeted Maurice from his front step. He could see her dark shape seated on the cold cement, with her knees huddled against her for warmth. Maurice didn't need any further clues to know who was speaking; he had imagined her voice over and over enough times, to know it was his wife.

"Maggie! You must be frozen. How long have you been waiting there?"

"Not long. An hour maybe."

"Usually I'd be in, it was just . . ."

Maurice felt the combination of self-consciousness and nervousness seize his vocal cords as he mumbled and flustered on.

"It's OK, Maurice. I met your neighbour five minutes ago. She explained you were watching her kids while she was at the hospital."

Maurice had never felt so relieved in all his life. This allowed him a few minutes to gather his thoughts.

"And what do you want, Maggie?"

Oh, no, that's not what he meant to say! That's not what he'd rehearsed.

"To be asked in would be a start. I've lost the feeling in my toes."

Maurice felt like an awkward teenager as he fumbled with the door key and tripped over the doorframe as he entered. Maggie's eyes had become accustomed to the night and as the hall light was switched on it temporarily blinded her. Maurice's eyesight had easily re-focused. Only a few feet away was his wife. The only other time in recent years that he had been this close was outside of her home yesterday – separated by the car window. As usual her long chestnut-brown hair hung loose on her shoulders. She had a few more grey hairs than he last remembered, but they only added to its luxurious sheen. A light tan radiated from her cheeks and her nose was slightly sunburnt. Her dress was floral and summery, with the hem only just above her ankles. Her bare arms were equally tanned, with the toning of a keen gardener.

Gradually she un-squinted her round hazel eyes and examined the hall before continuing her inspection in the living-room.

"So, this is where you keep yourself, Maurice. It's nice. Not your style, I would have said though. A bit, too . . ."

"Anonymous? Not as anonymous as you'd think."

"No, I was thinking suburban."

She continued her inspection of the empty glass cabinet and the plain beige furnishings. Maurice's nerves still hadn't calmed and he could feel his hands begin to shake.

"If you're here about yesterday, Maggie . . ."

'Jesus, not again,' he thought to himself. 'That's not what I had rehearsed. That's not my plan.' This time Maggie didn't bail him out and stood waiting for him to continue.

"If it's about me waiting outside the house."

"It's not, Maurice. It's about the letter. The one you posted for Matthew."

Maggie's gravity immediately stopped Maurice's internal debate.

"Did he read it?"

"No. But I did."

The pain on his wife's face was all too familiar – it was the very same as the many times he'd shouted at her, closed the door in her face and blocked her from his life. It was

364

only one step away from the last terrified expression he had seen as he'd walked out of the door four years earlier and told her to leave him alone, that he didn't love her any more.

"Does a person have to die of thirst before they get a drink in this house? Maurice, your hospitality leaves a lot to be desired."

The pained expression had shifted. For the second time in the past ten minutes, Maurice felt overcome with relief and hurried off to the kitchen. Maggie followed him and, as he began to fill the kettle from the tap, she searched for tea bags and sugar. The cupboards were almost completely empty.

"I guess I won't be getting a choice then?"

"Aye, you will – Spar own brand or nothing."

For a split second Maurice felt the years evaporate. But the sweetness of the moment only added to the bitterness of the truth. Maggie was the first person he had made tea for in the twelve months he had been living in Ashbury. His only other visitor had been Ursula yesterday and there hadn't been much time for civil hospitality.

Maurice took particular care in warming the mugs and squeezing every last drop of essence from the tea bags. They returned to the living-room, each pretending to warm their hands on the heat of the mug. Maggie sat where Maurice earlier had fallen asleep, staring directly at the glass cabinet. Maurice sat by himself on the sofa.

"Why've you no ornaments in there?"

"It's the minimalist look."

"Do you know what you need?"

"A woman about the house?"

Maggie didn't continue with her train of thought and

retreated into the arms of the chair. Maurice studied his visitor as she took tiny sips of tea. He was savouring the moment in his memory bank, to be recalled when necessary.

"Your garden's lovely though. Have you a gardener, Maurice?"

"No, I take care of it myself."

Maggie raised one eyebrow.

"I've become quite an expert."

Maggie raised both eyebrows.

"How are the boys? Who's minding them tonight?"

Maggie's gravity returned and yet again Maurice rebuked himself.

"The boys are fine. I can't keep Lewis away from computers or Matthew away from the girls. I asked my mother to look after them for me tonight."

"Did she know where you were going?"

"Yes, I told her. I couldn't very well leave the house at eleven o'clock at night and not give her an explanation."

"I bet she wasn't too happy."

"No, she wasn't. I'm her daughter – what do you expect?"

"But you still came."

"I had to, Maurice. I had to come when the boys were sleeping. And I had to come . . . if I wanted to be able to sleep tonight."

The tears swelled in Maggie's eyes, but her battle to control them was even more pitiful. Maurice stood up and made his way over to his wife, but she held her hand up abruptly.

"No, Maurice. Don't come over. I promised myself that you would never see me like this again. This is not what I'd planned."

Maurice stood still in his tracks, but didn't return to his seat. He crouched down on the carpet, a few feet away from her.

"Do you know, Maggie, what my plan has been? In my head, I've rehearsed this moment over and over. Don't you get it? This house is all part of that plan. For over a year I've striven to create a shell, a house waiting for your imprint to turn it into a home."

"Are you trying to trap me, Maurice?"

"It's not a web, Maggie. This house is a blank canvas. I can't give it texture or colour, but you can. I want to prove to you that I've changed, that I'm sorry for all that I've put you and the boys through. My life is nothing without you."

"I must go."

"I beg you, Maggie. Please don't."

Maurice's master plan scattered in tatters around him. He hung on desperately to the threads he had left – Maggie being here with him, right now. Her anguish and pain hurt him, as if it was his own, and his love for her weighed down upon him like a mighty rock.

"Maggie, I want to rebuild my life again and I want you and Matthew and Lewis with me."

"It's too late, Maurice. I rebuilt my life long ago. There's no place for you now."

Maurice slumped back down in his chair. With his dreams evaporating by the second, the vacuum of his life was now complete.

Maggie had achieved what she intended, which was to suffocate her threatening tears. With her husband shattered before her, she regained her composure and her self-defence barrier was reconstructed.

"I am happy for you, Maurice. I'm happy you've decided to move on. But you have to do it for yourself and for nobody else."

She leant forward and braced herself with a deep breath.

"I must go."

Maggie was final and absolute. Maurice was gutted by his dashed hopes and had to force himself to lift his head and trace the outline of his wife as she raised herself from the chair. But by forcing himself to look at her, he also faced the reality of the moment head on. He hadn't lived in his house, for fear of infecting it with his own self-loathing and insecurities. The paintwork, the few furnishings he had and even the driveway were pristine and protected. Any new weed shoots attempting to push their way in between the bricks were quickly and efficiently eliminated. He had dedicated his whole world over the past year to creating a cocoon for somebody else. His vision had always been the future and never the now. The occasional glimpse of his children playing football in their garden had been his only reward.

Maurice suddenly accepted that there was a full stop and a line drawn under his life up to this moment. The finality was crushing and terrifying but also, to some extent, liberating.

Maggie let herself out of the front door and walked down the brick driveway to her car. Maurice heaved his bulky body out of the chair and advanced after her, but when she reached the car door, she stopped and turned around. His wife held the letter he'd written to his son up in the air.

"Maurice, the reason I came to see you, the letter."

"Won't you let Matthew read it?"

"No, I won't, Maurice. He may look like a young man, but he's still a wee boy, our boy. I don't think he could handle it, not yet anyway."

Maurice had totally lost focus on the end of her sentence, as over and over he repeated to himself 'our boy', until involuntarily, it audibly burst out from him.

"Our boy, Maggie?"

"Yes, they're both our sons. They need a father. When I read your letter, I thought and hoped that maybe you were ready to be their father again. I came tonight to see if that was true."

"Have I blown it, Maggie?"

Maggie put the letter back in her pocket and pulled out her car keys. As she unlocked the car door and was about to step inside, she called over to Maurice.

"Next weekend I'll bring them over for an hour or so. We'll take it from there."

She pulled the car door behind her and drove off back along the cul-de-sac and onto the main road. Maurice was all alone and the night was dark and still. He pulled up two rocks from his border and positioned them eight feet or so from each other on the lawn. He strolled down to the far edge of his front garden and began dribbling an imaginary football around an imaginary defensive team. The fresh, lush grass, being crushed with each heavy step and clumps of turf flying with each sharp turn. Maurice took a giant kick and struck the imaginary ball. He stood and silently watched the ball's slow-motion trajectory as it curved, dipped and fell just a few inches short of the goal.

Chapter 43

Fergal and Frances were alone for the first time since the early hours of yesterday morning. The scent of stale beer and brandy mingled with those of leather furnishings and vanilla potpourri. Frances began clearing away the half-empty bottles and coffee cups.

"Leave that until tomorrow."

Frances ignored her husband and continued what she was doing. The domestic banality of this, in the light of all that had happened, served only to irritate Fergal further. He wished his guests hadn't left so promptly. The large, four-bedroomed detached house now rattled empty with the remaining two occupants busily trying to avoid each other.

"Leave it and I'll do it in the morning."

"But they'll smell bad then."

"So what, Frances?"

Fergal stood beside Frances in the kitchen and pulled the mug she was carrying right out of her hands. It fell crashing to the floor and slivers of ceramic spread along the slate tile.

They stood just looking at each other for a few seconds, before Frances ran out of the kitchen, crunching the clay fragments under her shoes as she went. Fergal heard the heavy thud of the stair door closing, followed seconds later by the heavy thud of the bedroom door.

Fergal remained, surrounded by the shards of ceramic. The glossy enamel glinted in the halogen kitchen lighting, whilst the exposed edges of the clay were dull and lifeless. Fergal used a dustpan and brush to begin gathering up the pieces. The larger fragments were easy to sweep up, but the smaller ones took refuge in the uneven cracks of the slate flooring. After five minutes or so, he was confident that he had retrieved all of the broken pieces. He ran his left palm gently over the top of the tiles, to confirm his success. A tiny sliver jagged into his index finger and he brought it up close to his face for inspection. The piece was balanced by its tiny nib jutting out of his skin. At the point of impact, a droplet of blood had gathered. The symmetry of the shard and the pellet of blood transfixed Fergal. He stood gazing at his finger, in complete silence and stillness. Between the fingernails of his right hand, he then released the fragment from its diminutive puncture wound. As he did this, blood gushed down his finger and down along his hand. He quickly ran the throbbing finger under the cold tap and watched the watery red blood dribble over the soiled glasses and cups in the sink.

Part of Fergal longed to follow the flow of the streaming water and escape down the plughole. How had he come to this? He'd asked himself this question two days ago and he still felt none the wiser. The truths that he had depended on all his life were nothing but mirages. He was going to have to start afresh and reconstruct his whole world.

And one thing was for sure, he didn't want to do this on his own. He hadn't given up yet.

The third door-thud of the evening echoed around the house as Fergal raced up the stairs. When he approached the bedroom door, he slowed down and opened it softly. The room was in darkness, but he could see the faint outline of the bed, which was empty. The en-suite bathroom was also in darkness and he soon discovered that it was empty too. As he was about to leave the bedroom and check the other upstairs rooms, he caught sight of Frances's head just peeping out from behind the bed. In between the bed and the window, his wife was sitting on the carpet, squeezed into the shape of a small shell. Her face was completely smothered by her folded arms across her knees. Her short, bob-style, fair hair fell like a crown and only the pink of her ears as any way visible. She was silent.

Fergal sat down on the carpet beside his wife; two huddled mounds in the blackness. He reached into his back pocket and pulled out the positive pregnancy test he'd discovered in Frances's drawer that afternoon. He hadn't returned it then and on seeing the group assembled outside of Maurice McAllen's house earlier that day, he'd shoved it into his pocket. He'd been conscious of its presence ever since. Fergal squeezed the tester into Frances's clenched fist.

"Do you really think I don't care?"

Frances remained silent, but she turned her head to the side and looked at the tester in her hand.

"Do you really think I wasn't affected by what happened to our baby and what happened to you?"

White flashes of plastic glimmered in the darkness as Frances rotated the tester in her hand. She still didn't respond to her husband.

"When they took you into hospital for the D and C, do you know what I did? I drove over to Belvoir Park, ran out into the middle of the forest and screamed like there was no tomorrow. I held my hands over my ears and over and over I filled the still air with my wailing. I cried to the point that I had no tears left and only dry sobs remained."

Frances lifted her head and gazed directly at her husband. She looked confused and dazed. Her pupils were fully dilated, making her eyes look large and exotic. Fergal knew this time, as always, he had to take the role of negotiator. But this time, unlike the others, he knew it was right that he should.

"Frances, I cry all the time, if that's what you want to know. But I think what's more important is that you know how much I miss talking to you and being with you. I've just been trying so hard to be this rock of support for you, but it seems I've been nothing of the kind."

Fergal had spent his life thinking that he was a child in an adult world. He had always been conscious that his bluff would soon be called. But up until now his older sisters and then Frances had always been there to nudge him onwards. Now the comfort of Eilish's matronly hip was miles away and Frances was lost in her own inner turmoil. He was on his own. Fergal was facing adult problems and it was time he faced them honestly. He acknowledged that his friend Brendan had managed to maintain his childlike world, but he had paid the price. For Fergal, standing still was not an option. It never had been.

"I love you, Frances. I always will, no matter what."

Frances stopped swivelling the tester.

"I'm all the things you said I am. And probably more

besides. But, let's get one thing straight . . . it takes me two, not one, mouthful, to eat a donut."

Frances's eyes sparkled and a delicate smile burst from her lips. Fergal had made the first advance in this battle. She responded to each word he said and he felt sanctioned to continue.

"Frances, we made the mistake of grieving on our own. Maybe sometimes, we should just cry together. Not all the time, of course, or they might carry us off to padded cells."

Frances dropped the well-stroked pregnancy tester onto the floor and lifted her head from her arms. Fergal's clumsy way of being serious and light-hearted at the same time was reassuringly familiar.

"Fergal, maybe sometimes, well, maybe all the time, we should move our lives forward."

Frances spoke precisely and with a confidence that Fergal hadn't heard for a very long time. Each word reverberated around his head and he could feel his spirits soar.

"I'd like that more than anything, Frances. These past few days without you, I've come to realise that it's important to look back at the past, but you're best not to stare at it too long."

"I know."

"You do?"

"I've been too busy wrapped up in myself."

"And I've been too busy wrapped up in a version of myself that wasn't me at all."

"So, all in all we've both been pretty wrapped up in things, Fergal."

Encouraged, Fergal leant forward and kissed his wife's brave smile. His soft kisses ran down her neck and back up to her mouth, which was open and welcoming. He hadn't really realised how much he'd missed this. They held hands and pulled each other up onto the bed. Fergal and Frances lay facing each other, meeting only at the feet, knees and hands. They lay for half an hour just innocently stroking each other's hands. They were discovering each other again after an absence of many months. Fergal curled Frances's right hand into a tiny ball and began gently massaging it until it was flat again. Attentively and exactly, he then set about creating a new hand, by pretending to mould new fingers, sculpting knuckles and painting on fingernails and delicate tracts of veins. The new hand was now complete.

"Frances, let's always talk to each other."

"Yes."

Fergal's wife was still mesmerised by the hand massage and barely able to communicate.

"And will you promise me one thing, Frances?"

The trance continued.

"What?"

"Will you not go telling everyone I wear my shirt tucked into my underpants? It was only the one time . . . and I was in a hurry for work."

"OK. But would you promise to buy an orange, or a purple, or a yellow shirt, next time you go shopping?"

"It's a deal. I might even try and lose a few pounds."

Frances half-opened one eye and looked unconvinced.

"I will. I've been a lardy arse ever since I was wee. It's time I did something about it. No wonder I never got the girls."

"What about all the stories of you and Brendan out on the pull?"

"Bullshit. It appears that my memories of the past are

slightly skewed. I was a boring fart really. I never had the money for dates and as for run-ins with the cops – I was too busy running away. I've an history as exciting as a packet of custard creams."

"That's not entirely true, Fergal. What about the flowers?"

Fergal's thoughts raced back to his and Frances's first date. They'd met at a university freshers' party. Their eyes met over two pints of cider and Frankie Goes to Hollywood bellowing 'Relax'. Within half an hour they were sucking each other's faces. An hour later they were studying tiny aliens dancing in the waves and two hours later, Fergal was lifting a very inebriated 'sure thing' into his bed. The aliens turned out to be plankton, illuminated by the full moon. And the 'sure thing' didn't turn out to be sure at all. Fergal had managed to undress Frances down to her bra and knickers, without her even opening her eyes. The temptation to take advantage was strong – he was nineteen after all – but his two-week stint as an altar boy when he was twelve kept Fergal in check. The following morning, the temptation was even greater; Frances was still unconscious and he had a teenage erection. But a two-and-a-half-mile walk to the nearest garage to get milk, bread and marmalade for breakfast, curtailed the urge. On his return, Fergal passed a garden brimming full of magnificent powder-pink carnations – all screaming out 'pick me, pick me'. Frances was foremost in his mind and the welcome he felt assured, if he arrived home laden with flowers.

Unfortunately, he didn't make it back that morning. Fergal spent three hours in the police station while they tried to get hold of the garden's owner, in order to ask if he wanted to press charges.

"I can't remember. Did the guy drop the charges, Fergal?"

"Did he fuck! I had to pay him fifteen quid first."

"Well, there you go."

"What?"

"You are reckless."

"I suppose so. I'd forgotten about that."

"I bet you've forgotten about the time you hit the lady RUC officer with the fifty pence too?"

The chants of 'Thatcher, Thatcher, grant snatcher', came hurtling from the past. As did the vision of Frances and Fergal wedged with hundreds of other students protesting outside the Belfast City Hall. Emotions and tensions were high and the student throng had started to squeeze against the police barrier. There was a lot of jostling and pushing. Fergal's only motivation to be there was to impress his politically inspired, new girlfriend, Frances. He'd already earned himself a good few brownie points by imaginatively crafting a huge homemade cardboard fifty pence. It was awkward to carry, but worth it for the effect. When he knocked the female officer's hat off with it, he was confident of even more credit points. The officer had a different perspective on the incident.

"Aye, that's right, Frances. I even got to court with that one."

"I suppose the judge peeing himself laughing and telling the RUC to stop wasting his time doesn't quite make you an outlaw."

"No . . . but I was arrested for assault in the first place."

"You were, Fergal."

"Reckless stuff."

"Absolutely."

"But the stories about poaching and stoning the army – they weren't entirely accurate."

"What about the fifteen-pound salmon?"

"Now, that one's true."

Fergal decided that his past was a jumbled mess of truths, half-truths and complete lies. And he'd enjoyed every minute of it.

The gentle banter would have continued if Frances hadn't halted Fergal's ranting by seductively running her tongue along his bottom lip, tenderly biting.

"And you got me, you know. Not a bad achievement."

"Aye, but you're only after my conservatory."

Fergal marginally leant away from his wife and looked her up and down.

"You're the most beautiful woman in the whole world. Do you know that?"

"I guess I'm not too bad."

"And I love you. Except for . . ."

"Except for what, Fergal Coyle?"

"Except for when you're running buck-naked through Dam Square. Don't you still have some explaining to do?"

"Tomorrow. Right now, how about something nice to go with this?"

Frances kissed Fergal fully on the mouth and he could feel her tongue tickle his lips before plunging inwards.

Chapter 44

The obligatory balloons denoting 'birthday party within' were strapped to the porch light of house Number 5.

Molly Watson came racing around from the back of the house on a sparkling silver scooter. She dodged the puddles, the result of an early shower, circled the front of the house and scootered around the back again. A few minutes later, she appeared again, continuing her lap of honour. This time she stayed at the front of the house and headed along the footpath. She stopped at the 'For Sale' sign outside of house Number 7, and used the pole to lean against and clear a few muddy tufts from around the wheels of her new birthday present.

"Hey, wee girl, go and play around your own house."

"Very funny, Sam."

"So what's it like to be nine then?"

"Same as eight."

Sam continued to badger Molly as he carried two heavily laden black plastic bags from out of the house and into the wheelie-bin at the side. Ursula then followed with two smaller bags.

"Hi, Molly, happy birthday."

"Thanks, Ursula. What's in the bags?"

"Clothes. I haven't space in our new apartment, so they have to go."

Sam tore a huge hole out of the plastic of one of the bags he was carrying. He pulled out a white viscose blouse, almost hidden by an abundance of frills and ribbons.

"Now, Ursula, tell the truth."

"OK, so some of them are old."

"How old, honey? When did you last wear this?"

"1985."

Molly tried to imagine what the old days must have been like, but found this leap into the past too giant for her young years. She decided to stick to the present.

"Is your new place nice, Ursula?"

"Lovely. Sure you'll have to come and visit. Belfast's only up the road and we've a park across from us with swings and slides and . . ."

"Can I bring my scooter?"

Sam had finished with the bin and came racing from beside the house, mimicking an enraged grouchy old neighbour.

"No, you can't. Clear off, or I'll stick a knife in your new wheels."

Molly's laughter, as she escaped Sam's clutches, filled the cul-de-sac. His chase was hampered by a purple suede miniskirt, hurled at him by Ursula. He abruptly altered the target of his pursuit from the quickly escaping Molly, to Ursula. When Molly eventually found the courage to look back, both Sam and Ursula had disappeared inside the front door.

"Watch out!"

Molly turned around to face forwards and soon realised that she was a few feet away from a collision with an open car door.

"Hi, Lewis. Are you coming to my party later?"

"Might do. Might not."

Molly was familiar with Lewis's 'hard to get' approach to life and she wasn't fazed by it.

"Don't then. Your big brother can come instead."

"No, he can't."

"Why?"

"Cos I'm going."

Over the past twelve months Molly had enjoyed her new friendships with Mr McAllen's two sons. She enjoyed playing them off against each other even more. She also enjoyed the fact that whenever Matthew, Lewis's older brother, was about, Ruth had taken to wearing skirts and girlie cropped tops. Their embarrassed conversations provided hours of entertainment.

Matthew's brother jumped out of the car and the two of them ran up the driveway to their father, who was waiting at the step.

"You guys better move it if you want to see the kick-off."

The brothers tried to push past Mr McAllen into the house. With pincer-like movements, he motioned to give them a playful nip on the ear with his fingers – almost like their entrance fee as they passed this giant turnstile. The boys were familiar with the ritual and ducked down to avoid the mock punishment. Matthew went for the dummy move to the left and then a sharp turn under his father's huge legs. But McAllen wasn't fooled and by clenching his mighty thighs together, the unfortunate Matthew was well and truly trapped. The boy tried to force his arms through and flew like Superman, motionless for a while as he struggled and squirmed. There was no escape and his father nipped his ear before releasing him. Lewis's tactics were manipulative, rather than physical. He attempted to distract his father with tales of his school football injuries.

"And look at the size of this bruise."

"Where?"

"It's one of those sore hidden ones, Dad, under the skin."

"Is that right?"

"Dead sore it is."

"Here's a wee nip to take your mind off it."

The conspiracy was foiled and Matthew, like his brother before him, paid the price. Seeing how boys carried on with their fathers was something new for Molly. She decided she liked it, not in her own house, but she liked it for others.

"Do you want to come in, Molly, and see the match?"

Mr McAllen used to frighten Molly, but now she just liked to imagine that she was from Lilliput and he was the mighty Gulliver. She thought to herself how different her opinions were of older people, now that she was that bit older. Of course it was her, rather than the people themselves, who had changed. Grown-ups don't change. While Molly considered Mr McAllen's offer, she held her hands over her ears for protection.

Before Molly could answer Mr McAllen, the boys' mother rolled down the front window of her car and shouted across to their father.

"I'll collect them at the usual time, Maurice. Can you take them on Wednesday this week?"

"No problem. I'll pick them up after school."

"Fine."

"Maggie?"

"Yes."

"Do you want to come in for a while?"

"I don't know."

"I've made burnt potatoes, runny mince and mashed-up veggies."

Molly didn't mind that Mr McAllen's invitation for her to join them had been blotted out. It was worth seeing his face light up when he saw the boys' mother get out of the car and walk up the driveway. There was something in the way the woman swaggered up the path, with her hips rotating all over the place, that was familiar to Molly. But she couldn't put her finger on it.

Molly was totally forgotten as the woman stepped into the house and Mr McAllen closed the door to Number 8.

Molly wasn't omitted for long. Her father was hanging a 'Happy Birthday' banner across the top of the front door and shouted across the road.

"Molly, to the right?"

"More to the left."

"Is that it?"

"Higher."

"There?"

"Higher still."

"Is that it?"

"Lower, Daddy."

Alex's adjustments and re-adjustments resulted in splurges of Blu-tack splattered around the brickwork. He just left them there. He was joined by Molly's mother carrying a bright yellow cotton dress, patterned with slight snowdrops and daisies.

"Molly, your guests will be here in an hour. Come and get your party dress on."

"Can't I stay as I am?"

'After all, look what you're wearing,' Molly thought to herself. The birthday girl knew that being older meant that she should now be embarrassed by her parents and by what they looked like. She decided her mother was too old for a tight white T-shirt and almost see-through, loose linen trousers. Plus, she had started wearing flat shoes, and on occasion, no shoes at all. Molly was faced with being another year older, another year closer to spots and, to top it all, her mother was slowly turning into a hippie.

"Mummy, can I? I'd much rather wear jeans."

Her parents whispered to each other – 'like kids', Molly thought with superiority. One of the balloons escaped and Molly's mother ran down the driveway after it. When she turned around and began walking back towards her husband, Molly instantly recognised the same swagger as that she had seen Mrs McAllen perform only minutes earlier. That's where Molly had seen it before. Her own mother had started doing it recently too. The connection satisfied Molly's innocent curiosity. The mystery was solved and the whys and what-fors of the puzzle were of no interest to her nine-year-old world.

The escapee was joined by thick string to its balloon friends and fixed a second time to the brickwork. Molly's parents then turned their focus back to their daughter. In unison, they shouted across to her.

"Go on then! Wear what you want!"

Molly then saw her father kiss her mother.

"Yuck! Not on the street! People are looking."

Like a catapult, Molly shot off in the opposite direction, with the aim of distancing herself from her embarrassing parents as much as possible. She scootered across to Number 2 and joined Fergal Coyle, who was cleaning the grass from his lawnmower.

"Need a hand, Mr Coyle?"

"Not today thanks, Molly."

"Isn't the grass a bit too damp for mowing? That's why it's all clogged up around the blades."

Mr Coyle didn't seem too impressed with Molly's advice.

"Molly, your Ma's calling you."

"No, she's not."

"Well, I'm off to the shop now anyway. You can help me next time."

Mr Coyle leant across his front step and pushed the front door, which was slightly ajar, wide open. He shouted into the interior.

"So, what do you want me to get?"

"Something nice."

"Like what?"

"You know something nice to go with a cup of tea."

Mr Coyle continued to release sodden clumps of grass from the blades. Specks were flying off and splattering the hems of his beige trousers. Molly tutted, but instead of looking up, Mr Coyle continued his task, only with added zeal. The added pressure, unfortunately, was too much for the wooden clothes-peg being used to scrape. It broke in two.

"Mr Coyle, you really need the right tool for the right job."

Molly couldn't understand why her neighbour didn't give up, but instead continued to persistently chip away at the stubborn grass with one of the broken halves. After a few laborious minutes, he appeared to whip himself up into a scraping frenzy. He then stopped and when he did eventually look up again, he looked totally surprised to see Molly still standing there. He reached across to the front door again and shouted inside.

"Aye, but what?"

"Something tasty."

"Could you be specific?"

"A Toffee Crisp, cheese and onion crisps and a tin of ravioli."

Mr Coyle's wife joined her husband at the door. No wonder her stomach was so huge, thought Molly. She must be having a juggernaut rather than a baby.

Her stomach was completely round and Molly tried to imagine the baby's arms, legs and other bits and pieces packaged in such a spherical space.

"Hello, Mrs. Coyle."

"Happy birthday, Molly. Are you looking forward to your party?"

"Yes. I had another baby myself this morning."

"Good for you. What's the baby's name."

"Felix. It was sore at first. But I don't want to put you off or nothing. Bye, must go."

Molly, as usual, departed at the same speed as she had arrived. Two large furniture removal vans had just driven past the end of the cul-de-sac and her mission now was to follow them. Fifty metres up the road, the vans pulled into a newly built cul-de-sac, phase two – Ashbury Mews, a recent extension to the development. Deliverymen started to unload furniture at house Number 14. Their cargo was an assortment of Mexican pine furniture, including tables, bookcases, television cabinets and chairs.

A massive pine picture-frame was the next to be unloaded and Molly caught her reflection in it. She did look a year older.

A very tall, smartly dressed man greeted the deliverymen and inspected each piece they unloaded for scrapes and chips. He peered through the gap created by some drawers having been removed from a heavy cupboard and spotted Molly.

"Hello, there."

"Hello."

Molly was particularly impressed with the very definite crisp ironed lines down the front of his trousers. They refused to crease, even when the man bent to inspect each leg of the pine dining chairs, one by one. When two trouser presses were the next items to be unloaded, Molly made a mental note of what to add to her next list for Santa. A pine bed, two wardrobes and a chest of drawers were unloaded next and Molly was starting to get bored with the parade of honey-coloured timber.

She slowly turned on her scooter and headed towards house Number 16, also only recently occupied. Outside, a couple with a new baby were hanging an outside light. The baby was propped up in a three-wheeler buggy, surrounded by any amount of soft toys and mobiles. At every whimper, the baby's father would leave his task and race over to the child. The mother was obviously annoyed, as she was the one left holding the heavy lamp at her full stretch.

"I'm always the flipping apprentice. Let me do it, if you want to watch the baby!"

"You'll get halfway through the job and then start crying ' I'm stuck'."

"At least I'll give it a go. I'm sick of holding this and fetching that."

"But look what happened the last time."

"I got the job started."

"You painted the ceiling."

"So?"

"What about the walls and woodwork? Who ended up doing them? Now, be a good girl and I'll be over in minute to show you how the job should be done right."

Molly could see the woman's stretched arms quiver under the weight of the lamp. There then followed a stream of profanities and words Molly had never heard before. She quickly raced across the road, making a mental note of the unfamiliar words, in order to impress her older sister later on when she got back home.

House Number 15 was much more sedate. A woman was planting grass seed on freshly rotavated soil. She battled with clumps of discarded cement, tutting every few steps. Molly toyed with the idea of sharing some of her agricultural experience with her new neighbour, but decided to keep quiet – for now. The new neighbour was a large woman and every time she bent down to spread more seed, her shorts spread so tight that Molly could see the patterns on her underwear. Bugs Bunny and Tweety Pie were being stretched in all directions. As she leant forward, two voluptuous breasts also escaped from her T-shirt. Molly looked down at her own very flat chest and imagined what it must be like to be burdened with such things. She wouldn't be able to ride her scooter, that was for sure.

Just as the woman was about to make a further lunge forward, much to Molly's anticipation, the front door flung open and four young boys came hurtling out. Now the woman had eight darting legs to contend with as she tried to continue her work. The youngest, who looked around two years old, also happened to spot the objects of Molly's fascination and grabbed at the woman's chest with two flailing hands.

"Mummy, I want booby."

Molly was spellbound. With all her years of experience of motherhood, with her own three babies in the last year, she'd never actually had a chance to see breastfeeding first hand. And here was a boy, not much younger than her own baby sister. Perfect. This was her best birthday ever. Molly stood transfixed as the woman threw out her last handful of seed and lifted the youngster up and under her T-shirt. This was getting better by the second.

Suddenly, one of the older brothers ran across the garden and out onto the road. An elderly woman from Number 16 came darting out from her garden and lifted the boy. She was just in the nick of time before a third removals van careered around the corner. Molly's interest in the near-accident was nothing compared to her disappointment as the mother dropped her young child back down again and ran after her other son. There followed raised voices between the older woman and the large one. From her distance, Molly could only pick up phrases such as 'too young to be out', 'should have been watching them' and 'mind your own business', but it was enough to warrant her departure.

Keeping to the newly laid pavement, Molly turned back in the direction of home. With the new houses behind her, she looked across at the last house to be completed in this new phase, house Number 17, perched on the corner of the cul-de-sac. A young couple had strapped a calico hammock between two sturdy-looking sycamores in their front garden. The trees were the last of the natural boundaries belonging to the old farm land. The couple were jostling each other and taking it in turns to stand up and keep their balance. The hammock swung and dipped haphazardly, causing, in Molly's opinion, a few near-nasty tumbles. Giggling and hollering, the couple just about managed to keep their balance. The old trees creaked with each rock, releasing tiny splashes of rain from the morning's shower. Molly had managed to hold her tongue when it came to advice on the large-breasted woman's lawn, but she felt compelled to question the revellers. She simply couldn't understand the fun in what they were doing.

As she scootered past, with her own home now in view, Molly shouted across to the couple.

"Why are you standing up? Isn't it much easier if you just lie down?"

The young couple waved and carried on regardless.

THE END